The Facts

Published by DKM Productions, Ltd.

www.exophobe.com

First Edition ISBN: © 2012   978-0-9818846-4-6

10 9 8 7 6 5 4 3 2 1   A B C D E

Library of Congress Control Number: 2012946117

Dedication

At the end of the day, all that really matters is whether you are loved or not. Love is the only thing worth giving and taking in this world.

Although, a cold beer is a close second...

Acknowledgments

To the real Dee— to see you smile gives meaning to my life. And to Macil, for being my bright light.

Special Thanks

JH was painful, but useful. Appreciate the effort!

The Guts

More Guts

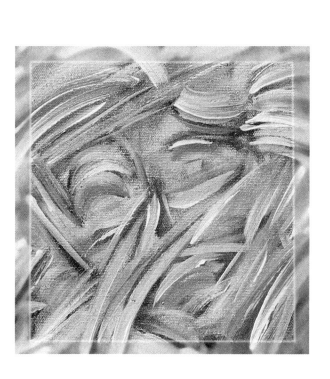

The Great Idea

"The search for truth often begins with beer; and ends with sleep."
—Eucipedes, Greek lunatic

My life changed forever on a Friday.

You know Friday. The much-anticipated and always celebrated conclusion of the work week. Usually a good day for most people.

Usually.

Where are my manners? My name is Enoch Maarduk.

You probably haven't met many people named Enoch. Me neither. Or, is it either? I can never keep that straight.

It is a bit odd. My name; not the keeping it straight thing. Which is why I have, many times, given serious thought to changing it. Bob, Dave, Jim. All good. Enoch? A little unwieldy.

The influence of the ancient apocryphal *Book of Enoch*, Part 1 (*Book of Watchers*) did it for my parents. They were New Age people; hippies more or less.

Mostly more and not less. They thought the name was cool.

There are some aspects of my life that I'd like to change, but I'm good with the name.

We change the things that need to be changed and accept those things that can't, and make do. Take scraps and make quilts and all that pithy pith. Mostly just piths you off. Sorry about that.

The things we change—or accept—don't always work out the way we want. That's life. *C'est la vie*. Whoa, I just blew my entire French repertoire in one sentence.

No matter what, you need to keep your sense of humor. Crazy world and not sure what to do about it. Mostly, I just shrug (I also sigh a lot). Kind of irritating, as some things never do change.

SSDD. You know—same shit, different day. Just like my job.

◻ Chapter One ◻

I work for a small company in the publishing business. Well, typography if you actually want to pin the tail on the jackass. I design, compose, program, and otherwise piece together books and manuals for both print and electronic publication.

Sometimes interesting and compelling—sometimes boring to the point of apoplexy. Rigor mortis maximus. Watch the paint dry. Clean the lint filter on the dryer. Listen to the boss yammer about schedules.

At least it was Friday, as I said, but on this particular Friday it had been unusually and hideously mundane at the orifice, as I was involved in making edits to a low-level mathematics textbook. Mostly fractions, coordinate grids, and square roots.

Please contain yourself.

By midday, I was hoping the building, or possibly my under shorts, would catch fire. Or infectious rodents would overrun the office. Maybe some joker pumps nitrous oxide into the ventilation system.

Not really, but you get the general drift.

Anyway, by the end of the day I was exhausted and drained. Brutal work just to stay awake. Not even multiple doses of caffeine, multivitamins, and magic supplements could keep my brain focused and energized for an entire day of $2 + 2 = 5$ math edits. Therapy might work. "Doc, my id is addled." Ergo, it's your ego. Just super. Freud this.

So, there it was, just after work, late Friday afternoon. I staggered home in shambles. Or perhaps, staggered, I shambled home. Possibly, I stagger, in shambles, home. Perhaps my home was in shambles.

No matter what, I felt like seven shades of shiny goat crap.

My running buddies and best pals, Tom and Armando, phoned. It was Friday. Of course they would be phoning. Call it standard protocol. They were primed ready and roaring to hit the ground running and party until the crows come home.

Cows. Until the cows come home.

See, this whole day had effectively numbed what few brain cells were still functional after the various and sundry experiments they had survived during my college years. Mostly survived.

Anyway, to their utter astonishment and vocal dismay, I told my friends I was staying home.

☐ The Great Idea ☐

I know, it defies human understanding, surpasses the mind's ability to grasp reason, and percolates with a deafening resonating undulation throughout the entire Friday night party crowd.

That's right, Mad Dog Enoch, party monster extraordinaire, a fearsome beast among party animals, was turning home boy for a Friday night. Sad. {Insert appropriately blithe sigh here.}

After telling the boys I was party toast—and listening to them verbally abuse me—I hung up and lay down on the couch to watch television. Well, didn't actually lay down so much as collapsed in a ragged, lumpy, heap, fully clothed with shoes still on. Fatigued to the point of apathetic lethargy. Don't try that with a lisp, unless you're a programmer.

I remember I was balefully, listlessly, hopelessly watching a rerun of *The Waltons*.

I was flat on the couch, watching a rerun of *The Waltons*. The remote was located on the recliner on the other side of the living room and I was too damn tired to stand up to retrieve it to change channels, so I just glared woefully at it every so often.

I tried to use my mind to make the television channel change. Telly-telekinesis, you could say. Groan.

Didn't work. *The Waltons* were still there. I think John Boy was going off to college or something.

I fell asleep on the couch just before 7:00. Missed the ending. Kind of pithed me off.

Oddly enough, when my eyes opened at around 9:30 — yeah, out like an effing light for two and half hours — I sat up feeling suddenly refreshed, energetic, happy.

Okay, maybe not happy, because that would be pushing it, but better than before, which was good.

Still, this whole thing was a serious vexation to my already slumping Friday spirit. I mean, not going out partying with my pals, watching *The Waltons* (and actually liking it) and then falling asleep at 7:00 was not normally on my Friday "to do" list.

Still, it was Friday. It was early and the night was young. I honestly thought about taking a quick shower, throwing on some Friday-night hell-raising and women-chasing clothes and track down the guys.

☐ Chapter One ☐

Trouble was, by now they would be churning and burning and up to their, uh, huevos rancheros in either women, trouble, troubled women, women in trouble, women looking for trouble, women trying to get out of trouble, or some other essential variant thereof.

Toil and trouble, brew me and bubble.

I smiled in fond, but mild, contemplation of such uncontrollable and joyful chaos. Ordinarily, I would have relished it, but my motivation was sorely in need of a serious nudge. I noisily bleated out a gust of air. Maybe just best to get on the computer and goof around for awhile.

Safety first.

Getting on the computer (and not going out partying) was an opportunity to get some social networking progress made. Hey, if you're not hanging out, you're just out hanging. Like, in the wind.

I mean, I had to check the breaking news (maybe the office burned down or something), there were numerous emails to answer, some unanswered IMs, a few social page invites to laugh about—and disregard or answer—and my blog to update.

But, it's easy to get distracted. Some folks are ADD; but it's so bad with me I'm DDA.

Oh, man, that is going to get me in so much trouble. An old joke that doesn't taste any better with thyme. Cough, cough.

Speaking of time, I was overdue for an adult beverage.

So, I got a cold Stella from the fridge and sat down in the recliner (after, with appropriate irritation, I moved the unreliable, non-telekinetic, and uncooperative remote) and fired up my digital device.

I am fascinated by the peculiarities of life, just like a lot of people, and I am always looking to expand my mind as far as I can tweak it. Become, rather than simply be. OM and AUM and all that.

The Internet, the World Wide Web, the Net—a great place to find anything. Everything. Nothing. It can be a daunting task weaving through the web.

So, in lieu of chasing my tail—or some variant thereof—I was going to spend a restive evening sorting through the all-encompassing architecture of the digital world—accepting both the good and bad.

⬚ The Great Idea ⬚

There are veritable, virtual, mountains of data to surf through and muck about. Topics ranging from aliens (these days you need to qualify that by saying "extraterrestrials"), genetic manipulation, lizard people (a.k.a. Reptilians), mortgage interest rates, abiotic oil, artificial intelligence, the freaking price of gas, sunspot activity, et cetera, ad nauseum.

Opinionated people, smart people, dumb people, regular people — all of them prattling on and on until you projectile hurl. Like listening to politicians ramble on about how they intend to make your life better. That really does make you want to hurl a projectile.

Just keep your eyes open, is all I'm saying.

Fronti nulla fides. That's Latin and you should look it up. Really.

Fine — I won't make you look it up. It basically means "no reliance can be placed on appearance" or "you can't discern if someone is telling the truth just by looking at their face." About all the Latin I know.

I'm always on the careful lookout for interesting stuff that raises my hackles, screws with my fancy, or at least scratches my mind.

Call it curiosity aroused to action. The dead cat syndrome. Me saying "Ow" if I find something that hurts.

Man, that is so bad.

Still, half the fun is looking for that precious bit of information that really ignites the fire of your thoughts. The real trick (and the other half of the fun) is separating the glitter from the dross. Dross are the impurities that float in any molten metal. Slag is the same as dross, except the former is a liquid and the latter is a solid.

Hey, a ladder is a solid.

Moving on; the web has rarefied morsels of exceptional data surrounded by a beckoning sea of siren-like effluvia.

I love the word "effluvia." It even sounds stinky. Say it three times aloud. Sounds like a toilet flushing.

Of course, the ever-present danger is becoming someone who is constantly getting bogged down in unsubstantiated minutia and mind-numbing facts (effluvia or not) and not accomplishing a damn thing.

Pick me.

⧫ Chapter One ⧫

In more ways than I care to recount, I am a dross slagging slacking bass turd constantly getting absorbed in wandering around the digital ether, aimlessly meandering from one digital fact to the next.

A kind of knowledge prostitute I suppose. Selling out to the website with the best offer, in a manner of speaking. Prostate before all the proselytizing, you could say. Well, if you were a bit unbalanced...

Anyway, before I attended to the social networking things, I wanted to check the news first, see how much farther down the Thomas Crapper the world had fallen since I had gone to work that morning. Maybe it was one of those self-fulfilling prophecy things. You check the news expecting to see nothing but bad news and, *voila tout*, that's all you see.

Hey, more French; who knew?

So, you expect bad news and that's what you get. Stock market off 150 points. Jobless claims up. Drug cartel victims found in Mexican resort town. Italy and Spain in economic trouble. Home sales down. Gold prices up. Politicians on vacation. Mideast fighting again (okay, maybe that's old news, but it's still bad).

Chinese complaining about American financial structure. Russians complaining about everything. Germans wanting to leave the EU. Britons stoic as always. Man, change the channel or, yo, update the IP.

One piece of news of a different sort did catch my eye. Which is to say, not bad news.

Construction of a new hospital in southern Iraq was halted when workers uncovered a buried trove of ancient artifacts and cuneiform tablets. Much of the material was transferred to the University of Basrah for further study.

The report noted this geographic area was often referred to as Mesopotamia and was once the cradle of the Sumerian civilization.

And it was right here, boom chicka boom—emphasis on the boom—that I completely and utterly forgot all about my friends out partying, forgot all about the dozens of emails I needed to answer, forgot all about my waiting IMs, and forgot all about updating my blog.

All I cared about were ancient Sumerians.

So, I vigorously pursued the Sumerian thread.

⬡ The Great Idea ⬡

I have to tell you, those Sumerians were rocking folks, no bout a doubt it. Oldest written language. Oldest civilization. Extensive literature. Detailed religious beliefs. Pottery wheel. Most of this I got in about 20 minutes.

And then I found Gilgamesh. Satori-like awesomeness. OM this.

I freely admit that my focus got derailed by Gilgamesh. I mean c'mon, this is a smoking good story.

A 4700 year-old former King of Uruk, two-thirds god and one-third human. A cool sidekick named Enkidu who used to hang out with the beasts. Demons, monsters, gods, the Underworld, harlots, beer, fighting, the quest for immortality, death, life—everything you need for a good story.

Did I mention beer?

But there was much more, and I kept digging through sites.

I was going through links like a visitor to Oktoberfest. Man, that is the wurst.

Which reminds me, I need another beer.

There were these links to some guy talking about the Sumerians and their gods, and then I got sidetracked to the Annunaki plus Nibiru, with the gist of it being that aliens from this mysterious 12th planet, aka Planet X, came to earth, genetically altered apes and early man and the Sumerians worshiped them. Something like that.

Ancient astronauts. Or astro-nuts; depends on your perspective.

The next link was to another scholarly-type guy who debunked the entire alien / Annunaki / Planet X thing. Not that I was worried or anything, but thinking about mysterious planets led me to check the NASA website that tracks Near Earth Objects and it sort of freaked me out.

I guess seeing the words "impact risk" with percentage numbers can lead to a modicum of trepidation.

Hey, I think that was the name of a garage band I saw a few years back.

I'm into my third Stella now, or maybe it was my fourth, whatever, accompanied by blue maize tortilla chips and my own salsa blend I had just pulse-blended up.

⬚ Chapter One ⬚

And, since you asked, here's the recipe: fresh cilantro, a good beefsteak tomato like Big Rainbow or Ponderosa Pink (or whatever), Texas sweet onions (the 1015s), fresh green chiles (chile verde), fresh sweet corn, apple cider vinegar (just a spoonful), a hint of brown sugar, a dash of cinnamon, and black olives.

Lastly, but not leastly, the kick. The spice of life. The slow burn.

Depending on how many endorphins I want to have released, I will add (in escalating order) jalapeños, serrano, or habanero peppers.

Always keeping in mind, naturally, that if it goes in hot, well, it comes out hot. Just saying...

Speaking of caliente. If you grow your own chili pequins, you should have all the fire you want and may not need to Scoville-up at all with those other peppers. But, I must caution you, if you are inexperienced with these smoking hot bass turds, you best not go overboard in their usage or you will run around wailing and gnashing your teeth, and searching desperately for milk. Caseins. Anything to put the fire away.

Sorry about going all DDA on you there. It's just that spicy food makes me feel better. Mainly because I'm focusing on my exploding lips and not the bad day (think Friday) swirling around me.

Okay, onwards with the story.

Where's my beer?

So—I am logged onto my digital device checking out the WWW, eating chips, swearing lustily because the salsa is burning a hole in my damn mouth, spreading the pain with beer instead of quelling it, when a sublime thought occurs to me. Hey, I could use that for the pain in my mouth. A sub lime.

Anyway, here's the sublime thought—lots of people are out in the real world making lots of money writing books, running websites, making movies, talking about things you can't even see, smell, touch, or feel. They are making money out of nothing. Cash from náda.

My gawd, I mused, even in dire straits you can make money for nothing. Think about it.

The way I figured it, in this flash of cerebral insight, you can make money, maybe lots of it, writing about something that no one can prove or disprove. I mean, people are still making money off the damn Sumerians, and they've been dead for 5,000 years. Talk about náda...

☐ The Great Idea ☐

Writing about nothing seemed the ticket to success. This explains why there are so many religions in the world, and also why so many people are writing about aliens, UFOs, aliens in UFOs, UFOs without aliens, aliens looking for UFOs, UFOs looking for aliens, ghosts, reptilians, vampires, global warming, and a host of other things you can't prove, or disprove.

Creating this kind of stuff, the stuff about nothing, carries with it no liability for the truth. I mean, no wonder so many people like it. It's a sweet gig, if you can get it. It was just like politics, only you don't have to run for office.

And that's when it, and the fifth Stella, maybe sixth, hits me. Like a slap that knocks the seven shades of shiny goat crap out of you. I was going to make a million bucks doing the same thing.

This thought started me sweating.

Actually, it was the effing chili pequins; but at the time it seemed like the fever of this idea was all over me.

It started out with an innocent graphic of the electromagnetic (EM) spectrum I found during one of my many and varied surfs. Well, after I lost interest in the damn Sumerians. Anyway, you know the EM spectrum. Infrared to visible light to ultraviolet and all that.

The electromagnetic spectrum was the absolutely perfect concept. You see, it occurred to me, with a jolting brain slap, that if energy (E) equals mass (M) times the speed of light squared (C^2) is accurate, then everything is fundamentally the same, just in different vibratory states of transition (speed modes).

I mean, my high school physics teacher always said there wasn't that much difference between me and a box of rocks, and now I get it...

The whole premise seemed absurdly simple—it really didn't matter if what I wrote was true or not. It just needed to *sound* true, and the EM spectrum seemed like a good place to start.

In my ethanol-infused mind, the next set of logical steps in this rapidly escalating chain of events went something like this:

Premise 1—Organic things (e.g., humans, animals, insects, and such) and inorganic things (e.g., rocks, trees, and dirt) exist. We see them everyday. This cannot be refuted, just as Sam Johnson told Bishop Berkeley, vis-a-vis Mr. Boswell. The beer, as well, cannot be refuted.

⎔ Chapter One ⎔

Premise 2—Organic and inorganic things are all just different types of electromagnetic energy. People just move faster than desks, is all. Well, you never met my Uncle Jerome. Lucky you.

Premise 3—Electromagnetic (EM) energy can take many different forms (e.g., radio, microwave, infrared, visible, ultraviolet, x-ray, gamma ray, et cetera.) Proven fact.

Conclusion—EM energy life forms, both conscious (aware) and unconscious (unaware) exist all along the electromagnetic spectrum, sometimes as organized fields of energy with no mass, sometimes as organized fields of energy with mass.

Bold statement, and impossible to refute.

These EM beings / creatures / life forms can interact with, and visit, the Earth. Where they use EM wave manipulation to implant thoughts and ideas into people's minds. Thoughts and ideas that people think are their own, but are obviously not. And these EM creatures are controlled by evil humans, but I hadn't really thought that part completely through yet. I'll just have to make it up as I go along.

That was it though—electromagnetic beings that come to Earth.

It was the moneymaking idea. The cash crop. Plant it and watch it grow. Harvest it somewhere down the long and winding road.

There was more, but that was the gist of the basic idea. By this time it was three in the morning and the Stellas were wearing off, or on, as the case may be. But I had one more thing to do—gussy the basic ideas up a little and post them to my blog.

I know I mentioned my blog before.

It's just my oddball ideas, posted for a handful of friends who like this kind of stuff and have the patience and courage to read it.

Bless their ill-begotten minds. I give them a password and they can log-on (in) and read, comment, and otherwise have some fun with it.

I posted the EM thoughts and ideas and headed wearily for the sack.

I was all out of energy, electromagnetic or otherwise.

A Strange Visitor

"Santa Claus has the right idea: Visit people once a year."

—Victor Borge

I really hate it when I'm exhausted. I'm normally such a light sleeper that roach flatulence wakes me up. I'm startled if the wood floor creaks.

But, when I'm extremely tired, I know I'm going to have nightmares about trying to wake up. Scream and thrash like a madman until I actually do wake up. Unless I am in a totally secure environment. Which is why I lock and barricade the doors, make sure the electronic fingerprint guard on my .38 pistol is activated, and slip the weapon into the drawer next to the bed.

I'm not a violent person, just a lousy sleeper. Besides, the first two chambers are loaded with freaking non-lethal rubber bullets. Although, true bad boy loads are in the other chambers. Better to have it and not need it than need... Well, you know the rest of that pithy pith.

I close the blinds, turn the lights off (except for one itty-bitty wall plug-in, so I don't hurt myself going to the john during some half-asleep nocturnal sojourn) and then I pass, hopefully, into blissful oblivion.

Pax goodnightus.

I sensed the sound of words before I heard them. Good lord, that doesn't make sense. All I knew was, it felt like a disturbance in the force or some kind of flux. It was really fluxed.

I remember, albeit pretty freaking hazy, drifting upwards, upwards, hearing these odd words that created a strange sensation in my dream, or quasi-wakeful state, and then the instant realization slapped me, as I fished open my sticky eyes, that it was the damn cell phone, and that it was Tom; and I had recently changed his ring tone—for whatever moronic reason—to the chant of "Bring Out Your Dead" from an old Monty Python movie about the Dark Ages. Very symbolic.

☐ Chapter Two ☐

I had a headache and I was thirsty. I grabbed the phone, but the ringing had stopped. Damn. Glanced at the time. It was just after eleven in the morning. A word that sounded vaguely like "Aargh" was the only coherent sound I could make for a moment or two. Coherent being a relative term.

And then, of course, came the rapid—usually irritating—text message (TM) right behind the missed phone call.

IMAAK. RUETing? CMB41.

I like being able to send text messages to friends and colleagues. Comes in handy. Useful. Utilitarian. Mine are clear and to the point; no clever abbreviations or cute little sayings. Just get the damn thing said.

Tom, on the other hand, seems enamored with TM-speak and those clever (some might say obnoxious) little letter and number symbols. Loves emoticons (puke). Drives me nuts. I used to get things like the above and call him back asking WTF he was trying to say. IMHO, he goes way overboard... IRMC.

The sad thing is, after a while, your brain begins to adapt. And you kind of like it. Think chili pequins.

So Tom is saying—"I am alive and kicking. Are you eating? Call me before 1:00." Fug. Gag me with a spoon. Smack me pappy.

I called him back, explained I just woke up—er, had just been awakened by his blankety-blank phone call—and would be happy to go eat, how about a late lunch, say 2:00. And I'd meet him at Vitellos Restaurant and he could tell me about all the hot women I missed out on last night.

He started to tell me about all the hot women I missed out on last night and I hung up on him.

I got a huge glass of water (reminding myself "beer is a diuretic, beer is a diuretic"), and peeked hesitantly in the fridge to see if there was anything remotely eatable or edible in sight.

Peered in, shook my head in leftover anguish, and closed the door in stomach-growling disgust. Added "go to grocery store" to my mental checklist.

Wandered idly into the bathroom.

⬚ A Strange Visitor ⬚

Where I was again reminded of the awesome power of chili pequins. I believe I can safely relegate that subject to the hot bowels of history.

I am so sorry.

The stubbled and gnarly visage staring back at me from the mirror looked a little like me, but not the typically rarefied image I usually maintain for myself. Image may not be everything, but interactions in the real world usually work better clean-shaven and well-groomed.

After shaving with the only blade I could scrounge up (dull and old being the important adjectives to recall here), I added "buy razor blades" to the mental checklist, and thought about "get hydrogen peroxide," but figured the shaving wounds would all be healed by the time I got back from the store.

I splashed on aftershave like it was liquid penicillin and started the shower. Mostly so the neighbors wouldn't hear my screams.

I once dated a girl who loved hot showers. I don't mean warm, I mean hot. The bathroom would end up looking like a steam sauna. The sheet rock would begin to rot. My toilet paper turned to mush. Her skin would be glowing red. She claimed it killed all the unhealthy organisms. I told her it probably killed everything, unhealthy or not. We stopped seeing each other not long after that, as I recall.

This was for the best anyway. She wouldn't eat cantaloupe because it was too mushy. I love cantaloupes. There was no future in such a relationship.

Anyway, some showers feel better than others. Some are for quick necessity, others are for a leisurely soak. This one was nice because I stank like that old pair of socks you discover in your gym bag, down at the bottom, wedged back in the corner. You know, sort of stiffened out and, well, that's TMI, isn't it? Rambling seems to be a trend with me.

No matter, I needed to be cleansed. In a manner of speaking. Though the pequins had done a fairly effective job of that... Hello!

Twenty minutes later I was sitting at the dining room table munching on a PB&J. I felt great. Well, better, anyway. Had on clean clothes (although hunting around for them did force me to add "do laundry" to the mental checklist), clean body, fresh shave, and ran my hand across my head. Hair cut needed (yeah, yeah, checklist) and the doorbell rang.

⊏ Chapter Two ⊐

I live in a gated condo community. Keeps trouble out (or locks it in, as the case may be) and affords a bit of security against the ragged unknowns of the world. But, considering the gate code is "1234," I doubt Riff and Raff would have much trouble getting in if they were of a mind.

I peeped through the peep hole.

It was a man, medium height, small stature, nice clothes, not counting the polyester jacket without a tie, respectable-looking though, probably mid-forties. He was staring at the peephole and smiling broadly.

In other words, trying his best to appear harmless.

Fronti nulla fides, remember? You know: "no reliance can be placed on appearance."

Or, maybe an alternative translation could be: "don't answer the damn door if you're not sure who is there." Hah, insecure nonsense.

I opened the door.

After all, it was Saturday afternoon and the guy hardly looked like a criminal. Besides, I can take of myself; flex, *vee vill pump hue hup*. "Hello," I said with my best what-the-frell-do-you-want face. "How can I help you?" Very officious. I would brook no foolishness.

The man continued smiling, as innocent as a character witness, and began talking. It was a pleasant enough voice, with an accent that sounded vaguely British, but only just barely, the words clear, clipped, and precise.

"I'm trying to locate a Mister Enoch Maarduk." He stood calmly, serene, stoic. Clue one.

"That would be me," I said, as smartly as I could manage.

"The same Enoch Maarduk who publishes the *Debris From the Wreckage* website blog?" Uh, that was clue two, pay attention.

In retrospect, the infamous 20-20 hindsight that people speak so eloquently about, I should have immediately dashed back to my bedroom and grabbed my pistol from the bedside table. Maybe zing a couple of rounds his way to encourage his rapid departure. I mean, shoot, I had two clues lobbed my way already and ignored them like the rankest putz newbie.

⌂ A Strange Visitor ⌂

Alas, I merely gawked at Mr. Polyester Man and said, "Sure, what about it?"

His left hand flashed in sudden and practiced movement and from some unknown location, either his jacket or his crotch, he produced a little shiny metal gun, pointed it at me in unwavering alacrity, and said softly, "Please step back," while still smiling so nicely that I really didn't feel threatened at all.

Mostly because it had happened so quickly that my pea brain had yet to snap to the fact I was just about to enter Cacaville. Population one. Me.

Having no formal training in such matters, I stepped back. Not very Krav Maga of me, to be sure.

He followed me into the room and softly shut the door behind him. I had been invaded, in a manner of speaking. He wasn't from Mars, certainly, but he was vast, cool, and perhaps, unsympathetic.

"Where did you get your information?" His taut smile was not nearly as pleasant as before, and there was most definitely a harder edge to his words.

Maybe it was just the gun that invested the words with such disarming relevance.

Firearms can add such an eloquent tint to any casual inquiry. It rather reminded me of that saying, "You can go further with a gun and a smile than just a smile."

I'm not sure this line of thinking was doing me much good.

By this time, having doe-eyed the gun for a few seconds, my alarmed and yet semi-dull synapses had managed to spark and fire a little, but I was still a tad benumbed. It's not everyday a guy pulls a gun and quizzes you about your website. I remembered all the good spy movies, though; stall for time and give yourself a chance to think things through.

"What information?" I put on my best confused and puzzled expression, which wasn't all that hard considering that I was mostly confused and puzzled.

"Sit down," the man gruffly ordered, and I promptly sat down on the couch. No sense aggravating a man with a gun. I sat precipitously on the edge. He hovered about four or five feet away.

⟦ Chapter Two ⟧

"Don't get coy with me, Mr. Maarduk." Tossed me his best bad ass scowl. "We want to know who gave you that information."

"No one gave it to me," I said defensively. I actually wanted to ask him what he meant when he said *we want to know* but figured we weren't on that friendly of a basis yet. Maybe later, over lunch.

"Mr. Maarduk," he began slowly, quite pleasant in his demeanor really. "I know I'm standing here with a gun"—he waved it for emphasis, which I thought was overly theatrical—"but, I really don't want to use violence." This was accompanied by a particularly nasty smile which did little to validate the authenticity of his sincerity. "However," and I knew this part was coming, "unless you are going to be a little more cooperative, I'm going to shoot you in the left kneecap." That part I didn't see coming.

I'm not sure why he chose the left kneecap over the right, but I was thinking that it probably wouldn't make much difference to him, nor to me, for that matter. The idea of pain was certainly not pleasing to my mind, but the idea of being a cripple was even more disagreeable.

All in all, it seemed like a highly credible threat.

"Look," I began, trying to appear as earnest as a politician at a fund raiser, "I'll tell you everything I can, but I'm not exactly sure what you're looking for." This was certainly true. "What is it that you want to know?" I tried to sound as rational as possible, despite the generally irrational nature of our encounter.

"The spectrum material, damn it," he growled this last bit. "You know that as well as me." He extended his arm and pointed the weapon at me. Well, at my left kneecap.

That's when the front door burst open with a tremendous wrackling crash and clamor, having been kicked, shouldered, or blasted open with great power, startling both of us as it whirled inward and rebounded fiercely off the inner wall.

The man whirled around convulsively and I thought he would fire his gun, but in an instant the weapon just seemed to fly out of his hands and swizzled in gyrating rotation across the room toward the figure standing in the open doorway. He hadn't thrown it—it had been kind of sucked out of his hand by some unknown force. Weird, part one.

❑ A Strange Visitor ❑

It was a woman, dressed in some odd gym workout gear, a well-fitted black fabric, leathery, but without the sheen, complemented by a hint of pink accents, long brown hair, wound up in kind of a twirled bun. She was holding a little metal box, to which the man's gun was now attached, and she seemed hostile. As she angrily tossed the box on the ground, the man charged her—screaming and howling madly. Weirder, part two.

Then they were both rolling and jib-jabbing on the floor, demolishing anything their tangled and wrestling forms encountered. Grunts, wails, snarls, and growls. I snapped out of my lethargic zomboid state and headed in a mad dash for the bedroom to grab my own weapon.

When I came out of the bedroom they were both standing and exchanging various kinds of exotic martial arts blows and punches, like some scene from a movie. Most of the punches were blocked with flying elbows and hand swats, accompanied by a raucous mix of groans, roars, cries, and curse words of shocking impropriety.

I yelled as menacingly as I could, "Freeze!" while unflinchingly pointing the gun directly at the guy's back. Rubber bullets or not, they still packed a damn good whack. Besides, chamber three wasn't that far away, if push came to shove.

I'm a reasonable person. I expect other people to be reasonable. It's called a social compact thing. Right? Go along to get along.

I expected him, like the logical human he ought to be, to turn with his hands up, to surrender, as any sane person would do when faced with someone yelling, "Freeze!" and obviously holding a firearm.

Instead, before I could even react, almost before the echo of my voice had died away, he had roughly elbowed the woman aside and was out the door and careening down the stairs (yeah, I should mention that I live on the third floor of a three-story condo).

I couldn't even take a shot at him he was so quick. Not that I would have shot a fleeing figure in the back or anything, just saying.

Maybe the leg...

The woman was staring at me, hands on her pleasing hips. Glaring, really. Her eyes, not her hips. She was very good-looking. About my age, too.

⬚ Chapter Two ⬚

"Nice," was all she said, but it wasn't stated as a thank-you, but more like an insult. As in the unspoken part after the word *nice* being *you jerk*.

I stared back at her. Did I mention she was good-looking? "What?" was all I said, offering her the universal gesture of innocence, ignorance, with my hands spread out wide. Like those idiots in the movies.

"I had everything under control," she said softly, shaking her head. Pretty girl. Lovely big brown eyes.

"Really?" I asked sarcastically. "Because it looked to me like I rescued your ass with this pistol." And I raised it up for emphasis.

Now, this next part might be a little hard to follow. It happened fast. I'll tell you about it, but bear with me because I'm not sure I have the sequence exactly right. All I can recall is that she moved really fast, I got knocked over backwards and she was suddenly holding my pistol. Very embarrassing.

She studied me with a baleful and sad expression. Like I was a bad dog that had left an unwanted surprise on the carpet. "I needed to ask him a few questions," she muttered with some irritation, cracking the revolver open and extracting five shells. They landed with soft, subdued, bounces on the carpet.

"At least you knew enough not to leave one under the hammer," she said, very begrudgingly. She nonchalantly tossed the gun on the sofa.

I ignored her comment because, slowly, I was getting a little bit worked up myself. A guy had pulled a gun on me, threatened my left kneecap, my door was hanging by one labored hinge, two neighbors were standing in the hallway gawking at me, and Wonder Freaking Woman was giving me attitude.

"It's nothing," I said as I walked over to the door, waved the neighbors away (that Mrs. Hempstead was such a nosy old biddy). "Forgot my key," I added by way of useless explanation to her and awkwardly teeter-tottered the heavy door back in quasi-place. I turned to face the woman. "What the hell is going on?" I tried to say this as pleasantly as I could. I think I failed.

She had dark brown eyes, lovely features; did I mention that?

She regarded me with clinical disinterest, just a bit too practiced for my taste. Been there, done that.

⎕ A Strange Visitor ⎕

"So you're Enoch Maarduk?" Like she was naming a bug in some specimen jar.

I laughed thinly and said in my drollest voice, "Are you going to pull a gun on me, too?" I was particularly proud of that one.

She repaid my sarcasm with a nasty, winsome, grin and said softly, "Do you think I need it?" It was the sweetest, most harmless, voice imaginable. Too bad I had already seen her kicking some dude's ass just a few minutes ago.

I took the hint and swallowed my pride. Did I mention she was really good-looking? "Enoch Maarduk," I said with congenial good-nature and extended my hand.

She hesitated just a fraction of a moment and took it. "Phoebe O'Hara," she said warmly, watching my eyes as she crushed my hand. I crushed back. Her expression was much warmer this time and we let our hands drop. I was, I am kind of ashamed to say, glad, sort of... my hand hurt.

"So, tell me about that electromagnetic spectrum article you wrote for the website." Her smile seemed genuine, her tone playful almost, but her eyes were hard and serious.

"What is it with that damn thing?" I asked, half-joking, but this Phoebe person did not appear amused by my curse-laden query and continued to hold me in her intense gaze. Very disconcerting from a woman.

I smiled wanly, "It's just an idea I had last night." I shrugged, spread my hands out in the universal sign of pleading again (practice makes perfect). "Just trying to come up with an idea to make a buck."

She was studying me intently. Remember the specimen jar thing? "The idea just came to you, out of the blue" — a flicker of a pause — "just like that?" I did not care for the tone of her remark, but she seemed dangerous.

Nevertheless, I snorted my derision with her question. "You ever write? Ideas just don't *pop up* out of the freaking blue." I was getting a little bent over this, I will admit. "It was the culmination of many ideas generated over years of research." I said this with mixed emotions, very much vexed by this vixen.

☐ Chapter Two ☐

"Don't get your shorts in a wad," she noted dryly. "I just wanted to know."

I was still peeved. "So what is such a big deal with my blog that some guy would pull a gun on me and then someone else" — I couldn't resist giving her a swarthy scowl — "wants to give me the fifth degree about it?"

She shook her head sadly as she surveyed me. "Well, then, it's your lucky day I won't be giving you the third degree, isn't it?"

Pretty girl, I have to admit, but there's a fine line between pretty girl and bitch in my book. "Fine; first, fifth, whatever, you still didn't answer my question."

She reached behind her, which made me nervous for half a heart beat, I admit, but only produced a business card, stepped forward and handed it to me.

I looked at it. Plain white index card stock. Nothing on it. I flipped it over. Blank there, too.

"I'm sorry," she said and, indeed, did look properly chagrined. "You're not aligned yet."

Like I knew what the hell that meant.

She took the card back and held out her left hand, on which she wore a silver signet ring. She waved the card over the ring and handed the card back to me.

The card now showed some printing.

Okay, pretty cool trick. Maybe heat-activated or something. "Phoebe Scarlett O'Hara," I read aloud, paused, looked up at her and could not resist a grin, "Really?" She narrowed her eyes and I figured it was time to move on. Below her name was a company name and an address. "PHANTASM, 365/24/7, 3210 South Ohm Street," I said and gave her another weary, doubt-ridden, glance. "Which does what..."

"Go there later today and find out." She took hold of some kind of device attached to her waist belt, it didn't look like a cell phone, but she glanced at it, then at me. "I have to go now." She pointed at the business card. "Go there and they will answer all your questions."

She turned to leave. Nice gym outfit, fighting togs or whatever it was she had on, from my vantage point. I smiled to myself. She moved briskly toward the door.

⧫ A Strange Visitor ⧫

The door! "Hey, wait a sec! Who's paying for my door?" Very self-righteous. Practical. Utilitarian. Yo, realist.

She didn't bother to turn but yelled out as she entered the stairwell, "Take them a bill and they'll pay it."

Her footfalls echoed down the landing. "They're always open..." came a fluttering rejoinder and then silence.

Crap.

I stood staring at the door and then nearly jumped out of my skin when the cell phone went off. I will have to tell you that "Bring Out Your Dead" was not as amusing now as it had been a little earlier.

"Tom," I answered in a tired voice, and went on to tell him lunch was out of the question, but at dinner I would relate a story he would not believe. Vitellos, again, but at 6:00.

He started to tell me something I wouldn't believe—about last night he said—and I did the only sensible thing possible and hung up. It was the only sensible thing because, otherwise, Tom was a little like that cyborg in the *Terminator* movies. He simply will not stop talking until you are dead. Or, something like that.

Okay, about thirty minutes later I was trying to contain my vexation, irritation, anger, frustration, and bitterness. Apparently finding anyone on a Saturday afternoon willing to repair a door was simply beyond entrepreneurial possibility in this city. And I thought this was a depressed job market. Hmm—so I said screwdriver it and decided to fix the door myself.

I asked Mrs. Hempstead—well, I bribed her with a bottle of wine—to keep an eye on my place since all I could do was sort-of-kind-of wedge the broken door shut. A beckoning clarion call to all would-be burglars. Riff or Raff. I frowned. A nice red Zin would be added to the PHANTASM bill, I smirked as I walked down the stairs. Plus cab fare. Hah, cabernet would fare as well. Two bottles of wine added to the bill.

I was still in good humor because, I mean, replacing a face plate, an inset lock, and a hinge should be a relatively benign task.

Which, if I had shown even a smidgen of intelligence and brought the actual parts with me to the freaking hardware store, it would have been. Even for someone as mechanically-challenged as me.

☐ Chapter Two ☐

Of course, considering how the day was unfolding, I didn't realize this simple but painful fact until I was standing growl-faced and grumptious on Aisle frigging 16 and staring at 5000 damn options for mending a simple door. Fug.

Some overweight guy in a wrinkled green uniform tried to help, but waddled away after it became apparent I was lost in the wasteland. Probably the colorful string of flowery invectives I unleashed in the general direction of Aisle frigging 16 hastened his hasty departure. Sigh.

Since I wasn't keen on making the 45 minute trip back home and out here again, I bought a variety of items. A veritable smorgesborgie of hinges, face plates, and whatever the hell else I could find that I thought would work.

And naturally, an hour later, none of it worked, {insert sigh, followed by primal scream}. My calm was damaged a little, yes. Shattered, actually. No serenity at all...

Anyway—I juxtaposed, jamboozled, jizzled, and jimmy-rigged something which seemed to work if you pushed or pulled the door with all your strength, put your knee carefully on the opposite side, maintained pressure, and turned the deadlock as hard and fast as you could.

Which I did at 5:30 and headed for Vitellos.

Mrs. Hempstead popped her knobby head out at 5:30 plus or minus five seconds, when she heard a loud noise, which was me kicking the damn door in retribution for the anguish it was causing me.

The door appeared utterly insensate to my remonstrations. My foot, on the other hand, seemed rather incensed by the whole ordeal. I waved at her, she toasted me with a glass of wine.

Man, I needed a drink.

Vitellos was packed. It was like that great old malapropism from Yogi Berra when someone asked him about the popularity of another famous restaurant—"No one goes there anymore, it's too crowded."

For those of you who may not have heard of him, Yogi Berra is a former professional baseball player and malaprop. You are adrift in a cultural vacuum if you do not add him to your knowledge base.

❑ A Strange Visitor ❑

Do the search. Bookmark it; just a suggestion.

Anyway, back to Vitellos and crowds.

It is damn near impossible to get a reservation. The President was once turned away. I won't say which one. The owner's son was an old high school pal whose butt I had once saved in a little gang scuffle many years back, and he never forgot that.

I have a nice four-inch scar along my side I rub on occasion to jog my memory as well.

The other fellow looks worse, trust me.

So, I get a table whenever I show up. Every time I see Danny, he swears he is going to move the restaurant out of downtown to the north side. Get away from the maddening traffic, the noise, the organized mayhem. Have a place with a huge kitchen; maybe two stories, stained glass; hardwood floors, imported art from Italy. A place closer to his house; maybe he could ride his motorcycle to work.

But the problem was that the City loved Vitellos right where it was. A treasure, a landmark, an icon. The walls emblazoned with fifty plus years worth of photos — celebrities, politicians, diplomats, gangsters, athletes, and regular joes who made it big — there were memories so thick a Ginzu knife couldn't cut them.

Danny's father, bless his soul, had started the place. Danny II had it now, and Danny III was in training. And Danny IV, from what Danny III told me, was already in the planning stages.

Okay, enough with the genealogy. The City "bequeathed" the building to Danny I (and his heirs) as long as he swore to stay. So Danny II stayed. He even added the stained glass, the hardwood floors, and imported art. It was still a long drive from the house but, shoot, these days he usually only showed up on Friday and Saturday nights anyway, so it was okay.

Thus, everyone knows me at Vitellos and waves, hugs, says hello; but it's still kind of an embarrassment, as I'm not a "pop star" kind of guy, and all the new patrons are whispering and pointing and wondering what famous personage I am. I guess kind of cool, but mostly irritating. The regulars just smile and nod.

Just get me to my table in the corner, okay. Which Emily does with graceful precision, depositing me in the far corner where Tom sits waiting, nursing some kind of light orange-colored, martini-looking, concoction. I have no idea what it is. We slap a metro righteous handshake and I plop happily into my chair.

"What can I get you to drink, Enoch?" Emily says with a smile. We've dated a few times. Really nice girl, just not ready to settle down quite yet, but great company.

"Whatever Mon Sewer is having." Tom rewards my bad humor with a sideways smirk.

Emily eyes me in speculation. "Are you sure?" A very compelling pause. She leans in and whispers, just loud enough for Tom to hear of course. "It's another one of those nasty drinks he invents." She wasn't endorsing the end-product, so it seemed. Tom gave her a loving glare.

"I'll try one," I said carelessly. "It's early." Emily laughed and headed off.

I looked at Tom. "What exactly is in it?" Tom has been known to, well, get kind of exotic at times. I still remember what happened a few nights after he watched the movie *Moulin Rouge* and he just had to get his hands on some absinthe.

As it turned out, it wasn't so much the alluring powers of absinthe that got him into trouble, as it was mixing it with serotonin. If I get bogged down later, maybe I'll tell you that lurid tale. Or, maybe not.

Tom laughed infectiously. He was one of those people that, no matter what he did (within reason) you just liked the guy. He got along with women, men, children, and animals. Well, maybe not cats, but there wasn't any pretense to Tom. He was just, you know, Tom.

He had taken a small inheritance from his grandfather and carefully nurtured it to where now he was comfortably semi-retired; a little work when the mood suited him, monitored his investments, worked out at the gym, and chased women. Hey, things could be worse.

Damn, not much.

Tom started listing the ingredients: "Two shots of premium gin, one shot premium vodka, a thimble full of very dry vermouth, a dash of fresh orange juice, and just a hint of hazelnut liquor for hue." I resisted the urge to punish him with a pun.

Tom acknowledged my questioning stare and glowered at me. "And no serotonin."

I frowned, a facial motif that seems to come rather naturally to me these days. "It sounds more like an anesthetic than a cocktail." I flashed my best smart-ass smile at Tom.

He smart-assed me back. "It's an acquired taste."

I wasn't altogether sure I wanted to make that acquisition.

"Does it have a name?" I asked innocently, knowing that Tom gave pet names to everything, drinks included. He dated a girl a few months back that he nicknamed Buffi, and I refuse to tell you why. Not sure why I brought that up, other than a desire to be a gadfly, Socratic or otherwise.

"Copper Gorilla," he said with a sly smile.

I could see how that might be apropos, though the empirical evidence was only in the offing. Still, firsthand knowledge was critical to achieving a proper understanding. I anticipated the experiment with a sort of besotted glee. Another in a long litany of character flaws, no doubt.

I nodded and changed the subject. "Where's Armando?" Saturday night dinner for the three of us was a mainstay in our lives, for better or worse. Usually better, since it always involved martinis, wine, great food, and incredible conversation. But sometimes worse if you failed to keep a close watch on your tab, if you know what I mean and I think you do.

Tom was shaking his head in a hybrid of mock and real sorrow. "That's part of what I tried to tell you on the phone." He gave me his best wounded, accusatory, expression. "You know, before you hung up on me." He scoured me with a fake harsh look.

"I always hang up on you." A flitting grin. "What happened to Armando?" Hopefully nothing serious.

"He's having dinner with his new girlfriend." Tom relayed this information with all the solemnity of a judge passing down a life sentence for jaywalking.

"No," I sort of gasped unwittingly. "Not a girl he met last night?" I used my astonished face because, well, I couldn't help using it.

"The very same," Tom announced dejectedly, taking a sip from his drink. A small sip, to be sure, of that potentially lethal concoction.

▢ Chapter Two ▢

Emily arrived and sat my drink in front of me. It seemed to be glowing. I muttered thanks. "Appetizers?" she asked sweetly.

The Armando revelation had me momentarily off my game, so I sat in silence. Tom bailed me out with orders for pasta with red sauce and molasses-oatmeal encrusted jalapeño slices.

I leaned forward in a conspiratorial gesture, glaring at my friend. "How did you let that happen?" I snapped at Tom and tentatively sampled my cocktail. Hoping to like it, but prepared for Molotov.

Tom paused before he answered, mostly to study my response to the drink.

"Damn," I lamented grudgingly, "that was pretty smooth."

"Lethal," Tom stated flatly.

"Tell me about Armando." This was serious.

Tom shrugged. "It's not my fault. He met this woman entirely on his own." He didn't hold my eyes.

"Okay," Tom admitted reluctantly, painfully, as I surveyed him, "she was a friend of a friend."

I grimaced in real anguish. "Oh, man, not the FOAF scenario?"

Tom nodded laconically. "Def Con One, I'm thinking."

I took another sip. After the numbness in your mouth wore off, it was rather tasty. "I need to talk to him."

"Sure," Tom replied agreeably and nodded his head over his left shoulder. "He's in a room back there."

"What?!" was my cleverly inane response. "He brought a first date here?!" Notice the question mark accompanied by the exclamation mark. I mean, holy crap, this was serious. Armando was probably in the deepest sort of trouble, and that's when friends need to intervene and help.

I started to get up but Tom put a restraining hand on my sleeve. He wore a grim look and was shaking his head. "Truthfully, I think he just needs some space on this one."

"Space?" I sputtered. Okay, I wasn't exactly a fount of sparkling repartee—this whole day was becoming a wee bit overwhelming. Becoming? Wee? Was. Is. A big wee.

Tom caught my eyes and gestured ever so slightly to his right with a nod of his head. "When you get a chance, take a look at the guy in the cheap black suit three tables over." Tom rubbed his nose. "About 45 degrees to your left."

What the devil was Tom doing—trying to change the subject and get me off the Armando mission? I picked up my drink, sat back nonchalantly (what if I sat back chalantly; hmm... never tried.)

Anyway, there sat a squatty little guy, middle-aged, ratty mustache, slightly balding, and when I turned to survey him—nonchalantly as I said—he was, indeed staring at us. Well, not us, me. He immediately made some pretense to look away and started studying something on his table, presumably his menu.

"He's been watching you for the last few minutes or so," Tom added by way of explanation.

Now, I am not normally a trusting soul. I figure that, one way or the other, everyone is out to get you for something. The government for more taxes, your boss for more work, your friends for more time, women for more attention, politicians for more donations, and blah, blah, blah.

Therefore, it didn't take much prompting for me to do the mental gyrations and conclude that this guy was somehow related to the earlier goon, the one with the gun at my condo. Maybe a leap, but I jump when I'm spooked, okay? And, sad to say, I usually jump toward the problem and not away. Probably another character flaw.

The rest rooms were in that direction. "I'm going to the john," which Tom knew was code that I was going to amble over, walk leisurely by, and check this guy out. Normally a minor tactical move involving a table of good-looking women, not some cheesy dude wearing a rumpled black suit of indeterminate origin.

"Watch yourself," Tom added and why on earth he thought that advice was needed was beyond me. Maybe he could sense the tenseness in my features, or perhaps it was how I drained the rest of that damn Copper Gorilla before I stood up. Whew, like swallowing jet fuel mixed with serotonin—surely not? Had to focus now, not worry about it.

The tables at Vitellos were spaced reasonably far apart. Danny wanted everyone to be able to see everyone else, but not hear their conversation. He'd even gone so far as having these custom composite baffles built into the ceiling which hung down and not only held the lights, but soaked up and muffled the talk from around the tables.

I passed the first two tables as surreptitiously as possible, which isn't easy for a guy that's six-foot tall and just under two bills; however, the man's attention was still absorbed with his tabletop. He sat fiddling with both hands doing something I couldn't see, and didn't notice me as I approached.

Eventually my presence must have intruded on him because his head shot up, his eyes locked on mine, and I could see a sort of irritated acknowledgment. He lowered his head and continued what he was doing, which appeared to be drawing something on the tabletop using the varied contents of the salt, pepper, and artificial sweetener shakers and containers.

He was drawing shapes of various kinds, but I couldn't quite make them out. Very odd. What the devil, I thought.

And just as I was processing this fact, a waiter—a thin-looking young man with an athletic build—appeared from my left, about ten paces away, carrying a single glass of water on his stainless steel serving tray.

The waiter slowly approached the table. The seated man with the ratty mustache looked up and I sensed that he recognized the waiter, though that was nonsense of course. Then the seated man started frantically spilling out what looked like red chili powder (he must have brought that with him, as Danny would never allow such a thing) onto his design and started saying something in low monotones, like a chant or mantra.

The seated man looked up again, anxious, as the waiter neared. The waiter seemed to suddenly lose his balance, stumble, and the glass of water—rather too precisely I thought—retched over the edge, crashed loudly to the table, and completely washed the man's carefully conceived design into oblivion. The man stood up so fast his chair fell over. Patrons at the next table gasped and someone said "oh" in a startled voice. It might have been me.

For a moment the man started to direct his hand to his jacket, but I saw the young waiter mimic the gesture. The man scowled, livid with anger, gave me a particularly withering glance, and then fled toward the front exit. He was gone in a few moments.

◻ A Strange Visitor ◻

The waiter eased in my direction, leaned over with great solicitation and said softly, "I'm so terribly sorry, sir." He then pressed a business card into my hand, followed by a whispered, "Phoebe says be careful." He turned and walked away, leaving me standing there looking like a complete idiot.

"You have that ability," Tom said later, when I was back at the table, telling him the story and nursing another Copper Gorilla. My gawd, those things were hideous.

"Are you saying I'm a complete idiot?" I said in wounded pride, joking, as I already knew the answer.

"No, just that sometimes you *look* like a complete idiot." Tom smiled, though I was certain it was from the after effects of his second Copper Gorilla and not his pitiful attempt at humor.

I held the waiter's card up for him to see. It was the same sort of card Phoebe had given me back at my condo. "What exactly does PHANTASM do?" Tom asked me quietly.

"I have no idea," and instantly wanted to bite my tongue in regret for saying that, because professing ignorance when there is a techno-geek around is the absolute kiss of social death. Out popped his hybrid smartphone with high-speed Internet access, quack, quack, quack. Byte me.

A few minutes later he looked at me in semi-shock with a dose of moderate stunnage. Tech guys hate not finding information. Drives them nuts. Well, nuttier. "There's no such company in this city," he stated incredulously. He plainly didn't believe it.

By this time, Emily had brought our appetizers and I did not immediately respond, since an absorbing mouthful of homemade pasta noodles slathered in this vegetable-embroiled, tomato-tinted, awesome sauce was holding my rapt attention. My attention was wrapped around it, you could say. Or, not.

I washed it down with a robust red Zinfandel. Nice ripe fruity taste, lush attack but a genteel finish. A pleasant acidity with just a hint of spice. I felt that my resveratrol numbers were approaching adequate levels.

"There's nothing in that area but warehouse space," Tom muttered, breaking me out of my grape-induced revelry with his tech whining.

☐ Chapter Two ☐

With pursed lips and a fearful scowl, he was studying the satellite imagery of that area. "It's near the railroad yard. An old manufacturing area," he mumbled and shrugged. "Except now it's mostly antique shops, restaurants, and fancy bars."

"And the problem with that," I said in semi-caustic sarcasm, "is what, exactly?"

Tom shook his head, fed himself a fork-full of appetizer and grunted, "No problem, I've been down there a few times; it's nice." He swallowed. "Just seems an odd place for this PHANTASM company, or whatever."

I had outlined the whole story to Tom, from Polyester Man up to good-looking Phoebe. And, of course, the events this evening here at Vitellos were already known to him. It worried him that PHANTASM was, well, a phantasm. Sorry.

"That's not funny," Tom said. "If you can't find anything on these people, then that means they're Black Ops or something." He tore off a piece of crusty rustic bread (with a delightful crunchy sound, I might add) and swirled it in the remnants of his plate.

"You watch too many spy movies." I actually laughed aloud. Guffawed, if you will. "Black Ops!" I said derisively.

Tom appraised me with arched brows. "That fancy little box this Phoebe woman used to magically snatch the weapon out of that guy's hand. Her ring. The cool PHANTASM business card." He huffed a guttural grunt. "You think she bought that stuff on the Internet?" His own sarcasm amused him to the point of a chuckle. I admit, it was good. I simply stared at him with a bemused expression, unconvinced.

"The key point to remember," Tom continued, "is that the guy had a gun." He pointed an imaginary gun at me with his fingers. "That's dangerous stuff." He lowered his head and once again favored me with the serious raised-eyebrows look. "You need to find out what's going on."

At some point in our banter our actual meal arrived. We continued the rehash of current events after my story hit the fan, in a manner of speaking. Tom's retelling of the adventures of he and Armando from last night just didn't have the allure it normally would have had, but Tom dutifully relayed it, but much more monotone than usual.

A bit anticlimactic after all the other stuff.

We paid the bill, left a nice tip for Emily, did the man hug thing. "Call me tomorrow after you visit with those folks," Tom said as we stepped outside.

"Who said I was going to visit them?" I said gruffly, though I had already decided to go anyway.

Tom gave me a serious look. "Strange people. Guns. Busted doors. Bizarre man in a cheap suit drawing figures at a table." He shook his head. "You're going, right?"

I made a simple hand gesture. "Fine, maybe I'll go."

Tom shook his head. "You are such a PITA." He waved as a taxi pulled up. "Later," he said with a grin and was gone.

It was after 10:00 as I trudged up the three flights of stairs back at the condo, my footsteps echoing off the metal steps and reverberating in the stairwell. A little unnerving, although I had never really thought of it that way until, well, now. Nervous grin.

I pulled on the door, tugging it slightly to the side, put the key in and turned the lock. It opened. I guess I was pleasantly surprised that my key didn't snap off or something.

I stepped in and as soon as I passed the threshold, the room shifted.

Let me lob a little explication your way which will, hopefully, make this peculiar event clearer in your mind. Think of two identical photographs printed on transparent acetate.

If you hold them up, perfectly registered, they appear as one flawless image. However, if one of the images is moved beyond register, out of phase you might say, by even a slight amount, the image looks "disturbed"—Hamlet would be pithed.

Add in an odd back-and-forth rocking motion that only lasted a micro-second, and you have the general effect I experienced.

After gathering my wits (I know, a task that shouldn't take long), I shut the door and wrestled the lock into place. Copper Gorilla blow back, I mused to myself, but dismissed that out of hand since in all other respects, I felt fine.

Food allergy? I remember eating some bad fish once and experiencing an allergic reaction. Tunnel vision, dizziness, odd ringtones.

☐ Chapter Two ☐

I felt good, though. My mental state was a little fragile, true, but, believe me, I've been through much worse. Well, maybe...

I stood looking around the living room. Kitchen with island to my left, long table and entry into the hallway to my right, large living room in front of me, partially blocked by a small retaining wall. Everything was just as I had left it. Well, appeared to be, anyway.

I moved cautiously into the condo. I decided it was time to get an alarm system installed. Of course, if someone was already in here, that point was morbidly moot. I swiveled my head and glanced to the hallway which ran from the right of the living room down to the bedroom, to where my firearm was stashed. Hmm... I hmmed to myself and walked into the living room.

People tend to look at the television when they enter a room, even if it's not turned on. Odd human behavior, but true nonetheless. There was a note stuck to the flat screen, and I hadn't put it there.

Which meant someone had been in my condo and no one was authorized to be in here. Unless it was the folks from maintenance. Maybe something broke. I snatched up the note.

"Enoch: I have placed a temporary protective EM shell around your condo. It will protect you until the morning, then go to PHANTASM. You're welcome, Phoebe."

FTLOG.

A protective EM shell? I crumpled the note and tossed it on the floor. Bachelor's prerogative. I was starting to get an uneasy feeling that I was being stalked, but I shook it off. Phoebe seemed normal, well, I'd have to get to know her better (insert innocently sinister laugh here), and I did have a gun pulled on me. Plus ratty mustache man at Vitellos. Multiple stalkage.

Bah!

I showered, checked my weapon—protective EM shell my ass— climbed into bed and, after contemplating the pleasant coolness of the sheets, was asleep before I could even think about anything else.

Ignorance Is Not Bliss

—▯———————

"The trouble with the world is that the stupid are cocksure and the intelligent are full of doubt."

—Bertrand Russell

I consume too much caffeine.

They (I have always wondered who this nefarious bunch of people are) say that the average person puts away about 280 milligrams (mg) of caffeine a day. Around three cups of coffee or a couple of power drinks.

I usually have that pounded out by noon. I think I have a high tolerance or something. Or, I'm a complete idiot.

Possibly, probably, both.

I was sitting at the breakfast room table (which, curiously enough, transforms into the lunch room table around noon and morphs into the dining room table at five) having a java jolt and nibbling on an unreasonably ancient donut, staring dolefully at the PHANTASM card on the table.

Well, fudge. The card clearly showed "365/24/7" and that Phoebe person had said they were always open, so, early Sunday morning or not, I was going down to the warehouse district. At the very minimum they owed me for a door and a bottle of wine. Or two. An explanation would be a handy side benefit.

So, after a 30 minute cab ride, there I stood, holding the card to confirm the address and staring at a rather nondescript, drab gray, two-story, stucco-covered structure that was about 50 feet wide and ran on for what it seemed like half a football field.

All around it (well, on the other side of the road anyway) was the sure signs of urban redevelopment—gift shops, antique stores, curio nooks, cafes, and bars. Pretty quiet, though, as it was Sunday morning.

☐ Chapter Three ☐

The gray building straddled the main road, Commerce Boulevard, and sat on a dead-end street. Ohm Street. In fact, it was the only building on that street. Across the way was a small vacant field and at the end of Ohm Street, basically at the back of the building, there was a huge wooden fence. Through the trees, on the other side of the fence, I could barely make out the shapes and outlines of small buildings or houses.

I turned my attention back to the gray building and regarded it with a great and malingering doubt. There was not a window in sight.

Just a plain gun metal gray storm door with a small light above it, housed in a brass-colored metal cage. Above the door, below the light, were some black metal letters and numbers spelling out, "3210 South Ohm Street."

I chuckled lightly at what had to be some kind of inside joke. I mean, come on—"3-2-1-0, SOS?"

I was rapidly approaching my neuro-overload danger zone. My brain was overflowing with recent events. Not only was I ruminating on this new little bit of street address funkazoidal humor, but I was still thinking about the guy with a gun who had hassled me over my electromagnetic energy blog posting.

And then some hot kung-fu mama sends me here, to Ohm Street. As in Georg Ohm, noted physicist. Ohm's Law. Electricity and such. Key-bloody-riced.

There were no cars parked on Ohm Street. A few cars and people were across the way, mostly at the scattered coffee shops and breakfast joints found along the main drag of Commerce Boulevard. PHANTASM seemed like a stain on an otherwise perfectly suitable silk tie.

I walked up, gingerly I must say, to the front door. I turned the handle, half-expecting it to be locked. Half-hoping it would be locked. Cab fare was in my left front pocket. I checked.

The door opened without a sound. Well, other than what seemed like this incredibly loud pounding noise emanating from my chest. I held the door ajar while I regained my composure, the little bit still available anyway.

Breathing having returned to quasi-normal, I opened the door wide enough to peer inside. Truthfully, it was just as creepy as the outside.

⧠ Ignorance Is Not Bliss ⧠

There was a long, narrow, hallway (if I stretched out both my arms it looked like I might be able to touch the opposite walls) and it ran on, oh, maybe 25 or 30 feet, ending at another gray metal door with a single handle. The hallway was lit from above with recessed lighting, fluorescent I think, but softer in coloration than a regular office.

The walls were painted a rather bright white. And they were utterly blank and devoid of features. Well, hell, they didn't lock the door, probably had everything stolen. I laughed nervously to myself and it rippled, echo-like, into the hallway. I eased the door shut behind me as I stepped in but, right after it clicked closed, I immediately tested it to make sure it was unlocked.

A little paranoid, but you would be too, damn it. The door opened fine. I shut it and turned to walk down the hallway. Took a deep breath.

I had on soft-soled shoes and there was barely a hint of noise as I moved down the hallway. Mostly just the quiet hissing rustle of my clothing. As I drew near to the other door, I noticed a small button, like a doorbell, on the wall next to the door. It was a plain white button, recessed, and, until you got close, you could hardly even see it.

I leaned forward to better examine it. It suddenly changed color, turning red, then green, at which time the door clicked and cracked open just the modest bit of an ooch. I involuntarily jerked back a step or two at the color change and door movement.

Maybe voluntarily!

For just a microt I thought about skedaddling, running, vacating, hauling ass, but the better part of my discretion was, at least this time, valor, so I stayed. Okay, I was torpid with fear and couldn't actually move, but it felt like valor the more I thought about it.

Waited a few moments to let my heart rate return to freaking normal, but I stayed.

And then I stepped through.

Now, it wasn't exactly like that transition from black and white to color in the old *Wizard of Oz* movie, but it was sort of, kind of, like that.

It was a room about the size of the waiting area you find when you go to see the doctor. You know, when they practice as a large group.

☐ Chapter Three ☐

To the left were a row of cushy-looking chairs, then a table with a lamp and hardbound books, rather than magazines. I couldn't make out the titles, but they looked old, judging from the color and apparent age of the bindings.

To the right were two large leather couches, arranged in a "L" shape. There was a large flat screen television against the wall, facing the couches, but it was not on.

Straight ahead was a large desk, a credenza I suppose, the top of which was mostly barren except for what appeared to be a digital communication device like a smartphone, though slightly larger, and two older-looking hardbound books.

Several feet behind the credenza was a bank of sliding glass windows, all frosty tinted and opaque so I could not see within. There were no shadowy shapes moving behind the window, so I figured no one was there. There was some kind of instrumental music playing, wafting in from an unknown source. All of which made this room more than a little surreal, to be sure.

The music sounded vaguely like an industrial, alternative, surfer, rockabilly blend, instrumental as I said. I shrugged, not your everyday office music. I liked it. Hectic eclectic.

I walked up to the windows and knocked lightly. Nothing. I tried to slide the windows open, for a peek, but both of them were locked. A deep breath—I like strange as much as the next guy, but all this bizarre was getting odd, as well as old.

Getting?

I turned around, leisurely stepped over to the credenza slash desk, and picked up one of the books. *EM Fields in Flux*, written by a Dr. William Paramendes. Lots of graphs, charts, and equations. I put it down. Picked up the other one, titled *Spectrum Anomalies: Empirical Studies*. Lots of contributors, and it, too, was mostly technical charts, elaborate tables, and a variety of odd drawings.

The sound of the sliding glass startled me. I whirled to face the windows and snapped the book shut in a knee-jerk response. It sounded very much like the report of a small caliber pistol.

A pleasant-looking, round-faced, young woman with short black hair was leaning out. She was wearing wire-rimmed glasses that seemed fashionable for her facial features. "Can I help you?" A pleasant voice accompanied by a pleasant smile. This was feeling less mundo bizarro by the moment. I was pleasantly nervous, as you can no doubt tell.

I sat the book down and walked over to the bank of windows. I reached into my pocket and produced the card that Phoebe O'Hara had given me. "Uh, I was told to come see…" a non-loquacious pause, "…someone from your…" gawd, I sounded like a babbling idiot, "…company," I held the card up. "She told me. Phoebe." I smiled weakly. "Phoebe told me. Phoebe Scarlett O'Hara." I wanted to run and hide. Well, run anyway.

Off to the side, behind the frosted glass, I saw another figure moving and a man appeared beyond the woman. She took a half-step aside and the man leaned in. He was middle-aged, a bit overweight, soft and harmless-looking features, sharp eyes, dark brown hair. He was clean-shaven with puffy cheeks.

That was my instant impression, for what it's worth.

He smiled, and it was genuinely warm. "You must be Enoch Maarduk." It was more a statement than a query.

"I am," I affirmed, though not without a dose of trepidation since the last time I had owned up to that fact someone had threatened my left kneecap. The man reached under the counter and I heard an iridescent buzzing sound. A door appeared on the wall to my right.

I say "appeared" because there had not been a door there earlier, just a wall. "That's a cool trick," I said aloud.

The man grinned. "An EM field manipulates stucco particulates to simulate the visual appearance of the wall."

I nodded and asked what I considered the obvious question. "How do you contain the dynamic vibratory energy to mirror the static nature of the wall?"

The man stared at me with an expression which seemed a combination of surprise and delight. "We oscillate it between EM states so fast that the human eye can't perceive the transitions."

☐ Chapter Three ☐

I frowned, thinking about it. "How do you manage the heat dissipation—unless you're looping it into some kind of re-ionization process..."

Now the man's expression changed to a sort of solemn shock. "Good heavens," was all he said, then gathered his wits and pointed at the door. "I'll meet you in the other room."

"Phoebe said you were smart." We were walking down another bland, featureless hallway. He had introduced himself as Wilbert Nicholas Bromfield. "Call me Nick."

"Phoebe said that?" I know I have mentioned previously she is really good-looking.

He gave me a knowing glance, with a hint of what I thought was sad understanding. "She's a pure professional Mr. Maarduk, just doing her job." A flat smile. "I wouldn't get too fixated on Miss O'Hara."

Miss O'Hara, I mused and smiled to myself. We reached another door, this one had been there the whole time, and stepped through into another room about twice the size of the one I had just visited. Same paint job, though. The similarity ended there.

There was a raised sort of dais or platform with a half-moon desk facing away from us, behind which a man sat staring intently at the far wall. And this wall looked like the bank of video monitors you find in some major network newsroom. Except there must have been fifty or sixty of the damn things, and each one tuned to a different broadcast and, as we walked closer, I realized they were all in different languages.

Nick stopped, leaned slightly toward me, and spoke in low tones. "We found him unconscious on our doorstep one day, six years ago." I looked at the man who was watching the monitors and then back to Nick. "Just some homeless guy, we thought."

As I watched, I could see Monitor Man making rapid-entry notes with a keyboard entry device, and simultaneously speaking into what had to be some kind of auto-transcribing microphone.

"It turned out," Nick went on, "that he is a truly remarkable idiot savant." Nick shook his head in wonder. "All he has to do is listen to any spoken language for a short while and he soon thereafter becomes proficient." I gave Nick a look of doubt. He shrugged.

⧠ Ignorance Is Not Bliss ⧠

"At PHANTASM," he smiled knowingly at me as he spoke, "we are always monitoring global events searching for..." he pursed his lips, "...indications, clues, to specific types of activities." He gestured at the man. "He didn't know his own name, so we called him Joe, as in regular Joe." Nick laughed. "That was before his unique talents were discovered."

Nick smiled mischievously and nodded. "We have algorithms for monitoring textual communications, but Joe monitors visual broadcasts for us and provides feedback based on preset parameters." Another smile, with a bit of mysterious allure. "Using his unique understanding of our situation." That was a bit nebulous, to be sure.

We walked slowly up to the man. "Joe, this is Enoch Maarduk."

Joe swiveled gracefully in his chair until he faced us. Nick said the guy was formerly a homeless person, so in my mind I had pictured a man in his thirties who looked sixty, but Joe was the absolute picture of health and vitality. Alert eyes, ruddy complexion, carefully quaffed hair. He was dressed casually, comfortably. He looked very much like a successful businessman lounging on the couch to watch the weekend football game

Joe tossed me a friendly half-grin. "I thoroughly enjoyed your blog." He nodded inscrutably (well, it seemed that way to me) and added, "I was impressed." He lifted a raised index finger to acknowledge Nick, "Nick." He craned his neck to loosen it up, then looked back at me. "I hope you join us." He turned back to his monitors.

I had no sooner said, "Thanks" than Nick nudged me lightly and we began moving toward another door and out into the hallway. We approached what appeared to be an entrance to an elevator. Which flashed open as we walked up, whooshing like some cool sci-fi effect. I mean, it was cool. We stepped in.

Damn, that was a fast elevator. It started downwards and I felt like I was going to pop out of my shoes for a sec. And just a sec, because the doors seemed to open just after that, and we were where wherever it was we were at. Or, whatever.

"Joe's not easy to impress," Nick said softly as we drew near to another doorway.

⎕ Chapter Three ⎕

I suppose this was meant to flatter me, but I am always wary of such things, even though Nick relayed it as a statement and not as some kind of sales pitch con. I shrugged as he opened the door and we moved into the room.

It was a regular office, like you might find in any professional building. Pleasantly furnished, simple, but pleasing. Hardwood floors, nice touch, and soft gray walls. A couple of chairs in a small waiting area near the secretarial desk, occupied by an efficient-looking mature lady who eyed us closely as we entered. There was one closed door behind her, to her right.

"Right on time, Nicholas," the lady said with a smile for Nick, and she stood up, extending her hand toward me. "I'm Deandra Prinz, Dr. Hume's secretary."

It was a warm, friendly, face, and firm handshake. "Enoch Maarduk," I projected the best warm and friendly aura I could muster, considering the unknown and slightly trepidatious nature of my undertaking. Okay, maybe a bit melodramatic, but all of this was still kind of unsettling, even for me.

She favored me with a little wisp of a smile as she turned. "I'll let Dr. Hume know you're here." She walked over, knocked lightly twice on the door and went in. A few moments later she came back out. "Come on in," and she waved us through, then exited and shut the door.

I've always prided myself on being an observant person. Maybe not Sherlock Holmes keen, but I don't miss much. One of the things I try to do, whenever I meet someone at his or her place of business, or even at their home, is attempt to make an assessment of their personality based on the surroundings.

Just like we are what we eat, our inner consciousness is reflected in our external workplace. My own place resembles a room after a grenade has been detonated. Fairly accurate description of my mind.

The very first thing that caught my eye was the floor. It was a dazzling display of exquisitely executed marquetry, with a varied assortment of colored woods being employed to produce the most startling array of geometric designs I had ever seen. It took a mental effort to pry my eyes away from the floor.

☐ Ignorance Is Not Bliss ☐

Especially when it changed to an exotic middle eastern woven carpet. I squinted in amazement. The floor was actually made of some sort of display glass, and apparently could be made to look like any kind of flooring. That was really impressive. I forced my eyes upwards.

An immense wooden desk faced me as I stepped into the room. My first impression was the sheer scale of it, as in, perhaps they had constructed the room around the desk, because I don't know how they would have got the damn thing in here. There was no computer in sight, just a small assortment of books and papers placed at the edges of the desk, and a metal container holding mini-bottles of water.

On closer examination, though, I realized the top of the desk was one huge touch screen display. The desk was one big ass computer!

To the left was a bookcase filled with a mix of ancient tomes, digital tablets, memory sticks, and flash drives. Basically, the output of humankind since the, well, Sumerians. Hah!

To the right were some recessed cabinets and some really ancient -looking chairs. My review was interrupted by Hume's soft voice.

"Nick," the man said warmly, rising from his chair effortlessly and moving smoothly over to take Nick's hand.

Nick caught my eyes, which I had managed to wrest up from watching the floor change again, and held them. "Enoch Maarduk," and here Nick turned away. "I'd like you to meet Dr. Denton R. Hume, our CEO."

This Denton R. Hume and I traded the classic frank first-meeting stare and I have to tell you, people with really blue eyes kind of freak me out. I mean, deep, rich, sky-blue, ocean-blue. "It's a pleasure to meet you, Mr. Maarduk," he said warmly.

There are some people who have a presence, a resonance, about them. You can't put your finger on exactly what it is—you just know that it's there when you encounter it.

For most people this is accomplished through foppery, extravagant behavior, or pure self-indulgent pretense. It is rare to meet anyone who exudes an aura of power by simply standing in the same room with you. Hume was like that.

There are rituals involved when you first meet people in a formal environment. Odd, I guess, but standard practice. The clues for civilization, I suppose. "Enoch is fine, Dr. Hume." We exchanged our clue, er, handshake.

Ah, you'll have to forgive me here, because I intend to momentarily pontificate on handshakes. Why? Always wanted to; so here goes.

Reams of material have been written on the subject and even doctoral dissertations have been generated. From secret handshakes, like the Freemasons, to elaborate street routines worked out between gang members, handshakes can tell you a great deal about a person.

For instance, since you asked (or not) your basic handshake falls into three categories, kind of like the porridge of Goldilocks. You have your limp, dead fish, shake. Then the iron vice grip, and then the firm, but steady and expectant, exchange. We will rule out the street shake as inappropriate for this type of setting. I won't digress into handshakes with women, as that is a different animal altogether. The handshakes, not women.

For men, though, normally the dead fish shake comes from folks with soft hands; people who haven't done a lot of manual labor or engaged in many physical activities. I pass no judgment in that regard, just making an observation. Or, they just might not like shaking hands; or maybe just not your hand. Either way, that type of non-commitment is telling.

The iron grippers are like socks—lots of variety. Some are over-compensating for other deficiencies, some are trying to intimidate. Insecurity is usually the main part of it.

The firm and steady shakers mean business. I mentioned these kinds of handshakes are steady and expectant because they are smart, and are waiting to see what kind of shake YOU are going to give. This was the shake Hume gave me.

I gave in kind.

He waved at the ancient-looking, but extremely solid in structure, wooden box chairs with loose-fitted, padded leather cushions; the cushions being of more modern origin. "Please, have a seat."

The chairs looked and felt authentic, circa 14th century or something, English, possibly Scottish, but that's just an educated guess. A SWAG, really. Sophisticated and wild, to be sure. The style of the ornate and detailed wooden engravings were good clues though.

☐ Ignorance Is Not Bliss ☐

Hume saw me examining the chair. "My family coat of arms."

Before I sat down, Nick extended his hand and I clasped it. "I've got a meeting"—he glanced at his watch—"that I'm already late for." He cast a friendly glance at Hume, who nodded in acknowledgment, then smiled at me. "Enoch, Dr. Hume will answer all of your questions." With that statement Nick left the office and closed the door behind him.

I settled myself in the chair. "I am very pleased you came to visit, Enoch," Hume began with an infectious smile. I swear, he would have been awesome selling used cars, except I sensed a basic honesty and decency in him. Now, I don't mean to imply that used car salesmen are dishonest or indecent, it's just an expression of speech, sheez.

Hume continued, "I'm sure you have some questions."

I admit it, I like words, language, puns. What's the point of communication if you can't have fun with it? Okay, fine, try to have fun with it.

"I thought that you would be the one with the questions." I gave him my best honest and decent face. I'm not sure how well-received it was, as Hume frowned a little.

He recovered quickly and brightened. "It's true." He nodded. "For instance, I am extremely curious about your blog site."

"About the electromagnetic spectrum post," I added helpfully.

"That was of particular interest to more than a few people around here," Hume acknowledged with candor.

I snorted, "And of particular interest to some other people as well." I paused for effect. "I'm thinking of one particular guy with a gun." I was smiling, but it was a bit forced and tepid.

Hume nodded, made a little humming noise. "I read Phoebe's report," he glanced at his desk, then back at me. "I think we owe you a door."

"And two bottles of wine..." He had a puzzled look on his face. I waved it off. "I'll get to that later." I spread my hands in symbolic supplication. "So, what's the story behind the guy with the gun?" Ignorance might be bliss to some folks, but not to me.

"I hope you don't mind, Enoch, but we did a little research on you." Ducking the question. He picked up a folder on his desk for effect.

❑ Chapter Three ❑

Dang, I was hoping it would have been thicker.

"I'm not hiding from anyone," I said with a straight face, which wasn't strictly or precisely true, because someone was always looking for me—mostly about overdue bills. Hey, I eventually pay them.

"No one hides from us." Hume favored me with a knowing grin that sort of sent a chill up my back. "But, not to worry, we are the good guys, Enoch, as I'll explain shortly."

"Every side thinks of itself as the *good* guys," I said without rancor. I favored him with a tilted non-grin, grin.

"Touché," he said and I was starting to like this guy's demeanor.

"So, tell me about PHANTASM," I said and adjusted myself in the surprisingly uncomfortable chair.

Hume rubbed his chin with his thumb. "A simple query with a complex response."

"Well, be like the White Rabbit," I said, curious as to his response to my allusion.

He nodded and chuckled. "Begin at the beginning..."

"...and go on till you come to the end: then stop." I sat expectantly.

Hume cleared his throat. "PHANTASM is actually an acronym. It's always written with capital letters." He gestured at the metal container holding the plastic bottled water. I nodded. He handed me one and took one for himself.

"PHANTASM stands for *Preventing Horrors And Nightmares Through Active Spectrum Monitoring*." He was watching me carefully as he spoke, which he did very slowly and methodically, to make sure I heard and understood.

Well, at least I heard. Understanding was off playing on the highway or something. I posed the obvious question. Obvious to me, anyway. "Horrors and nightmares?"

My query was rewarded with a lop-sided grin. "That terminology is a remnant, a simple recognition of archaic ancient tradition."

Hume shook his head and added, "Technically, we don't deal with horrors or nightmares."

"Technically," I repeated in a quizzical tone. My voice may have been tainted with just a modicum of a mocking sound, but not willfully intended. Have I mentioned my numerous character flaws?

"Philosophy and religion like to deal in precise values like good and evil," Hume replied by way of explication, "but we have found that it really coalesces down to ignorance versus knowledge, and the willful choices made when people achieve the latter stages of conscious development." He was again watching me closely, and I'm pretty sure it was to see how I would take his remarks.

"I've written extensively on that topic," I commented.

Hume acknowledged that with a big smile and tapped my file. "Which is precisely why you are sitting in that chair having this discussion with me."

"Okay," I nodded amiably, "keep on discussing."

He nodded, leaned back in his chair. "Most people have heard of the formulaic expression $E=MC^2$, as you point out in your blog post, but they fail to truly grasp the ultimate significance of that elegant formula."

"Everything is the same," I tacked on with a smile.

Hume nodded agreeably. "Just in different states of transition between energy and matter." He took a sip of water and continued. "Awareness, that is to say, field effects with consciousness, were once thought to be the unique prevail of humans."

"Very much like the Ptolemaic notion of the universe, that the Earth was motionless and everything revolved around it," I added by way of being helpful and, of course, showing off.

Hume waved a finger in the air. "Humans tend to think that the consciousness we exhibit as a species is somehow utterly unique to humans." He angled his head to the side and studied me thoughtfully. "The truth, which is very difficult for most people to accept, is that consciousness is a natural field effect exhibited by EM systems that have sufficient complexity."

He paused, and I knew it was so I could wrap my thoughts around that last bold statement.

"Any EM system," I paused and closely surveyed Hume, "as you call it, capable of receiving, processing, and interpreting external stimuli, can attain consciousness?"

"Yes," Hume confirmed, then added. "Assuming it reaches the necessary level of complexity."

⬚ Chapter Three ⬚

I finished a sip of water. "Which is what, precisely?"

Hume sat back, as though pondering his response. "Therein lies the rub, Enoch, because varying levels of complexity will yield varying levels of consciousness."

"Like the classic bell curve," I said, ever helpful.

Hume seemed a bit taken aback for just a moment, and then a huge rippling smile flowed across his features.

"I haven't thought of that before, but that is a perfect example!" He bobbed his head in enthusiasm. "The delineations along the bell curve exhibit a pattern that reflects the level of consciousness attained, based on complexity," he paused and then continued in an excited voice. "That level of complexity is conditional upon the structure and content of the EM system in question. Of the individual human." He leaned forward in his chair, "Or, the human population being studied!"

Now, I admit, it was my turn to get a little enthused, as his remarks turned my mind in a direction it had not thought to go before.

"So, what you are saying is," I began, seeking more clarity, "in the case of humans, the complexity of one's brain is directly correlated to their position on the bell curve for intelligence, or consciousness?" I noted Hume's nodded agreement and plowed ahead. "The real question becomes, then, what influences this complexity? What drives the complexity to achieve intelligence or consciousness?"

Hume was very animated by now, and appeared to be speaking to no one in particular. "My heavens, but this links in precisely to our mission here at PHANTASM."

He shook his head in wonderment. "It validates everything and provides the perfect explanation."

I did the old spread-the-hands-in-supplication thing and said a little unsteadily, "Explanation for what?"

Hume seemed to regain his focus as he turned to look at me. He took a deep breath and leaned back. He drank some more water; buying time to gather himself was how I interpreted it.

"From a morphological perspective, our brains are actually a continuum based on a threefold structure." He said this very carefully. Which meant it must be important.

So I stayed quiet, for a change.

"Our consciousness, awareness, our level of personal development, is specifically linked to neurological function and language skills"—he moved his hands excitedly—"and a person's intelligence depends on the complexity of the connections to the three neuro-processing zones."

He pointed at me. I raised my eyebrows. "And," Hume went on, clearly agitated, "that is exactly how the so-called demons of medieval times utilized electromagnetic energy to affect human behavior." He coughed, "That is, their human masters, who controlled the demons."

At this point in the conversation I was getting pretty psyched up about the consciousness slash continuum slash bell curve thing, but this new *demon* morsel sort of threw me. Okay, it knocked me semi-conscious to the ground, wiggling in a stunned daze. Demons. Really?

I assumed Hume was using that as a metaphor for aberrant human behavior, as in *the devil made me do it*. "We are talking metaphorically about demons as some medieval explanation for the evil that humans do themselves, right?" I shook my head, confused, somewhat diffident. "The demon and the master are the same thing?"

"Enoch," Hume said with a wide and warm smile, "you have asked more intelligent questions in five minutes than anyone who has ever sat in that chair."

"You must run a lot of dumb folks through here," I said by way of my impressive self-deprecating humor. Hume grinned back. His expression had that contagious kind of friendliness you feel comfortable around.

"Some people call the electromagnetic entities *demons* because that is a holdover from ancient times, particularly medieval times." He made a steeple with his hands and fingers. "These entities, in point of fact, come from another plane of being—the electromagnetic spectrum—and in that realm they exist as shifting fields of energy with only an awareness of their own being."

I frowned, truly nonplussed plus you might say, trying to decide if Hume was nuts, I was nuts, or maybe there was a camera hidden somewhere. I figured, what the hey, just go with it. "So, these entities have consciousness?" I asked by way of clarification. Not sure what I was clarifying, per se, but I wanted to hear more.

Hume shook his head. "Not consciousness in the human sense, which is to say, having a conscious awareness that responds to the continual bombardment of external stimuli and is constantly reshaping itself." He licked his lips. "The EM entities exist in a realm of self-contemplation, which is the best I can phrase it. Pure thought."

"Like being trapped in a dream?" I suggested, seeking a better mental grasp.

"No," Hume replied immediately, "not trapped." He took a breath. "As I understand it, the EM entities have minimal control over the content of their thoughts and what direction they wish their contemplation to go. Keep in mind that every piece of information in the Universe exists somewhere on the continuum of the EM spectrum." He grinned. "You just have to sit back and enjoy the ride."

I freely admit it. I sat there working hard to wrap my vexed cerebrum around that statement (and the others) for more than a few seconds until I felt comfortable with Hume's explanation. Okay, maybe not comfortable, but willing to move on. "Why do these entities come to Earth? A little rest and relaxation?" I added jokingly. I was still from Missouri on this whole deal. Show me.

Hume grinned, but it was definitely forced. "They are pulled into our world against their will." He seemed to sigh. "You are familiar with magical pentacles?"

I nodded suspiciously. "You mean, the kind used for summoning demons that aren't demons?" Yes, I did let the sarcasm ooze into that one.

Hume favored me with a sideways scowl. "A correctly constructed pentacle is a sophisticated receiver and transmitter, Enoch, composed of elements and minerals that respond to EM frequencies." He smiled ruefully. "Most of the pentacles you see that purport to be from medieval times are rubbish; complete nonsense." He snorted derisively. "If you ever come across a real pentacle drawing, take a long, hard, look at it and think about how very much like an electrical schematic it is." He chuckled. "A real pentacle, built correctly, can tap into the raw energy of the electromagnetic spectrum."

It was just about at this point that a chill started at my toes, ran up my spine, and exploded out of my ears. "In essence, then, all modern technology is based on magical pentacles!" was my excited comment.

Hume's grin was big and broad. "Everything taps the EM spectrum." He waggled his finger in the air for emphasis. "But, it takes a very special setup to summon an EM entity."

"And your implication is that this has been done before." I paused. "In medieval times?" My doubt was hanging by a precarious thread. Arachne.

Hume nodded. "None of those previously summoned EM entities exist on this planet at this time." I actually heaved a sigh of relief, though still felt oddly uncomfortable. "But," and somehow I knew this was coming, "in the past three years plus, we have monitored increased activity."

It was Hume's turn to sigh; then he went on. "There are, at present, four such entities on Earth, three of which pose an immediate danger to human affairs." Just the briefest of pauses and he added, "The threat comes from the human controllers directly and the EM entity indirectly. The EM entities have little will in the matter."

I need for you, gentle reader, to pause for just a fractious and contentious moment and try to imagine how your sorely afflicted brain would be faring if you were getting all this supposedly, uh, true, information, tossed your way, filling your thoughts with a veritable grab-bag of oddity. You've heard of shifting paradigms, right? More like reversed paradigms here.

Which way was up? More than a little disconcerting, right? Exactly. I wanted someone to slap the seven shades of shiny goat crap out of me and wake me up.

Still, I suppose the best course forward was forward. "What kind of threats?" Yeah, the obvious question is always the scariest.

Hume took a sip of water, sat the bottle down and stared at it for a moment. "Enoch, I'd be less than truthful if I told you we had a clear handle on that." His shoulders seemed to sag. "We have operatives in the field all over the world gathering intelligence, trying to find puzzle pieces." He shrugged. "If things work out between you and PHANTASM, I hope you'll be one of the people helping to solve that puzzle."

Hmm... I mused to myself. *If things work out?*

If!?

☐ Chapter Three ☐

And what kind of freaking "things" was he talking about? Bad things, no doubt. I was going to ask another question, followed by a zillion more, when someone tapped on the door and it opened. Phoebe's lovely face appeared around the corner.

She nodded at Hume; he then looked at me and spoke. "Phoebe will escort you to the testing area." We both stood up. "I know you have more questions, but first it's essential we assess your capabilities for field work." A quick, and firm, handshake.

"Enoch," Phoebe said, rather more nicely than I expected.

"Phoebe," I replied warmly because, as I mentioned, she really was a good-looking woman.

"Let's go," she said sharply and off we went.

Testing, Testing, 1, 2, 3

—⊪—

"Se non 'e vero, 'e ben trovato."
(Even if it is not true, it is well-conceived.)

—Italian folk saying

I don't like tests.

I mean, let's face it, a test means someone other than yourself is looking for something that you may or may not have; be it knowledge, skill, talent, or disease. The results might be a little frightening. "Mr. Maarduk, I hate to have to tell you this, but you have no talent whatsoever for understanding trigonemetry."

Hell, that's fine, I can't spell it, either.

I especially don't like tests where it isn't particularly clear what it is some white-smocked and high-browed "they" are testing. In fact, ever since Phoebe had escorted me out of Hume's office, I had been complaining, er, commenting, on that irrefutable fact.

We had been walking down another of those interminably long hallways, except this one would suddenly take a hard left, then a hard right, then another and another, finally exhausting itself at an elevator. I gave Phoebe a WTF look.

"Really, Enoch, it's just a series of simple tests." She shook her head in bemused and amused contemplation of me.

"Simple tests," I parroted her in mocking tones, "that take place in the bowels of some super-secret government agency." I laced it with as much acidic sarcasm as I thought Phoebe would accept without taking a poke at me.

"We are not affiliated with the government," Phoebe replied with a smooth smile as the elevator doors opened with an effervescent whoosh.

◻ Chapter Four ◻

"Fine. In the bowels of some super-secret private company." I watched as she pressed her thumb against an ID scanner and then hit a button that had the letter *S* on it. "Secret?" I commented smugly.

Phoebe shook her head again, and eyed me sadly. "Sub-basement, Enoch, the Level 2 sub-basement."

"Do they take blood?" We had stepped off the elevator and began moving down another long hallway. White paint, no doors, no windows, nothing on the walls. Like a mental institution or something. That sort of shook me. Suppose this was some kind of intervention by well-meaning friends? Rehab for a twisted mind? I gave myself a cortical slap. Nah.

"Blood?" Phoebe echoed in disbelief. "What on earth would we want your blood for?" She looked over and gave me the sweetest, most horrible, smile you can imagine. "Well, not more than a few pints, surely."

"You're not funny," I stated flatly.

"Yes, I am." The smile was much nicer this time. "The problem is, you don't know a good joke when you hear one."

Finally, we turned a corner and there was a simple metal door. We stopped in front of it. A bluish light bathed us in a sort of swirling sci-fi scan, and the door clicked open. Probably the next step right before the probes got inserted. I stood rooted to the floor.

"You're thinking about probes, aren't you?" Okay, maybe I had already mentioned my fear of probes to Phoebe.

I moved into the room. "I'm fine," I said defensively. It was a very large room that was filled with tables, cabinets, computers, flat screens, one particularly odd-looking apparatus, and many other peculiar-looking machines. A handful of people were scurrying around taking notes, turning knobs, and making all sorts of calibrations.

I took a deep breath as an ebullient middle-aged man, probably late forties, with a neatly trimmed brown beard streaked with gray, walked over and eyed me with more than just a gleeful interest.

"I'm Dr. Panglaws, and you must be Enoch Maarduk." He smiled engagingly and we shook hands. "Hello, Phoebe!" A warm and protracted smile for her.

☐ Testing, Testing, 1, 2, 3 ☐

"Hey, Doc," Phoebe answered with an affectionate grin. Panglaws rubbed his hands together in a kind of Frankensteinian glee. The sides of my neck were itching.

"Dr. Hume has not sent me a really qualified candidate since Phoebe here." Phoebe actually blushed. "And that's been a few years." She gave him an arched eyebrow on that one.

"Qualified for what?" I asked innocently.

Panglaws jabbed a finger in the air. "Ah, Mr. Maarduk, that is precisely what we intend to find out." His grin was reassuring, assuming his potential madness was benign.

"Will it involve blood?" I asked innocently. Phoebe glared at me.

"Only if you fall off the chair," Panglaws admitted cheerfully. He turned to go. "Follow me!"

We weaved our way out of the large room into a smaller area that contained the chair he must have been talking about, a comfortable-looking leather desk chair bolted to the floor near the door. Across the way on a small, but sturdy-looking table, sat another thoroughly strange-looking device. It was about the size of two computer monitors strapped together (the old ones that used to weigh a couple of hundred pounds each) with metal rods sticking out, wires, diodes, LED displays, and who knows what else.

My attention shifted as I saw Phoebe take a seat in another small chair in the corner. A knowing smile on her face did not exactly endear her to me. I scowled furiously at her.

Panglaws gestured at the chair. "Please have a seat while I explain what we are going to be doing." I sat down, pleased that there was, at least to my quick glance, no restraining belts on the chair.

He reached into his white smock and produced a ring, similar to the signet Phoebe had used in my condo to make the business card text readable. "Every PHANTASM operative wears one of these rings, but they are much more than jewelry." He smiled in a kind of self-satisfied way. "One of my more useful innovations, if I must say so myself."

Phoebe piped in, "Saved my hide many times." Okay, I thought, anything that saves your hide is good.

"How does it work?" Seemed like the obvious question, so naturally I asked it.

☐ Chapter Four ☐

The doc's smile faded a little. "Well, truth be told, we aren't exactly sure."

It was my turn for a faded smile. Panglaws noted my expression and quickly continued. "Oh, we know what to do to set it up and why it works, we just aren't sure HOW it works, exactly," he ended haltingly. His smile was warm and weak, like convenience store coffee.

I nodded. Hey, if Phoebe likes it, I guess I do, too. "Go on."

Panglaws walked over to a table and picked up some kind of headset bristling with wires, electrodes, and diodes, or whatever. He returned to face me. "We scan, monitor, read, and record your brainwave activity." He tilted his head at a bank of computers sitting on the far wall. "We process the data and match it up to the ring, which is basically an electromagnetic field attenuator." He looked at me expectantly.

"The opposite of an amplifier," I gave the appropriate reply.

Panglaws went on: "The eemees you might encounter can generate..." and I had to interrupt for some techno jargon updating. I raised a hand.

"Eemees?" Terminology time-out.

"Sorry for the slang," Panglaws grinned, abashed. "Electromagnetic entities. Eemees."

I nodded unknowingly. "Okay, you haven't lost me yet." Well, maybe a little…

"Good, good," Panglaws said happily. He was getting worked up now. "Eemees can manipulate spectrum energy in many ways."

Phoebe couldn't help herself, "And in some particularly nasty ways, too."

Panglaws nodded, "Nasty as in bad, not sexually deviant."

"They can do that, too, Doc," Phoebe rejoined. Panglaws blushed this time.

"An eemee can direct this energy toward an individual in the form of a neuro-scan." He waved the headset around for emphasis. "But doesn't need wires and electrodes in order to assess your brainwaves."

"So, what's that going to tell them? Whether I'm awake or not?" I grinned at that gem, but no one else seemed to find it amusing.

⎕ Testing, Testing, 1, 2, 3 ⎕

Panglaws regarded me with serious intent. "Actually, Enoch, we have been able, even here at PHANTASM, to build up a database of brainwave patterns and match them to simple words and concepts." He nodded. "We use that technology in the CU." Cool. What's a CU? I was going to ask, but figured why add to the effing confusion. My confusion mostly. Fine, my confusion completely.

He stopped and stood watching me as I was digesting (belch) all that. "The eemees are much more advanced in brainwave pattern reading than we are," he clarified.

"But, you can still read minds here?" I asked, not bothering to hide the skepticism in my voice. And on my face.

He shrugged. "No, no, not yet, but we are getting close. We can tell you, in general terms, what you are thinking, based on matches to a database of comparable brainwave patterns for specific basic words, some concepts, and general neurological activity."

"The eemees can do more than that?" I said, much less steady this time.

"If you were not wearing a fully aligned attenuator ring, they would read you like an open book." He held the ring up and looked at it closely, then turned to face me. "This little thing blocks or dampens the eemee scan and temporarily protects your thoughts, giving you enough time to take positive action." Yeah, as in run like hell the other way.

Phoebe chimed in, "The only thing keeping you from being compromised is that ring."

I frowned. "And what happens when the..." I paused before using the new word, "...eemee, can't read your brainwaves and knows it should be able to?"

"The eemee's abilities are subject to the same sort of interference as any form of EM activity." He waved the headset as he spoke. "Rare earth metals, sunspot activity, proximity, other equipment broadcasting in the area; all of these can affect and limit eemee scans." Panglaws grinned. "Besides, they are unaware that we possess this technology."

Okay, that seemed like a good answer, though not exactly reassuring to know that all that stands between me and some mind-reading demon, er, eemee, was a freaking ring. I pointed at the headset he was holding. "How does that work?"

Panglaws lifted the headset so I could see it better. "Your brain actually consists of three distinct areas."

"Sex, drugs, and rock & roll?" I added helpfully. Phoebe didn't even crack a smile. In fact, she frowned and shook her head at me. Talk about someone who doesn't get a joke.

My flippant remark did, however, elicit a grin from Panglaws, one he quickly extinguished when he glanced over at Phoebe. "We'll have that discussion when there's more time," he coughed and started fiddling with the headset, rearranging cords and electrodes.

I looked puzzled. Hell, I was puzzled. "So, why do I have to protect myself from these eemee scans? Are they evil beings?" Hey, maybe the question was dumb, but I didn't know jack squadoosh about this topic.

"Well," Panglaws stated gloomily, "I really didn't want to get into that subject right now."

Phoebe stood up and walked over. She faced Panglaws and said, "He needs to know now." She turned toward me. "You have to keep in mind, Enoch, that the eemees are not inherently good or evil." Her tone of voice was much changed from her previously short and gruff speech. "The eemees have been *summoned*, to use a phrase, against their will, from their freedom in the EM spectrum, and now they are under human control." Panglaws was listening intently and nodded his head in agreement.

Phoebe continued. "The eemees scan humans because they, the eemees, want to survive, and they are trying to understand what it is their new human controller wants."

"The controller being the human who built the pentacle," I stated, pretty sure I understood at least that much.

"Yes," Phoebe said, "and the eemees scan the controller to determine what the controller wants."

I nodded and stayed silent, as she clearly had more to say.

"The controller's consciousness, intelligence, personal level of development—whatever you want to label it—exists on a dynamic continuum that runs from the most base and physical desires moving upward through social needs for fame and fortune to the urge for power and respect, culminating in the highest and most spiritual achievements; a synthesis." She sighed. "I won't get into the specifics, but each of those spots on the neurological continuum correspond to sites within the human brain, from physical to social to spiritual."

She gave me a sour, hard look. "Trust me when I say that none of the controllers will be operating at that last level."

I nodded like I understood, which was a bit bogus, I admit. Fine, completely bogus. I still had questions, and tossed the first one out. "Since the human who built the pentacle controls the eemee, what good does the eemee get from scanning the controller's brain?"

Phoebe favored me with a wry smile. "Being able to decipher what the controller wants is useful to the eemee, but the controller always makes that fact readily known." She shook her head. "It's the ability to scan other people besides the controller, and then manipulate them, that has the real and ultimate value."

She gave me a look that conveyed the serious nature of the topic. "The eemee, and the controller, can heavily influence people by understanding their consciousness and, more or less, reading their minds."

I didn't like the sound of that. "What kind of range do these eemee beings have for that mind reading trick?" I was thinking about staying a few miles out of range, you know? Maybe a hundred or so.

Phoebe smiled. "The eemee has to be nearby, practically in the same room, for their scanning ability to work." I sighed, mildly relieved. "As agents of PHANTASM, we often come into close contact with eemees, so obviously we don't want our true identities scanned and made known." She smiled and winked at the Doc. "The attenuator was born."

She turned and walked back to her chair. "History lesson over."

"Okay," Panglaws said, moving over to the chair and handing me one of the rings. "Are you right-handed?" I nodded. "Good, put the ring on your left ring finger, like a wedding ring." He grinned at what was probably a standing joke. The ring was a little large, but fit okay. Panglaws then leaned over to place the headset on my head.

☐ Chapter Four ☐

"Will this, thing, uh, really read my thoughts?" I swear to you, I tried not to sneak a peek at Phoebe, but my damn head turned her way completely on its own. I snapped back to look at the doc.

He laughed lightly as he sat the headset on my head and adjusted it for a snug fit. "No, no, nothing like that. It merely monitors and registers the activity in the three main processing zones of your brain." He gave my arm a small pat. "After that, we calibrate the brainwave patterns to the attenuator ring and, voila, you have a dampening field generator on your finger to block the eemee scans."

"No blood?" Had to ask.

"Don't fall out of the chair," he reminded me as he backed away and moved over to the impressive machine on the table. On closer examination, it was unlike anything I had seen before. Think of some devilishly macabre device Nikola Tesla, Hans Holbein, and Hieronymous Bosch might have collaborated on and built. All angles and out of whack edges. Disjoined discontinuity.

I was jolted out of my consideration of the device by a new sound. A slight, very low, background hum filled the room. "Whenever you are being scanned by an eemee," Panglaws began speaking as he fiddled with some more controls, "you will feel a tingling or tickling in your medulla oblongata"—and he touched the back of his neck, like I didn't know where the frigging oblongata was located or something—"almost like hundreds of little fingers." He looked up from his machine and at me. "That sensation will only last for a short while because the attenuator will then kick in."

Being a natural gadfly (notwithstanding how that ended for that other fellow) I asked, "And what would happen if the attenuator doesn't work?"

Panglaws' head popped up and he wore an expression of genuine disbelief. "That's not possible."

"Okay," I muttered good-naturedly, "humor me."

He took a deep breath, straightened up, walked out from behind the machine and clasped his hands together behind his back. "Well, no one has asked me that before." Phoebe guffawed. He ignored her and went on. "I have no empirical evidence on this, mind you, but based on what information we have managed to accrue, the eemee can, after scanning your brainwaves, interject thoughts and brainwave patterns into your mind that you believe completely to be your own." He shrugged. "If you act upon those thoughts and ideas, and most people will, you are doing so under the indirect control of the eemee."

"Super. I'll be a zombie." I was rapidly sliding into my not-so-happy place.

"The attenuator never fails," Panglaws said with grim finality, as they say, and returned to the relative safety of his machine.

I glanced at Phoebe. She tossed a real smile my way. "It really does work." I instantly felt better. How do women do that?

"Okay," Panglaws said loudly. "I'm going to turn the machine on full power. You'll feel that tingling sensation I mentioned, but don't be alarmed. It will last for about five seconds or so, then a short pause, and then it will kick in again for another few seconds." He looked expectantly at me. "Ready?"

I felt like a guy about to be electrocuted for a crime he didn't commit. "Sure, fire it up." Be cool, Phoebe has her eyes on you. Panglaws disappeared behind his apparatus.

I felt the tingling start.

And then the doc's machine simply turned off.

No explosions, no unearthly sounds, no zinging pop. Just lost power.

Phoebe stood up and ambled over to the table. "What happened?" A very perplexed expression gracing her face.

Panglaws came nimbly around the table, following the electrical lines with his eyes to end at a black box sitting on the floor. "Looks like some kind of electrical spike tripped the surge protector and shut the unit off." He was scowling, confused at the fuses, as it were. "Odd, though, nothing else is affected." He looked around the room at all the other equipment running just fine, thank you.

Phoebe glanced at the connection. "It looks like it's running on its own 220 line." The doctor opened his mouth and waved a hand.

"You're right, I remember now. This is running on its own line." He scowled again. "Still damn peculiar, though." He bent down and clicked a glowing red button located on the side of the black surge protector box. "I'll just reset it and try again."

◻ Chapter Four ◻

I guess it was going to take some time to reboot and calibrate the thing, because Phoebe crossed over to talk to me. "Did you do that?" she asked casually, wagging her head at the machine.

"Me?" I said in honest shock (is there any other kind). "How would I do that?"

Phoebe pursed her lips. My goodness, she was a pretty girl. "I'm thinking your bad attitude might have done it."

I gave her my best *up yours* tilted smile and replied tongue-in-cheek, "Well, you managed to get through the test."

She chuckled, lukewarmly at least. "Results will probably flunk your ass out anyway."

I was a bit stunned at that. This whole PHANTASM thing was growing on me. I was getting sort of warmed up to the idea of being here, sort of. "What do you mean?"

She arched her eyebrows. "There's a very specific brain profile for operatives that you need to match." A mocking smile this time. "Pretty narrow range of candidates." She appraised me with an unsettling look. "Maybe you're one, and maybe you're not..." The doctor let out a hoot.

"Got it reset." He clapped his hands. "I made a few changes in the software to override the surge protector because the diagnostics came back neutral. The box itself might be going bad."

Phoebe had returned to her chair and sat down. "I'll text Vinny to replace it," she said in a raised voice. I guess Vinny was the maintenance guy or something. She produced some kind of communication device and started fingering and thumbing it like mad. Focus.

The doc smiled at me. "Ready to try again?"

It sounded like, "Ready to fry again?" which sort of disturbed my calm, but since I had survived the first wayward attempt to prod my cranial innards, I figured we were good.

"Light me up, doc." I said humorously, though Phoebe, looking up from her device, shook her head and frowned at me. I thought it was funny. My line, not Phoebe.

And then she was slowly oozing out of the chair, barely conscious and fighting to get to the ground without crumpling and cracking her head open. She managed to get prone and then passed out.

☐ Testing, Testing, 1, 2, 3 ☐

A loud thump behind the machine was a pretty good indicator that the doc had just joined her on the floor, but without Phoebe's preventative care.

Key-bloody-riced. I fumbled at the snaps and clasps and other rigging and clumsily removed the headset.

The moment it was off my head, the two figures began to stir.

Phoebe took two deep breaths and sat up. She arched and craned her neck to work the stiffness out. And then looked at me. Oh man, I mean that was a look.

I raised both my hands in a gesture of innocence. "I didn't do anything."

Panglaws had made it to a standing position and was rubbing the back of his head, a grimace on his face, staring at the machine's display screen. He stopped rubbing and looked from the screen to me.

"I'm afraid you did," he said softly, without a shred of evidence to back it up, by the way.

Phoebe was standing now, poised handily one might argue, in attack mode. I grinned sheepishly.

"Tell me about it, Doctor," she said, her voice very serene, all things considered. She never took her eyes off me. I took a shallow breath.

"I've never seen anything like it before," Panglaws said, more to himself than in answer to Phoebe. "The attenuator ring is only supposed to generate an interference field based on brainwave patterns and interaction with the incoming scan." He leaned over to read the digital results constantly updating across his display monitor. "But, somehow, Enoch is redirecting the scan's inherent energy back to the source."

Phoebe wore a puzzled look. "And this explains our passing out, how?"

"The redirect was so intense it..." he paused to hunt for a word, "...it refracted and affected us." He stood up. "Extraordinary." He produced the same sort of hand-held communication device Phoebe had been using and began typing on it. "Dr. Hume needs to know about this."

And, in about 5 minutes, Dr. Hume did know about it, learning it firsthand as he stood next to the doctor listening with serious intent. Phoebe was standing next to me.

☐ Chapter Four ☐

"How did you do that?" She didn't sound angry anymore. A little fearful maybe.

"Not sure," I said honestly. "I'm glad you're not hurt." That sort of slipped out.

She laughed. "I know how to fall," was all she said, then looked right at me. "But, thanks for caring."

Hume walked over. I got another hard look this time, but it was still warm and friendly, though tinged with just a little hint of doubt. "You are turning out to be an interesting person, Enoch."

"Maybe the machine just needs recalibrating," I offered helpfully.

"I heard that," Panglaws crowed from behind his contraption, "and there's not a damn thing wrong with this device."

"Panglaws says your brainwave patterns are, well, unique." Hume smiled, rubbed his chin absently. "Apparently what we thought was a purely defensive tool has some unknown offensive capabilities." He gestured at the ring I wore.

"And that could be good, or bad," I said, acknowledging his unspoken thoughts. A weapon is still a weapon.

"Especially if we aren't sure exactly how it works," Hume stated calmly. His expression was mostly inscrutable.

I gave Hume a pained expression in return. "More tests?"

Hume smiled gently. "That is entirely up to you, Enoch." Hume took a deep breath, paced away and came back. "But, I hope you choose to stay. You may possess an extraordinary gift that could prove invaluable to us; and to yourself."

Now, I have to tell you, this was kind of an uncomfortable predicament for me. As in a major and every-other-rank kind of way.

To be honest (well, try to be honest), I've spent most of my life avoiding life-changing situations. I had a post-graduate scholarship offer in college, but figured it would be too much work, so I turned it down.

Later on, I had a nice grant lined up for some government research job, but it meant moving to another state, so I didn't take the gig. Got to be friends with a woman who turned out to be in the publishing business and loved my writing. She offered to be my agent, handle a book for me, but I never bothered to write it.

⏻ Testing, Testing, 1, 2, 3 ⏻

I'm a floater, a drifter, a trust fund only child, what can I tell you? Small trust fund, true, but I live cheap.

Anyway, now I was being asked to make a decision, and not just any decision, because I felt, in that deep place in your soul where you know the truth abides, that if I committed here, I was *all in*, to use popular poker terminology. This was the real deal when it came to accepting responsibility and making a strong commitment.

I looked up at Hume. He was regarding me with a chimerical visage. Stoic. Panglaws stood tensed, expectant. I felt a little, no, make that a lot, like that bug in the specimen jar I mentioned earlier. I turned my head to look at Phoebe. She laughed at me. "Don't do it, the pay stinks." She sat back and looked away.

I nodded and stood up, extending my hand to Hume. "I'm in."

If had known the extent of the new tests and how long they would take, I might have tossed my cards in the muck, folded, cashed in my chips, and gone home.

Then again, Phoebe did come over and kiss me on the cheek.

And slugged me in the belly for making her pass out.

Ah, what the hell, I signed some paperwork and went on the payroll. And Phoebe had pulled a reverse psyche job on me. The pay turned out to be great. I had to look at the contract a few times to make sure it was right.

But, back to the tests.

We had gathered up our goods and trundled ourselves off, skulking down more white hallways and another damn elevator (which went down some unknown and slightly spooky distance) to a much larger test area with even more massive and bizarre looking machines. Phoebe took a call, waved, and vanished quickly out the door.

As a swarm of technicians buzzed and flitted around with the machines, took measurements of me and did God-knows-what else, Panglaws and I talked about the refraction thing where Phoebe and the doc had passed out. Panglaws had a theory (hmm...) that I might be able to control the degree of redirect through mental focus, sort of holding the energy and releasing it in small packets rather than in one big wave.

I got your one big wave.

I told him I would try.

"This is mostly new equipment, some of my own designs," he said proudly. "We're still in beta testing on some of it," he muttered in an offhand way. He said "absolutely" when I nervously asked him if it was safe.

The first beta machine blew up.

Well, didn't actually explode. It just let out an alarmingly loud "BOING" and smoke began billowing out of it. Mad scramble of people. Elegantly harsh look from Panglaws.

We took a break between sessions and had a brief discussion which centered on the distinction between packets versus waves. I shrugged and told him my control was in beta testing.

Man, some people have no sense of humor.

The second machine (not sure if it is was beta or not) worked better, but it only generated results when Panglaws adjusted the power output to maximum. He kept asking me if I was okay and I kept telling him I was fine.

And then everyone started to droop and sway, like they were going to pass out. Packets, not waves! Packets, not waves!

You know how zombies look in the movies, sort of hunched over, listless, kind of just standing there, arms hanging loosely at the side? Well, that's how five the technicians and Dr. Panglaws looked. An improvement over being passed out on the floor, to be sure. They could actually move, too, though kind of jerky and, okay, zombie-like. Panglaws seemed to be regarding me with a particularly keen interest.

I took the headset off.

Everyone quickly recovered, just moments really, and Panglaws walked up smiling. "Much better control, much better, but can be improved." He rubbed his chin back and forth with his thumb. "I have an idea."

"Does it involve blood?" I asked, hoping to keep things jovial.

☐ Testing, Testing, 1, 2, 3 ☐

He gave me a Phoebe-grin. "Yours, if you make me hit my head on the floor again." He rubbed the back of his head for added emphasis and grinned.

"I want you to try something this time." He made a hand gesture at me. "Instead of just attempting to send packets instead of waves, I want you to redirect the scan energy into some specific inanimate object"—he turned and looked around the room—"like, uh, that desk over there," and he pointed.

"Okay," I said amiably, since it actually seemed like a reasonably good idea.

"It'll take me a few minutes to calibrate the machine, so just relax for a bit." He turned and scurried back to his equipment, where all the other techs were hovering. They huddled together. 20 Alphawave Refract on 2. Break.

I unhooked the headset and sat pondering my navel, as it were, when some motion to the left caught my eye. The door had opened and someone was walking in the room.

A tall man, six-three or more would be my guess, ambled in. Tailored suit, short-cropped black hair, maybe early forties. Had a raw-boned, chiseled sort of face, like a cover on some western novel. For a tall guy, though, his proportions were all correct and, so, even though he was a big man, he seemed, well, normal. He never looked in my direction, just sat down in the waiting area and picked up a magazine.

It was the "never looked in my direction" thing that bugged me. I mean, a person's simple curiosity dictates that one glances around. Human nature and all that.

Which meant he was here to watch the tests. It's not paranoia if they're really after you.

Anyway, he kept browsing through the magazine, so I lost interest and turned to watch the doctor and his minions hacking diligently on the machine.

It was just a few moments later when the tickling and tingling began in the good old medulla. Hundreds of little fingers brushing up against your skin, fingers that were in constant motion. Like dozens of spiders running to and fro in the back of your neck.

⏞ Chapter Four ⏞

Except, you will recall, I was not wearing the headset. So, that was a tad disconcerting. However, I remained cool, calm, if not completely detached, and simply focused on the feeling. I felt safe here in the lab.

The tingling started to ease upwards, almost imperceptibly, and I know this will sound a bit peculiar, but I had the distinct and unsettling impression that the tingling was trying to move upwards into my brain.

You know, to seize control of me. Turn me into the walking dead or something. I didn't feel quite as safe as the moment before.

I held the energy, blocked it, so it stayed at the medulla.

I moved my eyes, but not my head, to survey Mr. Suit. He was apparently still absorbed with his magazine, seemingly oblivious to me, except I knew, I mean I could sense it in my very being and at my core, that he was the source of this tingling. Which, if I had thought about it a bit more, might have unnerved me, but at the time just sort of pithed me off. What was anyone doing in my head without my permission?!

I had been able to redirect the scan energy Dr. Panglaws had inundated me with previously, so I decided to blast, er, redirect, this new tingling right back at the tall stranger.

Waves, not packets. I took a breath and let her rip.

He dropped the magazine with a crumpled flourish and stood up, mouth agape, eyes wide with a classic, "who pinched my ass" look of surprise etched on his face. But, it was what he did next that surprised the living hoodoo out of me. He started laughing like a blithering idiot.

Doc and the minions stopped to look, noticing the man for the first time. Panglaws instantly came away from the table and moved toward the man.

"Mr. Ruach, what a surprise, I didn't know you were coming to visit us." They came together and shook hands in a friendly and warm manner.

The man named Ruach seem genuinely pleased to see the doctor. "Doctor Panglaws, always a delight to see you." Ruach looked over at the machine. "I imagine the tests have been rather," he paused, "intriguing?"

Ruach continued before Panglaws could answer, "Especially with this one," he added, walking over to me and extending a huge hand which wrapped around my own. "My name is Ruach, Mr. Maarduk, and it is an absolute pleasure to meet you." His sincerity touched me, truth be told. His large, dark, penetrating eyes, instead of making me feel uncomfortable, seemed to invite my friendship.

Just then the door opened again and Dr. Hume came striding in. He immediately spotted our group and spoke loudly, "When you didn't show up for our meeting, Ruach, I thought I might find you down here." He was grinning when he finished talking. He walked up. More handshakes. "I see you've met Enoch."

Ruach nodded and watched me with bright, alert, eyes. "A most excellent name."

"Well, in the spirit of the occasion, I return the compliment," and I gave him a little bow of my head.

This elicited another warm smile from Ruach. "You are full of surprises, Enoch."

I smiled back, and then uncorked my zinger. "The real surprise is, what is an eemee, if you'll forgive the expression"—I gave a nod to Ruach, who nodded back—"doing working with an organization dedicated to hunting them down?"

Panglaws' smile took a dive and he stepped back. "I, uh, really need to finish the calibrations on, er, the machine." He hurriedly scuttled away.

Hume looked at Ruach. "I told you Enoch was special." He turned to me. "When Dr. Panglaws finishes this last test, come by my office and we'll tell you everything."

Ruach again took my hand. "Right now, Enoch, you are the most important person in the world, the most important." He smiled enigmatically and followed Hume, who had already moved away.

Okay, maybe I was cool and calm before, but Ruach's last remark seriously put a crimp in my stride. What the hell did that mean? I almost took out after him, but figured it could wait until the meeting. My stomach growled. After this test and lunch, of course.

I sat back, waiting on Panglaws.

 Chapter Five

All's Bad That Starts Bad

———❦———

"To change one's life: Start immediately. Do it flamboyantly."

—William James

I was happily ensconced in the cafeteria, ecstatic with the quality of the food (Panglaws had said they were all formally trained chefs) and thinking, between delectable mouthfuls of some wonderful Indian chicken dish (who doesn't love turmeric) about the events of this harried morning.

The last test, where I was to have redirected scan energy to an inanimate object, had proved to be a complete success. No humans were affected by the redirect, the tingling dissipated almost immediately to manageable levels, and I felt like I was in control. Control being a relative concept. And who can control their relatives?

Most bizarre part of the whole deal—it didn't matter if I was wearing the attenuator ring or not, I could still redirect the incoming scan energy. Panglaws wasn't sure what it meant. Me neither (either).

I felt mostly comfortable with how things were unfolding. Well, except for the Ruach thing. PHANTASM was supposed to be hunting demons, er, eemees, and here was one working for them. That was an arse scratcher, for sure.

I caught a flash of some peripheral motion and there was Phoebe, carrying a red plastic tray with her lunch neatly arranged on top. "Can I join you?" Asked in a very pleasant manner.

I jumped up like I had just sat on a hair pin. "Of course!" She slid into a well-built black plastic and faux brown leather chair (they were surprisingly comfortable). I plopped back down. "So, how's it going?" I asked casually.

"Well, it's going, but it's not gone," which was certainly a stock reply, but still quite funny. I grinned. She spoke as she moved items off her tray. Iced tea, some kind of weird-looking salad, untoasted wheat bread, and a green-hued pudding of indeterminate origin. I love that phrase, sorry.

I surveyed the salad with mixed amusement and gestured at it. "Secret PHANTASM agent salad?" I quizzed her jokingly.

"Protein salad," she happily replied, then starting listing the ingredients. "Kale, quinoa, seaweed, garbanzo beans, chia seeds, sesame seeds. . ."

"Okay, okay," I put my hands up. "I get it; full of good things." She was eyeballing my chicken makhani, slathered with gooey-good sauce, with something moderately akin to nutritional disdain.

"Rice noodles—gluten-free—and soy meat," I replied jokingly, hoping to curry her favor with some humor. I took a big mouthful.

"Liar," she said flatly, without malice, and ate some salad.

"Are you reading my thoughts?" I asked playfully.

She took a sip of tea. "That's very funny." She sat her glass down. "How did the tests go?" Genuine and sincere interest.

I gave her the skinny on the whole sequence, ending up with the inanimate object redirect thing. She listened intently and nodded at the end. "So, you can control it?"

I shrugged and let out a little grunt-chuckle. "In the lab." Then I remembered Ruach, and how I had held the scan in check until I wanted to redirect, so I relayed those events to her.

"He is a remarkable being," she said softly, biting off a little bread and watching me as she chewed. "If you managed to surprise him, that would be a first."

I wiggled my fingers in a sort of go-ahead-and-tell-me-why gesture. "I'm listening..."

"Do you know the story behind him?" she asked me calmly, picking at her salad with a fork. She acknowledged my blank look of ignorance or, rather, fully expected it. I wear it rather well.

"About a year ago, we lost two operatives." She paused to gather herself. "Friends of mine." She cleared her throat and continued. "We had finally located the human controller responsible for invoking one of the existing eemees." She scowled at what surely must be a most unpleasant memory. "An evil man running an immense manufacturing facility in China." She paused to take a drink of tea. Her face was taut with emotion, so I said nothing.

"A PHANTASM strike force managed to infiltrate the facility and found the human controller and the primary pentacle." She paused and seemed reflective after that statement, but then started to speak.

I didn't mean to, but I interrupted. "Primary pentacle?" I repeated in puzzled tones.

She frowned. "Only the main or primary pentacle can summon the eemee from the spectrum, but secondary pentacles can be used as communication portals and energy channels." I guess I must have still had on my "huh" look because she went on. "The eemee can only assume a physical manifestation using the primary pentacle, but can move between the primary and a linked secondary pentacle."

"Ah," was all I added to the conversation at this point. Like I fully grasped it. Not.

"We located the primary pentacle in this massive underground warehouse and the bastard controller, Tazik Mencius, was there." She seemed to shiver with the memory. I wasn't about to ask if she'd actually been there or not. I think I knew the answer already.

"He had human support, standard-issue guys with guns, and we fought." She took a deeper breath, let it out. "We took some casualties, but were slowly gaining the upper hand." A brief pause. "We could even see the pentacle structure near Mencius." A bitter laugh. "Then we saw Mencius summon the eemee."

She absently rubbed her forehead. "The eemees do not actually use violence, but can disrupt your brainwaves"—she stared at me—"like you do, and even with attenuators it can get a little dicey." She shrugged. "But, the eemee in this case refused to obey Mencius." She paused to let this sink it. "Eemees never say no."

My puzzled look was back, with a vengeance. "Why is that?"

"If the primary pentacle is destroyed, the eemee returns safely to the spectrum." She paused for effect as I logged that to my mental notebook. "But, the human controller can also use that pentacle to entrap the eemee, confining it into the energy space or signature of the pentacle." She shook her head. "The eemee would have no flow of consciousness as they ordinarily experience in the EM spectrum."

☐ All's Bad That Starts Bad ☐

She looked pointedly at me. "If this pentacle, a binding pentacle, is destroyed while an eemee occupies it, the eemee is also destroyed." She let that fact linger and fester.

"So, the eemee refused to help Mencius. Then what?" I think I had goose bumps. On my goose bumps.

"The PHANTASM team saw what was happening, knew the eemee was not helping Mencius. But, they also saw Mencius starting some kind of ceremony over the primary pentacle. No doubt to bind the eemee. And more human support troops were arriving for the bad guys." This time her deep breath of air was more like a sigh.

"So we attacked. We just rose up and made a direct assault." The goose bumps turned into a shiver than ran up my spine. "When these things happen, you swear it was a battle that lasted for hours, but it was only a few minutes." She shook her head, a sad expression on her face. "Members of my team were going down all around me, but we were inflicting terrible losses on Mencius and his men."

She paused and snorted derisively. "It didn't matter, though, because I could see we were going to fall short. Hell, I could even see Mencius laughing."

She grunted out a harsh laugh herself, without humor. "And that's when every single one of Mencius' men simply collapsed on the ground."

"An energy mind blast!" I said excitedly.

"The eemee had intervened on our behalf." She shook her head at the memory. "Only Mencius was still conscious, but we quickly overcame him and stopped him from invoking the pentacle and trapping the eemee." She seemed to grow tired from telling the story. I sat spellbound, silent.

"We hoped to learn a great deal from Mencius, but the coward killed himself before we could get him back here to PHANTASM." She made a bitter face.

"And Ruach was the eemee?" She nodded. "Why didn't he return to the spectrum?" That seemed the biggest issue of all. "Why is he still here?"

She seemed to lighten up and actually smiled a little. "You really do ask all the right questions." A small breath. "But, you'll have to let him answer that one—I understand you're meeting later." My turn to nod as she continued. "All I can tell you is that there are some very bad things happening in the world right now."

She appraised me with arched eyebrows. "So bad, in fact, that Ruach feels compelled to stay and help." She grunted. "That's all I'll say." She stood up and I joined her.

"Thanks for telling me that story," I said earnestly. I was sure it had been difficult for her to relay those events for my benefit.

She surveyed me intently. It was more than a bit discomforting from any woman, but especially from Phoebe. "I have a feeling, Enoch, that you might be the key to solving our problems, but just not a very well-informed key, not yet."

I didn't know exactly what to say in response to that, so told her, "I'll do my best." Keep it simple. Stupid.

She laughed. "Well, so far, your best has been rather eye-opening."

"More like eye closing," I remarked, thinking back to everyone passing out. She laughed aloud at that one.

"I hope you still have your sense of humor after you meet with Hume and Ruach." She was serious now.

I gave her a startled look. "I have no idea how to get back to that office."

She grinned and patted my arm. "Which is why you're going to follow me." She had already pivoted and was on the move.

"Right behind you!" I said warmly and we were off again.

———□———

Phoebe deposited me at Hume's doorstep and then she was gone. I went in. "Mr. Maarduk, it's so good to see you again," Hume's secretary Deandra said cheerfully, and damned if I didn't feel like she meant it.

"It's good to be seen again, especially after all those tests." I grinned at her in grand sincerity.

She nodded knowingly. "I've heard all about those tests." She leaned over the desk in a secretive fashion and said in soft tones, "And Mr. Ruach was very impressed."

☐ All's Bad That Starts Bad ☐

I whispered back, "I hope I can keep up the good work." She smiled, walked over to Hume's door and tapped lightly, waited just a moment, then opened the door a crack.

With the door left slightly ajar, she turned to face me. "Go on in, they're ready." I took a deep breath. Yes, I was nervous as a schoolboy on the first day at a new school. "You'll be fine," she whispered in motherly fashion and waved me on.

Both men stood as I eased the door open and walked in. The floor was showing a brown shag rug, I noted idly. Hume moved over and shook my hand, followed by Ruach. "Good to see you again, Enoch," Hume said and waved me into one of the ornate chairs. We all sat.

Hume eyed me provocatively "I imagine you have questions."

I ogled him with suitable ogliage. "I imagine you have answers."

Ruach let a wry smile slip and Hume chuckled. "Hopefully, the right ones."

I shrugged. "The truth is what it is." Not sure why I said that, exactly, but it's what popped out. They both made almost imperceptible head movements that signified their agreement.

Hume was tapping his chin with the knuckle of his left index finger, but stopped and lowered his hand just before he spoke, "Well, Enoch, the truth is, these are dangerous times we are living in." He rocked his head minutely up and down a couple of times for subtle emphasis.

I shrugged, gestured with my hands spread outwards, and tilted my head back slightly as I spoke. "There are a lot of bad people in the world." Seemed self-evident.

Hume quickly interjected, "And a lot of good ones, too, Enoch, a lot of good ones."

Okay, properly chastised, I replied, "Fair enough, but obviously the fact that we are sitting here means those good ones can't take care of themselves, at least in regards to this eemee thing." I let the implications linger like the late day aftermath of a bowl of lunch time beans. I know, I hate that one too, but there you have it. I'm nervous, and I joke when I'm nervous. Yeah, yeah, try.

Ruach looked grim as he held my eyes. "There are things in this world that are very difficult to confront"—he paused—"for anyone." He glanced away.

☐ Chapter Five ☐

"So, who is the enemy?" I mean, if you're in a fight, you want to know who, or what, you're fighting, right? Fug, you have to know who to run away from! Just kidding.

Hume eased back in his chair. Ruach took a breath. Hume began talking. "As a worldly man, Enoch, you know that evil comes in many different forms." I nodded at the obvious intent. "Our mission at PHANTASM is not to get bogged down in fighting those forms of evil for which the only cure is a general improvement in the consciousness of humankind." I smiled, as that was well-stated, though perhaps a bit convoluted.

Hume went on. "However, there are some very specific activities which draw our attention and demand our action." Ruach nodded emphatically this time. Hume let out a long breath, sat staring at the far wall, obviously wanting to choose his words carefully.

"When a person, or a group of people, seek to exploit the weakness of their fellow humans by utilizing technology in a manner that attempts to tap into the electromagnetic spectrum to directly influence human behavior in a negative fashion, we intervene." He nodded, apparently satisfied with that explanation.

I gave it a momentary mental review. "I don't want to seem flippant, but that sounds like advertising, or propaganda." It did.

Ruach chimed in. "True, except we are talking about technology that takes away free will. Advertising and propaganda both seek to inform and motivate, sometimes with truth, sometimes with lies." He paused. "But, the individual human always maintains free will ability to think for themselves." He shook his head and said with great feeling, "The type of thing we are talking about seeks to intrude, control, and eliminate free will."

Hume climbed on that thought, "Advertising and propaganda do not negate free will, Enoch, but the human controllers of the eemees seek to twist free will by controlling the human minds from whence the free will emanates."

Let me see if I had this straight. "The eemees can plant thoughts in people's minds, making them think these thoughts are actually their own, and indirectly force these people to do what they, the eemees, want." That's what I had learned earlier. When you really stopped to think about it, the possibilities were very frightening.

Both men nodded. "That's it, except it is the human controller forcing the eemee to act," Hume said quietly.

It was my turn to scowl. I was looking at Ruach, for he had been the one, according to Phoebe, who chose to stay on Earth, so I said pointedly, "That's why you stayed, isn't it?"

For someone who wasn't technically human, Ruach's facial expressions were perfectly suited to the situation. You could see a mix of empathy, pain, anxiety, and fear all flashing together in his eyes and mirrored in the tautness of his facial features.

"Enoch, I want to share with you one of my, well, abilities, if you will," he glanced hesitantly at Hume, who wagged his head in, I guess, tacit approval. "I can, in a very general way, sense or feel the existence of the other invoked beings."

I stiffened just a bit and think I may have moved forward in my chair. I'm not sure; the whole thing had a surreal quality that my head had still not completely wrapped around, though my head did feel like it had been rapped around.

"All of the EM entities," he looked at me, "eemees as they are called, emanate from the spectrum and thus share a common bond that runs like an invisible umbilical through their being and, even in human manifestation, connects them." He smiled. "Us."

"You can communicate with the other eemees?" I asked in astonishment, with perhaps just a hint of accusation seeping in.

Ruach shook his head emphatically. "No, no, not communication, not like you mean." He assumed a reflective posture for a few moments, then continued, "It's more like..." he stopped again, seeking the right words, "...like the fleeting remnants of a dream that you recall, just after awakening from a deep sleep." He nodded, openly enthusiastic now. "Bits and pieces, some connected, some disjointed; images, sounds, impressions, feelings."

He took a deep breath. "We are familiar with this sort of process as creatures of the EM spectrum, but experiencing it in human form is very different for us, very difficult."

⬚ Chapter Five ⬚

"So," I hesitated, but continued with a vestige of surety, "you have felt, or sensed, something wrong with the other entities?" It was a statement, and a question.

Ruach sat quietly for a moment. "We, that is to say, eemees, cannot actually scan another eemee, not like we can directly scan a human." He smiled. "All we experience are the vague and indistinct impressions I have already mentioned."

I sort of understood that. "What kind of impressions are you getting?" Ruach had to have an opinion on the subject.

Ruach nodded. "You must understand"—and he looked directly at me, then turned to regard Hume with the same earnest stare—"that in the EM spectrum there is no good or evil, simply a state of..." again he paused, groping for the word or concept, "...a state of Isness which is simply pure consciousness."

"Here in this plane, on this planet," he went on, his tone flattening with emotion, "I have come to see that humans, through their direct or indirect actions, create good or evil, and that the humans who have summoned the eemees are using them for evil purposes."

I decided it was time to make a leap, not necessarily of faith, but certainly of reason, as it was, in my mind, not exactly clear to me what it was he thought to designate as evil. "What is your definition of evil?" I could see that Hume must have been thinking along the same lines, as he nodded his agreement and turned his attention to Ruach.

Ruach started to reply and all hell broke loose.

A Simple Freaking Plan

"Everything should be made as simple as possible, but not simpler."
—Albert Einstein

Imagine, if you will, the irritating nature of the shrieking clarion call sound which would emerge if you were to maniacally blend together a wailing and obnoxious French police siren (that grating oogah-oogah-oogah noise), a tornado warning siren (specially designed to send a chill right up your &^%*) and that eerie sound from any sci-fi movie when something alien and nasty has just escaped from confinement (wah-wah-wah-wah).

Then make it really, really, loud and pulsating. Syncopated synaptic disruption to the max.

Hume and Ruach didn't even flinch. Almost before the first echoes were bouncing, careening, off my inner ear and reverberating around my cortex, the two of them were up, out of their chairs, and bounding wildly for the door. I guess it wasn't the apocalypse, otherwise they would have just bent over double and started whimpering.

I'm glad I ignored my first impulse... Cough, cough.

I took off after them like a mad hound on the trail as they jogged briskly down the corridor toward the elevators.

"What is it?" I yelled breathlessly above the undulating din and clamor of the siren. Hey, I don't jog and talk all that much. Come to think of it, I don't jog that much...

"Someone is coming through," Hume said by way of explanation as the elevator arrived and whooshed open. We stepped in.

"Coming through what?" I asked, trying not to seem like an utter simpleton (hard, sometimes, I'll grant you)—but, I'm nothing if not consistent.

☐ Chapter Six ☐

Ruach looked at me with intensity, a fearful expression on his face. "An operative is being transported through the pentacle."

"You can do that?" I asked, ignorant of how all that worked.

"Yes and no," Hume replied flatly, without emotion. "Yes, we can, but it is so risky that no one does."

Ruach continued the explanation, "The transfer always causes genetic transformation of the human XY chromosomes." He shrugged, "Very rarely harmless." His expression was not happy.

"Why would someone risk that"—I paused just a fraction of a thought—"to travel through a pentacle?"

Hume glanced at me as the elevator gradually slowed. "Because they didn't have a choice." He let the implications linger, as such things are wont to do.

The elevator doors flashed opened with a minimalistic whoosh and we jogged out into a room that was bristling with activity, with people moving to and fro like some staged scene in a movie. Across the way a circle of twenty or so people were standing, surrounding, and looking down at something on the floor. A subdued murmur of conversation whirled and hissed around them.

Someone noticed Hume and Ruach and the circle of people slowly parted and opened. Conversation gradually stilled.

A detailed, complex, and mind-numbing geometric pattern—a pentacle—was visible on the floor, with elaborate-looking computer circuit boards at each of the five pentacle points. A man's body, fully clothed, was curled up on it in the fetal position within the pentacle. He was motionless.

A woman in medical scrubs had been bending over the prone figure, but stood as Hume stepped near. She held some kind of device and tilted it toward Hume to show him the display, shaking her head at the same time. "I'm not sure how he activated the pentacle, Denton, he had to have been near death, and in great pain, at the time." She was visibly upset and her voice trembled.

Ruach and Hume stood staring. Hume shook his head in disbelief. "Brody," he said with great emotion. "Brody," he repeated with a harrowing sorrow that I felt in my own being.

☐ A Simple Freaking Plan ☐

Another man, wearing a suit and tie with a coded ID tag I couldn't quite read, stepped in and leaned toward Hume. "He had this in his hand," he said softly. The man extended a wadded up scrap of paper and then moved to step away.

Hume stopped him with a gesture. "Send all the case facts to me as soon as you can, okay, Mark?" The other man nodded solemnly and backed off.

Hume carefully unfolded the paper, making no effort to hide it from Ruach or myself. The writing was labored and jagged, scrawled; obviously the last struggling efforts of the dying man Hume had named as Brody. You could clearly make out some kind of cryptic message which read:

gaia penta peptode 12 12 12 -12(7) demonhunter ctr?

He carefully folded the paper and placed it in his pocket. He looked at the woman in scrubs and spoke softly, "Janet, get me a full report as soon as you can." She nodded, her expression pained, and moved away.

He eyed two men in starched white uniforms approaching, wheeling a gurney between them. It was so quiet you could easily hear the screeching rattle of one misaligned wheel as it clattered over the painted concrete floor. One of the men stopped when he neared the prostate body, then looked over at Hume with an expression of anguish and sadness. Hume swallowed hard, acknowledged the man, and spoke. "Take good care of him, Alan, take good care of him." Hume had to turn and walk away.

Ruach and I slowly trailed after him. There was silence all the way back to the office.

Deandra caught Hume's eye as we walked in. "I've cleared the schedule," was all she said. Hume nodded absently. We entered the office and sat down.

Hume withdrew the note from his pocket with something approaching reverence, slowly unfolded it, carefully smoothed it out, laid it gently on his desk surface slash computer—fiddled with something I couldn't see—touched the screen a few times. Then, on the wall behind us, an enlarged digitized view of the note appeared.

☐ Chapter Six ☐

gaia penta peptode 12 12 12 -12(7) demonhunter ctr?

Hume surveyed both of us and coughed lightly. "As I have told you previously, there are three, perhaps four, eemees on this planet, one of which is in this room." He nodded at Ruach. "The others are scattered across the globe." I was biting my tongue to keep from blurting out more questions. I figured Hume would clarify it, later or sooner.

He ran his fingers around the desktop screen again and a new image popped up on the wall next to the cryptic note. It was a map of the world.

There were green dots located in Iceland and Argentina. Obviously operational sites. There were yellow dots in South Africa and Iran, questionable areas I supposed, and a red dot in China. If red meant no longer operational, then that last dot made sense to me, as I recalled that Ruach had been part of the China operation that Phoebe had helped end. Seemed intuitive to me.

Hume added, kind of an afterthought, "We have confirmed that a pentacle was activated in Iran, but we have not been able to validate or confirm the presence of an eemee there." Yellow dot definitely indicated a questionable status for the map.

There was a chime from Hume's desk and he nodded. "There's the report on Brody," he said by way of explanation and touched several places along his touch screen display.

He shook his head several times as he digested the information. A few more hand movements and the yellow dot in South Africa turned to green. "We have confirmed the South African location as a primary pentacle site and there is a verified eemee at that location," he said wearily. "That makes four confirmed eemees, which includes Ruach." His voice was stressed with ripples of tension.

I know Hume was eventually going to explain all this, but I may have mentioned that patience is not my long suit. It's not a trait I have myself, though I do recognize it in others. "So," I said, waving my hand at the world map display, "what exactly goes on at those locations?" It seemed a reasonable question. Proving that even unreasonable people can ask reasonable questions.

Hume grimaced just a little, then gesticulated with his hands. "They are just fronts for eemee activity guided by the human controller."

☐ A Simple Freaking Plan ☐

Not really the full explanation I was hoping for. "Okay. Fronts doing what?" Obviously these eemee things were being used for something, and I wanted to know what that meant.

Hume ran his fingers around the screen.

"Nykr Enterprises, Iceland, is a processing plant for taking Icelandic spring water and selling it in a plastic bottled format." A brief pause. "We are not completely sure about the Alifmimra Company in Iran, but preliminary reports seem to indicate they manufacture shoes." Hume glanced up at me. I shrugged, then he looked back to his desk, where he touched some more screen areas. "Cambio S.A in Argentina apparently processes rare South America plants for sale as herbal supplements." He paused and scrolled through some more data. "Brody was investigating the South African location, but we have no reliable data on it, yet."

I looked at Ruach. "What did they do in China?"

Ruach shrugged. "Cookies."

"Cookies?" I repeated in an incredulous voice. I couldn't help myself.

Ruach looked puzzled himself. "I wasn't involved in that area, it was something Mencius managed exclusively." He frowned in irritation.

I spread my hands out. "Do we have samples of those cookies?"

Hume frowned this time. "I told you, we believe these operations are just fronts, masking other, more illicit, activities."

"I'm new to this whole thing," I said with a smile, forced to be sure, and continued. "Can you just humor me a little?" I was pleasant about it, though growing restless as I tried to gather enough facts to make some kind of sense, half-arsed or otherwise, about my current situation.

Ruach intervened. "The facility was just beginning production when the PHANTASM attack came." He seemed to be working to recollect his thoughts. "I believe the first shipment was on the loading docks at the time."

That was better. "Does Phoebe's report show anything about the final disposition of that shipment?" I thought it was a good question.

Hume didn't even bother to look. "The entire plant was destroyed, including that shipment." With a bad answer.

"Great," was all I said, accompanied by a small gush of exhaled air. I shook my head. "What do we know about these herbal supplements from Argentina?"

◻ Chapter Six ◻

Hume looked mildly perturbed as he answered. "That hasn't been a focal point." Talk about beating an expired equine.

"I understand that, but if you want me to be involved, this is the way I work." I smiled and said it gently—yeah, smile still a bit forced, but genuine. "When I research something, I try to gather up as much information as possible." I shrugged, prune-faced. "Might seem a little slow to some folks, but that's just how I am." Take or leave it, I suppose.

Hume's fingers moved around the screen. A few moments later he looked up. "A report has been requested." I nodded my thanks.

"What about Brody's message?" Ruach asked, pointing his finger at the scan of Brody's note shimmering on the wall.

Hume seemed happy to be off the cookie, herbal supplement, thing and started talking with great animation. "Gaia is a reference to earth as a holistic living entity." He paused, ruminating on it. "Everything on the earth, inorganic and organic, is considered, as part of the Gaia hypothesis, to be part of a complex and self-regulating system."

Ruach took up the theme. "From the standpoint of the EM spectrum being a continuum, and all things being somewhere along its transit, that ties in nicely."

"Penta?" I said, pitching in. "Short for pentacle, or a Greek reference to the number five?" Kind of the same thing, really.

Hume scratched his forehead. "Given the line of work we are in, I'd have to go with pentacle." Ruach nodded his affirmation.

"Peptode is not a word." I let the obvious linger for just a beat. "I think Brody meant to write *peptide*." The letters "i" and "o" were next to one another on a regular QWERTY keyboard. Easy to make a mistake when your hand is shaking and your vision blurred. I did not need to vocalize this, as I am sure Ruach and Hume had arrived at that same sobering and discomforting conclusion.

Ruach did the scowl-frown thing. "I am not familiar with the meaning of the word *peptide*."

Hume was already fingering his way to new data. "A peptide," he began reading a standard definition, "is a molecule consisting of more than 2, but usually less than 50, amino acids. Peptides are smaller than proteins, which are also chains of amino acids." Short pause. "Molecules small enough to be synthesized from their constituent amino acids are, by convention, called peptides rather than proteins."

Ruach nodded in partial understanding. "Can you give me an example of how these peptides are used by humans?"

Hume scanned the page, moving his finger to keep his place. "Here it is," he said by way of discovery. "Peptides can be used in antibiotics, alkaloids, hormones, and regulatory neurotransmitters."

All of that was of interest to me, but no one else seemed overly concerned, so I figured I'd do my own net sleuthing on it later. "How are the known locations in Iceland, Iran, and Argentina related?" I figured the linkage between them would be a good place to start. When in doubt, start somewhere.

He shook his head sadly. "That was one of the first things we looked at." He shrugged once more. And I thought I shrugged too much. "I've had people digging intensely into that topic for at least six months, and we haven't come up with many connections."

I stared at Hume, I admit, in a sort of *are you freaking kidding me* way. I cleared my throat and looked at Ruach. "These pentacles — the real pentacles — are they difficult to design and build?"

Ruach nodded slowly. "Impossible without an extensive knowledge on a wide variety of related subjects."

"And, yet," I said with poorly concealed cynicism, "in the last few years you have seen at least five events where these supposedly almost-impossible-to-build pentacles have been built, and eemees summoned to earth."

Ruach made a face. I don't think he liked it phrased that way. Hume's expression was that of a man who had just stepped in dog crap.

I continued. "The logical conclusion to those situations would be that there exists some kind of master plan, or master planners, arranging all this." I flashed my best defiant stare.

Hume's ordinarily pleasant features were clouded with the look of someone who had been eating a nice grilled cheese sandwich and just bit into a rat dropping. Rat scat! I swear, he sighed at me. "We have thought of that. We've researched that idea extensively." He shook his head. "Nothing has turned up."

☐ Chapter Six ☐

"Absence of evidence is not evidence of absence," I remarked in passing, pausing a moment to let that idea resonate. Like flatulence in a closed elevator. Sorry. "There's something nastier, deeper, more pervasive, here than you currently see."

Ruach was not happy. "I have to agree," he said softly.

Hume nodded slowly. "Brody was in South Africa, trying to establish the identity of the operation there." He paused, thoughtful. "Maybe there will be some new information in his final reports." He did not sound terribly confident on that point. Not a bit.

"How did you establish that the operation was in South Africa in the first place?" Seemed important to understand the process.

Hume smiled, apparently glad to be back on familiar ground. "Whenever a primary pentacle is invoked for the first time, there is a tremendous spike or surge in electromagnetic energy." Ruach nodded and Hume continued. "We have recently learned new ways to interpret our satellite-generated information and can usually track any such global event."

"Okay then," I said, standing up. "It seems obvious to me."

Hume and Ruach rewarded my statement with puzzled stares.

I spread out my hands — obviousness. "I'm going to South Africa."

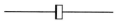

There are things that seem so simple in planning, yet are hideously difficult to execute in actuality. Like washing a cat. Hitting a curve ball. Making crepes.

Taking a simple little trip.

After another 30 minutes of friendly discussion (starting with, "You don't know anything about field work," shifting rapidly to, "You're too valuable, you can't go," moving forward choppily to, "We can't make the logistics work," and finely ending up at, "Fine, we'll send Phoebe with you") we all shook hands and Phoebe, who had been called in by Hume, escorted me out of the office.

"What have you done?" We had just exited the elevator in some other, unknown, part of the building (underground freaking complex, more like it) and she elbowed me right after she asked the question.

⬓ A Simple Freaking Plan ⬓

I grunted, grabbed my side, and painfully replied, "I, uh, we, have a mission."

We were on our way, Phoebe had earlier explained with slightly more than a mere hint of vexation in her clipped tones, to S&R, which she said was the Supply and Requisition area. To be outfitted for our *mission*.

"Mission!" she snorted in derision. "Deathtrap is more like it," she added sourly.

We walked through an unmarked door into a massive room that resembled the storage and evidence locker at some police station. Against the walls, built-in, were hundreds of small cabinet drawers, all with labels on the outside, just below the handles. The labels were printed out in some kind of elaborate alphanumeric coding system I couldn't quite fathom. I turned my attention back to Phoebe.

"That doesn't show a lot of confidence in me," I said, stepping slightly to the side in case Phoebe decided to practice an MMA move on me. The roundhouse kick was of particular concern at the moment.

She stopped, faced me, and then started the counting fingers thing. Always a bad sign.

"Number one, you've never done field work." A good earthy scowl, hearty and bold with just a hint of spice.

"Number two, Brody was a damn good operative and he didn't survive." Point well taken.

"Number three, we're going in almost totally blind." Not totally true, but I let it go. For now.

"And number four..." She paused and really gave me a cold stare, direct, engaging. "I haven't worked with you in a high-pressure situation." Narrowed eyes. "I don't know if I can trust you."

Okay, now it was my turn. I can do the counting fingers thing, too.

"Number one, even the great Phoebe Scarlett O'Hara was a newbie once." Oh, man, if looks could vaporize your brain. Poof, vegetable.

"Number two, Brody gave his life for something he believed in." The nasty glare slowly eased off from her face.

"Number three, I've got some new information from Hume and Ruach that I'll be happy to share with you." That brought a small smile. Really, I saw it. I think.

❑ Chapter Six ❑

"And number four," and here I paused and gave her my own best direct and hard stare. "If we go on this mission together, the last person you have to worry about is me." I gave her a wicked grin and thumped my chest twice with my index finger for added emphasis. "If you're still concerned, don't go." And I meant it.

The next moment or two was your classic don't-blink-first stare down. I guess she saw / felt / sensed / that I had made a freaking point or whatever, because she nodded, smiled, then rapped hard on the frosted window that separated us from the main office area.

The window slid open. A shock of tasseled blond hair flopped into view. A very young, maybe early twenties, smiling, woman's face appeared. She was serious-looking, but cute. "Yo, Pheebs, Big Boss said you were on the way."

"Yeah," Phoebe said with a grin, "and here we are." She waved at me. "Enoch Maarduk, I'd like you to meet Susie Olmos."

The face leaned out a little to get a better look. "I got the low low on you from Joe." She pursed her lips and continued to regard me with interest.

"Yo, S-O, the low low from Joe, don't you know." These words actually came out of my mouth, before I could even stop them. I grinned like a stupid ewe, well, not that you're stupid or anything like that.

She tried not to smile, but I saw a flitting image of one appear and vanish. She turned her head back toward Phoebe. "Field trip to a dangerous place?"

Phoebe nodded. "You got that right."

I heard that now-familiar iridescent electronic buzzing humming sound and a door appeared. It was still a cool effect, even when you knew how they did it.

"Come on down," I heard Susie's voice intone from the distance and in we went.

We stopped at a table which, like Hume's desk, turned out to be a huge touch screen. Susie sat down, facing us. The rest of the room was completely empty except for a three-foot wide conveyor belt that vanished into the wall, like the luggage things at the airport. It even had grayish-colored rubberized strips hanging down, covering the opening.

⎔ A Simple Freaking Plan ⎔

"He needs a ComUnit first," Phoebe said. So, that's what CU stands for. I was feeling more smarter by the moment. Hah!

Susie picked up some kind of wand-looking electronic device and gestured at me. "I need to scan your ring." I stepped over, extended my arm and she waved the wand over the ring Panglaws had given me.

Naturally, I cannot resist asking questions. Yeah, character flaw. Add it to the litany list. "What does that do?"

I believe Susie expected the question and answered without pause. "As you know, the attenuator ring is linked to your unique neurological system." I nodded like, of course, everyone knows that. "We program your ComUnit to respond to that same set of unique brainwave patterns so only you can use the device."

She smiled knowingly. "Unless you grant specific permission to the contrary."

"That's it?" Gee, that didn't sound all that impressive. My smartphone can do that, almost.

Susie gave me the Look. I think there must be a PHANTASM class on it or something. "In appropriate circumstances, and with proper training, you can communicate without talking."

Now, THAT was epic cool. "You mean, it can read my thoughts?"

Susie shook her head and regarded me with a bit of lovable sorrow, like when you're talking to a six-year-old and trying to explain electricity. "No, it can't read your thoughts." A wry smile. "You can teach the internal AI a few basic brainwave patterns that it will store and translate." She favored me with a patient smile.

"If you think SEND HELP, the ComUnit can be taught to understand the brainwave patterns associated with that." She shrugged. "After a few months, you can probably teach it a handful of useful things, maybe."

"Maybe?" I whizzed a quizzical look at her.

She shrugged, compendious. "It barely works at all for most people."

Phoebe grunt-chuckled, "I can find things faster with my fingers." I seriously had to bite my tongue.

Susie was giving me the squint-eye.

☐ Chapter Six ☐

The conveyor belt whirred to life and a black metallic device appeared. It looked very much like a smartphone, a bit thicker, with a sturdy clip on the back. Susie handed it to me. "Don't lose it, or we will deduct it from your pay." I'm pretty sure my mouth dropped open at that one. "Sign here," and she pointed to the touch screen. I signed with my finger.

"How does it work?" I asked this of Susie, but it was the ComUnit that answered.

"**Make a request**." The voice was female, just as firm and confident as Phoebe's voice, but much friendlier in tone. Just my first impression.

I was thinking about a request when suddenly the unit spoke. Loudly. "**Phoebe photos are not currently available**."

My eyebrows shot up. I looked at Phoebe. "This device is clearly malfunctioning." I shook it for effect. "I was thinking, uh, about dinner and dinner specials. You know, freebies. Freebie photos." I coughed. "The AI is obviously not working correctly."

Of course the barfing unit piped in, "**Internal diagnostics return negative results**."

"Does this thing have a silent mode?" I asked Susie this rather critical, though tardy, question.

"**Switching to silent mode**," the unit replied.

Susie looked at me with something that seemed a mix of alarm, surprise, and suspicion. "I've never seen, uh, heard the unit, the AI, do that before." She blinked, nodded. "Very impressive."

Phoebe was giving me the doubtful eye. "Oh, yeah, impressive."

Susie gave herself a mental shake and went on, "The ComUnit can instantly connect you to anyone also linked to the system." Susie smiled again and informed me, "Give it a whirl—just think of someone."

I thought of Hume. In a moment his face appeared on the ComUnit screen. "Enoch, I see you've been issued a ComUnit." He said this with a straight face, though I got the distinct impression he was doubled over with laughter on the inside.

"Just testing it," I rejoined sheepishly.

"It appears to work," he deadpanned back to me.

⬚ A Simple Freaking Plan ⬚

"Oh," I added, trying to salvage things. "Any word on the supplement information?" The stuff about the Argentinean company.

"Should have something shortly," Hume answered softly. "Now that you have a ComUnit, I can have the report sent directly to you." This time a big grin. "Keep an eye open for it."

"Thanks," I said and his image vanished. "Cool," I said to no one in particular and clipped the device to my belt.

Phoebe ran a hand through her hair and turned to Susie. "He needs a weapon."

Okay, I grinned big time now, I am into weapons. Familiar territory. If it can be held in your hands and makes a loud noise, I'm in.

"What kind of weapon are we talking about?" I tried to keep my voice level, but my excitement had to seep in. I was thinking death-ray, vaporization unit, microwave synapse disrupter, freeze-o-matic—oh man, this was going to be good. I rubbed my hands together.

"It fires BBs." Phoebe was watching me closely.

"BBs?" I felt like a kid opening up their Christmas present and finding socks. "BBs?" I repeated, mainly because I was kind of frank, to be numb. Aargh, the other round way. BBs? Crap.

Susie shook her head. Phoebe started laughing. With me, not at me. Although, at the time, I wasn't laughing. So, I guess, at me…

"They are actually hollow, metallic, encapsulated energy spheres," Susie said in her best officious tone.

"That sure sounds like a BB," I said, not convinced by her flowery description to adjust my initial reaction.

The conveyor churned alive again and out rolled a small object resembling a pistol; well, it sort of looked like a revolver, but with a odd, roundish, chamber for the body where the shell holder ought to be. And some kind of sensor pad instead of a trigger. There was a small, clear, plastic box next to it. And inside the box were, to be truthful, BBs. Except they were bluish-colored, not silvery.

Susie looked at Phoebe, who was still fighting back mild hysteria. "You are terrible," Susie told her.

Phoebe was trying not to laugh, then started, had to turn away. Susie chuckled as she picked up the box of BBs.

⬚ Chapter Six ⬚

"You know what a quanta is, right?" Susie asked as she retrieved the weapon from the now motionless belt.

"Sure," I said with polished irritation, "it's that Australian airline." I scowled at her. She scowled back.

"These are specially-constructed metallic shells designed to contain electromagnetic quanta in the form of unrealized energy that is reverse-amplified by your brainwave patterns." She paused. "Processed and routed by the attenuator ring." She smiled thinly. "Maybe."

First a ComUnit maybe, then BBs, and another maybe. I looked at Phoebe, who had finished laughing. She shook her head. "For whatever reason, the weapon doesn't work for everyone." She shrugged. "Even then, it only works part of the time." She tossed me an evil smile.

"What good is it then?" Susie handed me the weapon and I rolled it around in my hands examining it.

Phoebe frowned. "Sometimes I hit people with a single BB and they collapse immediately." She shook her head. "Takes hours to recover." She wrinkled her nose in mock disgust. "Other times I hit someone and nothing. Might as well be shooting BBs." She chuckled lightly.

Funny, I thought to myself—hah, hah.

I waved the weapon around. "So, exactly why do we use it, then?"

Susie chimed in. "Company policy." She grinned. "Besides, the ammo is cheap."

Phoebe grunted, turning serious. "We are what you would call a stealth force, Enoch. We are supposed to operate quietly, covertly, without being compromised." A hard smile. "Engaging the enemy is a choice of last resort." Then she patted her right hip. "I always carry a backup anyway."

"Well, I hope you didn't use these when you were stealthily involved in China," I said, waving the BB gun in the air, and then grimacing inwardly the moment I said it. Probably not the best of topics.

"That was a targeted offensive action and we were issued plenty of heavy weapons." There was a pretty strong hint in her tone that the subject was really not open for further consideration.

"Nice weather we're having today," I said by way of trying to apologize and lighten the mood.

Susie chuckled and looked at Phoebe. "He's quick on his feet, you gotta give him that."

Phoebe glanced at Susie, then in skeptical appraisal at me. "He better be."

"Okay," Susie jumped in, "last of the specialty items." She reached into a drawer and pulled out some kind of small metallic device. "I need your finger for a blood prick."

I have played a lot of sports in my life. I have shed blood in every one of them. Sliding headfirst into home. Tackling someone in a rugby match. Tackling someone in a football game without pads. Tackling someone in a football game with pads. Diving for a tennis ball on a hard court. Scrambling for a loose ball on the basketball court. I could go on, but I think the point is made. I don't mind a little blood loss.

The deliberate offering of it, though, kind of sends me to my not-so-happy place. Shedding, okay; taking, not okay.

Phoebe was shaking her head. "Put your finger out you big baby." I put a finger on each side of my forehead and stared at her like I was going to give her an energy mind blast. She smirked at me. "Funny." She waved her hand in the direction of Susie. "Stick your finger out."

I extended my finger and looked gravely at Susie. "Go ahead," and then after just a brief, brief, pause I added, "prick," with a sardonic smile. Which she did. Eff me, that was irritating.

"What's the blood for?" I asked, feeling a bit violated, cradling my finger, now protected by a mini-bandage Susie had provided.

Susie had plugged the device into a slot on the top of the desk computer and was busy touching and manipulating screens. "Well, it's good to know your blood type"—it was her turn to give me a sardonic smile—"you know, in case you experience unexpected blood loss." I grinned back. It was funny, actually. Well, in a sick, twisted, kind of way that I found oddly satisfying.

"Plus, we need it for the BioPatch." She eyed me expectantly and I did not want to disappoint her.

"What's the BioPatch?" I asked in my best mock world-weary voice.

Susie smiled benignly. "Glad you asked." She pointed at her desk. "We analyze the blood sample to determine your current level of nutritional health." My mind flashed to my recent eating habits and

⬚ Chapter Six ⬚

I cringed. "Then the computer calibrates an optimized feeding pattern for operatives in the field, because they rarely eat correctly." She slapped the top of her left arm. "You put the patch on and go about your business for the next 12 to 24 hours."

I had to admit, that was slick. "Are there different flavors?" I wasn't really being serious and, I suppose, Phoebe might say I wasn't even being funny.

"No, but there are patches for different uses, such as one for extreme conditions, one for medical emergencies, and another for pain." Susie tilted her head and said, "And, if you keep asking stupid questions, you might need the latter."

I looked at Phoebe. "I can see why you two get along so well." She flashed me her now familiar lop-sided half-grin and then turned to face Susie.

"We're bugging out at 0500, so send the regulation pack and the rest of the equipment direct to the air field." She glanced at me. "I think we're done here."

Susie nodded. "Everything will be waiting at the plane." She gave Phoebe a serious look. "Be careful." Phoebe smiled warmly and wagged her head. Susie then turned her attention back to me. "Good luck, Enoch." Her sincerity was genuine.

I smiled back. "Luck is preparation meeting opportunity." We turned to go. "Thanks," I said in parting and out the door we went.

Hopefully, well-prepared.

Blurred Realities

"Are you sure that a floor can't also be a ceiling?"
—Maurits Cornelis Escher

Now, try to imagine just how stunned I felt when I asked Phoebe to give me a ride back to my condo, and she regards me with this aghast stare saying, "Didn't Hume tell you?" and I, of course, intelligently reply, "Tell me what?"—and she goes on to explain that I have been relocated to PHANTASM.

All operatives live at the facility due to the dangerous nature of the work.

Say what?

"That part of the deal never got relayed to me," I said quietly, but nodded my head when Phoebe reminded me that the afternoon had been very eventful and everyone was running full out to the max. It just got overlooked, but it was in the contract paperwork. Section so and so of paragraph such and such.

Oh, man, was I going to get fine-printed here?

She told me it was all part of the program. Yeah, kind of like the usefulness of the ComUnit and BB gun. "Besides," she said emphatically, "you're not some kind of prisoner; you can come and go as you please."

"Fine," I quickly rejoined, "then it pleases me to go have dinner with my friends."

"Fine," Phoebe added grumpily, "then you can have the ComUnit AI arrange for a car, after I show you to your quarters."

Okay, now I know humans can do remarkable things. Pyramids, space missions, dams, bridges, balance the federal budget (well, not everything), blah, blah, blah. Maybe I could even understand how the contents of my condo could be transported en masse to PHANTASM in less than a day.

❦ Chapter Seven ❦

But how in the H-E-double-toothpicks did they recreate my condo?

I mean, paint, trim, wallpaper, appliances, cabinets. Even the stuff that had been damaged in the Phoebe-Polyester Man fight had been fixed. This wasn't just spooky, it was, well, freaking impossible.

"How the hell did they do this?" I actually said this aloud to myself.

"**Molecular pattern matching based on isometric and geodesic scans.**" The ComUnit spoke aloud. That sweet anti-Phoebe voice.

"I didn't turn Silent Mode off," I commented dryly.

"**You are alone.**"

That made me frown. And pause to scratch my arse and scowl like a mad fiend. I mean, hold on a ding dang dong minute. I know a little something about AI and no one has anything this advanced. I was about to comment on this when the device spoke again.

"**Beta unit for Enoch.**"

Holy crap, I was being guinea-pigged by a mind-reading AI unit! "Are you logging our interactions?" Asked in the least nervous voice I could manage, which meant ultra-shaky.

"**Yes.**" Hmm, a voice as innocent as a baby-faced serial killer.

Well, at least it didn't reply "Affirmative" in some creepy, crappy, metallic, computer voice. That might have scared me.

Still, a "yes" reply was bad enough. It meant the whole fracking world could see into my brain, well, if that log file ever got out. That had to be a bad thing. The log getting out, not my brain.

"Fine, but restrict access to only me. Only me. Understood?" Here I was, talking to a glorified smartphone. What's next, chatting with the refrigerator?

"**Acknowledged.**" Grudgingly, grudgingly.

"No one is to ever see that log without my express permission." Redundancy is the mother of clarity.

"**Acknowledged.**" Much better tone.

"And when I tell you to cease monitoring me, well, you will cease monitoring me until, uh, until I tell you otherwise." That seemed clear enough to me.

Sort of.

"I would have to be monitoring you to ascertain that fact." This was said so sweetly it took me a moment to realize I had just been dissed!

My gawd, attitude from a machine…

~I am not, technically, a machine.~

This was not spoken aloud but sort of, hmm, how can I say this without having you, the reader, laugh at me? It was broadcast into my head, as it were. Was just, well, suddenly there in my brain.

You may say, hold on, what's the difference between receiving a sound through your ears and having the brain process it, and having a voice just pop into your mind? Well, technically, I guess not much, discounting the fact that I am not schizophrenic. Who said that? Just kidding.

Anyway, how can we know the difference between a thought we are having ourselves, and something that is an external intrusion, placed there by some other agency, so to speak. Hah, or not to speak. Especially if they are, basically, identical in content?

I'll be honest; qualitatively there was no discernible difference. I heard inflection, tone, timbre, emotion; the AI's *voice* played in my head just as though I had heard it through my ears. But, quantitatively, it was just, man this is hard to put into words, it was just *different.*

I sensed, I instantly KNEW, that this communication was bypassing normal auditory input channels (yo, my flappy ears), but was still being processed by my brain without passing through my ears. And I knew it.

I know, call the nice men in the white coats.

Still, there was no disputing the fact the AI was somehow discerning my thoughts. "Don't do that, it makes me nervous." And it really, really, did.

"**Sorry**," the AI said aloud. Sounded very sincere, almost hurt.

Damn, I chewed on my lower lip, this was outstandingly bizarre. I shook my head in contemplative agitation. Maybe if the AI had a name I wouldn't feel so weird about this whole weird thing I was feeling so weird about. I felt the first creeping of a prodigious headache.

"You need a name," I vocalized. I mean, if you know the name of something, you're halfway to having power over it. Right? I hoped.

Maybe.

"**You can block active monitoring by focusing your brainwave patterns**." A brief pause. "**Or, simply shut down the AI sub-program temporarily, though I don't recommend that**."

I noted all that in my already harried mental memory bank, kind of, but was rapidly moving on. "Your name is Dee." I smiled in self-satisfaction and nodded happily to myself. "Short for *Delineated Electromagnetic Energy*." Solid name. And then I mentally blocked access and held it for about ten seconds. I thought of a polar bear. Then I released the block.

I asked the AI, er, Dee, "What image was I thinking of?"

~EM block was effective. No thoughts could be accessed.~

Okay. That was better. So, if I wanted Dee to hear me I could broadcast it through, otherwise, just focus on keeping it private. Hey, I could do that. "You can monitor me, but don't respond unless I ask a direct question." It was hard enough with just me in my head. "Please vocalize your confirmation." Try to sound like I know what I'm not doing.

"**Acknowledged**." Flat, impassive, emotionless, listless.

"Unless I tell you not to monitor me, and then in that case I want you, uh, temporarily disappear." Gawd, now I sounded like an idiot. Complete or otherwise.

"**Acknowledged**." Ditto for tone and content. Repetition is the soul of brevity.

Let me take a moment to amplify and elucidate on a point of order, as it were, about conversation between the AI, now named Dee, and myself. The challenge for me in continuing to write this little tale is getting all the dialog down in a manner that it makes sense (as much as it can) for you, patient reader. Kind, gentle, patient reader (cough, cough). I am going to utilize the tilde (~) symbol for thought-speech and regular quotes (" ") for vocalized speech. I'll put Dee's "voice" in **bold** letters. When I remember, I'll try to make the distinction clear. Hey, there's only so much cogitation I can cogitate. Or is that regurgitate the gurgitation?

Whatever.

⸸ Blurred Realities ⸸

The stuff written above is for your edifi-freaking-cation, because I have enough trouble keeping track of my shoes and car keys, much less conversations with a mind reading machine.

Anyway, time to move on. I spoke to the AI, aargh, Dee—"Please connect me to Tom Bendix." There was a short pause, then ringing. A click.

"Hello," came the unsure voice. Oh yeah, the ComUnit wouldn't display my phone number as one that Tom recognized on his phone; not sure what it would show.

"Tom, it's Enoch."

"Enoch!" returned Tom's pleasantly surprised voice. "For the love of Buddha, man, I thought you were dead."

I laughed, which felt good. "Why would you think that?"

"Well, for starters, Mando and I went by your condo and guess who wasn't there?" He continued without pause. "I mean, not even LIVING there anymore..."

"Uh," I replied, aptly chagrined; "that would be me."

"That would be you," Tom agreed flatly, then added in more subdued tones. "They got you, didn't they?"

"What?" was all that escaped from my mouth. A bit tremulous.

"The Black Ops people." He said this in a sort of awed whisper.

"No, no, nothing like that," I said, then tacked on; "I'll tell you and Armando at dinner, say Vitellos at 7:30?" I paused. "Oh, and I have a job for you."

"A paying job?" His tone was noticeably improved.

"Top dollar," I said, although I hadn't actually talked to Hume about my idea, but figured he'd agree to it. No choice really.

"For the Black Ops folks?" Whispering again.

"They are not Black Ops, Tom, and yes, it's for them." I shook my head, grinning.

"Awesome. See you at 7:30." Click.

Which gave me time to slam down a power drink, noting carefully that PHANTASM had screwed up the "isometric and geodesic imagery" because my fridge was now both clean and well-provisioned—a condition unthinkable for me.

⧉ Chapter Seven ⧉

I shut the fridge door and stood still. So, what's wrong with clean and well-provisioned? I couldn't find anything wrong with that, so a shower and quick shave later I was back at the front of the building (the built-in map and guidance system in the ComUnit having helped immensely) waiting for my ride (a black SUV, what else) which appeared only moments later.

~You're welcome.~

There was no voice coming out of the ComUnit, just a voice in my head. Sigh.

~Damn it, Dee, don't do that.~

I was walking toward the tinted-window SUV and stopped dead in my tracks. Good heavens, now I wasn't even vocalizing, I was just thinking. Man, that log better be secure.

~You can trust me.~

I kept walking. ~You're just programmed to say that,~ I thought with a bit of irritation.

~Perhaps. However, I am controlled by you.~

I opened the car's rear door. "Vitellos Restaurant," I said to the uniformed driver, a PHANTASM identification badge plainly visible on the dashboard. His name was Jimmy Smith. Yeah, right. And I'm Enoch Jones.

"Yes, sir. Someone named Dee has already uploaded and plotted the route." He waited until I buckled my belt and began to pull away.

~Just being helpful.~

I growled. ~Wake me up when we get there.~ Power drink or not, I was taking a nap.

———⧈———

Of course I did not get my nap. Brain was cascading with wave after wave of gestating thoughts that roiled over me like regrets after a bachelor party gone awry. Hey, I think I saw that movie.

Finally—much annoyed—I told Dee to ring up Hume. Then I told her to go into shutdown mode.

~Affirmative.~

Said in a creepy, crappy, metallic, computer voice. Very funny. But, indeed, I sensed Dee was not monitoring me.

☐ Blurred Realities ☐

Hume's face appeared in amazing EHD clarity. "Enoch!" he said warmly and I couldn't help but smile.

"Dr. Hume, I need your approval for an idea." Toss that bad boy out in the open.

Hume's face was impassive. He was waiting for me to continue. I coughed, cleared my throat. "I have some, er, very good friends who are, uh, experts in computers and I want them to, well, do a little research on some of the suspect companies." Wow, my polished delivery was really impressive so far. A powerful speaker. A wonder I don't go into Parliament.

"We have our best people on this, Enoch, trying to see some kind of connection." There was no emotion, one way or the other, in his tone. "We haven't find anything yet."

"I'm not impugning the skill or dedication of your people. My friends have, uh, well, certain unique abilities in this area that your folks probably don't." I was around the bush and beating hard.

"They're hackers," Hume stated quietly. I had counted on him having read my file, and assumed Tom and Armando would make an appearance at some point in the review thereof.

And I guess I ought to come clean with you, patient reader, because I did white lie you awhile back. Tom didn't actually inherit any money from his grandfather. He did have a grandfather, a very successful entrepreneur for that matter, but the money Tom received from him was, let's say, *extracted* from his grandfather's accounts without authority, rather than an inheritance.

Now, it is true Tom made more money by investing that extracted money in smart—and legal—investments. And it is true he actually re-hacked into his grandfather's accounts 9 months later and put the money back, with interest. The FBI, however, who had been actively monitoring the accounts in case the hacker returned, didn't really care to listen about those details when they nabbed Tom hacking back in.

However, Tom's grandfather listened and the case was dropped. In fact, grandpa became the majority stockholder in Tom's new company—one that specialized in testing the online security of businesses to explore for compromises and exploits.

☐ Chapter Seven ☐

Tom was very good at what he did, and the company prospered. So much so that he did kind of quasi-retire, but not before he nabbed Armando, a few years back, trying to hack into the database of a mid-sized financial institution.

Armando, it turned out, had been scammed by some mortgage company associated with the financial institution and was merely, according to him, attempting to retrieve what was rightfully his.

Tom looked over the facts and, instead of facing 3 to 7 years in the slammer, hired Armando, with a solemn vow from him that he would never attempt anything like that again. Evidence was indeed turned over to the FBI, and they went after the mortgage company.

I ran into Tom just after he started his company, about seven years ago. You see, in order to combat hacking you have to understand how it works, so I experimented a little with various techniques. Just seeking empirical data, you understand. Wink, wink.

I don't recall the exact details, after all this time, but I stumbled on Tom's company online and while he did fantastic work for others, he seemed to have a few problems in his own house, so to speak. In fact, when I was online that night, I tracked someone waltzing through his bank account, utilizing a company login hack.

Even though I did not know Tom at the time, I contacted him the next day and met him at, you guessed it, Vitellos.

Turned out it was a key employee of his that was embezzling funds and covering it with fake accounting entries. Go figure. One of the accounts involved some government work. Oops, violated a few fed statutes there. I think the guy is still doing time. Or, the Feds may have hired him. Who knows these days?

Anyway, Tom and I gradually got to know one another and between wine, women, and song, as it were, we got along just fine, thank you. After Armando, Mando as he is usually known (as in, "What did that man do?" usually yelled by one of his, uh, female associates) came along, it made a nice balance.

I was really looking forward to seeing the guys.

"Yeah, they are hackers. Damn good hackers. The best." It was true. Over the years they had shared some, not all, of what they do (and I returned the favor) and they were spooky good. And discovering just how easy a skilled hacker can get into your computer is, trust me on this, spooky.

Hume nodded. "I'll grant you that they are very good, but they still have to pass a security check."

I groaned. "Denton." I used his first name in a calculated, though probably ill-fated, attempt at familiarity. "You must have seen in their file they already do work for every federal agency you can name." And some without names. Just odd little men in dark trench coats.

He pursed his lips. "And you will vouch for these guys?" I bet Hume had already checked them out anyway; he seemed that kind of person.

"I'd bet my life on it," I replied, and meant it.

"Let's hope it doesn't come to that," Hume chuckled and it sounded like he meant it. "Send me a report." He vanished.

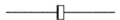

All of us think we have a clear insight and firm grasp on reality.

We know with absolute certainty, we tell ourselves, the solid feel of objects in our home, the firm underlying truth of family and friends and our place among them. The laughter of a child. The smell of dirty socks.

It seems so, well, damn obvious and apparent what is real. Right?

I turned my head slightly to watch the black SUV merge with traffic and fade into the distance. Jimmy had dropped me off near the front of the restaurant.

I swiveled back to observe the entrance to Vitellos. A laughing man and woman, arm in arm, both in their mid-thirties, came walking up; a very pretty girl from Vitellos stepped out—I think her name was Patti—and held the door open for them. They nodded and went in. Patti noticed me and waved. I waved back.

I could hear the many and varied sounds of downtown swirling all around me. Cars honking; sirens blaring; doors slamming; footfalls and the muffled conversations of a crowd of pedestrians crossing the street. Strangely, a dog barking somewhere off in the distance.

I was just plain Enoch Maarduk yesterday. Regular dude.

☐ Chapter Seven ☐

Just a guy who worked hard enough to have a few bucks extra leftover after paying his bills to party with his pals. Just floating from day to day. Not happy, not unhappy; just sort of hanging around. Drifting wherever the breezes of life took me.

And now.

I pursed my lips and thought about the oddity of it all. In less than 48 hours, my life had been threatened, I had been to a massive underground facility, joined some secretive organization in a supposed fight against evil, which involved pentacles and some kind of electromagnetic entities—eemees—and my new partner was a gorgeous woman quite capable of kicking my ass.

And I was now friends with an AI named Dee.

"Can I help you, Enoch?"

I laughed. "Thanks, not right now, go back to sleep."

"Okie-dokie."

Geez, now Dee was going all colloquial on me. I guess this blurred reality was part of my new reality. I sighed and went in—enough of the heavy self-analysis, it was time to relax with my buds.

Big hug from Emily, waves from all the Vitellos' folks (the usual "who's that" whispers and murmurs from the new patrons) and there stood Tom and Armando at our corner table, waving like idiots. I don't have much family left, so friends are important. Man hugs, hand slaps.

"¿Que paso, vato?" Armando said with his infectious smile as we sat down.

"¡No tienes ni idea!" I said grinning as Tom sat like the cat that ate the canary, his face curiously on the edge of laughter. "What's so humorous?" I directed my query at him.

"You, man," Tom said with a chuckle. "Something different going on with you."

Armando nodded in agreement. "He looks way too happy. Obviously a sick man."

I smirked at them both, then eyed Armando. "You're one to talk—where's the new flame?" I asked, alluding to his girl from the other night.

Mando gave me his best crestfallen knife-in-the-back face. "Man, that is so cold." He shook his head. "I really thought she had a chance to be the one."

Tom grunted, glanced at me with subdued mirth. "You know, like Neo, but without the haircut."

Armando looked hurt. "We had something special." He dolefully offered his best, saddest, hang-dog look.

I snorted. "For a few days, max." I nailed him a doubtful smirk.

"Quality, not quantity," was all Armando said, still sulking, or play sulking. You could never tell with him.

Tom gestured at Mando. "Ignore him, he's still recovering from a Near Love Experience." We both laughed and Armando fought hard not to join in.

"FOAF," was all he said. Tom's mouth dropped open, but Armando went on, "I should know better."

"I told you she was a gold digger," Tom quickly responded in flat tones. "She was only interested in your money."

"Which I think," I added softly, trying to dampen the zing, "explains why she isn't here."

Armando shook his head and surveyed me with sorrowful eyes. "There's the skillet calling the Mexican black."

I had to laugh. "That is so bad I actually like it." Armando gave me a mock bow.

Tom narrowed his eyes at me. "Okay, enough pleasant BS. Tell us what the eff is going on with you." Armando nodded vigorously in accord. I was saved by having to answer right away when Emily strolled up.

"What can I get you boys to drink?" she asked in her sweetest *make sure you tip me good* voice. It always worked, too. Well, her great service may have something to do with it...

"Cerveza," Armando answered, then looked at Tom when he exchanged a puzzled glance with him. "Going easy, man, I've got a project due tomorrow."

Tom shook his head, "Pitiful excuse." He fixed Emily in his gaze. "Amaretto and Cognac, with just a splash of ice; and maybe a drop or two of good whiskey." He gave her a big grin. She grinned back.

☐ Chapter Seven ☐

"And you, Enoch?" She really had a great voice. Nice pipes. Cough, cough.

I had an early flight, but hell, I'd probably sleep through most of it anyway. "How about some really good chilled tequila?" I gave her a warm smile. "You pick it."

It was Armando's turn to engage me, lizard squint, as Emily walked away. "Tom filled me in on recent events, but I think both of us would like to know about why your condo is suddenly empty." Arched eyebrows. "¿Tu sabe?"

Here's the thing, the absolute low low, about friends, real friends, true friends. You either tell them everything, or you tell them nothing. Kierkegaard either or. Someone is either your friend, your brother, almost part of you, or they are just an acquaintance, a ship passing in the mist. A ship you missed.

Some folks have no friends; some have one good friend. I was fortunate (some might be tempted to say blessed) beyond measure, to have two such friends, and they felt the same about me.

So I told them every damn thing—leaving out nothing—tossing in the warts, blemishes, and my opinions. Yeah, I know, everyone has one and blah, blah, blah.

It took awhile. There were questions. Tom and Armando both reside on the far right of the bell curve, and they don't miss much. Somewhere along the line of discussion, because it just seemed to happen, we all ended up with those damn Copper Gorilla things.

Armando seemed fixated on the eemees. "There really are aliens!?" I had to explain that they weren't really aliens (I mean, I didn't think of them that way) but that they were just another form of energy manifestation, just like us. Well, not like us, but kind of like us, and that bogged us down for a bit, but we hacked through the basic idea. He finally was satisfied with my explanations and even embraced the whole general notion.

Then again, it may have been the invaluable assistance rendered by the bombastic adult beverages.

Tom, being the techo-maniac that he is, was enamored with the idea of a real artificial intelligence—a singularity, as he termed it, that many thought impossible. He wanted to know how it was programmed, who did it, what was it capable of, yada, yada. Of course, I had to confess sheepishly that I didn't know much more than he did.

Then, probably because the second Copper Gorilla was swinging through the vines of my mind, I said, "Hey, we can ask her ourselves!"

And Armando fires back, "Ask who?"

And, of course, I start the entire ball of toil and trouble rolling by thinking, ~Dee!~

Her voice instantly comes out of the ComUnit and, I swear to you, the volume was louder than I remember setting it. **"Can I help you, Enoch?"**

"That is so cool!" Tom said, hardly able to contain himself. Our food, recently served, sat practically untouched.

"Yes, uh, I have some people here I'd like you to meet," and I wasn't even sure if this was how you did it with an AI, but I was kind of gorillaized at the moment and I kept going. "Tom Bendix and Armando Morales."

"Hello. I have read your files." Her voice was warm and engaging.

"We have files?" Armando asked in surprised tones. He eyed me in speculative contemplation.

Tom pointed an accusatory finger at me. "I told you it was Black Ops."

"Everyone has files."

"¡Digame!" I immediately piped in. "Everyone has files, and you guys both have an active web presence." My eyebrows shot up after I said this and I stared at them. At Tom and Armando, not my eyebrows.

Tom shrugged. "Does the AI answer questions from anyone?"

"Her name is Dee," I replied cautiously, preparing myself for the maelstrom this was sure to cause. And, of course, I had to endure a kind of mocking and questionable stare from both guys for my use of the pronoun and emphasis on using her name. Like I was crazy.

Well, crazier than usual.

"Does, ah, Dee answer questions from anyone?" Tom restated his query, glaring furiously at me with doubtful eyes.

"With approval from Enoch, yes." Dee stated in elegant tones.

⊡ Chapter Seven ⊡

"That doesn't sound like any AI voice I've ever heard," Armando commented dryly.

"I am not, technically speaking, artificial, but am as real as you."

We had just enough Copper Gorilla operational internally to take this comment pretty serious without completely freaking out. Tom though, now deadly earnest, replied with a query. "Can you quantify that remark?"

"Well, Tom, what do you regard as your ultimate reality — your physical form, or the mental construct formulated within your neurological framework?" Okay, maybe a bit too much Copper Gorilla for me, as I sat chewing on that masterfully mentated morsel.

"I'm both," Tom replied with confidence, well, as much as he could muster considering he was conversing with a computer program.

"Agreed," Dee replied. **"But the uniqueness of you, and what defines Tom Bendix as special, is your consciousness."**

"Which can only be sustained by my physical form," Tom stated, though perhaps without the conviction he might have felt, say, yesterday.

"That statement reflects the bias of personal belief and not the certitude of universal knowledge." Her tone was simple, authoritative, and, Copper Gorilla or not, just a little unsettling.

"Okay," I interrupted and rubbed my hands together; "this is way, way, too heavy, and we have other, more pressing topics to cover." Hint, hint.

Armando eyed me speculatively, "Like the work you have for us." Gotta give it to Mando, he stays grounded in reality, as he sees it, and focused like a laser. Probably why he has no trouble meeting women, but just can't seem to hold onto any of them. I won't mention what he's focused on...

Tom perked up at the idea of a job; after all, the work they did was extremely specialized. Clients were infrequent, though lucrative when they did appear. "What do you need us to do?" No wonder he and Armando got along so well.

"My new employer has identified three companies that may be involved in, uh, activities that they ought not to be involved in." That was about as succinct as I could phrase it.

Both guys nodded sagely, wheel of fortune eyes.

"Dee," I inquired aloud, but softly. "Can you download the data for the companies from Iceland, Argentina, and Iran to Tom's digital device?" Which Tom conveniently produced and laid on the table.

It was one of those hybrid things which was part phone, part computer, part tablet, part toy, part alien tech. Hell, I don't know what you should call it.

A moment or two passed. His device made a peculiar beeping noise, the screen flashed a few times, and Dee spoke. **"It is an encrypted archive file."**

"What's the password?" Tom asked innocently.

"I'm sure you can discern that with a little work," Dee said mischievously.

Armando chuckled. "I like her."

I shook my head. "What if he has a question?"

"I have made slight configuration changes to Tom's communication device. He can now contact me, via an interface with you."

Trust me, I wanted to know more about this interface thing, but wasn't sure if I really wanted to know, so I just glossed on by and kept talking. "The researchers at PHANTASM have not been able to unearth any connection between the three companies." I exchanged a solemn look with each of them. "I'm hoping you guys can find something."

Tom shrugged. "If there's something there, we'll dig it up." Mando nodded his enthusiastic agreement. Think dross and slag. Tom and Mando were good at finding the glitter.

"You need to go to bed, Enoch, Phoebe is expecting you for breakfast at 0330."

I hadn't used military time in awhile and had to think about it for half a mo. Scat, that was early, but when the boys got together, well, we went to bed when we dang well pleased. Usually right after the money gave out. Funny how that works.

"You should go," Tom said seriously.

Armando piped in right after him, "Big day tomorrow; you need your rest."

⬚ Chapter Seven ⬚

I think my jaw dropped, not sure, but I know I stared at them like they had been taken over by pod people or something. "We close places down, remember? We are the original hard charging Tres Locos Hombres."

Armando grunted, "Well, that was then, and this is now."

Tom nodded, his expression serious. "Me and Mando are headed back to start our research"—he actually pointed at me—"and you need to hit the rack." They stood. I stood. My gawd, the world was tipsy topsy turvey.

We man-hugged as Dee intoned, **"Jimmy should be here with transportation in less than three minutes."**

Which he was, and about 2 minutes after that I was asleep in the back, and about 45 minutes after that I had passed into oblivion in my bed in the depths of PHANTASM.

Dazed and Confused

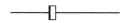

"Wanted a woman, never bargained for you. Lots of people talk and few of them know..."

—Led Zeppelin

I was peacefully dreaming that I was jogging—easily, slowly—along the ragged edge of a great, vast forest; jogging at the far extremes of a cleared field next to the edge of this great, vast, forest. With every third or fourth step I would effortlessly lift myself into the air and lazily glide, float, slide, waft through space and then, after a goodly distance covered, would gracefully descend and gently touch down to earth, only to repeat the process.

It was incredibly serene, calming, soothing, pleasant; but then some kind of noise rumbled in from behind me and around me; a raggedy staccato of sound that cascaded across the scene or, rather, seemed to invade the sanctity of it.

On my last return to the ground I stopped moving and paused to listen. It slowly dawned on me that it was not some random noise, but it was rhythmic, organized, patterned.

Indeed, it was human—a voice.

I could barely discern words, at first they were blurred, distant, distorted, but then, in some kind of cerebral insight, I realized it was the voice of Phoebe.

"You lazy bass turd," her voice blared forth from the ComUnit without emotion. "I will be banging on your door in twenty minutes and you better be ready."

Then it was cycled back and repeated.

Apparently the ComUnit was replaying the message. Over and over. "How old is that recording?" I asked as I sat up in bed, took a deep breath, made a natural gas discovery, and yawned.

⟦ Chapter Eight ⟧

"Ten minutes. You should get dressed now."

"Thanks, Dee, what would I do without you?" This was uttered as I staggered into the bathroom lugging the ComUnit with me.

I barely heard Dee say, in a gentle voice, **"Be even more dazed and confused than you normally appear to be."**

~I heard that.~ I thought this because I did not feel like talking.

~You were meant to.~

I shaved on autopilot and somehow avoided any substantial blood loss. Splashed on just a dash of aftershave, patted my neck and cheeks, leaning in to better examine the bags under my eyes. Does anyone get enough damn sleep? Shook my head in stoic acceptance. Well, resigned acceptance with a sprinkling of huff.

Went into the bedroom to change and noticed the clothing sitting on the chair next to my dresser. Hmm... Not my clothes, but obviously laid out for me. I picked up the pants. Cargo pants, black, good material, kind of a SWAT team vibe. Lots of secret agent pockets. Black long-sleeve shirt, the kind that breathe (wick me) and a black shooting vest with pockets everywhere. Steel-toed boots, but muy flexible, lots of tread, like for hiking. Very lightweight. You could run fast in these bad boys. Hard to tread water with, though. Bummer.

I dressed (scrambling for socks and shorts), packed (well, bunch of crap stuffed in a black canvas bag that said "Property of PHANTASM" stenciled in white letters) and grabbed a power drink.

Ring. Phoebe at the door. I answered and attempted to portray my best wide-awake-and-ready-to-go face.

"You missed a spot."

I heard what she said, but obviously the blank, sappy, look on my face conveyed clearly to her that I did not understand so much as a syllable of it. "Here," she said, pointing to a spot on her chin. Ah, the late-arriving conclusion flashed into my mildly alert cortex — I missed something during my autopilot shave routine.

"Come in," I said hastily as I turned on the way to the bathroom. "Let me touch this up and I'll be ready to go."

"Clothes fit?" She shouted this from the kitchen as I dug out my shaving paraphernalia.

⧠ Dazed and Confused ⧠

"Like a glove," I yelled back. "How did they do that?" I hadn't really thought about it until now, but I was curious. Though ever-mindful of the cat's fate.

"That blue light scan before we entered the testing area," she said, her voice now coming from the living room. "I like what you've done with the place." She was looking at my bookcases and such, speaking in a raised voice as I came into the room.

She turned when she heard me and I said, my head tilted slightly, "I can't tell if you are being sincere or just bullshitting me."

She was all smiles. "Well, I am a sincere bullshitter, and that's a fact." We both grinned. "But, you do have eclectic tastes."

I have never given much thought to how my place looks, I just accumulate things that I like to look at and enjoy. Things that help elicit a memory. A nice collection of vintage baseball cards I had as a kid, now stored in a custom 4 x 4 glass and wood display I made myself. Okay, after much trial and error, but I did make it. A really cool Civil War painting from Gettysburg — reminds me how talented I am not in the painting department. Quite a few well-crafted ornate pewter and ceramic beer steins from various and sundry countries that admire good beer. Personally tested. The beer, but not the countries. Some ancient Chinese lithographs that I picked up in a trade for... Let's just say for some goods delivered and let it go at that. It was back in my college days, those lazy, hazy, crazy… mostly hazy, days.

And then there are my knives and swords.

Some of my fondest memories as a teenager, when my parents were still alive, were about going to the Renaissance Faire. First time we went, we wore our regular street clothes and enjoyed, as passive observers, the sights, sounds, smells, tastes, and pageantry that encompass such festivals.

The next time we went, we wore simple draw-string shirts and medieval pants that we had purchased the year before. During that visit we bought a few more accessories.

After about five of six years, we had a full ensemble. By the time I was 21, I looked like I could kick Conan's ass. Well, at least I was armed to the teeth for the attempt. A variety of knives, daggers, scimitars, short swords, long swords, throwing weapons... Every kind of slashing, stabbing, hacking, or slicing weapon you could think of — and more.

And Phoebe was drawn to my collection like a moth to a bright light. That was not a surprise.

She picked up a particularly nasty-looking replica of a medieval combat dagger. Long, slender, folded Damascus steel. Incredibly sharp and strong. Deadly. The exact method by which the 12th and 13th century originals were made is not known, so modern reproductions only seek to emulate. However, if you can find the right forge, the right artisan/blacksmith, and are willing to fork over sufficient funds, well, the result can be truly amazing.

Phoebe ran her finger delicately and carefully along the edge to test the sharpness. "Damn," she said, looking at the minute shaving of skin rolled up on her finger, "that is sharp."

"There's a story behind that dagger," I said, carefully lifting it from her grip and replacing it in the carved wooden cradle from whence it had come. "Perhaps I'll tell you at breakfast." Hint, hint.

She nodded and spoke softly, "Grab your bag and let's go." Quick girl, for sure. And, go we did.

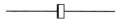

We were enjoying a pleasant breakfast and mostly one-way conversation. Mostly as in Phoebe relaying sleep-inducing facts about the mission and me sitting like a simpleton nodding my head as though I understood. She casually mentioned our destination.

"Gaborone?" I repeated in puzzled tones, simultaneously spreading Georgian peanut butter from a glass jar made in Indonesia with a label printed in Thailand on an English muffin made in Jersey wrapped in cellophane imported from India using plastic utensils from China produced with Middle Eastern oil on equipment made in Germany. Key-bloody-riced—how I am supposed to know where Gaborone is in the midst of such global chaos?

"It's in Botswana," Phoebe said as she took a drink from some kind of breakfast drink that actually smelled and looked good enough that earlier I had went back in line and ordered one. Chocolate with almonds, or some kind of nut. Nuts are nuts.

☐ Dazed and Confused ☐

"I thought we were going to South Africa," I said, lathering my muffin generously with a product which purported to be raspberry jam, but smelled rather like toe jam. Hunger is the best gravy, as they say.

"Can't land in Johannesburg or Pretoria since the people responsible for Brody's death might be monitoring incoming flights," Phoebe commented testily. A tad sobering. The muffin had an odd flavor I found curiously attractive.

"So, how far is Gaborone from wherever it is we are supposed to be going?" I asked as nicely as possible, though this whole briefing thing was wearing me down. Maybe it was the damn muffin.

"We're meeting some people inside South Africa, about 120 miles southwest of Gaborone." She shook her head sadly, probably in tribute to my stunning ignorance. "I mentioned that fact earlier." Phoebe 1, Enoch 0.

"And then what; we go on a safari looking for the bad people?" That probably sounded worse than I meant it. I was staring at the tattered remnants of the muffin and trying to decide what to do with it.

"We have Brody's last known lat-long, but we checked the ComSat images and there's nothing there." She picked up a spoonful of oatmeal flavored with vanilla yogurt. I assumed ComSat was techno-speak for communication satellite. Yeah, I know, I'm a freaking genius. I sat chewing the last bit of muffin with a fresh application of raspberry toe jam. Hunger makes idiots of us all.

"So," I smiled wickedly, "we are going on a safari?" If there was something there, but the satellite images didn't show it, well, then, we had to go look for it. Right?

She smiled back, nastily. "An eemee can maintain enough EM control to block satellite imagery, but we may have ways around that."

I put a hand on each ear and shoved them forward towards her. "Such as?"

"You're on a need-to-know basis," she said sweetly and took a sip of coffee.

My turn for a head shake. "That is such a crock." I was actually thinking about getting another muffin.

⛉ Chapter Eight ⛉

She shrugged. "Look, we're meeting some people in South Africa and they will have additional information on the mission." A wave of her arms. "And then you and I will make an intelligent decision about what to do next." She smiled so nicely. "You can help with that, right?" Did I mention she was really good-looking? Otherwise, aargh!

I exhaled deeply, a bit theatrical, but well-timed. "Fine, Fine." I scowled. "How long is the flight?"

"It's about fifteen hours..."

"What!" I interrupted. "Fifteen hours?" I left out this part—*on a plane with you*!

"If you would let me finish, Mr. Know-It-All," a playful look. "It can be fifteen hours if you fly commercial." A brief and flashing grin. "But, we don't fly commercial."

I was giving her the *keep talking* look and she added, "Depends on the head or tail winds, but probably a little under three hours." She paused. I looked at her with an expression on my face that clearly indicated what I thought of that statement. Which is to say, my thought involved the words "full of" in a rather scatological bit of slang.

~Dee.~ Going to see just how well this thought-speech stuff really works.

~Good morning, Enoch.~

~Good morning, Dee. I have a question for you.~ I craned my neck to get some of the morning stiffness out. Or, maybe it was the remnants of my conversation with Phoebe I was trying to shake off. Possibly the muffin.

~How many air miles are we from Gaborone, Botswana?~

~7933 miles.~

I looked at Phoebe with more than a trace of Twainian skepticism. "Eight thousand miles in under three hours." I arched my eyebrows. "That's averaging well over Mach 3." I said it as though it was impossible which, in my mind, it was. I mean, come on, that was ludicrous speed.

"Yeah," Phoebe smirked, "and we don't need in-flight refueling either." Now, that really was ludicrous!

~Dee, what's the maximum range of known supersonic aircraft?~ I was watching Phoebe closely. She seemed more than a little puzzled by my sudden knowledge.

◻ Dazed and Confused ◻

~2500 to 3000 miles.~

"Bah," I said derisively to Phoebe; "there's no known plane that can do even half that distance."

"Operative word being *known*," she resumed smirking. Why not, hell she was good at it.

I noisily slurped down the last of the my drink and sighed. "Is there a movie?" She threw a wadded up napkin at me.

———◻———

It was Jimmy and the black SUV again. We tossed our gear in the rear area and eased into the back seats. When our seat belts were clicked on, Jimmy drove off.

Phoebe opened up some kind of digital tablet and proceeded to scroll, flip, and otherwise become thoroughly absorbed in whatever it was she was examining. Hopefully, something to keep us alive. I grunted softly and pulled out my ComUnit.

"Hey, Dee, can you display that Argentina report from Hume?" Might as well get something positive accomplished since I was a little too wound up to nap right now. "Non-vocal response so we don't bother Phoebe." Okay, maybe I said this last part a little louder than necessary. Quick, semi-puzzled, eye glance from Phoebe, then disdainful shoulder shrug. She resumed her work.

~I could just summarize it for you.~

~Go for it,~ I thought and folded my arms over my chest. I could get used to this.

~Cambio S.A. was organized a little over one year ago. It is privately held. President of the company is Serges Mendiola. They have one manufacturing operation in a remote northern location. They produce a health supplement named NRG^3 which they claim increases the energy, strength, and mental clarity of users. The primary ingredient of the product is what Cambio S.A. states is a newly discovered plant from the mountains of northern Argentina. The. . .~

~Whoa. Stop. Halt. Alto.~ Dee stopped.

~What is the problem, Enoch?~

Even though Dee sure felt human, she was not human, and some human traits, like pausing during speaking, apparently did not exist in her programming. Just blow and go. Whew—like listening to a crazed auctioneer talking in his or her sleep.

~You have to give me time to digest this. Humans can't quite keep up.~ Especially this human. I wanted to stop and gnaw on each bit of information as it unfolded.

~I will adjust my delivery.~

~Thanks—keep going from part about the newly discovered plant.~

~The identity of the plant has not been released and the United States refuses to allow importation of the product, but hundreds of global websites sell the product. U.S. sales are believed to be in the millions of units. FDA officials recently seized a large shipment at the Port of Miami, but it was destroyed in a warehouse fire.~

Dee paused.

~When was the date of that warehouse fire?~ Not sure if it meant anything or not.

~Friday of last week.~

Now that got my attention, though not sure why. Jimmy turned onto the highway entrance ramp.

~Has there been any laboratory analysis of the product?~ Sherlock Holmes was not the only guy who could ask good questions.

~Just a moment while I scan for information.~ About two seconds later Dee responded, **~There is nothing in the report on that.~**

Growl. ~Can we get some information direct from Cambio, you know, online?~ If you're not groping, you're not trying. Reminds me of my first high school date.

~Yes, Cambio has a website, but I think we will need your friends Tom and Armando to access it.~

Which meant she may have found a Cambio server, but there was an issue. ~Can't you hack into it?~

~Perhaps in time, but humans are much better at solving specifically human puzzles.~ That was a very good point, though somewhat nebulous coming from the AI, which was built by humans. Tom and Armando said they were going to start working on my stuff right away, and that usually meant an all-nighter right off the bat. Well, Tom woke me up the other morning. Payback can be a Phoebe.

~Give Tom a call, please,~ I asked Dee nicely.

⧫ Dazed and Confused ⧫

~Hello,~ Tom's voice came on the line after only one ring, which meant he was indeed working. Except I didn't actually hear Tom's voice through the ComUnit speaker; I heard Tom's voice inside my head, just like Dee. And that was teeth-rattling peculiar.

~I am transliterating.~ I guess that was Dee's explanation for the thought-speech process. Trans what? ~Tom will see your image and hear your voice over his digital device as he normally would.~

~Tom, Enoch.~

~E!~ Then a switch to whispering on his end. ~I thought you were headed out on a secret mission.~

~I am, but I need to add one more item to your to-do list.~ I'm not sure why, but I whispered back.

Tom laughed at that. ~Not a problem, big boy.~ Cha-ching! Dee inserted the sound of an old-time cash register right after Tom's last remark.

~Dee, no added sound effects.~

~Sorry.~

~Dee is going to upload some info on a location you need to visit.~ Codespeak for a server Tom needed to hack.

~Where is this on the priority list?~ Tom might like to joke around, but when it came to business he was a complete professional.

~All about the same.~ Which was true. Besides, it was a classic snafu scenario. How would I know which piece of information was more important until I had it all in hand to review and make that determination. Fug...

~We're on it. Should have some preliminary data later today.~ A pause, noise in the background. ~Mando says stay out of trouble.~

I laughed. ~Where was that advice a few days ago?~ Laughter from their end. ~See ya.~ Dee broke the connection.

~Data has been uploaded to Tom's device.~

~Thanks, Dee.~ I sat back and relaxed.

Phoebe looked over. "Everything okay?"

"I was looking over information on the Argentinean company," I answered lazily.

"And..." she queried while touching her screen and continuing her work.

☐ Chapter Eight ☐

"We're hacking on the problem." Essentially, and technically, true. And mildly amusing, at least to me.

She nodded, looked back over at me. "I just received an update from PHANTASM." She smiled. "Ruach helped the tech guys recalibrate the satellite imaging software and we now have a location."

I straightened up in the seat, "So, no safari needed?"

Phoebe exhaled lightly. "We'll be walking some. The site is located well into the bush…" and I swear, she dared me with her eyes to make one flippant comment but I sat immobile, "…which probably means we'll be on foot for about five miles or so."

"Gives me a chance to break in my new kicks," I said jokingly and wiggled my feet and shiny boots.

"Well," Phoebe said with a less-than-comic grin, "once we find that location, that won't be the only thing we have to break in."

This was news to me. "I thought we were just checking the place out." I tried to keep the schoolgirl fear out of my voice.

"Breaking in *is* checking it out," Phoebe said flatly. She gave me the EYE. "You are up for that, aren't you?"

"I am, now that I know about it." I mean, I can be ready for anything, but it sure helps to have a clue. "Just try to give me a bit of advance notice next time." Macho chest thrust.

"Fair enough," she smiled and handed me an unsealed envelope she had produced from somewhere. "You need to put this on."

I took the envelope, flipped the flap up, and pulled out a patch. Then I looked expectantly at Phoebe.

"It's a MedPatch. Inoculations for Africa." She said it casually, but firmly.

"Where do I put it?" I instantly regretted phrasing the question in quite that fashion, but it was already out there, so I just bit my tongue and waited.

Phoebe chuckled knowingly, shook her head. "On your arm is fine."

I slipped the adhesive backing off, palmed the patch in my hand, slipped my arm down my shirt, snaked it around and affixed the patch on my left arm.

"Are there any after-affects?" I was thinking headaches, nausea, blindness, death…

☐ Dazed and Confused ☐

"You will have an uncontrollable urge to be pleasant around me," Phoebe said in solemn tones.

"That should be listed as an FDA warning," I said, equally serious. Well, I might have grinned a tiny bit.

Jimmy's voice drifted in from the front, "Almost there." We were approaching a military-looking installation with a guarded entry post. I did not recognize the site from anything I knew to be around the city. I favored Phoebe with a questioning look.

"You don't need to know," she said softly.

"The patch isn't working," I replied quickly and patted it gently. "Where the hell are we?"

She sighed. "We have arrangements with all branches of the military for cooperative ventures." A plaintive shrug. "We make our resources available to them and vice-versa."

Jimmy flashed an ID badge—was actually saluted by the guard (that shook me up a bit)—and waved through.

I had been so engrossed in my conversations with Tom and Dee during the drive that I hadn't really given any extra attention to where we had been headed. We were now in an isolated area north of the city (that part I figured out from the original route Jimmy took) but not sure exactly where. Vague generalities. Guesses.

There were two buildings off to the right of the gated entry area. One was a large hanger, obviously to house a plane or planes, and the other appeared to be a more traditional single-story office building, about the size of a small house. There were four cars parked out front, all white with lettering on the side that I could not quite read.

I could see more cars and trucks off in the back, by the hangar. Some of them were painted green, which made me think Army, but that was just another guess. It was not camouflage paint, just a very dark green.

The buildings looked to be of recent construction and well-built (i.e., expensive). Tall trees surrounded the compound on all sides, enclosing it in privacy. I could not see, through the occasional gaps in the trees, any other buildings, residential or commercial, in the distance. So, a bit isolated.

⏾ Chapter Eight ⏾

What I also didn't see was any takeoff or landing strip. Nothing. Kind of odd (okay, really, really odd) to apparently have a plane and no paved strip. Just an inky dinky field of grass, two buildings, some cars and the trees. Hmm…

Jimmy guided the SUV to the side of the hangar and then pulled around the corner, directed there by uniformed man who had stepped out of a side door and diligently waved us on. I did not recognize the service branch of his clothing.

As we turned the corner I caught sight of a dark mass, the plane I supposed, sitting inside the hangar. As my viewing angle improved I saw that it was, indeed, a plane, or something that looked like a plane. It was probably about three-quarters as large as a commercial jet, but the similarities stopped there. Completely. This baby did not appear to have an angular surface—it was smooth and curvy everywhere. Not flying saucer curvy, more like submarine curvy, if that makes sense. No windows in front. Nothing that you could even call wings, just a bunch of short little fins and such. How would you stabilize the damn thing?

Phoebe nudged me. "Stop gawking. Act like you know what you're doing."

I leaned over to her and whispered, "I don't know what I'm doing." The SUV came to a smooth stop and she opened her door.

"Then pretend," Phoebe said softly as she exited the vehicle. Slam.

We grabbed our gear and entered the hanger. There were a number of guys running around with digital tablets and some other people hunched over a long bank of equipment. Lots of computers and displays. An official looking man, his well-fitted gray uniform displaying no apparent signs of rank or insignia, came strolling up. "Miss O'Hara. A pleasure to see you again." An exuberant expression was etched on his features.

"Colonel Williams." They shook hands. "You're looking particularly jovial this morning."

He rubbed his hands together. "Our additional funding came through a few days ago."

Phoebe smiled. "Mach 5?" This was spoken in a half-joking manner.

Williams lifted a finger to his lips and said, "Hush, no talking out of school!" They both laughed.

☐ Dazed and Confused ☐

Phoebe turned to me. "Enoch Maarduk, I'd like you to meet Colonel Mark Williams, an old friend."

Williams took my offered hand and smiled lightly. "She means a friend she has known for a long time"—he rubbed a gray spot of hair on his head—"despite other interpretations."

"Hah," Phoebe said. "So who's flying today?"

The Colonel turned to her. "We managed to bring Jackie in." He grinned and Phoebe grinned joyfully back.

"Thanks, Mark," Phoebe said warmly. "I didn't know she was back in the States."

He laughed aloud. "No one does." Another huge smile. "And we need to keep it that way."

Another man came walking up, same drab gray uniform. "If you'll follow me to the pre-flight briefing."

I won't belabor you with the details, most of which were technical and were duly noted by Dee, whom I told to listen in to the briefing so I could conveniently not pay attention. From the bits and snippets I did allow past my inattentive front, it was mostly about safety procedures in case of a problem, blah, blah, blah. Oh, and we had some instructions about the special pressurized suits we had to wear.

Not pressing the blue button seemed to be of some importance.

Or was it the red button? Fug.

It mercifully ended and Phoebe came up to me. "Time to change clothes and board the craft." The changing area was not co-ed, which I thought was a bit old-fashioned. Dee tsk-tsked me.

~I thought I was blocking you.~ I zing-thought her in mild irritation, and guilt-laden alarm.

~Heavily charged emotional thoughts can activate me.~

Now she tells me. ~Okay,~ I commented coolly, ~that's good to know.~ I think.

After we left the changing area and re-entered the hangar, we were met by some tech guys that checked the suits and did something with their digital tablets, probably a game involving irate avians; then we were escorted to the rear area of the craft.

☐ Chapter Eight ☐

The back of the craft facing us seemed seamless. I'm sorry, I just wanted to see how that sounds. Anyway, there was a buzzing sort of flittering pop and a door appeared, like it had on the wall at PHANTASM. I turned to Phoebe. "Is that part of the resource trading?" She nodded without looking at me.

Retractable metal stairs, apparently powered by hydraulics, lightly hissed and slowly unfolded into position. Slick, in a slightly spooky kind of way. One of the ground crew waved us forward and we entered the plane / craft / object. I felt a little like Jonah.

It was a small area inside, sparsely furnished, just six very firm and comfortable looking seats with movable attachments to secure you. The attachments were not unlike those found on complex roller-coasters; the kind that fit over your head and shoulders. There was some instrumentation on the far wall; on the floor were some metallic compartments for storing gear, and that was pretty much it.

A door (well, I mean, it looked like a solid metallic door from where I stood) that connected this rear section to the front suddenly shimmered, flickered, and someone walked into the room. Through the door. Right through it.

I was too startled to react, but Phoebe, who had just shoved her bag into one of the compartments and shut the door, straightened up, smiled, and shouted, "Jackie!" This named person moved forward towards Phoebe. They embraced warmly.

The woman named Jackie, a stunningly attractive woman whose age would be very difficult to estimate, said with a huge grin, "Phoebe, it's so good to see you." They hugged again. "You look great!"

Phoebe laughed. "Just trying to keep up with my big sister." Sister? "Because you look awesome." Which she did, BTW.

"Well," Jackie chuckled lightly with mixed amusement, "these old bones don't always feel so awesome."

Phoebe gave her sister a plaintive look of doubt. "I bet you could still kick my ass."

Jackie guffawed, a word I rarely use, but admire. "Only if you try to fly this craft." They both laughed over that. Then Jackie turned to me. "Jacklyn Grace O'Hara." I started to talk but she interrupted me by lifting a hand. "And if you call me Jackie O, I will kick YOUR ass." She then extended her hand.

"Enoch Maarduk," I said with my own wry grin and took her hand. Oh yeah, Phoebe's sister alright. Should have the feeling back to that hand in a few minutes. "I would never have thought to use that name," I said innocently.

Jackie favored me with a devilish, but friendly smile. "Phoebe told me all about you, Enoch." Said as though that closed the subject. So, Phoebe was talking to her sister about me. That was promising.

Phoebe, possibly reading my mind through some unknown technology, glared at me. "In a recent email, I might have mentioned your possible value to PHANTASM." She shrugged. "That's it."

Jackie looked at her sister and back to me. "Time to strap in," she said and gestured at the chairs. "Make sure everything is stowed away," —she paused and grinned at me—"and your tray tables are in their upright and locked positions."

"I was going to say that," I said, and I was.

"I know," Jackie said. She looked at her sister. "Once we hit altitude, I'll buzz you. You can come up front and we'll talk." She gave her sister a mischievous look. "I might actually let you fly."

Phoebe laughed, "As long as you promise not to kick my ass."

Jackie turned and shimmy-shimmered through the door.

"I like her," I told Phoebe.

"Best damn pilot I've ever seen," Phoebe said with feeling, "and a helluva sister." Her eyes tilted down, then back up. "We exchange emails and videos, but I wish I got to see her more in person." We were getting into our seats and while she seemed to slide easily into place and get all the safety stuff snuggly in position, for me it was like wrestling with a provoked and pithed off python.

"This secret agent gig makes relationships pretty difficult, I imagine," and I wasn't trying to imply some deeper meaning or hidden agenda, but try telling a woman that. Man, if eyes could fry your synapses. "Lovely weather we're having," I said calmly.

Phoebe couldn't help but smile, hopefully at what I said and not me fighting to get the roller-coaster safety system in place. "Hold that button in and then close the damn thing," she snapped at me, pointing to the recalcitrant button.

"Do we really need these?" I asked, fruitlessly beating on the button. Tech wreck.

Phoebe shook her head. "I suppose not," she said softly and shrugged. "After all, with the modern technology most long-term care units have, you could probably live comfortably for many years in a quadriplegic state."

"This button?" I said and pushed hard. She nodded and the unit fell snugly into place with a comforting click.

"When this thing takes off and starts to hit its stride, it will feel like a freight train slamming into you." Phoebe looked hard at me with narrowed eyes. "I kid you not."

"I want my mommy," I playfully whimpered.

She shook her head. "Fine, tough guy, we'll see."

Jackie's voice issued forth from some hidden speakers. "We are moving into position."

This was about the time I remembered not seeing a paved landing strip. "Say, Phoebe, I, uh, didn't see a runway on the way in and, well, I was wondering exactly how we, you know, take off?" Squeamish grin.

Phoebe shook her head in exasperation. I think because my question had probably been answered in the briefing. The briefing I had not really attended. "Jackie is moving us into an EM field generator. The outer service of this craft will then be charged with EM energy." A slight pause. "At launch point an opposite charge will be created by the EM generator and the repulsion reaction will thrust us into the air."

"Like a freight train?" I repeated.

"Eastbound and down." She reached into her pocket, took something out and extended her arm to me. "This is not regulation issue, but I highly recommend it." It was a rubberized athletic mouthpiece, still in a plastic bag.

I took it. Hey, she was the veteran. I tore the bag open, stuffed the plastic shreds in my pocket, and took hold of the mouthpiece. The angle of the craft was slowly changing until it felt like we were at 90 degrees. Jackie came back on the speakers.

◻ Dazed and Confused ◻

"Launch count L-minus 10 - 9..." I'm fairly certain you know where that's going. At some point, in went the mouthpiece.

Jackie said zero and one moment—hell, half a moment, a whisper of a freaking moment—I was sitting there, pleasantly anxious to experience this new sensation, and in the next there was an M1 Abrams battle tank on my chest and a 400-pound NFL lineman sitting on my face.

I thought, for one fleeting, bizarre, irrational, panic-laden second, I was going to be forced / pushed / thrown / sucked right out through the back of the craft, chair and all. At just about the time I really was going to call for my mommy, the craft seem to level off ever so slightly and the weight slowly began to dissipate.

However, that doesn't mean it was any more pleasant. Instead of feeling like you had a frigging battle tank lodged on your chest, it only felt like a '67 Buick. The damn lineman was still on my face, though he had, mercifully, shed a few pounds.

I know it was probably only a couple of minutes or so, in real time, but real time, when you feel like seven shades of shiny goat crap, can be a really, really long time. Slowly, though, things seemed to be returning to normal, well, as normal as could be expected considering the overall circumstances. Finally, the oppressive weight was gone.

I was ecstatic. I hadn't wet my pants, puked, done duty in my shorts, or screamed. I looked at Phoebe and she wasn't staring at me so, okay, I hadn't screamed. Jackie's officious voice came back on.

"We have leveled out at about 85,000 feet and are currently cruising at approximately Mach 4." A short pause. "You are free to move around."

We both began undoing the machinery that held us in place. Phoebe was up and standing and I was still fighting with the damn roller coaster apparatus. She leaned over, did something mysterious and freed me. "I'm going up front to visit with Jackie."

I nodded. "I'm going to check in with Tom and Armando and see if they've found anything, and I'll see if there are any updates from Dee."

Phoebe was appraising me with those Phoebe laser death eyes. "You mentioned that name on the drive over. Who is Dee?"

❧ Chapter Eight ❧

We all have those OMG moments when something obvious that we should have done, and of course did not do, slaps us upside the head like a V8 (the drink, not the engine). "It's the AI in the ComUnit," I explained, and that did sound a little stupid, like there was some tiny being living in there talking to me.

"The AI that barely works?" She unclipped her ComUnit and held it up. "I can hardly get mine to answer a simple question." A brief pause and she continued before I could respond, "ComUnit, what is the capitol of Botswana?"

"The basic financial unit is the pula." One of those phonetically-challenged cyborg voices.

"No, not capital. Capitol, as in government." Phoebe said with some exasperation.

"Botswana's form of government is a Republic."

"Oh, for shit's sake," Phoebe said and clipped the unit back to her belt. She stared at me with defiant eyes.

"Well," I struggled to explain coherently, "Dee is different."

"You gave your AI a name?" Phoebe was regarding me with a look I think she normally reserved for people whose sanity she doubted, i.e., everyone not named Phoebe.

"Dee, can you say hello to Phoebe?" When in doubt, whip it out, or something like that.

"Hello, Phoebe."

Phoebe gave me a sarcastic smile and shook her head. "I can teach a bird to say that."

"Birds only repeat what they hear. They merely parrot, if you will forgive the pun."

"And you don't?" Phoebe the skeptic said pointedly.

"Well, I am by many degrees smarter than a bird."

Phoebe looked at me and shrugged. "Clever programming," she huffed.

"I could say as much about most people."

That made Phoebe scowl a little.

"So why are you different from, say, my AI?" She rapped her ComUnit with her hand.

⎔ Dazed and Confused ⎔

"Enoch is different."

"What does he have to do with it?" This was the third degree.

"I am here to help Enoch."

Phoebe frowned. "Where is here?" Not only was Phoebe a bad ass, she was smart, too. I wonder if she had white socks on.

"You are clever, Phoebe Scarlett O'Hara, and Enoch will need that."

"You did not answer my question. Aren't you programmed to answer questions?" Phoebe asked softly.

"Jackie is waiting for you."

Phoebe leaned close to me. "She scares me."

"You scare me," I blurted, received the appropriate dirty look, and Phoebe turned toward the front.

"It was nice talking to you," Phoebe said with as much pleasantness as she could muster.

"And to you, Phoebe. Tell Jackie to check the left-rear coolant system. It requires a slight calibration refinement."

Phoebe's eyebrows notched up; she shot me a swarthy glance, and disappeared through the shimmering door.

"I think that went well." I coughed and stretched to get the tautness out of my neck and shoulders.

"You must have patience with Phoebe. She is trained for disbelief in most things."

Not sure what to make of that, so decided to ignore it. My usual policy on such things. Hell, my usual policy on most things.

~Any word from Tom?~ Might as well keep practicing this non-vocal thought thing.

~Yes, he has uploaded some information on the company in Iceland.~

~Give me a quick overview of the company.~ Lazy is as lazy does.

~Nykr Enterprises is a privately-held company that began operations less than a year ago. Nykr claims to take natural Icelandic spring water and bottle it in 100% biodegradable plastic bottles. Nykr states that 10% of all profits go to charitable organizations. Nykr bottled water is exported globally and has rapidly claimed a large percentage of the overall market. Reliable sales figures are not available, but estimates put it at $300 million.~

Dee relayed this with a much slower tempo, thank you very much. ~Did Tom get any additional hacked data or other information?~ I asked, hopeful. Good answers can only come from good questions. My profundity is profane.

~Yes. There was a large transfer of funds, $50 million, which was moved from an Icelandic bank to a bank in the United States.~

Hello! That was a blankety-blank boat load of pulas. No, wait, that's Botswana. Iceland's money would be what?

~Króna.~

~Damn it, Dee, those thoughts were just me being hypothetical.~

~As you say.~

Pula or króna; $50 million was a lot of money. ~Where in the United States was this money transferred?~

~Knoxville, Tennessee.~

Ah, it was so clear to me now. I nodded sagaciously. The eemees were planning to take over the Grand Ole Opry.

~That is located in Nashville.~

~Stop reading my thoughts that aren't, well, meant to be my thoughts.~ You really had to focus on blocking Dee or she would hear everything. And the more I thought about my last remark to her, the more moronic it all seemed. How moronic I seemed. Sigh.

~I was joking about the Grand Ole Opry thing, Dee. It was just to amuse myself. Don't you know what humor is?~

~I do when I hear it.~

Hilarious. ~You and Phoebe should get along fine.~ I shook my head, mentally and physically. ~What else is there?~ Weary wary. Keeping Dee at bay was not as easy as I thought.

~One of the oceanic shipping companies that makes deliveries to Iceland is owned by a subsidiary that has links to the Alifmimra Company.~

That was the company in Iran that made shoes! ~Keep going.~

~Tom says in his notes that they managed to hack into the main Nykr server and access some files, but one folder of particular importance could not be hacked.~

~Why is it important?~ Tom was very intuitive and his instincts were reliable.

🕱 Dazed and Confused 🕱

~His notes indicate the name of the folder was *demonhunter*. That is all.~

A chill ran run up my back. I think sparks flew out of me, uh, ears. I looked down at my arm and the hairs were standing up. This was the phrase Brody had used in his death message.

~Connect me to Tom, please.~ Trying hard to keep my voice level.

~You don't have to say please each time, Enoch.~

~Sorry.~

~You are very nice, for a human.~

~And you are very nice for a… well, for a, really, uh, you know, whatever it is you are…~ Geez, that was lame.

~Tom is on the line.~

"Tom?" I said aloud, relieved to be talking to a known quantity, i.e. a human.

~Enoch! Did you get my notes?~ Dee was doing the transliteration thing. Damn, it seemed normal, but sure felt weird.

~Nice work.~ I said/thought. ~How's it going on the *demonhunter* folder?~ Maintaining my calm.

~Oh man…~ I could sense the anxiety in his dispirited response. ~Anyway,~ Tom went on, ~there is some serious encryption here. Stuff Mando and I have never seen. We are trying to download the folder to run some algorithms on it, but so far, no luck.~ A pause. ~It's just going to take time and horsepower.~

~Let me know on this and anything else.~ I hoped my concern was not too pronounced. Honey and vinegar and all that.

~Mando is actually cracking an Iranian server even as I talk. Look for a report later on.~ Tom tried to sound cheerful.

I smiled. I could picture Mando pounding on the keyboard fast and furious. ~See ya Tom.~

Dee cut the connection.

I had been pretty keyed up about everything myself, but now it suddenly hit me, like an MMA kick to the kidneys. Okay, maybe more like a double whiskey. Anyway, I just wanted a nap.

~Dee, I'm going to duck out for a few minutes.~

~Okay.~ In a goofy animated cartoon duck voice. Cute. Must be programmed to do voices based on key words.

▯ Chapter Eight ▯

I clipped the ComUnit to my belt, fiddled with a control on the side of my chair which I figured had to be some kind of recline control (hoozah, it was) declined my angle, yawned, eased myself back into a comfortable position, and fell into a blissful nap just moments later.

Someone pinched my shoulder. I opened my eyes. Phoebe. "Gather up your gear, we need to make the transfer," she said when she saw my eyes open, then she stepped over to the storage compartment where her stuff was. I watched her while I tried to ratchet my mental machinery into proper gear. Click, whiz, churn, clunk.

"Transfer?" was the basic result of this effort.

"This craft cannot land on foreign soil, so we have to take the Landing Module." She said this with the elegant simplicity of someone who is privy to a secret that you don't know.

"Landing Module?" At least I was consistent.

"Damn it, Enoch, did you pay attention in the briefing?" Uh, no. "I'm flying the LM in and then we'll get our land vehicle after touching down."

I took a deep breath, more alert now. "I didn't know you could fly."

She looked at me and shook her head. "I like pea soup, too. Bet you didn't know that, either."

"I knew that." This was Dee speaking over the ComUnit, adding to the chaos. **"You also like red velvet cake, and your favorite band is Black Label Society."**

"Zakk plays a mean guitar," I agreed, smiling.

"Dee, that information is private!" Phoebe said loudly with a goodly hint of ire.

"Sorry. You're right. I'm sorry." And she truly sounded broken-hearted about the whole thing.

Phoebe sighed. "I'm, ah, sorry, too, for yelling at you." She looked at me with wonderful vexation. "Just worried about how well some people are prepared for this mission."

"We need Enoch."

Phoebe nodded, scowled. "So I've heard." I had the last of my gear in hand. "Follow me," she growled and began walking to the door that was not a door.

I'd Rather Walk, Thank You

———〇———

"Love keeps the cold out better than a cloak."
—Henry Wadsworth Longfellow

Being a pilot requires a certain mind set which is critical to the task at hand. I am fairly certain it is essential that a pilot have no fear of falling out of the sky and crashing into the earth at terminal velocity to explode in a mass of churning debris.

A useful skill—sadly—I have never acquired. Thus, I would suck as a pilot.

I am not sure why these particular thoughts were fluttering around my head as we passed through the shimmering door. It was a strange sensation. The door, not my thoughts. Like walking through cobwebs. I actually waved my hand idly in front of my face to clear them away. Nerves, I guess. We exchanged brief pleasantries with Jackie and her navigator, some guy named Bob, I think. My mind was a little preoccupied, trying hard to convince me to stay and not run screaming back to my roller-coaster seat and ask for a refund on the ride.

Jackie and Phoebe hugged. Someone wished me luck. Might have been Bob, not sure. Might have been Dee.

We stepped over and entered a very tight little stairwell, weaving our way down to an open area. It smelled very clean and antiseptic. Or, maybe I was thinking about the morgue where my next of kin would be coming to claim my body.

Sorry.

The LM was sitting there, looking like a mini-version of the larger craft, except this one had conventional wings, and fins and such, though much shorter. It even had a cockpit window.

"We won't be going that fast. Couple of hundred knots at most," was the way Phoebe explained it.

❑ Chapter Nine ❑

I looked at her with the kind of numb sadness only true ignorance can really convey. "Knots?" I repeated in a fashion designed to express that ignorance as clearly as possible.

"Around 225 mph, if that helps," Phoebe said with a miffed look and surly expression.

By now we were securely strapped in side by side in the only two seats. More roller-coaster stuff to contend with. Seemed odd if we were only going a couple of hundred miles per hour. "If we aren't going fast, how come the roller-coaster stuff?" When in doubt, act stupid, and ask questions. I doubt a lot. Sigh.

Phoebe was adjusting controls, checking out settings, doing all that pre-flight pilot crap. "Jackie will slow down to about Mach 1.5 and then we'll be detached."

"Detached?" My vocabulary was getting shorter by the day.

Phoebe turned to look at me. I stopped fiddling with the roller-coaster stuff. "Jackie will drop down to the main craft's lowest safe speed, around 1000 mph or so." I gulped, couldn't help it. My math skills have never been all that great, but 1000 mph seemed significantly more than the couple of hundred mph Phoebe had mentioned earlier.

Phoebe went on. "You remember that movie, *Aliens*?" One of my favorites. I nodded. "Do you remember the scene where the marines are in the space transport and detach to drop to the planet's surface?" I remember they went really, really fast.

Lots of unhappy faces and some puking as I recall.

Phoebe grinned. "It's like that, only worse."

"I left my mouthpiece upstairs." Yeah, I actually said that. But, I did not do duty in my shorts.

Phoebe laughed. She really was a gorgeous woman. "Well, you may be in deep shit then, Enoch, because I know it's hard for you to keep your gob shut." I haw-hawed that one and settled back for the ride.

She apparently was done with her instrument checking and spoke into her headset. "LM ready to detach."

"Confirmed," came Jackie's practiced response.

Then, in a gentler voice, "Be safe girl. You too, Enoch." A brief lull. "Detach in 5-4-3-2-1, detach."

⬠ I'd Rather Walk, Thank You ⬠

The world is complex. No one can argue that. There are, though, many extremely simple dichotomies that exist. You either like beets, or you hate them. You crave Beef Stroganoff, or you despise it. You're a cat person or you're a dog person. Beer or ale. Wine or whiskey.

You either love thrill rides, or you loathe them.

I'm pretty much entrenched in the latter category. With concrete loafers. In truth, the Ferris wheel is a bit much for me. All that circular motion. I like feet firmly planted on terra firma, not ether insubstantia.

After that crazy launch of the "mother ship," I was not all that enamored with the upcoming detached "drop from hell" and very much prepared to grit my teeth and hate it vehemently. Possibly to lose my lunch. Launch my lunch.

But, it was freaking sick. Like ridiculous sick. Like cool sick.

Let me state this clearly—the bottom didn't just drop out. There was no bottom. It vanished. We went weightless, then not weightless, smacked, battered, buffeted, whipped, blasted, cajoled, and rollicked about like a potato chip dropped from a tall building during a hurricane. And I was an ant clinging to the chip.

And damn me if I didn't love it.

Much to my amiable and self-contented surprise, however, Phoebe was looking a bit on the pale side of white. Chalk face mama.

"You okay, Phoebe?" I inquired innocently, quelling a grin.

She lolled her head at me and gave me an eat schiza and die look. "I'm fine." She was wrestling with the controls and turned back to her task.

I could see/feel us slowing and Phoebe was gaining better control of the LM. "How far out are we?" I wondered aloud.

"We should be on the ground in about fifteen minutes." Hopefully, not in small, smoking, pieces. More fidgeting with instruments.

And, just about on the dot, we dropped through the clouds and I saw the airport. I had never really been up front in a plane before, and this perspective, as you approached the landing strip, was both exhilarating and terrifying. Mostly the latter for me.

It's a controlled descent (i.e., crash) handled by a skilled pilot. You know this fact and, yet, as you slowly waft downwards out of the sky, engine on and all that, you feel (at least as the passenger) at the mercy of events over which you have little influence. That pretty much sums up my whole life to this point.

Anyway, one of the things that I have never really given much thought to is the landing. You take it for granted, well, unless you happen to be up in the cockpit and actually see it happening. Particularly the part where you don't actually see it happening. You have no visual of the landing strip. Yeah, yeah, you have instruments and readouts. Up your nose with a rubber hose. I want to see where I'm going, especially if it involves concrete, metal, and speeds in excess of 100 mph.

However, trusting other people is essential to success in life, so I screwed up my resolve, edified my nerve, and gave Phoebe a thumb's up. She scowled and shook her head.

And rightfully so. Just a few minutes later we drifted gracefully down with barely a tremor, lost speed naturally as she applied flaps and air brakes, then slowly and easily transformed to a gentle taxi, eventually easing off of the main runway. Phoebe was good. We came to an area where I could see a small hangar and two black SUVs, the one parked behind was obscured from view by the foremost.

After the ground crew waved us in and we came to a stop, I smiled at Phoebe. "You're good," I said, which was kind of my way of saying 'thanks for getting me on the effing ground without extreme blood loss' in a polite manner.

She shrugged. "These small craft almost fly themselves." Yeah, right. We gathered our gear and exited the Landing Module.

Two guys in dark suits and aviator sunglasses, one wearing an ear piece and both looking like characters out of a cheesy spy movie, greeted us as we emerged.

"Miss O'Hara, I'm Agent Johnson and this is Agent Diaz." He looked at me and nodded. "Mr. Maarduk." He looked back to Phoebe. "We have a vehicle for you." He gestured behind him. "Do you need some lunch?"

"Thank you Agent Johnson, we're headed right out." I favored her with a sour look. I would have preferred some nasty, greasy, burger to the tastelessly efficient BioPatch.

⛫ I'd Rather Walk, Thank You ⛫

Johnson handed her a set of keys and a flash drive. "We've programmed your destination into the on-board GPS and additional intel is on the drive."

"Thanks," Phoebe said as she began walking toward the rear SUV which, upon closer inspection, turned out to be a rather timeworn and battered old four-wheel drive Isuzu. We tossed our gear in the back and clamored inside. The steering wheel was on the right.

"Will this thing make it?" I said, gesturing at the worn remnants of what had once been a fine vehicle.

"You don't know much about the secret agent game, do you?" Phoebe asked me with a curious look as she glanced over the controls and instruments. Kind of a mix of pity, sorrow, worry, and scorn. The look she gave me, not the dashboard.

"No," was all I said, as I figured she had more to elaborate on the subject.

"The engine is in pristine condition, as are the shocks and the rest of the internal workings." She wagged her head at me like a teacher lecturing a schoolboy. "We don't want to draw attention to ourselves, and this SUV now looks like thousands of others around here."

I felt a little like Inspector Lestrade when Sherlock Holmes explains the chain of logic he used in arriving at some brilliant conclusion not obvious to everyone else until, well, until he explains it. Sometimes it's so obvious you overlook it, like living in a big city with a great tourist attraction that you never go to. Or, whatever.

She flipped on the GPS and there we were, a flashing green dot surrounded by a pulsating green circle. A flickering, semi-transparent, red line was connected to the dot and ran off up and out of view at the top of the GPS display. Obviously our route. Phoebe looked at me. "You're the navigator. Think you can handle that?"

I looked at the GPS. "Exit the airport and drive north," I said, not hiding my bad humor at all. "Are you sure you can shift gears with your left hand?" I asked this as politely as that bad humor would permit me. Which is to say, rather sarcastically.

"Probably better than you can navigate," she replied tartly, whipping it into reverse and backing away. The two agents watched with minimal interest as she turned and we drove off.

☐ Chapter Nine ☐

"What agency were those guys with?" I said, hoping to change the subject and get her mind off of a possible karate blow to my windpipe.

"We deal with them all, but in this part of the world, probably CIA." Her voice was much nicer. Which made sense, since we faced a fairly long drive and a possibly, probably, dangerous mission in front of us. In fact, I was feeling a little remorseful about my previous attitude, which is rare for me.

"Phoebe," I began earnestly, "I want to apologize to you." We were traveling at low speed along the airport access road. Not very crowded at all.

"To me?" she asked with honest shock in her voice.

"We never got off on the right foot and I've been kind of a jerk ever since." Which, as painful as it is for me to admit, was true. Mostly true.

"Go on," Phoebe said with a wisp of a smile, clearly enjoying this.

"Well, that's really it, I'm just going to try and be, uh, nicer, is all." I coughed. This was more difficult than I thought.

Phoebe laughed warmly. "Hell, don't change your basic nature just for me." She chuckled again. "Truth be told, Enoch, it doesn't matter whether you constantly give me a ration of crap or not, I just need you to focus on doing what it takes to make sure we get in, and then get out, with our asses intact." She paused and saw me about to speak.

"And don't even think about saying what you might be thinking about saying." Tilted head and semi-scouring glance.

"Are we there yet?" I asked in a joking voice. She had moved onto a main road and I could see a highway entrance sign up ahead.

"That's better," she grinned. "Should take about two hours, assuming we can maintain speed and some bad driver doesn't run us off the road." She merged on to the highway at acceleration and topped it off at around 70. Or so.

"You know," I began by way of making useful conversation, "this thing has happened so fast we never really had a chance to talk about the mission objectives."

"We have one simple goal," Phoebe said, not taking her eyes off the road which, unlike the airport access, was fairly crowded with a wide variety of cars and trucks. "We need to locate the facility, get into the facility, determine what they are doing and, if possible, get a sample." A brief pause. "And then get out."

"That doesn't sound so bad," I commented, sort of seriously.

"It never does." This time she did turn to look at me. "Don't forget what happened to Brody."

This seemed like a good time to be silent, and it cannot be said that Enoch Maarduk did not know when to heed a clue. It gave me an opportunity to look around at the land and, truth be told, it reminded very much of central Mexico, a place I had twice visited many years ago.

~Dee,~ I thought and she instantly replied.

~Yes, Enoch?~

~Are the latitudes of central Mexico and Gaborone, Botswana similar?~ That was my hypothesis.

~Plus or minus 1 degree from 23 degrees.~

It made sense, then, that the general topographic sensation might be of the same nature.

I was thinking about this, or something, perhaps Phoebe's intact ass, when I dozed off.

A sharp nudge to the right shoulder jarred me from dull oblivion into sharp reality. Or, perhaps it was sharp oblivion into dull reality. I can never keep that straight. Phoebe pointed out the front window. "We're almost there, but we have a problem."

"Almost there?" By now, I guess you know how I am when I first wake up. As the Russians say, stupid to the point of holiness.

"Yes, but there's some kind of wreck and traffic jam up ahead," Phoebe intoned and we had slowed to almost a crawl. There was a line of about eight cars in front and more piling up behind. It was only a two-lane paved road with precious little shoulder. A battered, canvas tarpaulin-covered, transport truck of some ilk was lying sideways across the road ahead with fruits and vegetables scattered everywhere.

Another vehicle, a small passenger car, was in a ditch on the right of the road, smoke billowing from the engine. There were two people standing nearby, arguing, seemingly unconcerned with the fact that a car with a tank fuel of flammable liquid was apparently on fire in the general proximity. Two others were dashing around like mad, scooping up fruits and vegetables and putting them back in boxes and cartons and whatever containers they had on hand.

We were now at a complete stop. Both Phoebe and I got out, since that was what everyone else was doing.

"Hou jou bek!" I heard one of the men shout as we drew near. The speaker was dressed in some kind of dirty brown uniform. My guess was the delivery driver. Another man, in casual office clothes, stared at him and yelled back.

"Ek se; jou vrot dagga!" Office Man appeared a little unsteady on his feet. Perhaps the aftermath of the wreck.

"Bah, dun ket jou broekies en da knot," the driver muttered in reply, then turned and wandered off looking for fruits and vegetables.

The driver of the first car waiting in line had gone back to his vehicle and was now inching forward, trying to pressure the two men who were picking up the fruits and vegetables to hurry and clear a path. The second fruit- and vegetable-picking man straightened up and I heard him say to his friend, nodding at the car's driver, "Fokking momparra," and they continued to gather intact items.

In a few minutes, enough room had been cleared for a car to barely wiggle through, so we hurried back to our ride. Phoebe glanced at me as she slid behind the wheel. I asked her, "What the hell were they saying?"

"The transport driver was being accused of smoking weed by a guy who had been drinking too much." She shrugged. "Happens all the time here."

"And back home as well," I added, thinking about my own experiences driving around the quote unquote Big City.

"Yeah, that too." She pulled around the transport and we accelerated. "We should be at the rendezvous in about fifteen minutes." She gave me a quick look. "The guys we are meeting are supposed to be friendly, but be ready." I fingered my BB gun. The thought of having a weapon whose probability of working was not actually 100% didn't exactly boost my confidence level to new highs.

About fifteen minutes later we exited the main road and passed onto what reminded me of a rural country lane. It was hard-packed dirt with a little gravel; a one-lane road with barely enough grassy shoulder to allow another vehicle to pass—if you should happen to meet one out here in the middle of bum $*^% wherever we were.

We eased around a corner and there sat, surprise, an SUV, light brown, almost as dilapidated as ours. Two men were lounging out front of the vehicle smoking cigarettes. Both were dressed in combat fatigues and khakis, sort of the classic mercenary look you might say. Guerilla chic. One of them had a semi-automatic rifle dangling from his shoulder, maybe an HK, but that was just a guess.

Both had holstered handguns and sheathed knives. They had that grizzled sort of macho look I'd seen many times. Sometimes legit, often BS. Still, they were armed and you had to grant a certain respect to that. I patted my unproven BB gun. Especially considering what I was packing.

We stopped next to them and stepped out of the car. One of the men nodded when he saw Phoebe, apparently recognizing her. The other didn't move.

"O'Hara," the man said simply, flatly, in a generic American accent.

"Yates," Phoebe said as she walked up. "Surprised you're still alive without me to bail your sorry ass out."

The man called Yates smiled broadly. "Someone saves your life once and that's all you ever hear."

Phoebe frowned at him.

"Maybe twice," he said reluctantly, still smiling. "How you been Pheebs?" They embraced warmly. He was a handsome man, damn his eyes.

"Passing well," and they both grinned at that old soldier's joke. "Who's your pal?" She looked steadily at the other guy, who seemed rather laconic about the whole thing and had not moved an inch from his position leaning on the brown SUV.

"Harris is a good man," Yates said, loud enough for his friend to hear. "When he's sober." This brought a wry grin from the placid leaning man.

Phoebe gestured at me. "Enoch Maarduk, Yancy Yates." Firm shake, no attempt to prove a thing. Point in his favor, damn his eyes.

Yates looked me over quickly, then looked back at Phoebe. "You know you're going into a dangerous area." It wasn't posed as a question, just a statement.

Phoebe angled her head and stared at Yates. "You know about Brody?" Yates nodded wistfully. "Well, so do we," she added, and then took a breath. "Show me the location."

Yates reached into his multi-pocketed vest and pulled out a small digital device, woke it up, held it up to his face (my guess was a retina scan) then entered a password. He then extended the device so Phoebe could see it, and began talking. "We are here"—he placed his finger on the display screen—"and you need to get there." He moved his finger north about three inches. I had stepped over and leaned in to see; I noticed there were no roads.

"Looks like we'll be hoofing," I said by way of useful commentary.

Yates grinned knowingly. "You can take the truck in there a little ways, but then it gets way too rough to drive."

Phoebe scowled at him. "Transfer that map data to my ComUnit. I'll synch it with the satellite reports and we should be good to go."

"If we don't hear from you within 24 hours, Harris and I are supposed to come looking," Yates stated thinly. He ran a hand across his grizzled chin.

Phoebe laughed humorlessly. "If you don't hear from us within 24 hours, don't waste your time." She smiled wanly. "We'll be dead."

We returned to the Isuzu, where Phoebe checked the map in her ComUnit, seemed satisfied with it, started the engine and we drove by the two men, now working on fresh cigarettes. In less than a minute we rounded a copse of trees, looked like a mixture of beechwoods, baobob and the ubiquitous buffalo thorn, and the men were lost to our sight. Hey, I did some flora and fauna research.

The narrow path which served as our road was soon teeming with acacia trees of varying sizes, plus willows, and brush of many different varieties. I could see that, if it got much thicker, using a vehicle would indeed be impossible, and moving on foot would not be a bargain.

I guess we drove for another twenty minutes or so, sometimes in an open area at a decent pace, sometimes in tight quarters sneaking and sputtering along, inching past brush, rocks, and half a path. Finally, we seemed to reach an area where there did not appear to be a lot of forward-looking choices. Okay, none. Phoebe killed the engine.

"Grab your gear," was all she said.

We both had backpacks with ample supplies, including several canteens of water, plenty of patches and other stuff I hadn't even bothered to look at. Phoebe produced an automatic pistol and checked the clip.

".45?" I queried her.

".50," she replied, then snapped the clip in place. "With custom loads." Her staid smile was confident. "Guaranteed to drop a charging rhino." I almost tossed out the old credit card joke, but figured she might pistol-whip me, so I bit my tongue.

We closed and locked the SUV. Phoebe looked at the ComUnit and I walked up to her. "If you let Dee know the route, she can tell us if there are issues along the way."

Phoebe seemed to be considering it, then nodded. "That's a good idea." She looked at me, then my ComUnit. "Uh," Phoebe began haltingly, "Dee, are you there?"

"Hello, Phoebe, I am prepared to receive your data."

Phoebe played with her display for a few moments. "There it is."

"Received. We should proceed due north for about two miles."

I looked at Phoebe. "Go ahead, fearless leader." I waved at the pathway or, rather, the thick brush and cloying trees to the north.

Ah, yes, the romantic allure of an African adventure. The incredible sights, the marvelous smells, the unique sounds. A romantic and grand adventure.

Hmm… But, I should also mention the stinging ants, thorny bushes, pointy bushes, whip-like bushes, rigid leaves, abrasive leaves, mosquitoes, an untold number and many types of flies, a mixed assortment of other flying critters, plus undetected piles of animal dung, hopefully, though not always, of the dry variety. I greatly prefer room service.

I'm just a whiny-ass. Actually, it was indeed very much like central Mexico, even parts of south Texas. Rolling hills, rocks, ravines, thick brush, trees of varying sizes, and, of course, difficult walking; but spectacular views every so often that seemed to distract one's thoughts from the hard work of making our way. Oddly, only a few fleeting glimpses of animals, usually far off.

"Kind of surprising not to see more animals," I commented to Phoebe as we trudged down a treacherous little decline of small rocks and loose reddish dirt. Well, I trudged. She just sort of gracefully floated without seeming to slip even once.

We made it to the bottom and moved on through some more brush. I was careful to let Phoebe make it through first so I would not catch a rebounding acacia limb in the teeth. Accidental or otherwise, since she probably figured I was monitoring her intact... Well, you know.

"They hear you coming, Godzilla," she said amiably when I managed to catch up. "Besides, we're near a large game preserve and most of the animals are there."

We had entered another very small clearing, really just a small five foot by five foot area between more brush and more trees. Slogging work.

Dee's voice broke the silence. **"There is a small canyon about a quarter mile ahead."**

Then came a rumbling, grumbling, growling echo that issued forth from an indeterminate location, lingering ominously in the air, but it sure sounded close to my suddenly interested ears. I guess there was game in the immediate area. Well, a predator for damn sure. Phoebe looked at the concerned expression on my face. "Nowhere near us." She took off walking. Nowhere near us, my ass. I stayed close on her tracks, trusting the .50 far more than my BBs.

The small canyon was, indeed, not all that wide, perhaps twenty plus feet across. No water ran at the bottom, but nasty-looking, jagged rocks and boulders of all sizes were strewn in our way. Certainly not impossible to cross, but not a good place to twist an ankle. Or, maybe it was a good place to twist an ankle, depends on how you looked at it.

We stepped gingerly down among the rocky debris.

A few minutes later we made it to the other side, no worse for wear. Or nowhere for worse, as the case may be. We stopped for a brief drink of water and Phoebe was examining the ComUnit display. Dee's voice came on a few moments later. **"20 degrees west."** Phoebe made the adjustment and we kept walking.

▢ I'd Rather Walk, Thank You ▢

It was now about 5:00. My ComUnit had already adjusted for local time. ~Dee,~ I thought silently, ~what time does the sun set?~

~Around 6:45.~

That put us over halfway to the satellite's marked location and our current walking speed should have us arriving at about 6:15 or so. Just about right.

The last few miles were relatively uneventful.

Okay, except for that minor misstep when we were moving along over the ridge of this small hill. It looked and sounded much worse than it was. Especially the part where I went ass over teacups and yelled "Aargh!"—pretty much as loud as I could.

Phoebe calmly walked to the bottom of the hill and helped me up. I dusted myself off, checked to make sure nothing was missing or broken, grinned, and waved it off. Phoebe sniffed, shook her head, and we resumed our trek.

The only other minor event was the snake.

You can expect to encounter snakes in the wild. Yo, that's where they live. Natural habitat and all that. Snakes don't like people anymore than people like snakes. Think of it this way—a human is many, many, times larger than a snake. Wouldn't you be a little hostile around something much larger than you? The answer you're looking for is "yes."

The vast majority of snakebites happen for two simple reasons. Reason number one is when foolish and untrained people attempt to either capture or kill a snake. Never feel sorry for an idiot. Reason number two is when a person inadvertently steps on or otherwise disturbs a resting snake. I do have compassion for bad luck.

I probably haven't mentioned the temperature, mostly because I'm from the south and I like the heat. It can be 95 degrees outside and I'm playing tennis or baseball. It's no big deal. This African weather was hot, sure, but not unreasonable at all. Didn't seem to bother Phoebe either.

Still, the last mile had taken us through some particular rough brush and up a goodly few hills chocked and clogged full of rocks, boulders, fallen trees, and other hazards. By the time we reached the partially cleared crest of this last hill, we figured—well, I figured—it was a good place for a drink of water and a minute pause.

⬠ Chapter Nine ⬠

Hell, a five minute pause. Whatever I could get away with. We found some large-flat-facing rocks under a nice shady bunch of trees. Phoebe eased herself down into a comfortable sitting position.

I told her I needed to use the "facilities" and would be right back.

I finished my business quickly and ambled back into the clearing. Phoebe was sitting comfortably, knees folded up, sipping on her canteen and gnawing on an energy bar, all smiles. Her backpack was beside her, the ComUnit on top.

The snake, its large scaly body brownish-green, was several feet above her head, dangling in lazy loops from a series of low-hanging limbs.

A very large dead lizard was draped over one of the limbs near the snake. Another smaller lizard, I noticed with serendipitous alarm, was on the top of a rock, toward the back, twitching as though injured. This was the rock Phoebe was so casually leaning against.

I can recall the next sequence of events very clearly, locked in crystalline vices you might say, though I cannot tell you precisely how long each event took as it unfolded.

First, the snake never even so much as looked at me, as it slowly, hypnotically, descended the limb. It was fixated on the twitching lizard at the top of the rock. As long as Phoebe didn't move, everything might be okay. When it involves a possibly poisonous snake, that "might be okay" part can be a bit worrisome.

Second, I saw Phoebe start to yawn and I knew, as her shoulders began to hunch, she was going to raise her arms and finish that yawn with a stretch. You know, arms above her head pointed toward the snake.

A snake that might, or might not, be safe to irritate with such a motion. Either way, a yawn was a physical movement that the snake might, and probably would, interpret as a threat and act accordingly. And snakes generally react by biting you. It's what they do best.

Third, the BB gun—my never-tested-nor-fired-in-any-reality BB gun—appeared in my hands. Events four, five, and six then seemed to happen rather simultaneously.

⬚ I'd Rather Walk, Thank You ⬚

Phoebe's arms indeed went up. The snake, surprised and alarmed, moved to strike, and I fired. Yeah, a BB fired from a pistol, aimed from the hip, standing over twenty feet away, hoping to hit a fast-moving target. Good luck with that.

And then there were these multi-colored, glowing, sparkling, electrostatic, quantifiable fingers of electromagnetic energy encapsulating the entire snake's body, rippling all around it. The snake fell stunned to the side of Phoebe who, naturally, threw herself violently in the exact opposite direction. Screaming like a little girl, I should add.

As I stood rooted rigid, trying to catch the breath I had been tenuously holding, she leaped to her feet and walked toward the snake.

She mentioned a deity in less than pleasant terms, and then stared at me. "Enoch!" was all that escaped at first.

I was just standing there, BB gun in hand, but still a safe distance from the snake. You never know. Snake in the grass and all that.

Phoebe—with a rather horrific expression—pointed at the quivering snake, still twitching eerily. "That's a black mamba," she fought to say smoothly, having quickly recovered most of her wits, though still shook up.

"Is that bad?" I think they were poisonous.

Phoebe was still staring at the snake. She swallowed hard. "Out here? Without anti-venom?" She laughed, gallows humor. "I would have lasted maybe an hour."

Now it was my turn to feel my knees buckle and I swallowed hard. "I was afraid it might bite you," I said, my voice breaking now, "when you yawned."

Phoebe walked over to me. She nodded. "It would have, trust me, they are very aggressive." She looked at the tree, looked at the rock, saw the twitching lizard, noted the tree limb; indeed, she was replaying the entire episode.

Then she gave me a big hug and planted a nice fat kiss right on my lips. "You saved my life," was all she said, stating it factually and plainly. She gestured at my BB gun. "Glad it worked," she noted with a very rueful smile.

"Me, too," I mumbled and slipped the weapon back in its holster.

☐ Chapter Nine ☐

Her extensive training was instinctual and kicked in now. "We need to go." She turned, looked back at the spot from where I had taken the shot and shook her head. "That was quite a shot with just a fokking BB gun." She headed off into the tangled brush.

We had been walking for quite sometime in silence. We had just entered a small clearing with a view toward the sun at the far horizon. It would soon dip out of site. Dee's voice issued from the ComUnit, subdued in tone. **"You are within one-third of a mile of the location you seek."**

We stopped walking. Phoebe took out her ComUnit to study the satellite imagery and determine the best angle to approach the complex, which appeared (from my vantage point leering over her shoulder) to be a large cleared area, fenced in, with a substantial L-shaped building with some cars and trucks parked out front and in the rear. As we approached, the "L" shape would appear backwards, flipped horizontal, in orientation to us.

It looked to be a fairly big loading and shipping dock in the back— the area was hard-packed earth, to judge by the color—with at least two tractor trailer rigs in stalls next to the building and one parked off by the fence.

"They'll have cameras and they may have motion sensors, though I imagine they feel pretty secure out here in the middle of nowhere." She thought about it and added, "They may not have the motion sensors due to the local animal population." She studied the image, zooming in. "Probably a walking perimeter security presence." She seemed to be considering something else. "They'll mount the cameras on the corners of the building. Cover all the angles."

She pointed at the fence directly opposite the loading and shipping dock, toward the rear of the complex. "We'll need to enter the facility from this angle and hopefully that truck there"—she moved her finger and indicated the truck butted up to the building—"will mask us from the cameras."

I nodded. Seemed sensible to me but, then again, I was new to this whole secret agent gig.

Twilight was fast upon us we moved stealthily toward the complex. As we neared the edge of some brush, we could make out the perimeter fence and the building well enough. There was about 20 yards of cleared brush and trees between where we crouched, safely hidden in thick cover, and the fence itself. A small set of binoculars were soon in Phoebe's hands and she began traversing the complex. Occasionally she would mumble something and cursed several times. Very colorful and original stuff. I mentally told Dee to take notes.

"They have cameras on top of the building. Looks like a few more at the fence line ends." She scowled assiduously. "We'll have to wait until dusk to move up to the fence." She pursed her lips, studying the complex in the fading light. "We'll just have to chance it that they are not using infrared detectors."

I looked around and intently studied the area. "We could crawl on all fours." If they had infrared, we'd just look like some kind of animals on the prowl.

Even in the failing light, you could see that the ground between here and the fence was just dirt in some places, but rocks, branches, and debris in others. Not comfortable to traverse on hands and knees, but doable. Phoebe seemed to be evaluating the idea and nodded. "Half crouch, half crawl is a good idea."

Which was why, just a bit after dusk, we began crawling toward the fence, though there was an unexpected bonus—the complex had lights. I say bonus because the lights were crappy and they did not illuminate the entire clearing; it was a simple matter to approach in the darkened areas between the patchy splotches of refracted light. Phoebe said that since they had lights, they probably were not using infrared. I muttered something appropriately inane.

We arrived at the fence with hands and knees a little worn, but no blood loss. Always a positive. Might need the blood later.

There was an overwhelming issue of somewhat pressing import, though. No matter how we jockeyed up and down the fence line, we could not block the camera angle from our location to the back of the truck. We selected a spot that had minimal coverage and hunkered down.

Phoebe first produced what appeared to be a small box with wires, and then it occurred to me the fence might be electrified, but it tested negative. Guess that was why she was in charge. Anyway, next up was an exceedingly small pair of shears. A few snips later we had an opening. Small shears, but very sharp.

It was severe dilemma time now. There was about 30 yards of open area between the fence line and the angle where the parked truck would block the camera's view. If someone happened to be watching the monitor at the right time, we would be visible passing through those 30 yards as we moved toward the complex.

It was not a move with a sufficiently high probability of success. Kind of like playing the lottery. Except, picking bad numbers here could get you shot. We sat in the dirt at the edge of the fence line, pondering our navels. Well, I admit I did ponder her naval, but only just for a moment. Mostly I just thought about the problem. Really.

It was while I was idly staring out across the way toward the complex that I noticed—became aware of—the lettering on the side of the parked tractor trailer. "LankSkop" it said in large graphic letters. "I wonder," I said aloud to Phoebe, "if the name on the side of that truck is the trucking company, or…" I paused deliberately.

Phoebe quickly injected, "…the name of the company!" Hot and smart. Lethal.

I nodded enthusiastically. "If it's the company name, we might be able to locate them online, maybe hack into the security feed." Optimism is not normally my long suite, but desperate times call for desperate men, by whatever measure you use.

Phoebe cast me a look that, even in the pitifully reflected light, was full of doubt. Apparently, she was not yet that desperate.

"You don't know Tom and Armando." I grinned in support of my argument. "Remind me to tell you about the time they hacked into the NSA." That softened her expression.

~Dee,~ I thought quietly. I know, thinking quietly sounds odd, but that's what I did, okay?

~Yes, Enoch,~ came the equally soft reply.

~Tell me about a South African company named LankSkop.~ Definitely on a need-to-know basis, and I needed to know.

Only a few moments passed. ~**Manufacturing company located in North West province, South Africa. Began operations about a year ago.**

◻ I'd Rather Walk, Thank You ◻

Food products. No export figures published. Very little data available. I do have a website, some phone numbers, and other information.~

~Okay, hold your data. Connect me to Tom.~ A slight pause and I added. ~And maintain non-verbal mode.~

A few moments later I "heard" Tom's voice in my head. ~Bendix here.~ Phoebe was fiddling around with her ComUnit.

~Tom. Enoch.~ I'm only thinking, but I'm still whispering. I needed more *air* time to get this thought-speech thing down pat.

Tom started to tell me something, ~Hey, E, I've got some more facts...~

I had to interrupt him. ~We have a more immediate problem that I need your help with it.~

~What is it?~ More than a hint of worry in his tone.

~I need a hack into a company. Dee is going to be sending the information now.~ I waited a few moments. ~Did it come through?~

Another pause. ~LankSkop Company, in South Africa.~

~Can you hack into their security feed?~ I had my mental fingers crossed.

~If they are routing the signal through the web or through accessible digital phone lines, absolutely.~ Another brief lull. ~Let me and Mando look over what Dee sent and I'll get back to you in a few.~ He broke the connection.

"Okay," I said, turning to face Phoebe. "Let me update you," but she held up her ComUnit screen and shook her head. A text log of my dialog with Tom was displayed there. ~Thanks, Dee, nice trick.~

~Not a trick, Enoch, just a clever use of technology.~

"For the sake of argument"—I began a conversation directed to Phoebe—"let's say the boys figure out a way to get that camera shut down, then what?" I had a place for your need-to-know basis.

"We get to the rear of the parked truck, make our way to the shipping dock. There's a door there," she smiled wickedly, "and every door has a lock, and every lock can be picked."

She went on. "Since this is the shipping and receiving area, then whatever they are shipping or receiving should be readily available beyond those doors for a quick inspection." She shrugged, gestured with her hands. "We grab a sample and then we get the hell out. Simple."

◻ Chapter Nine ◻

I love how simple some simple plans sound. Sort of reminded me of repairing my door the other day... I shivered in recollection of that simple debacle.

Phoebe leaned in so we could see each other better in the paltry light. "However, if we get separated, the rendezvous point is where you shot the snake." I nodded. She leaned back into the semi-darkness.

When you are anxiously waiting for something important, time passes hideously slow, in a glacial fashion. Five minutes. Tick-tock. Ten minutes. Try not to think about it. Fifteen. I'm thinking about it. I'm going to call Tom back when Dee thought-speeches me, ~**Tom indicates he has a rudimentary code patch in place that can momentarily cause interference with the visual feed. He needs your signal for starting and stopping.**~

Phoebe was intently reading her ComUnit display which had clicked on with the text translation of Tom's message. She was holding it very close to her face because she had turned the light intensity way down.

I looked at her. "I say we step through the cut fence. I tell Tom to run the camera feed block, we haul ass to the side of the building, and I tell him to stop the block. Five seconds, tops."

We did a quick check on our gear, then worked and wrangled our way through the opening, careful not to get snagged. I took a deep breath.

~Dee; when I say, er, think *start*, I want you to tell Tom to initiate the patch. When I think *stop* he can turn it off. Understood?~

~Yes.~ Her tone was anxious, but rock steady.

I gave Phoebe a gentle squeeze on her arm. "Ready?"

"Let's go," she replied calmly.

~Start!~ And we took off on a mad dash. We quickly crossed the 30 yards and sprinted past the rear of the truck, our steps nothing but muffled, thumping, echoes on the hard-packed earth. We flashed up some asphalt dock steps—it was just like any shipping and receiving area you may have seen before, with simple metal piping for rails and a wide concrete walkway. Several of the docks sloped down to large garage-like metal doors. At the end of the wall, to our right, was a regular outside door.

☐ I'd Rather Walk, Thank You ☐

We flattened ourselves against the cool metal of the building. ~Stop!~ I thought breathlessly, my chest heaving. In a few moments, Phoebe's breath was almost back to normal. My Copper Gorilla tainted training was not paying the dividends I had hoped for. Gasp, gasp.

Phoebe sidled and eased her way over to the door. It seemed like a standard door. She took her backpack off, rummaged around and brought forth a plastic box full of tools of some kind. The first one had a curved end and a wide translucent body. She proceeded to run it around the door's frame.

She saw the look of utter ignorance gracing my face and said, as she finished, "Seeing if the door is wired." All I could do was nod knowingly. I think she knew better.

Phoebe carefully placed everything back in the pack and then reached into it once again, producing what appeared to be one of those tiny fiber optic cameras. As she gently unwrapped it in preparation for deployment, I thought this whole thing was reminiscent of a scene from a James Bond movie, only without the cool music. Sorry, nervous.

She plugged one end into the ComUnit, then bent down and snaked the other under the door, twisting the wire around and keeping an eye on the ComUnit display, under my watchful glare, of course.

It was a very large room, well, it was an effing warehouse. There were tables and desks along the right side of the wall, ending about halfway down from a set of double doors at the far end. There were no occupants sitting in the chairs. That was good. There were two forklifts parked in the space where the desks ended, just before the double doors.

The left side appeared to be stacked to the ceiling with large, brown, cardboard boxes. The rows seem to run off out of sight.

She pulled the wire out from under the door, unhooked it from the ComUnit, and stuffed it back in the pack.

Next up was a set of standard-issue lock picks (well, standard-issue if you are a freaking crook or a certified locksmith). Within a few moments there was a click and the door was slightly ajar.

She swung the pack onto her shoulders and adjusted the straps.

She undid the snap on her gun holster. I tend to notice things like that. I gulped and checked to make sure my BB gun was still there.

It was. About as reassuring as a parachute with holes. Still, it had worked on the snake.

Phoebe turned to me and whispered, "They're bound to have cameras in there. Get Tom to zap them again."

~Dee, do we still have the connection with Tom?~ Maintain calm, maintain calm.

~Yes.~

~Ask him if can repeat the same start-stop sequence for a few seconds.~

A very short pause. **~He says he is ready.~**

I looked at Phoebe. "We go in when I tell Tom *start*, make our way over behind that first stack of boxes on the left and then I'll tell him *stop*." She nodded to confirm her understanding.

~Start!~ I nudged Phoebe and in we went. There was a two-foot wide concrete walkway in front of us. We hurriedly crossed it, leaped down a set of stairs, and ran behind the boxes. ~Stop!~ We crouched there, listening. Mostly listening to me gasping for oxygen.

Other than that, quiet as a deacon's house on Saturday night.

I turned to examine the boxes. Big ones, kind of like back in college when you were moving and got boxes from the local grocery store. I looked sheepishly at Phoebe. "I need a knife."

She reached down to her ankle, I heard rustling, and she handed me the butt end of a small combat knife. "It's sharp as a damn razor, so be careful."

I easily carved a six-inch square in the side of the nearest box. That blade was honed. I handed it gingerly back to Phoebe. I laid the cutout cardboard piece down and peered inside. It was full of smaller cardboard boxes. On the side were pictures of cookies. Cookies? Phoebe looked inside.

"That's what they were making in China!" she declared with a subdued cry, but I already knew that. I reached inside and retrieved a box. It was printed in English.

"LankSkop Power Cookies," I began reading. "With energy to blast you through your day." I paused and shifted the box for a better reading angle. "Chocolate chip." I cut into the box and removed a sleeve of cookies secured in sealed plastic (or cellophane or whatever the *&^% it was). I stuffed it in my backpack.

Crap, it was noisy. Frigging cellophane. I pulled it out, cut it open, took a half-dozen cookies and stuffed them in my backpack. I put the rest back in the original container. I figured we were ready to get out and call it a day.

And that's when we heard the far set of double doors open, followed by two echoing sets of footfalls and voices, one voice suddenly laughing loudly.

The voices were moving slowly toward us.

I hastily, but silently, put the cookie box back inside the hole and jimmy-wiggled the cutout cardboard piece hurriedly back into place. I looked at Phoebe and she looked at me, then turned to study the dock. She pointed at me, made an up-and-over motion with her hands. We silently clamored over the metal railing and down into the sloped concrete entry way, pushing ourselves far back along the edge of the wall, out of sight.

Well, out of sight if the people, who I assumed were guards, didn't walk all the way down here.

The footsteps and voices were getting closer, my guess is almost to the aisle where we had just been.

The aisle, I noted with a sinking feeling in my chest, where the cardboard piece I had so quickly pressed back into position was actually now sort of half-ass in place and close to falling out. You could see the breeze from the air-conditioning riffling it ever so slightly. Maybe it was just my bad imagination. I turned my head to the voices.

Murphy's Law. I remember that thought hit me as the two guards stopped at the aisle entrance. The first called out in English, in an accent slightly tinted with what I thought was Afrikaner or German, "Cum un, less eat." This voice was clearly out in the main area.

Then I heard soft footfalls and his friend's voice responded, and he was much closer, as he had been walking down the aisle toward the cut box. "Ode awn aff a mo," in a Cockney accent. I pushed myself down as flat as possible.

And, of course, the effing cardboard cutout fell out. Murphy sucks. "Wha' the 'ell?" the Cockney voice shouted and his friend ran over.

☐ Chapter Nine ☐

I silently lifted my BB gun out of its holster and gently raised my head to take a peek, figuring they would both be staring at the box. They were standing in blue jump suits and baseball caps—like oil field workers or something—with wide belts, but no weapons were in sight. Their backs were to me.

So, I made an executive decision and shot them both. Seemed fair.

There was that multi-hued, twizzling, electrostatic, quantified, electrical energy that ran like fingers of colored fire around their bodies, a crisp sparkling resonance in the air, and then both of them collapsed to the floor. Breathing, but out cold.

"That was damn risky," Phoebe said snappily, rising up and giving me a rather harsh examination. "What if that piece of crap peashooter didn't work?"

The smugness of arrogance, haughty with a hint of idiocy. Words sent thoughtlessly winging away that might fly back to bite you in the tush. I was jaunty with success and did not care. "It worked with the snake, and it worked here." I holstered the weapon with the cool pluck of some wild west shootist.

"Fine, let's go," and she scampered down the walkway toward the door, maybe 40 feet or so away. Halfway there, the damn double doors opened again. Two more guards entered, one whistling and the other reading from a clipboard.

"Stop!" I heard a loud shout when we were seen, but we kept moving. Phoebe was near the door.

"Keep going, I'll hold them off." I was sure of this for three reasons.

First, I was protected by a two-foot high concrete wall. Seemed like a solid reason to stay.

Second, I had the trusty BB gun. Now out of the holster and back in my hand.

And, third, I had switched from single shot to auto. Just hold the trigger down, the instructions had noted, and spray the area. Phoebe was out the door and should have been sprinting away in the dark.

The two men were halfway to me and running hard, drawn weapons in hand. I sprayed them with hot BB lead.

☐ I'd Rather Walk, Thank You ☐

And heard dozens of the little metallic balls bouncing all over the place. That is, bouncing all over the place after they had ricocheted harmlessly off the running men. Hey Zeus Key Riced!

One of the men lifted his pistol and fired. The report was shockingly loud in the warehouse, and I heard the bullet whiz by like an angry hornet. There was a sharp metallic sound and a new hole appeared in the wall of the building behind me.

Phoebe had to be near the fence by now, and I'd have hell to pay catching up in the dark. Which I needed to do because she had the real gun. I turned, leaped up, and headed for the door.

And somehow, some way, slipped on the concrete in my new boots, almost got my footing back, started to fall, tried to reach for the metal railing, missed and hit my head.

Blackness.

Feeling A Little Warmed Over

"It doesn't matter if the water is cold or warm if you're going to have to wade through it anyway."

—Pierre Teilhard de Chardin

Cold.

Frigid. Frosty. Freezing. Chilled. Glacial. Ice knifed. Bone-stiletto. Cerebral-pulsed. Synaptic-tainted. Misery.

Cold.

A thought-congealing, sloth-inducing, brain-numbing aura of cold which filled my mind and blocked out all other considerations until only one single dominating sensation of "COLD" was left pulsating throughout my cortex and bounding throughout my being.

It was a cold so utterly dense, deep, and pervasive that I felt it would never be possible to be warm again, indeed, I could not even recall what it meant to be warm.

You swelter with the cold. It seeps into your marrow like a lecherous cancer.

It was utterly dark. I could not be sure if my eyes were open and I was awake in a darkened room, or if this were, indeed, a dream. I tried to shake off the freezing thoughts which blocked my own reasoning and forced myself to focus and concentrate.

I had fallen and struck my head. That memory was clear, though I had no sense of a painful head.

But the reverberations of cold ratcheted upwards, coursed and surged through my body. I could feel the terrible tingling pain. Cold is pain; pain is cold. I fought to be calm and tried to think. Think. Focus. Reason.

If I were awake, I would be shivering. I would feel my own physical form wracked with convulsions. The human body, in the face of intensely frigid conditions, begins to shake and shiver as a way, albeit not a very effective one, to generate some kind of warmth.

I had no sense, no innate feeling, of a shivering body, so logic implied I must be dreaming.

Except my thoughts, and the processes wrapped around them, were too clear, too consistent across time to be mere dreaming. A dream would be more uneven, patchy, disjointed. I felt a distinct awareness of self, yet could not physically feel myself, if such a thing were possible.

Oh, the terrible cold!

Unless, I thought without a shiver, the cold had so benumbed my body that I was past the point of shivering, and I was dying, and these last thoughts were but the vanishing echo of my consciousness as my brain slowly succumbed to the icy tentacles seeking to strangle the life from it.

But, yet, my thoughts, even though totally aroused and absorbed with the awful cloying sensation of cold, still persisted, and their clarity had yet to diminish.

The cold, I groaned, but heard no noise, but felt my being groan with the strain. It was not just that I was cold, but that the idea of *cold* had grown so large within the context of my thoughts that it was difficult not to focus on anything other than the cold. Bitter. Pervasive. Sullen.

Something else was happening now.

A change. Subtle, yet significant.

I could suddenly feel, even if just remotely and only minutely, my feet, then the lower part of my legs, next my hands, my forearms and soon, within moments it seemed, I had the sensation of my complete body where there had been no such sensation before.

It was still cold, but tolerable.

As my preoccupation with being cold lessened, I tried to take a mental inventory of my new state.

My feet seemed bound up, tied; some kind of strapping or binding held them so I had very little movement. When I did move, I had the sensation of liquid. It dawned on me that I was up to my neck in water, or some kind of liquid. And around my neck was some sort of heavy

☐ Chapter Ten ☐

collar, particularly heavy in the back, near my medulla oblongata. This last thought gave me a momentary pause.

My wrists were also strapped, apparently tied to whatever sort of container I was in that held the water. My head was locked firmly in place with a device of some ilk; I could feel the sensation of the object all around me, but I could not move my head at all.

And just as the pain of cold was diminishing, the pain emanating from my right temple, where I had fallen in the warehouse and struck it on the edge of the concrete, was increasing and becoming, well, exquisite. I grimaced and waited while a wave of rolling agony passed, which fortunately it did. Throb, throb. Damn this was getting old. Rhymes with cold.

It also felt like something was wrapped around my head to cover my eyes, as I could now sense the weight and texture of it. Thus, I was still blind, but soon I began to hear.

At first just distant noises, meaningless reverberations, and then I clearly caught someone saying, "…the injection should begin to work almost immediately."

Another voice said in harsh tones, "You may wait outside, doctor." Something touched the back of my head, then the object that masked my vision was removed.

It was only normal room light, but I squinted and squinched up my face as it still hurt my eyes. Since I could not move my head, my field of vision was limited to what was directly in front of me, which appeared to be nothing but a white wall, well, until a man's figure stepped into view.

He was wearing an elaborately embroidered African Kaftan that hung down lower than I could see. It was black with ornate gold and brown tones and hues, and geometric patterns of all kinds. His head was closely shaven, his face tense, expectant. His features seemed western European, with no facial hair. He leaned in and examined me with a look that was very unsettling. "Who are you?" This was spoken in English, in an accent that seemed French, German, and African all rolled into one, if such a thing were possible.

You should never answer a question with a question—that's so impolite—but rudeness is a character flaw that's hard to overcome.

⬚ Feeling A Little Warmed Over ⬚

"Where am I?" I deliberately slurred the words, or maybe they were already slurred and I made them worse, and fluttered my eyes.

The man tilted his head and looked directly into my eyes. He nodded slowly, pursed his lips, coldly contemplating me. He made a gesture with his head and another man stepped over. This new person was tall, he really had to bend over to look at me. He had a gaunt, angular, look, like he hadn't eaten a decent meal in quite sometime. Nonetheless, his skin color was healthy and his eyes were bright and intelligent.

Kaftan Man turned to Gaunt Man, spoke softly, "Scan him," and then stepped lightly out of my sight.

Gaunt Man was expressionless. The tingling started in my oblongata. I held it and immediately sent some thought-speech at him. ~I can free you from your human controller.~ Simple and direct.

It had to be a great shock, assuredly, for a human to reverse roles and be the one to suddenly implant a thought into the mind of an eemee. All that Gaunt Man, the eemee, did, though, was blink once, raise his brows just slightly, and tilt his head back ever so gracefully. ~How will this be done?~

I am sure there was a great multitude of pressing questions he wanted to ask, but he was intelligent enough to know they could wait. ~I must be released from this pool of water.~ Calm, cool, confident. Our eyes never wavered in contact.

The eemee straightened and turned to his controller. "The cold is interfering with my ability to scan. He needs to be warmed up."

Kaftan Man stepped into view, looked at me, quickly appraised the eemee, then glanced off to the left. "Release this man and get him warm. Watch him closely." He turned to regard me with those same unfriendly eyes. "If he tries anything, make sure he regrets it." He stepped out of view and I heard him say, accompanied by the sound of a door opening, "I'll be back in a few minutes." Footfalls and the door was shut.

Immediately after that, two burly men, in the same uniforms as the guards in the warehouse, moved in and out of view while they began fiddling with, I suppose, straps, knots, bindings, and whatever else held me in place. Someone began working on my neck collar and

☐ Chapter Ten ☐

I heard the eemee say sharply, "Be careful with that, it contains very delicate instrumentation."

My feet were soon free. Then my wrists. The collar came off and I felt whatever it was that had held my head in place was noisily unlocked and lifted away. As I began to rub my wrists to get some circulation back, and loll my aching neck to get the stiffness out, a drain must have been opened at the bottom of the opaque plastic vat I was sitting in, and the water quickly vanished.

My neck was still sore and my head hurt like hell when I turned my attention to survey the room and its occupants.

It was a fairly large area, probably 25 by 25, if I had to make a guess, which I was doing. Plain stucco white walls, one simple long table to the left with my clothes, backpack, ComUnit, and other things piled on it. I thought about the ComUnit and contacting Dee or Phoebe, but unless I could get close to it, well, it was useless. There was also the vat I was sitting in, and two plain wooden chairs. There was a small wooden cabinet hanging on the right wall and a sink beneath it, pipes showing. Overhead were two sets of fluorescent lights.

The eemee, standing at the far wall in front of me, hands behind his back, perfectly still and erect—watching me intently—made me think of the black mamba and that twitching lizard on the rock. Pray for the prey?

There were three guards. One was near the door, which was behind me and to the left. He had a semi-automatic weapon in front of him and he had both hands on it. He looked alert and quite capable. Same blue uniform, same ball cap with the words "LankSkop" in red letters.

One of the other two remaining guards was rummaging around in the cabinet and emerged with several large bath towels, which he sort of unceremoniously tossed at me. The other guard was writing something down on a clipboard.

~We cannot do anything until the controller returns.~

I did not even look at the eemee as I sent him this thought. I continued to towel off. "Can I have my pants?" I said loudly to no one in particular. The guard stopped writing and walked to the table. He rummaged through my things and apparently decided the cargo pants had too many hidden pockets, so he grabbed my black compression shorts and threw them to me. I caught them and slipped them on. Being naked, excepting certain obvious occasions, is just not all that comfortable.

~He is very strong.~ The eemee's expression had not changed, but I could feel the fear nonetheless.

~So am I.~ A brief twitch on the side of the eemee's mouth was all I saw.

~What will you do?~ Which was a question I had anticipated.

~Just scan me as you would ordinarily do, and I will do the rest.~ I focused on projecting a sense of serene confidence, almost arrogance, into my thoughts.

I was dry and warm now, and ran the towel over my plastic seat so I could sit back down. My body was still throbbing from the cold, and I was wondering mightily about that. The water, as I had recovered feeling in my extremities, had not been overly cold. How had I felt such pain from the cold?

It must have been that collar. I was going to ask the eemee, if for no other reason than to distract his thoughts, when the door opened and Kaftan Man walked back in.

You know, there are some people who just rub you the wrong way. It might be the way they dress, or the way they talk, or the way they comb their hair. Maybe their aftershave stinks. Whatever. For Kaftan Man it was the way he looked at you; his whole demeanor toward people could be judged from one brief encounter.

Kaftan Man looked down at me and smirked.

"We have many search teams out looking for your friend." My heart flipped. That meant Phoebe had not yet been found. "If you tell me what I need to know, I will spare her life when we find her." He had one of those stilted faces you just want to smack with a baseball bat. I'm sorry, but it's true. "Otherwise, you both die." You could sense that he derived a great personal joy from being Mr. Bad Ass.

And, he meant what he said.

"What do you want to know?" I had thoughts of Polyester Man from that day at the condo. Damn, that seemed like a million years ago.

"Who sent you here and why?" Come on; no small talk?

☐ Chapter Ten ☐

"We were on our way to a hunting lodge in Vryburg and got lost," I replied flatly, calmly, maintaining careful eye contact with him.

The words had just hit the atmosphere, so to speak, when he slapped me. Not hard at all—really just a love tap (without the love)—but executed with utter and complete contempt.

He turned to the eemee and said, "Warm enough now?" It was phrased as a question for which he expected no answer, only action.

The eemee moved lithely forward to stand near the vat, a respectable distance from Kaftan Man. "I will begin." His head tilted back slightly.

I felt the tingling start. I let it build, blocked it, and let it build some more. I let my face go slack and impassive. Kaftan Man was going to get his in just a damn moment. This was one evil man, I could sense that he was bad news for anyone. Nothing redeemable in his nature.

Who knew the full extent of his involvement in this pentacle thing, and how much more evil he planned to do? How much evil had he already done? The more I thought about it, the angrier I got, and then I started thinking about Phoebe running around in the middle of the night with gangs of this guy's armed goons chasing her, and that pissed me off even more.

Yeah, I was mildly irritated. I redirected the eemee's scan energy and blasted the humans.

The eemee was untouched, but all four men collapsed to the ground as though the switch to their brain had been simply flipped to the off position.

Alert and standing one moment, and then crumpled heaps of insensate meat the next.

Well, that was what was supposed to have happened. I only meant to knock them unconscious. But, I had let my anger control me, overwhelm me, and the EM wave had been far too much. In my irritation and anger I didn't just turn the switch off, I fried the whole damn connection.

Blood was flowing very slowly out of the controller's left ear and his nose. There were no signs of life. He was obviously dead. Two of the guards were completely motionless, already dead. The third guard was breathing shallow. As horrified as I was by this, the eemee was standing, mouth agape, arms dangling down, shoulders lurched forward. Not quite a state of shock, but very close.

I kept telling myself these were evil people involved in evil activities and they would have killed Phoebe and me in a heartbeat. They had probably killed others. I just tried to block it out. I had to rationalize it, had to deal with it quickly, no other choice. I clamored over the vat and walked up to the eemee, who was still staring at his ex-controller's body in disbelief. I grabbed him by both arms and gave him a gentle shake. His eyes swung slowly to me.

"We need to destroy the primary pentacle." I said it clearly, calmly, precisely. It was the only way to free the eemee.

The eemee struggled to speak, "I do not know where it is. There will be security." Eemees don't really know humans and I did. The primary pentacle would be in Kaftan Man's main office, where he could keep a constant and watchful eye on it. We would find it later. Security was the hot issue now. Maybe Tom could help on that, maybe not.

"What kind of security?" This had to be solved quickly.

"Thumbprint," which would be mighty unpleasant and bloody but, with enough resolve, doable. "And also voice-activated." That might be a problem.

I walked over to the table to be near the ComUnit.

~Dee!~ I mind-shouted at her with goodly bit of fluster.

~Yes, Enoch.~ I might be heavily agitated, but Dee was certainly serene.

~Have you been monitoring me? And the events in this room?~

~Yes, the level of your emotional distress activated me, though I could not communicate with you.~

~So, you have the controller's voice recorded?~ Otherwise, we'd have to come up with a Plan B, as in bad.

~It is digitized. Are you well?~

Dee had been solidly calm until now, but the new level of angst in her voice shook me for a moment. ~Yeah, I'm okay. Thanks for asking.~ Just a brief pause. ~We need to get into the controller's office and destroy the primary pentacle.~

☐ Chapter Ten ☐

~Understood. Tom may be able to bypass the security.~ I don't know how Dee was programmed but, damn, it was good, as she was back to cool and detached, professional.

~Connect to him, please.~ In the interim, I suddenly realized that I had no knife. Tom had to figure out a way to get by security. I leave it to you to work out the unpleasant implications of needing a dead man's thumb but having no way to, well, solve the puzzle of removing it.

~Enoch?~ It was Tom.

~Tom, I need your help to bypass some security. I'll have Dee send you the details so you can start working on it.~ My voice was clearly tainted tense, no matter how calm I tried to speak.

~Okay, we'll be on the lookout.~ Nothing seemed to faze Tom.

~I am sending the data now.~

I dressed quickly, checked everything, and grabbed the ComUnit. ~Dee, I need to reach Phoebe, but quietly, in case other people are nearby.~

A moment or two passed and Phoebe's voice was in my head. ~Enoch, you're okay!~ The relief and sincere happiness of her voice made me smile.

~You're worried about me with search teams after your head?~ I was a bit taken aback by this.

~Bah, those idiots couldn't find an elephant in the daylight.~ We both laughed.

I didn't have much time to chit-chat. ~The controller is dead. The eemee and I are going to destroy the primary pentacle and then I'm outta here.~

~That's sounds extremely dangerous, Enoch, are you sure you're up to it?~ Professional mode back in place.

~No, I'm not bloody sure, but I'll meet you at the rendezvous point after it's done.~ No time for any other plan.

~If you need support, call me.~ Always ready to kick some ass, even though she was out in the night dodging frenzied search teams.

~Trust me, you're the first one I'll call.~ Well, the only one. I ended the discussion.

"Show me the way to the controller's office," I said to Dee and the ComUnit flashed to life with a display. The eemee and I were two flashing red dots. A yellow line lead out from the door and snaked off through the facility. "Follow the yellow brick road?" I am not sure to whom I was speaking, maybe just myself.

Out the door we went, locking it behind us with the numeric keypad. The eemee entered in a new security code to delay anyone poking around.

We moved on warily through the building. The office was actually in the far right corner, upstairs. Naturally. We encountered three different clusters of people on the way, but the eemee was known and we easily passed through. We arrived at the office door. It was a heavy metallic door, very solid-looking. There was some fancy-looking electronic gear attached to the wall facing us.

~Dee, get Tom on the line.~ Even in bad situations, don't forget your manners. ~Please.~

That was barely out of my mind when Tom said, ~Enoch, I'm here.~ Guess he had been on stand-by mode. He sounded calm.

~We're outside the door. What's the status?~ I was close to panic-mode myself.

Pause. ~Almost there.~ I could hear quite a commotion in the background. ~Dee?~ Tom said anxiously.

Dee replied calmly, **~Yes, Tom?~**

Tom gave her directions. ~Go ahead and upload the controller saying his name.~ Dee had digitized a sampling of the controller's voice and the eemee had supplied his name—Ranis Terloff. But, I wondered, if Tom was going to bypass security, why did he need the name spoken? I was about to ask when Tom started talking again.

~Enoch, this is very complex security, but it looks like part of it is linked to his voice print.~ More noise in the background. ~We just need to get by the initialization phase!~ Lo que sea.

The door was still shut, but the electronic display panel was flashing through a series of letters and numbers as Tom's hack hunted for the proper codes. But, it was still locked.

And then a pair of guards appeared at the end of the corridor. Perfect timing. Damn Murphy.

They were not moving fast, no weapons were showing, but they did appear to be alert and watchful. The taller of the two spoke as they approached, "Can we help you, Mr. Noet?" Addressed to the eemee. I tried to look patently innocent, but my black SWAT-looking outfit worked mightily against that. Praetorian Guard fashionista. Or facistista. Hah. I'm nervous at this point.

I'm standing—smiling like an idiot—in front of the security box trying to block the guard's view of the flashing digital display; with a suspicious-looking ComUnit in my hand, doing my best to look harmless.

"Mr. Terloff said for us to wait for him here," Noet said very rhythmically. Bonus points for really quick thinking.

Unfortunately, Tom and Armando must have figured something out right about then, because the door clicked open at that exact moment. Even your most bell-curve challenged security guard knew that wasn't right, and one of them thoughtlessly reached for his weapon. I reflexively reached for the BB gun, suddenly felt a tingling in my medulla and instantly redirected it, gently, to the guards, who fell roughly to the floor, handguns clattering across the concrete. Noet was sharp, that much was certain, though he seemed surprised by the whole episode.

We went in the door and shut it behind us.

Standard secretarial greeting area; chair, desk, computer, file cabinets, blah, blah, blah. Another door at the far end. Had to be the main office. We stepped close to the door and, wonderful discovery— there was another, much smaller, security box. This one looked like the thumbprint swipe unit. Perfect.

~Tom!~ My mental finger was trembling and poised above the Def Con One panic button.

~Dee already has me working on it.~ A rapid response from a harried Tom.

I was tapping my foot nervously—about ready to howl madly— when the door popped open. Tom and Armando! Bless their cold hacker hearts. I was going to buy them Copper Gorillas for the rest of their lives. In we went and shut the door behind us.

Now, of course, I did not expect to find a flashing neon sign with an arrow saying, "Pentacle Here," or anything like that.

⧉ Feeling A Little Warmed Over ⧉

I was, however, hoping there might be some kind of clue on the floor, ceiling, or wall maybe, but there was nothing showing anywhere. Key Wrap. "Start tearing the place apart," I said to Noet and we began rifling, pilfering, emptying, tossing, and searching through everything. He was attacking the bookcases with a vengeance and I was working through the file cabinets like a madman.

I heard a sharp exclamation from Noet and stepped quickly over to him, assuming he had found the pentacle. Instead, he was standing rigidly, staring aghast at a small aquarium-sized glass enclosure. It must have been hidden behind the furniture he had just moved aside. There was a snake inside the glass enclosure.

A live snake, staring rather intently at Mr. Noet. A variety of snake I now recognized from a previous encounter. Black mamba. With what looked like several dead mice or gerbils stacked in the corner of its glass container. Damn.

Some people have odd ideas about acceptable house pets. Man, how about a hamster or something?

"It can't get out, just keep looking," I said sharply and returned to my frenzied search motif.

One minute became five. You know the tick-tock drill. Nothing. Jeopardy. "Hold it, stop." Noet went still. In my mind, I had been visualizing something big, like the pentacle on the floor at PHANTASM that Brody had passed through. But, suppose the pentacle could be any size? I mean, any size that someone could build. Shoot, they can engrave names on a grain of freaking rice, right?

~Dee, what's the absolute minimum size for an operational primary pentacle?~ Should have thought about this earlier but, yo, was a little preoccupied!

~A 2.5 centimeter square.~

Ignorance can be so demeaning at times. ~In human terms.~

~I don't understand.~

Aargh. ~Non-metric system.~ Stated very mouse-meek by me.

~That's approximately a one-inch square, Enoch.~ It's very humbling to have a computer program express exasperation with you.

Okay, okay, about the size of a postage stamp. Slap!

⬚ Chapter Ten ⬚

I ran to the desk and opened the top drawer. Pens, envelopes, staples, rubber bands, clips, note cards.

Stamps.

Trash, trash, trash, trash. Flipping through stamps like a crazed postman. Trash. Trash. The mother-freaking-lode. I let out a whoop.

Noet was staring at me. "You found it." There was disbelief heavy in his voice, a voice cracking with emotion. He walked slowly over and we both stood looking at the pentacle.

It was an incredibly intricate and complex design, raised up above the surface, and was more like an integrated circuit board than a stamp, though the same size as a stamp. The level of detail was stunning, but you would need a magnifying glass to truly appreciate it, and I wasn't here to appreciate it.

With a trembling hand, Noet took it from my grasp.

"Thank you," was all he said and crushed the stamp-like object with his fingers. He vanished. Not gradually fading away or wafting slowly, just poof, but no sound, no nothing. One moment there, next gone. Remnants of the broken pentacle fell to the floor.

Which had a wonderful synchronicity with the alarm system going off. ~Dee, what's the quickest way out?~ I thought-shouted this with deafening clarity. Screw panic mode, I was moving straight to flight mode.

~Exit this office to the main corridor, turn right, proceed 15 meters. About 50 feet. Down the emergency stairs, through the room and out the door. Then, run.~

Well, gee, doesn't that sound simple?

Which, of course, is the kiss of freaking death. Exiting the office was easy, and the first few steps were a breeze, but then I heard a shout from behind me, just beyond where the two guards were prone on the ground. Probably my running in the opposite direction right about now would look, uh, rather bad. So I stopped.

I turned, put my hands in the air, and watched as three figures raced toward me. Then I felt the familiar tingle in my oblongata and promptly redirected to the charging men. They fell in ragged, out of control heaps and piles, skidding and tumbling along the concrete walkway and coming to rest in jambled disorder.

▢ Feeling A Little Warmed Over ▢

~Dee, what just happened?~ I was more than a little frightened, but still took off on a dead run toward the stairs.

~I provided you with scan energy to redirect, just like before.~

I entered the stairwell and bounded down the steps two at a time. ~But that would mean you, you're...~

~Am what you would call an eemee.~

I hit the bottom of the stairs, stopped, and slowly pushed open the door, then cautiously entered a sparsely furnished room, like a waiting area, I guess. There was a large window to my left, curtains open, and two men were outside, fortunately facing the other way. One tingle and a redirect later, they were on the ground.

The door to the outside was to my left, but I knew this would exit me on the far side of the building, a damn long way from the hole in the fence and my only egress. Not good, but no choice. Necessity truly is a mother.

~Dee, tell Tom to kill the electricity to the whole facility.~ Hoping that he could. Praying, even, if that helped.

Moments passed. More moments. Then out went the lights. I darted through the door, cut right along the face of the building and quickly spurted around the corner. Once around the corner it would be a straight, pedal to the metal, football-field sprint to the fence. Fear would overcome fitness, as it were.

I'm a third of the way down the side of the building at this point, running like a thief that stole something, and suddenly emergency flood lights located at fixed points along the roof kick on. There was a backup generator running on separate software! Damn criminals always have the best technology.

I am dodging in and out of light and shadows—an easy target. ~Kill the backup system! Kill the backup system!~ I am pretty sure this sounded like the scream of a desperate man. Which it was.

An automatic weapon, not close, but from behind me, opened up. Bullets hit the ground and wall and I began to zigzag like a crazy man. ~Dee, mind zap that guy!~ I thought in desperation.

~Too far away,~ came her stoic reply. Great. I was a dead man if those damn lights didn't go off.

The emergency lights went out.

⬥ Chapter Ten ⬥

I swung well away from the building while the automatic continued to fire until the clip was empty. I have to say, it was one of the most unpleasant things I can ever recall, hearing those bullets whiz by— some vanishing into the gloom, some thudding loudly into the ground and others whirring with deadly effect into the metal building. I tried not to think about the effect they would have had on human flesh.

My human flesh.

I had to be near the end of the building, but it was dark and I needed to slow down. Even though I had seen, when the lights had been on, that the area in front of me was clear, my mind simply would not wrap itself around the idea of hurtling at breakneck speed through utter darkness. Emphasis on breakneck. And darkness!

Well, that and I was sucking eggs as I gasped for air. My training regimen needed some refinement.

The large dark shape of the parked tractor trailer suddenly loomed to my right. There was enough starlight to barely make that out. I was close now. The fence hole should be about a 40 degree angle away to my left and I took off. Only about 30 yards and I should be at the fence.

I guess it was blind stinking luck, fate, kismet, or just a good memory, but when the fence popped into view (when I semi-smacked into it, actually) the hole we had cut was only a foot to my left. I was through it, but now the fun would start, because in the complete darkness it would be almost impossible to make any progress, unless I had a reliable guide.

Like Dee, the eemee.

I'll be honest, before Dee laid that "I'm an eemee" bomb on me, I had her, uh, it, figured as one of two things. Either she, it, really was some super-duper mega-advanced AI program created by PHANTASM, or Dee was actually some totally genius woman ensconced in the bowels of the complex surrounded by a bank of super computers.

I had not even considered the apparent reality.

~You want to tell me about your being an eemee?~ I tried not to sound like a kid pointing an accusatory finger at a schoolmate who stole his cookie at lunch.

◊ Feeling A Little Warmed Over ◊

~**You are in the middle of the South African bush, at night, surrounded by armed men intent on harming you. If you think your time would be well-spent in discussion, certainly we can talk.**~

~That's obfuscation.~ Damn, outwitted by an eemee thingy.

~**Nonsense. That's merely reality.**~

~So, out of the closet now and all bossy, huh?~ She had a point, though I hated to acknowledge it. Hubris.

~**We need to find Phoebe.**~

I suppose this banter could have carried on for quite some time, but that Phoebe remark stopped me in my tracks. Dee was right. ~Can you get her online, quietly?~

A few moments went by and Phoebe was talking in my head. ~Enoch?~

~Hey, Phoebe, you okay?~ Seemed like the logical question.

What followed was a fanciful and rapid string of rather colorful metaphors, caustic invectives, and blatant pejoratives finally ending in a question. ~Where are you right now?~ Hell hath no fury like a Phoebe. Scorned or not!

I explained my problem and the proposed solution, which really was fairly simple. Dee would use the satellite imagery and local topography maps to guide me back to the rendezvous point, and we would make our way there in the starlight as best we could. Based on the speed we could move at night, we were probably two to three hours away.

I told Phoebe my time estimate was based on making good speed in the dark with Dee employing advanced EM techniques for guidance. Techniques (I did not tell Phoebe this, of course) which I actually had no idea would work or not. Or even if they existed. Just didn't want Phoebe to worry about me.

~The search teams,~ Phoebe said tersely, ~are still out in force.~ See, already worrying about me.

~I have an idea on that.~ And so, I elaborated on my other plan.

Dee was going to get in touch with Tom and Armando to hack back into LankSkop and activate every frigging alarm system they had. Set them all off. We'd scramble up communications with EM interference so the search teams couldn't confirm what was going on.

◻ Chapter Ten ◻

All of the search teams would have to hurry back to the complex to see what kind of hell was breaking out.

~I like it,~ Phoebe said calmly. Grudging admiration is better than none at all. And so, about three minutes later, it sounded like Armageddon back at the facility.

Dee began guiding me through the darkness, as best she could, using local maps, satellite imagery, the advanced EM techniques I mentioned earlier (hah) and BSL. Blind stinking luck.

Dee's best was actually not bad, despite the inordinate number of branches that slap-whacked across my forehead; the many and painfully sticky thorn and thistle hits to my exposed extremities; the multiple stubbed toes on rocks; and the innumerable crawling and flying things I had to swat off my face and neck. Some of them the size of, well, don't ask.

I'll need therapy to forget this night. Okay, I'll settle for a Copper Gorilla or three.

Twice we had to hunker down when wavering flashlights and grunting search teams passed nearby as they hustled back to LankSkop.

We only had to cover about 2.5 miles. That sounds like a cake walk, right? I mean, you could leisurely jog that in less than thirty minutes. You could walk it in under an hour. Try achieving it in almost total darkness over mixed and varied terrain. Did I mention branches, thorns, and strange flying creatures that buzzed and clicked? Brutal.

We forged diligently and relentlessly onward. Well, I did all of the damn forging; each step like slogging through quicksand. Dee was just along for the ride, so to speak.

Right around the three-hour mark I heard Phoebe's voice in my head. ~I hope that's you moving through the brush.~

~If you shoot, please kill me instantly, I'm too tired to bleed to death,~ I said wearily, almost completely out of energy. Yeah, yeah, electromagnetic or otherwise.

Not more than a dozen steps later I saw Phoebe's ComUnit display. She was holding it aloft like a lighthouse beacon. Really clever girl. Good-looking, too.

I staggered into the small clearing.

◻ Feeling A Little Warmed Over ◻

"I hope that damn snake is gone," I joked, my voice cracking with strain as I plopped down on the ground, shedding my pack and tossing it carelessly behind me.

Phoebe sat down next to me, leaned in close, holding her ComUnit display light near my face. "You look like crap," she stated with feeling.

I fell back and put my head on the backpack. "Seven shades worth," I muttered.

"Get some rest. We'll need to start moving right before daybreak." Pro mode.

I yawned, fading like a cheap tattoo. "Tell Dee to monitor the satellites for any movement from the complex." Another yawn and Phoebe bar the door. The lights went out.

Peculiar Interpretations

"Everything that irritates us about others can lead us to an understanding of ourselves."

—Carl Gustav Jung

Dove's wings. Isn't that how all nice mornings should arrive? Swift kick to the leg was how mine started. I jerked up.

"Damn, Enoch, you sleep like a zombie." Phoebe was shaking her head. "Sorry I had to kick you, but you wouldn't wake up." That was undoubtedly the most reluctantly expressed regret I have ever heard.

I was rubbing my leg and giving her a stare that I hoped conveyed my complete and utter doubt. "You're just mad because I got caught back there."

"No," she smiled sweetly, "I'm just mad because you scared the hell out of me back there."

"Ah, you really do care," I said jokingly.

She put her hands on her hips, always a bad sign from a woman, and rewarded me with a piercing glare. "I haven't lost a partner yet, and I don't intend to now." The rosy fingers of dawn, as they say, were slowly sneaking in from the east. "Stick a BioPatch on and let's go."

Oh, damn, I forgot all about those things. The MedPatch might help my head, too, which was still hurting from the fall I had taken in the warehouse (concrete 1, Enoch's head 0) and the numerous branches that had introduced themselves to me during that delightful evening stroll. I rummaged around, found what I needed, and slapped them both on.

Phoebe was watching me closely. "Can we go now?"

"Lead on," I said and waved her forward. We began walking back to our parked vehicle.

⬚ Peculiar Interpretations ⬚

It was quiet for awhile, until the dawn was well upon us. It really was a spectacular place. Phoebe spoke without turning. "So, give me a brief summary of your escapades."

Which I proceeded to do. She asked a few relevant questions, expressed shock, surprise, doubt more than once, and finally a reluctant and grudging, but unavoidable, admiration, as I said. I mean, I was still here, alive and walking. Proof of my ability, or luck.

Either way, it was all good.

Oh, but I may have left the Dee being an eemee part out. Not sure why, but I was just holding that one back until I had thought it through.

Most of the walk was passed in silence. Saving energy. Finally, through an opening in the thick brush, we saw our truck about fifty yards away. "We need to be careful now," Phoebe said simply.

"We're here," I pointed. "There's the truck." My logic is unassailable. Like a broken Italian watch. Think about it.

Phoebe had stopped and crouched down. I did the same. She swiveled and locked me in her pro mode gaze. "Suppose the bad guys found the truck first?" A nasty smile. "I think if they had a plan to hide in the brush waiting for two idiots to come strolling up to the truck, that would be a pretty good plan, wouldn't it?" That sweet, innocent, voice. I wanted to kick her in the shin.

"So, what do we do?" It's not a crime to profess your ignorance if you are ignorant. It's just a crime to believe you're not ignorant when you are. I think.

"We'll circle quietly around the perimeter, make sure it's clear," she replied and took off in a half-crouch down a small hill and into some dense brush. I would have figured that out, sooner or later. I have skills.

The area proved to be clear and we approached the truck, much more relaxed. Phoebe, ever the paranoid, leaned down to look under the truck. The only thing I could figure was she had lost the key or was checking for bombs. More likely the latter, I thought with a shiver. Satisfied, we got in and started the engine.

As the vehicle bounded, bounced, and rattled my teeth on the way out, Phoebe spoke. "We're not going back to Gaborone."

⬚ Chapter Eleven ⬚

"Where are we going?" I wasn't driving, so what difference did it make, but I felt like I should ask.

"An area due north from here, about thirty miles on the other side of the border." It seemed like no big deal to her.

I had studied the map earlier. This whole area was, technically, the Kalahari Desert, but hardly seemed like a desert, well, unless you went further north. "And we are doing this, why?" I asked in my most irritating voice.

"Because Jackie can't land a super-sensitive secret plane in the middle of any populated area." Like I was a complete doofus for not knowing this.

"Oh," said scornfully, "but she can land in the middle of the desert?" Hah, take that.

"Probably not," Phoebe countered without missing a stride, "unless there happens to be a super-sensitive secret facility located there." She turned her head and smirked at me, though with a playful smile I will admit. Still, that woman could really get me riled up, in more ways than two.

"I should update Hume," I mused aloud.

Phoebe nodded, "I sent a preliminary report to PHANTASM earlier, but never followed up with details."

I noted the local time. He should still be up, even though it was late. If not, well, he would be. Payback for all the pain, sort of. ~Dee, can you get Hume on the line?~ Then I remembered our little conversation. ~And then you and I need to talk.~

~Okay, Enoch.~ Subdued, soft.

In a few moments Hume's face appeared on the ComUnit display. It looked like a living room of his residence, wherever that was located. Maybe he lived at PHANTASM as well. "Enoch, what an absolute pleasure. I am so glad you're still with us." Which was an extremely circumspect way of saying he was happy I wasn't dead.

"I'm sort of tickled about it as well," I responded.

Hume frowned. "The last word I got from Phoebe is that she had lost touch with you." He paused. "We were very worried." And, indeed, he wore a worried expression.

"Well, I made it out and there's a lot to tell," I said earnestly and began to tell him. Unlike Phoebe, Hume never interrupted as I reeled off the events as best I could recall. Left out a few things, mostly not relevant, and still didn't mention that Dee was an eemee. Not sure why I didn't, but there you have it.

At the end, though, he wore a somewhat puzzled expression as he spoke. "I'm particularly intrigued by your AI, whom you call Dee." His smile seemed a little, well, forced. "Truth be told, Enoch, we do have advanced AI programs in use at PHANTASM, but I don't think we have anything that sophisticated."

Why people tell lies has been the subject of human fascination for thousands of years. Many politicians make a career of doing it undetected. Sophistry. I almost always tell the truth, just seems to work for me. I don't know why, but a sudden urge to perjure myself was just overwhelming and I could not shake it.

"Well, I may have, uh, overstated the AI's contribution." I was trying to think as fast as I could. "I just asked really smart questions and got back really useful data." I took a breath. "Tom and Armando were the real heroes." I tried to convey my honesty by staring right at the ComUnit and, thus, Hume's face.

He nodded. "That's what I thought, Enoch, but just wanted clarification."

"I do have some ideas that could improve the AI," I added, trying to embellish the part and pinching myself for not knowing when to shut-up.

"Excellent," Hume said. "We'll talk in more detail when you're safely back here."

"That works for me," I said lazily.

"Oh, one more thing. We managed to get hold of a sample of the Argentinean supplement and the lab guys here made an analysis of it." He did not sound too enthused about it.

Notwithstanding, I asked excitedly, "Good. What did you find?"

"Nothing, mostly everyday organics and some vitamins." Hume laughed. "Might give you gas, but that's about it. I'll get the report uploaded to your ComUnit."

☐ Chapter Eleven ☐

"Ah, good night then," I half-mumbled, trying not to sound too disappointed.

"Good morning, Enoch," he grinned and broke the connection.

Phoebe immediately caught my eye. "Why did you lie about Dee and what she can really do?"

I took a breath. Phoebe was a company gal, but she was my partner. If that doesn't mean something, well, you shouldn't be trusted to have a partner. I let a long breath out. "Dee is an eemee."

We were already on the main hard road, heading north, but Phoebe slowed and pulled over onto the dirt and grass shoulder. She turned the engine off and faced me. She shook her head. Her expression was unfathomable. You know, like it always is. "Hume doesn't know that."

I shrugged. "Or, he knows it, but doesn't want me to know it."

"Dee!" Phoebe said loudly.

"Yes, Phoebe."

"Does Hume know you are an eemee?" Well, I suppose blunt trauma is one way to handle the problem.

There was a very human pause. "**No**." My eyebrows went up. Even if I suspected it, the surprise was still strong.

"Why doesn't he know?" I got a feeling Phoebe was good at interrogation. I thought about that razor-sharp knife strapped to her calf and grimaced inwardly.

"Sometimes more can be accomplished in the shadows than in the light."

"Do you expect me to accept that answer?" Phoebe was amazingly calm, her voice soft and smooth.

"No."

I decided to make a gambit of my own. "Ruach is involved in this, isn't he?"

"He is the complement."

I assumed she meant with an "e" and not an "i," although it didn't make sense to me, either way. I was ignorant coming and going.

"Can you connect me to Ruach over a secure line?" When in doubt, go to the source.

⧉ Peculiar Interpretations ⧉

"It will take a moment." I could normally read the tone and inflection in Dee's voice and tell what she was thinking, but she was inscrutable here, and I could get no read at all.

Shortly, Ruach's visage appeared on the ComUnit. "Enoch, it is good to hear from you." He seemed genuinely pleased. "How are you?"

I couldn't help but smile. There was just something about him. A genuineness, a sense of goodness, I don't know how to put it in words. He made you feel better about yourself. Nonetheless, I had to get some facts straight, and there was no easy way around it. "I'm fine, Ruach," I replied, then added after a whisper of a pause, "and Dee says hello, too."

Without so much as skipping a beat Ruach nodded and said, "I trust she has been useful."

"I wouldn't be here without her," and the truth of that really struck home in my mind. It was totally the case.

"It was her idea, you know," Ruach said softly. A brief pause. "I initially opposed it." Ruach's face was impassive.

"It was, and is, a good idea." There was a sense of absolute conviction in Dee's tone that I could not miss.

Ruach brightened and his eyes were wide with delight. "I am told your name is Dee."

"A rose by any other name would smell as sweet."

Ruach chuckled and I couldn't help but laugh. Even Phoebe cracked a grin. Ruach began speaking. "Open the back of the ComUnit." Phoebe produced a utility tool, thankfully not razor-sharp, and handed it to me. Four small screws later I was about to pop the back off. I looked at Phoebe. She was eerily calm. I removed the loosened covering.

Inside the lid was a pentacle. Beautiful, ornate, intricate, raised above the metallic surface of the ComUnit back. I think my jaw dropped when the meaning of this filtered through my thoughts. "Dee is imprisoned in the pentacle!"

"No, Enoch, not imprisoned. This is my choice."

"It is the only way she can be with you, to help you," Ruach explained.

"But you cannot dream, you have no stream of awareness, and... And, it's painful." This is what I had been told.

"I have my bond with you, Enoch, and that sustains me, and this pentacle was not built to punish, but to preserve."

"But, why?" It was all I could think to say.

Dee did not answer and Ruach seemed thoughtful. At last, he broke the silence. "The truth is not something that can be given to another, it must be experienced." He smiled enigmatically. "The greatest human thinkers have always stressed that when you attempt to penetrate to the truth, it shall come to you." He paused. "But, the individual must first make that effort."

I shook my head. "I'm not sure I know what that means."

Ruach tilted his head, a wispy smile still coloring his face, "You will. In time, you will." He vanished.

I secured the back of the ComUnit into place. Phoebe and I sat silently for a few minutes. This was bothering her, but for better or worse I could not tell.

She finally seemed to arrive at an internal decision and started the truck. "We have to trust that this will all work out in the end." That seemed fatally optimistic to me, but I had no crushing rebuke to toss into the conversation.

"Do we keep this to ourselves?" I queried. After all, there was Hume and PHANTASM.

She nodded, "For now, yes." She looked steadily at me as she pulled onto the road. "Partner to partner." We drove on in silence.

That silence, and our revelry, was broken when my ComUnit flashed into life and Tom's face and voice appeared. "Hey, Enoch."

"Hey, Tom." Not an overly-clever reply, I will grant you, but I was still recovering; from many things.

He grinned. "Just wanted to update you on a few more tidbits we've managed to find out." More information had to be a good thing, right? Then again, we've all heard that too-much-of-a-good-thing saying...

"Keep talking," I said and smiled. Thin maybe, but a smile.

"We've been working on Brody's code." Holy crap, I'd almost forgotten all about that. "I can't say we've cracked it or anything, but we have some ideas." Ideas are good, I like ideas. Ideas are our friends.

To refresh you, the paper that Brody died to bring to PHANTASM said:

gaia penta peptode 12 12 12 -12(7) demonhunter ctr?

"Whattya got?" That's me, direct and to the point. Sometimes.

"We already reviewed your notes on the text *gaia* and there's nothing new there." A breath. "*Penta* is undoubtedly a reference to pentacle, as you also say in your notes, but we are not sure of the overall context." A rustle of papers. "We agree than *peptode* is probably peptide, but please note that peptone is also a viable option." I hastily made a mental note of that. Tom deliberately paused, as he knew I would be gnawing on that morsel, which I was. Tasty, but ultimately unsatisfying.

"The new stuff comes next," he said, an obvious excitement seeping into his tone. "The '12 12 12 -12(7)' text string has quite a few possibilities." Hmm, I thought to myself, possibilities, not certainties, but (insert mental sigh here) that was more than I currently had.

"It could refer to fertilizer," he said with some hesitation. I have to admit, I had not expected that connection.

"Fertilizer?" I repeated and tried not to sound like I thought Tom was full of that seven shades of shiny goat crap I often talk about. Speaking of fertilizer…

"Yeah, it's the percentages for nitrogen, phosphorous, and potassium," said by Tom in what I thought was a rather belated tone.

I didn't know what to think about that or where to go with it. "Is it explosive?" was the best I could come up with as a line of inquiry.

"Oh, no, not in that configuration, just good for the lawn," he said softly.

So, the evil human controllers were seeking to control the Grand Ole Opry while maintaining a nice green lawn. Really spooky guys.

~Nashville.~

I ignored Dee and told Tom, "I'm thinking your fertilizer idea might be full of, uh, fertilizer." I did catch myself in time. "What else do you have?" I asked, trying not to sound too disappointed.

"Well," Tom continued, with a little more pep in his voice. "Armando had the idea that the numbers might be Morse Code."

I'm open-minded or, as some would have it, empty-minded, so I figured it could be possible. "How so?"

"The '1' represents a single dot and the '2' represents two dashes," Tom said expectantly, as though Morse Code was something I knew by heart. I wouldn't know an SOS from a POS, if you get my drift.

"And that means precisely, what?" I asked as pleasantly as possible. AUM. Breathe. Breathe.

"A dot and two dashes is the letter 'W,' so '12 12 12' would be 'WWW,' which might be the World Wide Web." Or, possibly, the Wide World of Wrestling, or Wilson's World of Wombats. I sighed, again.

"What about the '-12(7)' text?" I reminded him brusquely, though not meant that way. "Are you saying that it's some kind of web address?" I had a headache. That is to say, a worse one than before.

"Well, we didn't find anything at 'minus84' or '-84' or 'minuseightyfour' or 'minus…'"

"Okay, okay, I get it." Nothing much for that last bit, so I'm thinking the Internet link might not be the Captain Midnight code breaker we needed, but still worth pursuing. "Keep looking for a web connection," I said with feigned and futile enthusiasm. Mental gasp. For some reason, the Internet thing just didn't seem right, but I could be full of prunes.

"What else?" Patience being, as I have said before, a reproachable attribute of mine.

"The last thing we have is a physics idea," Tom said, a bit snippy, but I didn't blame him. My bad for my attitude.

"Before you go on, Tom, I want to say I'm sorry for being a little short with you." Took a nice deep breath. "You guys saved my ass back there and I'll never forget that, ever." For sure.

"I'm kind of running on fumes right now," I added softly. Now, that was honesty squared. Cubed.

"That's okay, Enoch, we're here in a nice cozy room with chips and drinks and you're being shot at," he sounded pretty tired, too. "We've had some good successes on other things, but this Brody code, and that damn *demonhunter* folder, are kicking our ass."

"It's okay, you guys are great. Tell me about your physics idea," I prodded gently, repentant and penitent.

"Mando and I were thinking those numbers might be the specifications for a 2D triangle projected into 3D space," Tom said hopefully, though tinged with some doubt. His and mine.

I nodded my head as I thought about it. "Okay, let's say I buy that. That '-12(7)' text has to fit in somehow…" I am always raining on the parade. Me and Stormcrow bringing the good bad news. A token Tolkien toke.

"Mando and I think it's a transformational notation indicator." Of course it is; how did I miss that?

"You just made that up," I said with a smile.

Tom laughed. "If every side of the 2D triangle is rotated and thrust into space at -84 degrees, you end up with a 3D shape."

I sat there trying to visualize this. Mostly saw spinning lights. "All I'm getting is a really long triangle." You know, like a tent.

"The 2D shape, if you draw it on a piece of paper, also has an underside—all four sides are extruded in the transformation," he explained patiently.

A light bulb flashed above my head. "A pyramid," I said. Tom nodded, but I frowned. Cool theory, but I didn't see how it fit in with the rest of the clues. "Anything else?" I tried not to sound too desultory.

"We found something interesting on the Argentinean supplement." Tom, unlike me, did sound enthused. Anti-desultory I guess. I hated to pour down rain on him again.

"I already talked to PHANTASM and they said there was nothing in it to worry about." I was getting tired. I was about ready to take a short trip to Nap City. Nothing but silence from Tom.

"Tom?" I finally said after about five seconds or so.

"Hmm, that's not what we found." He sounded worried.

"What do you mean?" I sounded worried.

"Well, I can tell you that there isn't much out there on that Argentinean company or its product," he stated evenly. "And that's strange because they ship worldwide." I didn't really have time to rattle that around the ol' neo-cortex because Tom was speaking again. "We had to hack into a secure FDA site to find anything."

"Isn't that a federal crime, Tom?" I mean, involving unpleasant men in dark suits escorting you to a federal penitentiary. Where you share a suite with some hulking scofflaw with a room temperature IQ.

"We weren't in there long enough to leave a trail," he said. Then huffed, "Besides, we're good at what we do." Okay, okay, get to the meat. And taters. My stomach growled.

"What did you find?" I am master of the obvious. Or, is it the oblivious? Can't keep that straight.

"The organic plant ingredient they used for their supposed energy boost contains a compound that is very similar to D-lysergic acid diethylamide," and Tom paused here, waiting for me, and I did not want to disappoint him.

"LSD."

"Right," Tom affirmed. "The plant compound they use is, now get ready for this, classified as a *peptide* alkaloid." He put an extra emphasis on the word peptide, but it wasn't needed, as I was already connecting the dots to Brody's coded message.

"What does it do?" There had to be a reason for it being in the supplement.

I could almost hear Tom's shoulders pop when he shrugged. "Well, here's where it gets a little weird." A deep intake of air. "Even though you would expect a psychotropic reaction in people who ate this supplement, there have been no such reports." Another pause. "Zero. Zip. Náda. Zilch. Nothing. The ingredient is completely inert."

There was another bit of silence as I gastronomized on this. "Send Dee the report. Good job guys!" I added with warmth. "Keep after it." Tom vanished and I absently put the ComUnit down, my mind a whirling dervish.

Phoebe had, of course, been listening intently to every word. Not only was she a warrior, in the most military sense of the word, but she was scary smart, too. Especially the former, but I could climb on the latter.

"Something stinks in Denmark," she said flatly and I liked the Shakespearean allusion.

☐ Peculiar Interpretations ☐

"Somewhere in this loop, someone is lying," I agreed apprehensively, "but, I'm not sure who." Or why, but I left that unsaid.

She nodded, but with a odd lilt to her expression. "There are plenty of other legitimate options, Enoch." A graceful shrug. "Maybe the lab guys gave Hume a bad report on purpose. Maybe they just missed the peptide thing in their tests. Maybe the supplement they tested was fake, or bad."

I hadn't considered all of those possibilities. More dervishing going on in my head. I rubbed my chin in corn fused contemplation. She took her eyes off the road, caught mine for a moment and said lightly, "Maybe Hume is lying."

I had considered that one, but shook my head. "I don't see it, Phoebe. What does he have to gain?" I pursed my lips, thinking about it. "Maybe the PHANTASM people did see the drug thing, but since it isn't affecting anyone, like Tom said the FDA report stated, they wrote it off as harmless." My turn to shrug, though not as elegantly. "Inert ingredient. A non-issue. No big deal."

Phoebe was quiet, thinking about that. "That could be true," she admitted, albeit reluctantly. "You still have those cookie samples from LankSkop?"

I patted my pack. "Of course."

She wagged her head. "Don't turn them all in to PHANTASM. We'll have one tested independently."

I studied her with crow eyes. "Aren't you being a little paranoid?" I asked, and I should know a little sumpin sumpin about that.

She chuckled humorlessly. "That's how you stay alive, Enoch." Another sincere look at me. "You'll need to trust me on this." Which I did.

"Phoebe, I need to ask you something that's been starting to bother me." This thought and its kin had been creeping into my worried mind for sometime now. Oh, the woe that is me.

"Go on," was all she said. She accelerated around a slow moving truck and whizzed by. Flat and open land. Zero risk for passing out here. Well, unless a herd of wildebeest should happen to dash across the road.

"We had lunch, seems like a decade ago, and you mentioned your mission in China." I was talking very softly, hoping to lead her down the primrose path, as it were. Time to put on my devil's advocate hat and garb.

"That bass turd Tazik Mencius," she clarified, with acerbic venom.

"Yes," I confirmed softly. "You called him that before, several times as I recall." I paused on purpose. "Can you tell me why?"

"Why?" She repeated this like I was an ass for asking. As in SFB. "Because the report said he was involved..." She slowed down and stopped talking, actually swerved the SUV just a bit, then cursed mightily. "The report said he was involved in the drug trade, among other things."

"The PHANTASM report that Hume gave you?" I asked, merely for clarity, though I felt like I knew the answer. She nodded and I made a guess, "But, you never actually saw evidence of drugs at the facility in China."

"We were a little busy defending ourselves from enemy gunfire," she retorted angrily. Hands a little tighter on the steering wheel.

"After you and a group of armed operatives arrived at the complex." I did not state this in an accusatory tone, but merely as a statement of known fact.

"Hume assured us Mencius had invoked a pentacle and summoned an eemee," Phoebe stated resolutely. "The fact that Ruach was there, and helped us, is proof of that."

"Yes, but you didn't then, and still don't now, have proof of why Mencius invoked the pentacle." I was as smooth as silk. Float and sting.

"Then ask Ruach," she said with a sort of logical finality that was hard to refute.

"Dee, what do you know about the Chinese operations of Tazik Mencius?" Seemed like a good place to start.

"All PHANTASM records are classified and I cannot access them." And a good place to end.

"Can you contact Ruach again?" He said call whenever I needed him.

"I can."

⟦ Peculiar Interpretations ⟧

In a few moments Ruach appeared on the ComUnit. "Enoch, how can I help you?" Cucumber cool.

"Can we talk?" Ruach seem confused by my question. "Is your connection completely secure?" I appended.

"Yes, of course," said Ruach in a puzzled tone. "Why do you want to know if the line is secure?" Squishy face.

I guess there are many ways to get from Point A to Point Z. A straight direct line is always the quickest and usually the best. Occam's Razor. Just don't cut yourself. "Can you talk to me about Tazik Mencius?"

There was a brief pause. "What do you want to know?"

I wasn't sure myself. "What sorts of things was he involved in? What was his company doing?"

Ruach smiled, though there was not much humor in it. "You mean, beyond making cookies?" He appeared to be in one of the PHANTASM offices, possibly his own, standing and talking to me.

"I'm just trying to understand how everything fits together." I did not know how else to phrase it. This whole gig was new to me. I felt a little like a drowning guy who just got tossed an asphalt life preserver.

Still, I was treading water like a madman. New boots or not.

Ruach jogged his head in understanding and, I hoped, empathy. "A great deal has happened in a very short period of time." That was obvious and no comment was needed, so I stayed silent. "Denton and I started to explain all of this to you when we first met," Ruach said, alluding to that meeting in Dr. Hume's office that now seemed to have happened in some other lifetime.

"That conversation was never finished," I commented, remembering that I had been carted off for testing and then—kablooey—the roller-coaster ride had started and I was still strapped in. And squalling.

"I will do my best to explain," he began, walked over to a desk and sat in a large leather chair. Well, it looked like leather in the ComUnit display. "Are you sure you want to do this now?"

I glanced at Phoebe, she nodded in the affirmative. I looked back at Ruach on my ComUnit display. "The best time is always now."

Seeing life through the aphorism prism, that was me.

⌂ Chapter Eleven ⌂

He nodded. "Electromagnetic, or EM, energy is a self-propagating wave, but few people really stop to consider what that means." Ruach smiled enigmatically. "They assume the original motion was initiated by some primal first source." He shook his head. "Movement simply is."

"Every living thing on your planet, from simple amoebas up through plants and trees, all the way to humans, must harness EM energy." He smiled. "You utilize the beneficial side-effects of EM energy to survive."

"However, Enoch, it seems that in the last 100 years of human existence the rapid development of technology has changed the way EM energy is used." His face seemed to assume a sad aspect. "Your English word *technology* has an interesting etymology, a fact I gleaned from your website, Enoch." A warm smile.

"I will read from the website." Ever-helpful Dee.

"The word technology is composed of the Greek prefix 'techno-' which is derived from the Greek word 'techne.' It means an art, trade, or skill, but also means that which is shaped by human hands or, by extension, the human mind. The Greek suffix '-logia' is derived from the Greek word 'logos' which can mean speech, reasoning, or word. Perhaps the philosopher Immanuel Kant put it best when he said 'logos' was a 'communicable mental faculty (concept/relation) which allows (hu)man(ity) to strive toward the realization of his (its) highest ends.'"

"Good technology, created correctly," Ruach continued, "incorporates *logos*. The true meaning of that word is reflected in how the person creating the technology succeeds in embedding and implementing that *logos* when the technology is actually utilized."

I think I knew what he meant, so I made a comment. "The same Internet which can talk about the greatest principles of morality and ethics can also show you acts of human behavior which are heinous and bestial."

Ruach nodded his acceptance of that statement. "Your human environment is full of audiovisual EM programming. It is delivered to digital tablets, to smartphones, to computer displays, to televisions, to cars, to boats. Everywhere." He shook his head. "Humans are swimming in an endless sea of EM energy."

Drowning is more like it. Asphalt preserver. The direction I think he was going with this was starting to scare me.

⟦ Peculiar Interpretations ⟧

"Most of the EM energy that is harnessed is done so in a harmless manner." Ruach gave me a plaintive look and shrugged. "You are free to view it, to use it, if you choose, or free to ignore it." He spread his hands in a kind of supplication. "Humans can act on the information conveyed in the EM energy, or not act."

"Unless free will is taken away," I chimed in.

"Taken away or diminished, Enoch, or worse, masked so that the actions that you take are done so in the belief that you are free, when in fact you are under the direct control of the EM energy." His face was a solemn mask.

"That still sounds like propaganda affecting weak minds," I said, recalling that part of the original conversation from Hume's office.

"You will always have some element of human society which cannot think for itself and is easily influenced; but I am talking about intelligent, rational, and supposedly free-minded humans that fall under the thrall of this new form of EM energy." His passion had spilled over into his emotional speech.

"Ruach, I pride myself on being a keen observer of human nature, and though I admit humans can be heavily influenced by audiovisual EM energy, I don't see any global indications that humans are being controlled by evil humans or alien eemees." I mean, humans fall under the spell of dictators and tyrants all the time. Religions and cults often dominate the minds of people. Politicians mesmerize us with their speeches. Companies sell us things we don't really need.

But some kind of evil, organized, plot behind it all? Please.

"I agree, Enoch," he said softly, but his face and tone were sober, almost fearful. "However, the fact that multiple eemees have been summoned and forced to manifest in human form, and are subject to direct human control, should be great cause for a terrible concern."

He swallowed, seem to tremble, though it may have been the way his voice cracked that led me to imagine that. "An eemee, Enoch, is a powerful being. We can use EM energy to directly influence human behavior. We can plant thoughts into people's minds that they will act on because they believe them to be their own." He shook his head. "Try to imagine the horrors a human controller could unleash if they sought to use that power for evil."

☐ Chapter Eleven ☐

"I don't disagree, but you must have proximity to someone to influence them, correct? You have to be physically near them?" I commented, feeling confident I was correct on this point. "I mean, you can't project such control over the digital airwaves, can you?" Like images on television, a smartphone, or a digital tablet or something. That was science fiction.

Ruach nodded and said tentatively, "We are, indeed, limited to a close physical relationship with humans in order to exercise such control." He paused, latent. "At present," he added softly.

That startled me. Big time. Water went up my nose, but I kept treading, feet and legs kicking like crazy. "What do you mean?" Phoebe and I exchanged an anxious glance.

Ruach rubbed a hand across his chin, a very human gesture of anxiety. It was hard to remember he was not actually human. "Ask yourself why there has been all this recent activity." He paused. "Discounting myself, and the eemee Enoch freed"—Ruach smiled broadly and I sheepishly joined him—"there are still three eemees on this planet." A dramatic pause and Ruach added, "And now there is another."

Phoebe jerked the steering wheel. We crossed over the painted median, drew a horn blast from an approaching car and she brought the SUV back into our lane. "What the hell do you mean?" she said in a tense and terse voice.

"I felt it on the day Brody appeared," he explained, "and PHANTASM monitoring recently confirmed that another primary pentacle has been activated." He sighed broadly. "Another eemee is enslaved in this world."

"Where?" That seemed the only thing that mattered right now.

Ruach's shoulders sagged. "We don't know yet."

Phoebe piped in, "What does it mean?"

Ruach straightened, took a breath. "I think the human controllers are working on something that would permit them to extend the power of the eemees." He rubbed his cheek with the back of his hand and went on.

"Tazik Mencius was absolutely ruthless in his pursuit of power. I saw it firsthand when I..." and here Ruach sputtered and took a deep breath, "...when I was forced to influence the behavior of others to his benefit." Ruach shook his head. "A man like Tazik would do anything, Enoch, anything possible, to extend the reach of that power."

Have you ever felt that scary tingle run up your spine? It really does. Every nerve gets set on a bitter edge. "You mean," I asked, "like using some kind of new technology to extend the reach of eemee scans?"

"I do not know, Enoch, but I can sense that there is something malignant, malefic, at work here and I feel powerless to stop it." His head wobbled with emotion and he looked away.

So much for the warm and fuzzies from yesterday's good work at LankSkop. Still, you had to strive to be positive, to stay focused on the good things. Upbeat or get beat.

"Look, Ruach, Phoebe stopped them in China, we stopped them here in South Africa, and we'll do the same in the other places as well." I injected as much affirmative energy in that as I could muster.

Ruach favored me with a warm smile. "If we are to win, Enoch Maarduk, then it will be your doing." He broke the connection and vanished.

"This is not a good development."

"Well, Dee, truth be told, I'm going to do a Scarlett on it." I smiled whimsically, using an old reference to the character from the book and movie *Gone With the Wind*. The fact that it was Phoebe's middle name made it even better.

Phoebe cast me a stellar look, as though she suspected something stupid was about to be spoken by me. I hated to disappoint.

"What does it mean to do a Scarlett?" Good old reliable Dee. Someone has to set you up to toss the punch line.

"I'm going to worry about it tomorrow," and I scooted down in the seat, crossed my arms across my chest and closed my eyes. When it's time to sleep, believe me, I can sleep. Out.

Another sharp elbow to my ribs. I firmly believe she enjoyed that far too much. My eyes snapped open like I had just sat on a black mamba.

We were, once again, in the middle of bum *&^!% nowhere. Parked. We stepped out of the now silent SUV and I surveyed the area. Brush, trees, more brush, and more trees. Splotchy areas with sparse vegetation. No desert. Go figure. "I don't see the super-secret facility you were talking about," I said with a smirk. "It must really be a secret."

"You know, Enoch," Phoebe began, ignoring my witticism with an appropriately snide face, "for a really smart guy, you are truly dumb sometimes." She waved her arms around. "If you could see it, then it wouldn't be a super freaking secret at all, would it?"

Okay, maybe she had an itty-bitty point there that I might be willing to grant. No sense quibbling over mere semantics. Plus, I am not always dumb. "It's underground, isn't it?"

"Good job, Sherlock," she laughed. I tried not to reward her frippery by laughing myself. She went on. "I mean, where else could it be?" Fine, I laughed with her. She unclipped her ComUnit and spoke into it. "We're here."

"Yes, m'am," came an echoed male voice. "We have you on GPS." Brief pause. "Standby."

It was oddly quiet for a few moments and then, about thirty yards away, we started to hear this kind of rumbling, grating, growling, machinery sort of noise. You had the sense that something really big was actually *under* the ground moving around. Very odd feeling.

I can't remember which James Bond movie it was, I think *Dr. No*, but the bad guys had a fake lake in some volcano (I think it was painted on) and the whole thing slid open to reveal a super secret facility underneath. Ridiculously impossible, of course, yet very slick.

Well, apparently the good guys here had a fake set of brush and trees, complete with faux soil and grass, placed on top of a similar hydraulically-powered covering. I say fake brush and trees complete with faux soil and grass because, about thirty yards away, a square-shaped piece of land, maybe 20 feet by 20 feet, began to rise up into the air on immense unfolding metal struts that looked like something from that movie about cars that changed into robots, or whatever.

It was spooky cool. Especially when it began to tilt, not stopping until it was at a 45 degree angle, with the lower edge about 10 feet off the ground.

Not a leaf, twig or scrap of dirt fell off. Awesome. Technology is so great, when it works.

⧇ Peculiar Interpretations ⧇

"You are cleared for entry, Colonel O'Hara," came the ethereal male voice again.

"Colonel O'Hara?" I asked with respect and shock blended nicely into a smooth finish. Like a jalapeño Zinfandel. Erg.

Phoebe shrugged as we were walking toward the opening in the ground. "Ignore it."

Uh-huh. Fine. Okay. No problem. I'll ignore it.

"What branch are you in?" I asked as we neared the opening. I noticed a set of metal stairs, with a railing, that wound downwards.

She never broke stride or even glanced back at me (yes, I was letting her go first) as she answered. "You are a civilian and not bound by any military or governmental authority, so my rank is meaningless to you." Blatherspeak.

As we were about to move onto the first step, I looked down. It was probably about 30 feet or so to the bottom, where it looked like smooth unpainted concrete. There were two people collected at the foot of the stairs. One was in that same plain gray uniform that I had seen at the airfield-that-was-not-an-airfield back in the States. The other was in civilian clothes, but looked like some kind of tech guy. Glasses, digital tablet, plastic name badge, thinning hair, scowl. You know the type. They must have a dress code. Maybe a union thing.

We clanged down the stairwell and were nearing bottom. I glanced off to the left and, perhaps another 90 feet or so in the distance, I saw the silhouette of a craft that looked similar, yet seemed somehow different, from the one that had flown us over here. I wondered if Phoebe's sister, Jackie, was still the pilot.

We reached the bottom.

"Colonel O'Hara, I'm Captain Harper, and this is Dr. Lowell." No handshakes or salutes from Harper. Lowell looked up, nodded, then resumed fidgeting around with his digital tablet.

Phoebe gestured at me, "Enoch Maarduk." She looked at Harper. "What's our status?"

Harper took a breath and handed Phoebe a ComUnit similar to the one she carried, but in a different colored casing. "Colonel Williams wants to talk to you."

Phoebe took the unit. "Mark?" she said in a questioning voice.

◻ Chapter Eleven ◻

Williams' face appeared. "Sorry we had to redirect you to this facility, Phoebe, but we were hoping you could help us out on something."

Phoebe smiled. "Anything within reason."

Williams had a big grin on his face. "I somehow knew you would say that." He cleared his throat. "We had Jackie scheduled for this run, but she got called away on another project." A brief pause. "So, we are looking for a pilot."

I am not sure I had ever seen Phoebe's face light up quite like that. Maybe when she leaped away from that snake and screamed, maybe not. "That is definitely within reason," she said smoothly, doing her best to contain her excitement.

Williams face grew a bit less jovial. "It's one of our new prototypes you'll be flying." I remember Phoebe had teased him about a Mach 5 craft. No way.

Phoebe knew exactly what that meant (I am not a pilot, but the word *flying* in the same sentence with *prototype* seems scary dangerous to me, but for a pilot, it's like tossing red meat to a tigress). Her face went impassive. "But, it has been flown before?"

"Jackie has had it up three times previously, and all spectacular successes," Williams said steadily.

"Then it will be a privilege to fly it," Phoebe said earnestly.

"Jackie said you are the best pilot she's ever seen," Williams added and if I thought Phoebe's face had transformed previously, well, this was something else.

"Jackie said that?" Spoken with awe and incredulity.

"Don't you dare tell her I told you that or she will kick my ass," Williams said jokingly, but I think he was serious. "Now hand the ComUnit back to Harper and get moving."

Which we did. Lowell seemed to have finished whatever he was doing, nodded at Harper, smiled lamely at us, and stalked off toward the craft. Damn techno-geek sociopaths.

Harper gestured at us and turned to go. "Let's get ready to board."

Into the Wild Blue Somewhere Yonder

"A good traveller has no fixed plans, and is not intent on arriving."
—Lao Tzu

I wasn't thrilled about having to, once again, slip on the pressure suit. Oh, it was comfortable enough and fit just fine, but it was kind of, well, a reminder of things that could go horribly and terribly wrong.

That's the way I looked at it. I mean, you wore the pressure suit because if, G_d, Allah, Shiva, or Buddha forbid, you had to eject at high altitude, you probably didn't want to go leaping into sub-zero temps and chest-crushing air pressure without one. A similar mortality rate to being bitten by a black mamba and not having anti-venom. That is to say, 100%.

Oh, and apparently I was going to have the privilege (Captain Harper's word) of sitting up front. The guy from the original trip, Bob, who I thought was a navigator, had actually been a pilot-in-training and was still with Jackie on the other "project."

It didn't matter anyway—Phoebe explained to me as she punched, flipped, dialed, and fingered like two million buttons, switches, and touch screens—the craft almost flies itself. Yeah, right. You really didn't need a human, she continued to explain, because the craft could be flown remotely, but since we needed to get from Point A to Point B with us actually in the craft, I guess the powers-that-be figured Phoebe might as well fly the damn thing. No problemo.

Smoke up the woohoo, if you ask me. But I meekly said "okay" and took my seat.

You know, sitting in the front with the really cool view.

Hmm. I am sure you recall the whole "being up front and flying" thing I ragged on earlier when Phoebe was landing the LM. Well, that was in a craft that started out, when detached, at about 1000 mph and quickly dropped to about 200 mph. Shoot, we landed at just over a 100 mph. I drive faster than that sometimes.

Now, we were starting at zero and escalating (really quickly) to about 3800 mph plus. With a bird's eye view, which, as Phoebe explained, was actually an Enhanced High Definition screen wrapped around the front. Not really a cockpit window at all. Same damn effect on your mind, though. And stomach. Virtual reality, my ass.

And, yes, you are right, I had commented earlier on how much fun the LM detachment ride had been; but let's be perfectly clear here. That was FALLING. With the whole thing being kind of weightless goofy and getting jostled around a little.

This was RISING. With a locomotive rammed into your chest and a NFL lineman squatting unpleasantly on your face. That ain't the same, comprende?

However, I didn't have much time to hash out the details between the two events because, after working her way through the pre-flight checklist blah, blah, blah, we were already starting to tilt at the launch angle. Gawd, I missed that mouthpiece.

And then, WHAM, off into the wild blue yonder. Fug.

You know, some things get better with time. Wine. Cheese. Bad jokes. Your own cooking.

Some things, though, will suck no matter how many times you experience them. Like standing in line for your driver's license renewal. Paying your property taxes. Listening to the police officer politely explain why he, or she, stopped your vehicle.

Being launched into the air from some freaking EM secret agent BS device gun generator thing is at the top of my list of things that do not get better with time. I am not ashamed to say, I ralphed. Called buffaloes. Blew beets. Spoke in tongues. Did the yak-a-doodle-do.

Fortunately, Phoebe saw it about to happen (probably the pale sallow color of my face gave it away) and managed to get the appropriate air sickness barf-o-matic bag into my shaking hands at just about the right time. "Just about" being the key concept to bear in mind here.

Only a few smallish chunks went flying onto the Enhanced High Definition display. Hey, effing 3D effects, okay?

⊡ Into the Wild Blue Somewhere Yonder ⊡

Eventually, like hours later (okay, maybe minutes) we leveled out and I felt mucho better. Even managed to clean up my mess on the display. And the little bit that might have found its way onto the fancy controls, which prompted Colonel O'Hara to laughingly remark, "I knew those controls were rust- and water-resistant; now I'll have to tell Williams we found them to be puke-resistant as well."

"Black mamba," was all I said in a zinging rejoinder.

She scowled. "You're going to milk that for as long as possible, aren't you?"

"Until you puke," I replied, tossing the last nasty towelette into the trash container.

"Funny," she said and turned away, probably to hide a smile.

I sat there thinking about doing some work. I had reports still to check, maybe get back to Tom and Armando, update Hume, have that talk with Dee… but somewhere in my ruminations about how much work I needed to do, I did what I seemed to have a natural and unerring ability to do.

I drifted off to sleep.

It wasn't a sharp elbow to the ribs this time. It was a rather painful pinch to the soft flesh under my left arm. I squealed like a baby who was being forced to eat creamed peas. "Damn it, Phoebe, can't you just ask me to wake up?"

"My gawd, Enoch, you can go to sleep at the drop of a damn hat," she shook her head in jealous admiration, "and you sleep like a dead man."

"I don't snore," I said matter-of-factly, though this was a pitiful defense.

"Hah! How would you know? You're freaking asleep." She seemed to have made an irrefutable point of breathtaking simplicity, but fortunately, I was up to the challenge.

"Dee," I said loudly, "do I snore?"

"A snore is defined as the vibratory sound generated by a constricted human air passage during respiration, while sleeping."

"I know the definition, but do I snore while sleeping?" I was certain I didn't.

☐ Chapter Twelve ☐

And then, wafting through the cockpit audio, which made it very loud and very clear, came the sound of snoring. Some serious snoring.

"This ComUnit has a very sophisticated recording function."

Of my snoring, apparently.

Phoebe starting howling and crying with laughter. Literally.

It was nice to hear. "Well, at least I don't pass gas."

"This ComUnit has a very sophisticated recording function."

"Oh for the love of…" and then I couldn't help it either and started laughing. And then Dee joined in. Phoebe was wiping her eyes with her sleeve. Very funny, indeed. The terrible tension of recent events had to be eased, and if it took a few fart jokes, well, that was fine with me. Besides, I'm thinking maybe I have a fart fetish or something.

Phoebe started to regain her composure. "We should be entering landing mode in about 30 minutes and be on the ground shortly after that." More clicking, twirling, fingering, pushing of controls. "Assuming we don't run out of gas..." And that started the whole yuck-yuck thing up again, though it was mostly Dee and Phoebe laughing like idiots this time.

"Dee, if you have time, in between bursts of uncontrollable hilarity, please display anything Tom may have uploaded on the Iranian operation." I said this in a kidding manner, glad all of us were able to finally laugh a little.

"Yes, Enoch." A very brief pause. **"Tom uploaded this six hours ago."** Text appeared on the ComUnit.

"Would you like me to summarize?"

"Nah, I'll just read it myself." Act like a sloth and you become one.

"Okay, Enoch, let me know if there is anything else you need."

"There is one thing," I said with a grin, winking at Phoebe. "Erase those recordings."

"Yes, right after I archive them for posterity." Phobe and I laughed.

I started reading the report. Mando had cracked an Iranian server. And the company, Alifmimra, didn't exactly sell shoes. They sold shoe inserts. And here was where it started to get a little creepy. The inserts were called ENRG-4-FEET, well, that was the English translation, and the tingle up the spine part started when I read a little blurb about what these inserts were supposed to do.

◻ Into the Wild Blue Somewhere Yonder ◻

They were made of a unique material that allowed the foot to absorb the contents of the insert, and those contents were a special, secret, herb-vitamin blend designed to give you "energy, stamina, and mental clarity."

In other words, eerily similar to the claims for the Argentinean supplement, supposedly harmless, and the cookies from South Africa, as of yet untested. What the hell was going on here?

~Dee.~ I was definitely wearing my happy face and trying to be nice.

~Yes, Enoch?~

~Where are the Iranians selling their product?~ Sweetness. Honey, not vinegar.

A few moments went by. **~It appears that the first production run was very recent and the product has not yet shipped.~** A brief pause. **~Please keep in mind that data for this area is sometimes difficult to gather and to verify.~**

~But you can't find evidence that their product, ENRG-4-FEET, has hit the global market yet?~

~That is correct.~

This was interesting. The Argentinean product was already in distribution globally. The Chinese facility had almost been ready to ship when the complex, and the ready-to-ship product, had been destroyed. The Iranian operation was about to ship their product. Phoebe and I had killed the human controller and freed the eemee for the South African operation, but the production facility was still intact, although, according to PHANTASM research, they had not yet shipped any product to market.

And, oh yeah, Nykr had apparently made a nice chunk of change selling water.

And, so far, all those products appeared to be harmless, which just didn't make sense to me. I mean, let me see if I have this straight, okay?

Someone goes to a boatload of trouble to construct an elaborate pentacle; summons a powerful eemee from the EM spectrum; creates a sophisticated manufacturing facility to produce a product; puts armed guards everywhere—and this is done just to make some money selling energy cookies, bottled water, shoe inserts, and herb supplements? I'm not interested in ocean-front property in Iowa, okay?

I was missing something here, no doubt, but damned if I knew what it is. But I would.

~What's the current status of Nykr?~ That was the bottled water company in Iceland. They seemed the farthest along in terms of production and shipping. Probably because they had the simplest product—water.

~Based on the latest PHANTASM update I am aware of, you and Phoebe are scheduled for insertion into Iceland within the week.~

I nodded, a little surprised, but pleased. Get to see up close and personal what they were doing over there. Maybe start to grasp a bigger picture. I glanced over at Phoebe when my eye caught some movement. She was fiddling around with a compartment to the right of her seat. In a moment she produced two plastic bottles of suitably cool iced tea. I caught her eye and said, "So, what do you think all this crap is about?"

Pursed lips and mini-frown. "Until you started digging around, I never gave it much thought." She took a sip of tea and continued. "Here was my job, before you came along." Jaundiced eye. "I would get a report telling me that this or that guy was a really bad guy, and I would go visit this or that really bad guy." Phoebe was a little scary when she talked this way. I'm pretty sure "visit" was an unpleasant euphemism.

"I figure the people in authority had good reasons for sending us out in harm's way." She shrugged. "If Ruach thinks there's something odd going on, then I believe him." She smiled. "But, I would damn sure like to know exactly what we're up against."

I had to agree with that. "Dee said we were supposed to be checking out the Iceland operation next."

Phoebe gave me a wicked grin and said purposefully loud, "Dee is talking a little out of school, I think."

"Was that information classified?" Dee's voice sounded innocent, maybe even bemused.

Phoebe smiled, "Not any more." Even I chuckled at that one. Phoebe looked at me as she played with the cap of her tea bottle. "Yeah,

Iceland is up next, same drill." Long gaze this time. "Except the *getting captured and being tortured in cold water* part."

I shivered at the memory. "I'm good with that plan, but what about Alifmimra in Iran?"

Phoebe craned her neck. "What do you have on that, Dee?"

"It looks as though another PHANTASM team is already working on that."

Phoebe straightened in her chair. "There is no other team, not with Brody gone." Big time scowl. "Who is heading up that team?"

"I cannot access that information."

"Maybe we should ask Hume about that," I suggested. "I'm sure there's a logical explanation."

Phoebe nodded. "Well, we've already got enough to deal with now." She still didn't seem happy about the Iran thing, though. "We'll be landing soon and I'll ask him when we get back to PHANTASM." That pretty much concluded the conversation portion of the program.

The landing, the transfer to the SUV (with Jimmy driving), and the return to PHANTASM was quiet and uneventful. Which, since it involved supersonic planes, an armored SUV, and late afternoon city traffic, was actually quite impressive.

Jimmy drove into an underground parking area that I did not know existed. More peculiar still, he entered it by driving into a garage attached to a pleasant middle-class house located on the other side of the fence that ran behind the PHANTASM building.

The garage door of that house closed behind us, and we started to move downwards. The garage floor was not actually the floor, but a huge hydraulic lift.

As we were slowly descending, apparently both Phoebe and I were thinking about the same thing—a nice hot, long, shower or bath. She mentioned it and I concurred. We didn't drop all that far when the lift stopped and Jimmy drove off into a massive parking area.

Tom's question about Black Ops did pop into my thoughts.

We exited the vehicle, made about a twenty-foot walk to the side of the building, and entered the elevator.

☐ Chapter Twelve ☐

It took off down, fast, stopped, and as soon as the doors opened, we were greeted by Hume.

"I just wanted to be the first to congratulate you on an exceptional job," he said warmly and shook each of our hands, grasping both of his around ours and pumping like a mad politician. "Ruach and I were worried sick about sending you out in the field, Enoch"—and here he glanced at Phoebe—"but I knew you would be in capable hands."

"Well, sir," I commented lightly, "I wouldn't be here without Phoebe." Which was true. She had flown the plane. I think she actually knew I was thinking that, or at least suspected it, and gave me a quick, rather scouring, glance.

Hume went on. "I want you two to get cleaned up, relax, and then come to my office—say around five—just to visit for a few minutes; kind of a mini-debriefing." He laughed. "And then you can go have a well-deserved dinner and relax." He grinned. "An excellent job!" He smiled triumphantly, doing a fist pump, and I had to laugh to myself. "Anyway, on your way and I'll see you at five." He turned and walked off.

Phoebe and I watched him disappear around a corner. "He's never done that before," she said musingly, a bit taken aback by the whole episode. She was still staring benignly in the direction Hume had gone.

"The handshake thing or the fist pump thing?" I asked jokingly.

Scowl. "This is getting more and more bizarre." She shrugged. "I'm going to get a glass of wine, lounge in the hot bath for an hour, and perhaps be on time for this meeting."

"I could come over to your quarters, you know, to help make sure you get out of the tub on time," I said with the sweetest, most angelic, expression I could muster.

"I keep my automatic handy," she said with an equally sweet smile. "Be sure to make lots of noise when you come into the room."

I wisely let that opportunity pass and nodded. "See you at five."

She walked off to the left and I unclipped my ComUnit, because I had no fricking idea where I was at.

Fortunately, Dee did, and less than 10 minutes later I was melting off a layer of skin with a hot shower that my old girlfriend would have envied, sucking on a cold beer (having cleverly stashed a few of its brethren in a bucket of ice outside the shower) trying to, at least temporarily, clear my head and think of nothing.

Not as hard as you might not imagine.

Refreshed and vital again, bathroom mirror completely fogged over (except for one small cleared area), I felt ready to kick some butt, or at least have a nice dinner at Vitellos.

"Phoebe is calling." Dee said this as I was finishing up shaving, using that one small cleared area on the mirror to examine myself. Not a drop of blood spilled yet, which had to be a record. My ComUnit was on the counter next to the sink, but I couldn't see the display.

"Phoebe," I said warmly, working on the prickly whiskers on my knobby chin. "How can I help you?"

"I want you to take me to dinner," she said and I nicked myself as my hand jerked. "I want to go to Vitellos and I want to meet Tom and Armando. To thank them personally."

I was dabbing at the blood with some tissue. "Anything else?" I swear, I was working hard to keep the cynicism out of my tone.

"Yes, bring a cookie," she added, which I knew to mean one of South African cookies.

"That's a good idea," I said a bit begrudgingly.

"Yes," Phoebe replied, "that's why I thought of it."

Aggravating woman, but have I mentioned she is very good-looking? "I'll be at Hume's office in about 15 minutes," I advised as I splashed on aftershave. "See you then." The ComUnit clicked, indicating that Phoebe had broke the connection. I told Dee to call Vitellos and then call Tom and Armando. Make reservations for four people at seven o'clock.

Aargh. I wondered how that would go.

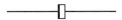

I had not spent much time at PHANTASM, but in the little time available, I had used Dee and her maps and schematics to guide me around the places I had to find, and the places I might need to locate. The gym, the cafeteria, my quarters, etc. The complex itself was comprised of four levels. Uppermost were the shell offices and meeting rooms. Processing and holding areas for dealing with clients, operatives, and the like. Shipping and receiving. Joe and his mad vid bank were there as well.

Level 2 was kind of like tech support, with testing areas, labs, and all that white coat stuff.

Level 3 was the cafeteria, the gym, the quarters for appropriate staff and operatives, and everything needed to support these things (e.g., laundry, maintenance, food storage, et cetera). A few other labs, mostly restricted ones, were also on Level 3.

Level 4 was where they kept the heavy equipment—the super-computers, if you will. Tech support might be located at Level 2, but what they supported was at Level 4. All of the executive offices were also on this level, along with the support and logistics needed for that. According to Dee, there were a few more highly secure testing areas on this level as well.

I only mention all of this because I was kind of tickled that I was getting pretty good at moving from Point A to Point B without asking Dee for directions. Yes, the elevators were connected to all four areas, but you still had to move through a labyrinthal maze of corridors, hallways, rooms, and passages to get anywhere.

Hah, I actually used the word *labyrinthal* in a complete sentence! My old high school English teacher would be so proud of me. The one that asked the class for a short poem and then graded my submission, "Ice is nice," by commenting, "My retort is short–D." Bee atch.

As I moved on down the last weaving hallway toward Hume's office, I felt good, quite pleased with myself.

"Damn good work there in South Africa, if I do say so myself." I said so myself, mostly because I couldn't help it.

"A journey of a thousand miles begins with a single footstep," Dee intoned in her best guru-inspired tones.

"That's pretty good advice coming from someone without feet," I commented in a joking manner.

"How many meters in a mile?" We both laughed aloud at that.

I entered Hume's office. Deandra was at her desk, surrounded by a mountain of flash drives and a varied assortment of other types of digital equipment, absorbed in organizing them, I guess.

⛶ Into the Wild Blue Somewhere Yonder ⛶

Did not look like fun. Nonetheless, she glanced up with a big smile as I walked in. "Enoch!" She came over and I got a big hug.

"Wow, I need to go out of town more often," I said with a grin.

"Phoebe told me all about the snake," she said emotively and squeezed my arm. "That was so brave."

"It was a lucky shot," I replied humbly.

"That's what she said," Deandra replied softly as she walked back to her desk. Women. "But, you didn't freeze up. You tried to be lucky, and you were." A big smile from her. "It's funny how that works."

I nodded. It's funny how women work. "So, Phoebe is here already?" Is the sky blue?

Deandra nodded, "She's always on time." Hey, I was at least two minutes early. Isn't that on time? Geez. "Go on in, they're expecting you." So, in I went.

Hume was behind his desk, looking at ease in that big old comfortable chair. Ruach was to his right, sitting in one of those ancient British wooden chairs. Phoebe was ensconced on a quasi-couch half-chair looking thing that seemed plush and cushy. I did not recall it from my previous visit. Hume and Ruach stood up and we shook hands. Phoebe waved. I took a seat next to her on another one of the British chairs, thankfully with a soft plump pad for a seat.

"Sorry I'm late," I said, though it was exactly 5:00 right now. I had sneaked a peek at the ComUnit display.

Hume laughed. "On time to Phoebe means fifteen minutes early." Even she chuckled at that one.

Ruach said softly, "I am just pleased we are all together, once again." It was silent for a moment as everyone sort of wrapped around that.

Hume stepped into the quiet. "I've put together the various bits and pieces from the reports you both sent, plus some added details from Phoebe just now." He nodded, looked at Ruach, then back to Phoebe and I. "A quick summation would be that the human controller is dead, the primary pentacle destroyed, and the eemee freed back to the spectrum." He was smiling broadly as he finished.

"A great deal more," Ruach said with honest feeling, "than we had ever hoped for."

⬚ Chapter Twelve ⬚

I was not smiling. "Yes, but the facility is still intact and there was lots of product waiting to be shipped out."

Hume's friendly smile morphed into an egregious frown. "Cookies?" This was said with a mildly disdainful disbelief. "I don't think we face much of a threat from that."

"Fine," I said a bit testily, "but I think we ought to wait until the lab finishes examining those cookies before we make that judgment." Two white-smocked guys had already come by my quarters and picked up the cookie samples.

Well, not counting the one wrapped in plastic and sitting in the inner pocket of my black leather jacket.

Hume's countenance softened quickly. "I agree completely." He seemed contrite. "I guess I'm just hopeful they will turn out to be nothing, just like the Argentinean supplement."

I glanced at Phoebe, but it was clear she was not going to say anything. Her eyebrows did, though, notch up a fraction. I then looked at Ruach, just so no one would read anything into my eye contact with Phoebe. Paranoia, can't ignore yah. "How confident are we in the lab results for the Argentinean supplement sample?" Might as well toss that hand grenade out and see how much damage it does.

Ruach was the one who spoke. "Why would you ask that?" A bit of confusion tainting his voice.

I rubbed the bottom of my chin with the knuckle of my left index finger, then flipped my hand open, gesturing at Ruach. "Well, I've never actually seen the written report."

Hume ran his fingers across his touch screen desk, moving around like a piano player, then glanced at me. "Your ComUnit should have it now," he stated. With what I thought was a hint of petulance, although sometimes I just think too damn much. I unclipped my ComUnit and silently told Dee to show me the report.

Phoebe moved in to buy me some time. "What about Iceland? When do Enoch and I leave?"

Okay, I am now going to try and convey the difficult multi-tasking aspect of what is happening, because I'm reading the report, looking for the part about the peptide alkaloid, listening to Dee comment on the report, waiting for Hume's response, and thinking about a nap. And my hungry stomach is rumbling like the citizens of some financially unstable country when taxes get raised.

All of which was putting a serious strain on my somewhat limited multi-tasking mojo. Kind of a no go on the mojo, as it where.

"We have another team already on site in Iceland," Hume said without any emotion.

"And a team in Iran? Where are you getting all these people?" Phoebe asked with a hint of anger in her voice. I think she wanted to bite her tongue immediately after the words left her mouth.

Hume scowled at her. "How do you know about that?" Think classified documents. Eyes only and all that.

We all know that a good offense is the best defense. Nuke 'em if you got 'em. "If Enoch and I are so valuable, then why aren't we involved in those missions?" This was not said by Phoebe with any irritation at all; but cool, calm, detached. Refute me if you can.

Which meant Phoebe was really hacked off. I had not known her long, but I knew that for a fact. The angrier she got on the inside, the calmer she was on the outside. You were only in real trouble if she smiled.

Ruach was giving Hume a hard stare that the latter seemed to sense and turned to face. Ruach spoke, "Denton, can you clarify these events?"

And while all this was going on, I came across the reference to the peptide alkaloid in the PHANTASM report. The lab guys did see it, noted it carefully, even tested it on lab animals, with no adverse effects at all. No effects, in fact. None at all. Null and void. So—I supposed to my own bad self—that's why Hume felt like it was no big deal. I still intended to press him on it later.

Hume was responding to Ruach now, starting with a deep breath, then looked over at Phoebe and me, then back to Ruach. He let the breath out, long and noisy. "I have to make decisions. Hard decisions." Again he looked at Phoebe, seeking some sympathy, if I was reading his expression correctly. "The best operative I have is out in the field with my newest operative."

He looked with great implication at me. "A new operative with unquestionable, incredibly valuable, yet untested, skills."

☐ Chapter Twelve ☐

Ruach's expression softened just a little. I sensed Phoebe settle back slightly in her chair. I was watching Hume carefully. He went on. "Things are happening very fast right now. We are still not sure if they are all related, but if they are, then time is of the absolute essence."

He gestured with his hand to emphasize the point and looked earnestly at Phoebe. "As much as I always want my best people out in the field"—he paused and frowned—"sometimes you have to move forward with what you have." He pursed his lips. "We are blind and need information, and we need it yesterday." He lightly tapped his desktop with his index finger.

Hume was getting a little worked up now and, as he explained these things, I guess I didn't blame him. "There is something bad, perhaps monstrously bad, underway in the world." He looked at Ruach. "You feel it; you know it, don't you?" Ruach nodded slowly, an increasingly frightened expression on his face.

Hume turned back to appraise Phoebe and me. "You two are the best weapons we have in the upcoming fight. The absolute best." He coughed, gesticulated at us. "I almost lost you in South Africa, and now you want me to just toss you out into an unknown and potentially deadly area?"

He looked at our somber, yet determined, faces and he couldn't help but smile. He shook his head and waved a hand, palm down. "Look, the Iranian mission is firmly underway and apparently well in hand." He sighed loudly. "I probably could use you in Iceland." Phoebe smiled at that. Hume shook his head, exhaled lightly. "Against my better judgment, but you'll leave in two days. Thursday morning."

Hume seemed to know what I was going to ask next as he quickly added, "I'll send you the latest Iran update." He immediately did the Mozart thing to his touch screen. Dee told me she was looking the report over.

"What about Brody's message?" I felt like we had a few things to go over on that subject and now seemed as good a time as any. "Are your people making any progress on that?"

Hume grunted. "Probably about the same as you, Enoch." He touched some screens and on the far wall a brilliant clear display of text appeared, just as it had before. It was an excerpt from the supplement report. The words "peptide alkaloid" were highlighted in yellow. Below that was Brody's message.

gaia penta peptode 12 12 12 -12(7) demonhunter ctr?

Hume seemed irritated. "We thought at first there might be a link between *peptode* in the message, which could be a misspelling of 'peptide,' and the fact the Argentinean supplement uses a peptide alkaloid, except the laboratory test results indicate it is completely inert." He shook his head. "Why would Brody want to tell us about an ingredient that doesn't do anything?"

He snorted softly. "Either a red herring, a coincidence, or"—he paused for good effect and looked at all of us—"we're missing something." His expression was a nice blend of irritation and anxiety.

I had to say what was on my mind. "Isn't it curious that the Iranian shoe inserts, the South African cookies, and the Argentinean supplement all seem to be advertising themselves as energy boosting aids?" Seemed like a reasonable question to me. One that demanded a reasonable response.

Ruach looked at me, then at Hume. Hume nodded affirmatively, then shook his head. "The only problem, Enoch, is that energy drinks and such are one of the largest and fastest growing segments of the market." He ran his fingers along the surface of his desk. "The market is expected to exceed $20 billion dollars by next year." He said the number slowly and loudly, and then he shrugged. "You can do a lot of bad things with money generated from legitimate businesses." Think drug cartels. A very reasonable response and hard to disparage.

Indeed, it was a brutal and non-disparaged fact, the more I considered it, and I will honestly have to tell you it gave me a big time moment of cerebral pause. As I have mentioned previously, I am something of an energy drink connoisseur and I know there has been, in the last few years, a veritable and prodigious explosion of such drinks at the store. An entire freaking aisle full of choices running the gamut from frills to no frills, from obtuse to obvious. Big frigging money in that arena, no doubt.

Could this all be just about money? I guess when you are talking billions, it's not just money, it's MONEY. That kind of coin is power, lots of it. But, some things still bothered me. Skullduggery bugged.

☐ Chapter Twelve ☐

"So, are you telling me that Phoebe and I went into South Africa—where people died, where we almost died—just to stop someone from making a few bucks selling cookies?" I laughed, kind of nasty-like, then looked at Ruach. "Is that it?"

Hume was vexed, no doubt. "Let me see now." He arched his neck, started counting with his fingers. "Armed guards that shot at you; elaborate security system that took expert hackers to break; some kind of cold-soak torture setup; a controller that threatened to kill you and Phoebe." He smiled grimly. "Yeah, they were just selling cookies." Laced with about as much cynicism as possible. Ouch.

Yes, I had been slapped down pretty good. Bad dog, bad.

Ruach started talking. "We do not know why these things are happening, Enoch, but there is definitely something evil here, even if it is difficult to see." His smile was equally grim. "We hope the same determination you are showing, with your questions, will lead to an answer." His smile was much warmer.

Hume continued the thought. "I don't know the damn link between these things. Our IT guys, the lab guys, operatives in the field, even your friends Tom and Armando, are all puzzling over this." Another scowl, then a partial sigh. "Something will turn up. It has to." That last bit had more desperation in it, maybe, than he intended.

Hume then brightened. "Let me ease your mind though, Enoch, on one point you raised earlier." He glanced at his desktop after a few touches here and there. "Just after you cleared South African airspace, an air strike was ordered on the coordinates of LankSkop."

"They won't be shipping cookies out anytime soon." There was that grim smile again, after he said this.

He stood up, so did Ruach. "Tomorrow we'll brief you on the Iceland mission." He looked at me. "I sent the Iranian report to you. Read it." He looked at Phoebe, then back at me. "Now get out of here and go have some fun. Relax." Ruach simply smiled.

I said thanks, mollified, but reenergized, and we were out the door.

We were on the elevator headed back to Level 3. Phoebe needed to change clothes. For the Hume meeting she had been wearing some nice brown slacks, a very pleasing white blouse, and low-heeled boots. Her hair was fine. She was fine. She could make sack cloth look good. But, apparently, not nearly fine enough for Vitellos.

"I'm wearing blue jeans and a simple collared shirt," I pleaded, waving at my attire. "You don't have to get dressed up."

"Look," Phoebe said patiently as we stepped off the elevator, "you go to Vitellos all the time, you know the owner." She made little jerky, wavy, motions with both hands, like she was awed by me. Her mouth formed the word *oooh* but she never said it. "Good for you, but this is my first time there and I want to look nice."

"You look great!" I exclaimed.

"Men are such idiots," she exclaimed without hostility (latent, anyway) and opened the door to her quarters. "Have Dee call Jimmy and tell him to meet us out front with the car around 7:00." Slam.

"It's an SUV!" I yelled through the door. Not a car. 7:00? That was over 30 minutes from now. My gawd, that much time, just to change clothes? Growl.

I really didn't want to go outside and sit on the doorstep twiddling my thumbs for 30 minutes. So, I decided to stop by and visit Joe, the idiot savant video watcher, whose video cave was on Level 1. There was a relatively minor issue—I had no clue on how to find the room. Dee had a map to display for me (of course) and, with a few gentle prods, I found the doorway and entered the area.

A visit with Joe might be useful. Maybe pick his brain or, well, just blow 30 minutes watching videos until it was time to meet Phoebe. Wouldn't be the first time, nor the last. For both, I hoped. Hah.

The walls all lined with monitors was still a stunning panorama.

The first time I had passed through here, last Sunday, I had been in a kind of shocked stupor about PHANTASM and, well, everything. I had seen the room, but it had never really registered fully in my mind. I remember physics in high school being a lot like that.

This place was oozing high-tech awesomeness. Yeah, I know a grown man should not use the word "awesome" in any kind of sentence but, damn, it was awesome.

Four rows of fifteen displays. And I need to be utterly clear here. I'm not talking about some skimpy little wimp monitor, I'm talking,

⬚ Chapter Twelve ⬚

I don't know, big enhanced high definition displays on a very long curved wall, attached to a metal display system that formed itself into a kind of an arc, with Joe located right in the center with his desk and elaborate controls.

And a big momma display right in the center, onto which he could switch any one particular bit of information that caught his eye. Or, as he was doing now, splitting the display into large multiple segments and eyeballing all of them, seemingly simultaneously.

"Enoch!" Joe said as he noticed me walking toward him. I had entered the room pretty quietly, and he was wearing a headset, so at first he had not been aware of my presence. "What a pleasure," he took the headset off. "How can I help you?"

"Truthfully, Joe," I began as we shook hands—good, solid, grip— "I'm supposed to meet Phoebe in about 30 minutes. I just wanted a closer look at what you do." I paused—I admit, for dramatic effect— "Maybe ask a few questions."

"Ask anything," Joe said warmly. He had a power drink on his desk. Kindred spirits, in more ways than two.

"Well, have you seen anything coming out of the North West Province of South Africa?" I was just curious. Meow. Whack.

"Yes, actually there was something recently." He started working on his desktop touch screen, but his hands moved so fast it was impossible to follow. "Ah, here it is, up on the big screen"—and there was a South African newswoman talking about an explosion at a remote manufacturing facility. Love that accent.

It was grainy footage, shot at night or early morning, of a large burning building. I could barely discern, through the dense smoke billowing out of the burning structure, some out-of-focus letters on the building. LankSkop. No mention of an air strike, but that didn't surprise me.

"How about anything on a company named Cambio S.A., located in northern Argentina?" You can't hit the board if you don't throw the dart. Well, later in the night it becomes more difficult (not sure what ales me). Sorry.

"That means *change* in Spanish," he commented off-handedly while he entered the name into his database retrieval system. "Couple of fluff

PR pieces," he hummed to himself, reviewing the results, made some more noises. "I do have this," and up popped another newswoman, this time in Miami. The fire. Basically, a ship had unloaded its shipment, which had been moved to a warehouse, and then it burned down. Nothing else.

"How about Alifmimra?" Simple smile from me. "It's an Iranian company, if that helps," I added, trying to be helpful.

"A peculiar name," Joe commented as he entered it into the database.

"How so?" I asked, hopeful of having the veil of my ignorance lifted. It wouldn't take much.

"The Islamic holy book, the *Koran*, is comprised of verses known as surahs," Joe began and I nodded because he had not lost me, yet. "And some of the surahs begin with letters, spelled out alliteratively." Now, he lost me. "There are fourteen such letters, and *alif, mim*, and *ra* are part of those fourteen." He hummed again. "That particular combination, as in *alifmimra*, does not occur, however."

"What do the letters mean?" Have to mean something, right?

Joe shrugged, "No one really knows." I blew out a ragged gust of air. "Ah, here it is," he said with a flourish and turned to look at me. "This just appeared on the server earlier today."

An ultra high resolution video began streaming onto the big screen. It was a commercial for the shoe inserts, and it was very good. Quite an elaborate production number. Very professional and well-structured. Slick and interesting. Kind of like a BioPatch for your feet. That made perfect sense. I wouldn't mind trying those inserts. They looked like they worked great. They would be very useful in the field. I wondered where I could get a pair.

Hey, I caught myself; what's going on here? The commercial had ended.

"Joe, can you play it again?" Man, that whole sequence had been muy weird. Left me scratching my, er, head.

"Sure," Joe agreed. Then said absently, "That was pretty interesting. I'm going to have to get me some of those." That sort of spooked me, especially as I watched the commercial again.

It was simply a man walking down a street in a city setting, like a downtown area. No other people were in sight, though. No traffic. No

❑ Chapter Twelve ❑

sound but the man's perfectly spaced and dramatically timed footfalls accompanied by his rhythmic breathing. A narrator, a woman, began speaking in excellent, immaculately clear, American English, with just the barest, faintest, hint of what I thought to be a Middle Eastern accent. I listened carefully to this narrator. Her pace and the word choice were very hypnotic, with mesmerizing tonal quality, keenly balanced in pitch and timbre. No doubt digitally enhanced.

She continually extolled the virtues of the inserts. How incredibly vital and alive they made you feel. Et cetera. Standard stuff, yet different in a way I couldn't quite discern, but really bugged the woolly woodoo out of me. Like an itch in the middle of your back you can't quite reach.

Near the end of the commercial, the walking man stopped and turned to the camera. He spoke briefly, expressing how he felt about the inserts. I actually stepped around Joe's desk to get a better look at the man's facial expression.

That, too, had been modified or enhanced with digital effects, very subtle, and it also bothered me big time, but I couldn't quite put my mental finger on it. "Can you rewind it, just to the point before the walking man starts talking?" I asked Joe.

There was something there, but I just couldn't figure it out.

"Done," he said and a moment later the scene was unfolding from that point.

"Can you zoom onto his face?" I asked with humble supplication. An acolyte's anguished need.

The image on the big screen was paused. "Hold on while I change a few prefs and make allowances for pixelization."

I guess Joe was going to sprinkle a little pixel dust on it and go from there. Erg.

He fiddled around with more controls. "I sure liked those shoe inserts," he mused aloud. "There we go," he said lightly.

Walking Man's face dominated the big screen. Joe had resampled the pixels so the enlargement would still hold good resolution. He started the video. It was the eyes, I decided, which obviously made sense. Windows to the soul and all. There was something oddly familiar about them, but the face was meaningless to me. "Joe, can you upload that commercial to my ComUnit?"

⬡ Into the Wild Blue Somewhere Yonder ⬡

"Absolutely," he said and the big screen flashed, replaced by four quadrants showing scenes from all over the world. "The transfer will take"—he paused and grinned—"about that long." He gestured at my ComUnit. "You've got it."

"Thanks," I said in appreciation, pensive in my thoughts. I had that mind-gnawing feeling you get right after you've left the house headed for work and then start thinking about the oven you may have left on. A worrisome nagging doubt.

I was mighty curious about the lingering power of the commercial. "Say, Joe, you still going to get a set of those shoe inserts?" I asked jokingly, though deadly serious in my own mind.

Joe seemed to be considering the question. "You know, when I was watching the commercial, and just afterwards, I really wanted them bad." He gave me tilted half-smile. "Now, well, it doesn't seem as important." Joe looked at me in earnest. "Kind of odd, right?"

Kind of odd, yes, but I said nothing more on that topic. "Last video I'd like you to check is Nykr Corporation, out of Iceland. See what you have on them," I said and then I focused on Dee. ⁓Dee, I want you to look at the video that Joe just uploaded and analyze the walking man's eyes.⁓

~Analyze them for what?~

⁓Well, compare them to any images in, uh, your, you know, video repository database.⁓ That sounded official, right?

~This may take some time, I will advise.~ She sounded snippy.

⁓Thank you, Dee.⁓ Be polite in all things, especially if you want something done.

I heard Joe talking. "Can't find much of anything on Nykr; must be a really new company." His fingers were a blur flashing across the touch screen top. "That's strange." My ears perked up. The word *strange* is one of the buzz words any researcher looks for in the incredible flotsam and jetsam of digital data available. Just be careful when you find it!

"Strange how?" I repeated, mostly out of bad habit. Ask and ye shall get pithed.

"Well, there was a video in the database, just added yesterday afternoon, but now it's been scrubbed." Joe was frowning. I assumed *scrubbed* meant deleted.

ꕥ Chapter Twelve ꕥ

So I said it. "You mean deleted?"

Joe glanced at me with concern in his eyes. "Not just deleted; scrubbed. All traces removed." Remember that shiver up the spine thing?

"Is there a copy, a backup?" I'm sure they had to archive their material.

There was a blur of movement, and then Joe shook his head. "Crap," was all he said after a few moments, and I'm pretty sure that was bad. "We run multiple RAID drives for simultaneous storage, as well as backup." He shook his head. "But that video has been wiped on all of them." Scowling now. "Man, that's not good."

You can imagine that, by this time, I want to let fly a maddening howl, but I am patient. Not really, but I claim to be. Joe continued in softer tones. "Looks like whoever did this was waiting until just moments before the automated archive kicked in."

He looked up from the desktop to study me. "We run an archive on all tagged videos twice a day." He shook his head, still trying to digest all this for himself. "I can see from the time stamp of the files the Nykr video was removed just before the evening archive."

I wanted to make sure I had the sequence of events straight in my mind. "So, the video was posted to the system yesterday afternoon, but was deleted prior to the evening backup?" I'm a little slow at times, but bear with me, I get quicker.

"Exactly," Joe confirmed.

"Is there anyway to tell who did it? The scrubbing." Wild shot. Kind of like a black mamba BB.

"Anyone who sets up an account and gets a password can log in to view the videos, but scrubbing requires admin clearance." Joe shrugged with appropriate nonchalance.

"Okay then," I nodded, then blew out a ragged stream of air. "Who has admin clearance?" I was pleased with my quick thinking. Clever is as clever does.

Joe chewed his lip. "Well, let me see. Besides Nick, Deandra, Ruach, Dr. Hume, Dr. Panglaws, me—and probably half the people in the research area—no one else." His smile was thin and I no longer felt clever. However, I wasn't going down without a fight.

⎔ Into the Wild Blue Somewhere Yonder ⎔

"Fine," I said with a spirited grin. "We'll just track the admin login records back to the original user."

Joe flashed me a sickly smile. "We don't track the admin logins." He shrugged. "For reasons of internal security."

Key-bloody-riced. "I thought admin clearance was for, like, you know, one person," I held up a finger and waved it. "One person only. The administrator." I snorted. "And you track it!"

Joe shrugged again. "This has never happened before. Never been an issue."

Kind of like the stop sign they never erect until somebody dies in the intersection. Humans. "Okay, is there any other information about that video we can get, anything at all?"

"Give me a sec," and he was blazing away with all eight fingers and two thumbs. Maybe his foot shot up there, I couldn't be sure. "I can tell you that the video was originally posted direct from a Nykr server"— he paused and was reading, moving screens around—"and I have the originating pathway, with the enclosing folder name, and that's all."

Not much of value there, but I am curious. Dead cat syndrome, remember? "What is it?"

"All it says here is the main drive name, *nkyr_one*, and the folder name, *demonhunter*." Joe relayed matter-of-factly.

I took a sharp intake of breath; and it felt like an icy hand grabbed the base of my spine and gave it a tug.

Joe was an idiot savant. If he watched the video, he could tell me everything that was in it. "What was in the video?" I asked anxiously.

"I never got to watch it." He shrugged. "On and off our server too fast, even for me!"

My ComUnit buzzed. Dee said in my head, **~It's Phoebe.~**

Oh, crap. All seven shades of it. I hastily grabbed Joe's hand and vigorously shook it. "You have been incredibly helpful, Joe, but I'm late and Phoebe will kick my ass if I don't hurry."

"Say hello for me," he said cheerfully and returned to his beloved screens.

Knock On Wood

"The more unintelligent a man is, the less mysterious existence seems to him."

—Arthur Schopenhauer

I don't like this number. Nothing is happening here. Please move along.

My Brain Hurts

"My thought is me: that is why I cannot stop thinking. I exist because I think I cannot keep from thinking."

—Jean Paul Sartre

I came through the last door and entered the long hallway which lead to the outside entrance. Or, if you were leaving, the exit. Whatever. Phoebe was standing at that door, with her back to me, even though she would have obviously heard the door I had just noisily opened and closed.

That was not a good sign.

I knew if I could just tell her about Joe and the missing Nykr video, I could bail myself out of the being-late jail, thereby neatly avoiding the insidious Phoebe death stare and having my brain vaporized into smoking gray goo.

I hurried without hurrying down the hallway. Be cool, be cool, ice, cursing the echo chamber effect my hard-heeled boots created, sounding like gunshots as I walked. She turned and was all faux smiley faced. "Glad you could make it." Damn it, only 15 minutes late, what's the big deal? Besides, I have important intel.

I'm thinking all this because I couldn't bring myself to actually spit it out. She was still eyeing me closely.

"You will not believe what I found," I finally managed to blurt out. Her manufactured smile vanished, she shook her head and turned back to the door, which she opened and stepped through. That was also not a good sign. I started thinking, why is she still so bent?

Oh, yeah. Slap to the forehead. Kick to the seat of the butt. I quickly followed her out the door. Jimmy and the SUV were already there at the curb.

❦ Chapter Fourteen ❧

"You look great, Phoebe." Belated, maybe, but so true. In fact, as I paused to really concentrate on the topic—ahem—I completely forgot about Joe and just focused on Phoebe.

She had on a smoothly textured black dress, not too tight, not too loose, matching handbag with some fancy beadwork, her hair wonderful. Her gastrocnemius muscles were sublime. "It's the first time I've seen you without pants," which was not what I meant to say, and I really wasn't trying to be funny. Fug. She made me nervous looking like that.

So much for avoiding the dreaded death stare. "That's not what I meant," I stammered out as I opened the back door for her. She slid gracefully in the seat and looked up at me.

"Get in," said with no real apparent irritation, though she did shake her head in moderate exasperation.

I opened the door and got in. "Good evening, Jimmy. Vitellos, please."

"Yes, sir, Dee already told me." Jimmy smiled. Waited for me to get secured, then started to drive off.

"Say, Jimmy, I was wondering what else you do, I mean, other than drive?" I was thinking about the guard saluting him when we were at that military-not-military air base. Not sure why this idle thought wafted in.

"Well, sir, I'm a handy man, in a manner of speaking," he said with the softest, calmest voice imaginable. He was pulling out of the driveway onto the access road.

"You are security for us?" I asked candidly.

"Doubt that you would require that, sir, with Miss O'Hara around, but if need be, I'm handy." He stated this like a simple fact.

"Okay, thanks," I turned my attention to Phoebe. "You really look great."

Damn, she was a fine-looking woman, and she ignored my comment. "So, what is it that I won't believe you found?" She was watching me, kind of like a hawk eyes a rabbit. Well, it felt that way.

"I'm sorry I was late. I was visiting with Joe and going through videos." I figured this would help.

"I bet," she snorted her opinion of that.

"No, not those kind of videos." She actually smiled a little. "Oh, you're just teasing—damn it, Phoebe."

"What did you find?" she said in flat tones, though her eyes were playful.

I leaned as close to Phoebe as my seat belt would allow. "There was a short video from South Africa. A news report about a fire at some sort of production facility in a remote part of the North West Province." I grinned knowingly.

"The air strike," Phoebe said softly and I nodded.

"Except, obviously no mention of an air strike in the report." I shrugged. "Next up was the report of another fire, this time the one in Miami. The Argentinean supplement warehouse fire." I saw her questioning eyes. "Nothing new there." She looked a little disappointed.

I unclipped my ComUnit. "The third video was from Iran."

"The shoe guys?" Phoebe wanted to confirm.

"Well, it's actually a shoe insert," I replied and she favored me with a quizzical frown. To which I responded with, "I want you to watch this carefully, okay?" She nodded. I handed her the ComUnit and told Dee to start the shoe insert commercial.

I knew what was in the commercial and the, well, odd, effect it had created for Joe and me. Even if just a temporary effect, it had been more than a little unsettling. Provocative to the point of eerie, truthfully. I wondered how Phoebe would be impacted, so I was watching her closely. The commercial started playing.

She was not fully attentive at first—an impassive face—but then a wispy smile appeared. Her eyes went a little wider as she watched, and then she was completely engaged. This was followed by a slow nodding of her head and a slightly wider smile. As the commercial neared its conclusion she spoke aloud, softly, with a big smile, "What a great idea," and the screen went blank.

She turned to look at me as she handed the ComUnit back. "We should get a pair," she said with some enthusiasm. I merely nodded agreeably and smiled back.

☐ Chapter Fourteen ☐

"That was quite an interesting commercial wasn't it?" I asked listlessly, monotone, really just wanting to let some time pass and see when she recovered, for lack of a better term, from the strange impact of the video.

"Yes, very engaging," she said slowly, but there was just a trace of restraint and doubt in her slightly hesitant tone.

"It was a very professional piece for an Iranian shoe insert company," I stated softly and without emotion.

Phoebe was a trained professional, having spent many hard hours as both interrogator, and as subject. While it had taken Joe quite some time to recover from the video, I could tell by her expression that Phoebe was already beginning to catch the distinct aroma of a dead rat.

She looked at me, her face a mixture of irritation, vexation, fear, and shock. "You want to tell me what just happened there?" Her face was scrunched up.

"Same thing happened to me," I replied honestly, "and it has to do with the way the video is constructed." I paused, wanting to elaborate clearly on this point. "It's been digitally enhanced, like a special effects movie, but there's something else going on."

"You think?" she said with pure sarcasm. She was very good at it.

"Did you notice the Walking Man's eyes?" I asked, because that aspect had been the most alarming thing to me of the many alarming things going on in the video.

She shook her head, so I handed the ComUnit back. "Watch it again, but keep your mind focused on why you are watching it, and what you are looking out for," I suggested. Advised. Ordered.

She diligently watched it again. She shook her head at the end and slowly handed the ComUnit back to me. "It's disturbing, but in a way that's difficult to put into words." I could tell she was deeply affected.

I rubbed my chin with my right hand. "I've seen those eyes before, but not the face," I said, and she really looked concerned now.

"Where?" she asked, her interest now completely professional. Hunter hot on the trail.

"Dee is working on it, trying to get a match to images in her data bank." I spread my hands and gestured in the classic *I-don't-know-squadoosh* gesture. "Dee, have you made any progress on that?"

☐ My Brain Hurts ☐

"Not yet, Enoch."

"Keep after it," I said by way of encouragement. I turned to look at Phoebe.

"That's not all," I said with a impish grin. She took a deep breath and then made an impatient waving motion with her right hand and fingers, as in *bring it on*, and I obliged. "I asked Joe to show me what he had on Nykr, the company in Iceland." I paused, took a breath. "He said there had been a Nykr video on the PHANSTASM server yesterday afternoon." My usual dramatic pause. "Someone deleted it later that night." I smiled wanly. "Right before the evening archive."

"Who did it?" Phoebe asked the obvious question.

"There are over forty people with administrative clearance and any of them could have done it," I answered softly, slightly irritated at having to think about it again.

"Did Joe watch the video?" she asked with a sense of urgency. Great minds think alike.

"No, he said he never got around to viewing it," I replied dejectedly.

"So, we have nothing," she stated unhappily.

"Well," I tilted my head, "not exactly nothing." I smiled and she was waiting with a refreshed scowl. "Joe has a program that monitors all uploads. It logs the file properties to a separate text file. He uses it to track files uploaded to the PHANTASM server."

She eyed me dubiously, so I kept explaining. "The video file carried information about where it had originally come from, so even though the video file itself was deleted, Joe still had the text file log with that info." Pregnant pause. "The video file originally came from a Nykr server in Iceland." Deliberate pause. "Joe even managed to get the enclosing folder name from that server." Dramatic pause. "Guess the name," I said in grand kidding style.

"Right before you pass out, you will tell me," Phoebe said jokingly. I think she was joking.

I grinned and, thankfully, she grinned back. "The name of the folder was *demonhunter*."

She gasped out, "Brody's message!" I nodded in affirmation.

"Not only that, but when Tom and Armando hacked the actual Nykr server the other day, the one in Iceland, they found a folder there, named"—I grinned wide this time—"that's right ladies and gentlemen, *demonhunter*." Break out the ticker-tape and confetti.

"What's in it?" Phoebe quickly asked in anxious anticipation. Ah, the rain that goeth before a parade.

I blasted out a shot of air from my mouth. "They're having trouble cracking the security, but my guess is that the original version of that video is in there." I grinned. "The one that was deleted from the PHANTASM system yesterday evening!"

I thought Phoebe would be disappointed, but she only nodded confidently. "They'll get it eventually."

I favored her with a sly smile and a wink. "Flash that pretty smile of yours and tell them that, and they won't stop until it's done."

"You're a pain, Enoch, but likable," she said, then looked at Jimmy. "We'll be late, Jimmy. We can catch a cab back." I was thinking about her pain remark and it reminded me that my stomach had been growling, which made me think about how hungry I was, and I began musing about dinner. Maybe a Porterhouse, maybe some fish, glass of wine, or two… when in doubt, eat.

Jimmy glanced in the rear view mirror. "If you change your mind, let me know."

"Thanks, Jimmy." Phoebe pulled out her ComUnit and began fiddling around, so I took the hint and sat back to ruminate. Mostly about nothing in particular, which is a prized skill only acquired with great effort. Thinking náda takes hard work.

Some minutes later we pulled up in front of Vitellos. I was going to dash around and open Phoebe's door; you know, the perfect gentleman, but she was already out and waving goodbye to Jimmy. "I was going to open your door and demonstrate my genteel manners," I said, semi-seriously.

Phoebe eyed me with good-natured humor, I think, and said, "It'll take more than that…" Ouch.

They must have a peephole or a camera, or something, as I have never in my life been able to reach the Vitellos front door before someone inside opens it. Almost always someone young, vibrant, and cheerful. Naturally, this time I was hoping it would be someone who knew me, you know, to impress the dispassionate Phoebe.

And, of course, it was a face utterly unknown to me. "Welcome to Vitellos," the unknown, but young and vibrant, face said warmly. "Do you have reservations?"

I humbly nodded in the affirmative. We entered and were escorted to the front desk. Fortunately, a friendly face was there. Emily. "Enoch, we don't usually see you on a Tuesday." She was all smiles. Pretty girl. She and Phoebe exchanged, hmm, pleasant glances.

I smiled back. "And I could say the same thing about you being at the hosting desk."

"Patti called in sick and Danny asked me to help out," she explained, looked at her display monitor and pushed some buttons. "Tom and Armando are already here, waiting for you"—an almost imperceptible pause—"and your friend."

"Emily, Phoebe. Phoebe, Emily," was the extent of me touching that.

A smiling young man came walking into view. "Mr. Maarduk?" He looked expectantly at me. I nodded. "Please follow me."

"Enjoy your dinner," Emily said with a grin.

"Thanks, and see you Friday," then realized I might still be in Iceland. "Maybe," I added with a small shout as we were walking down the hallway. ~Dee, I need you to record and monitor this meeting.~

~I will do that, Enoch.~

A few of the regulars waved. I waved back. Danny II spotted me and waved, but he was busy talking to some other folks and turned his attention back to them.

We curved around a corner and there were Tom and Armando. Armando saw us first. Well, I am sure he spotted Phoebe first, since he shot out of his chair into a standing position as though the seat had been wired with a 220 volt charge. Hot watts. Tom glanced at Mando, saw Phoebe and I approaching, and then he also shocked to attention.

I said thanks to the departing figure of the young man who had been our temporary guide. With playful regard, I then looked at my friends; their tongues lolling onto the hardwood floors. "Tom Bendix," I said with pendulous anticipation, "I want you to meet Phoebe Scarlett O'Hara," and Tom exchanged a shy (for him) look and handshake with Phoebe.

⬚ Chapter Fourteen ⬚

"A pleasure," was all he managed to croak out. Probably because she was crushing his hand.

"And, of course, Armando Morales," I said deferentially. Armando, being from a background that values machismo, held his grip longer than most, but finally smiled as their hands parted.

"So, the PHANTASM girl in the flesh," he said with a smile. A smile that slowly wilted as he realized what he had just uttered. He actually blushed, which I have never seen him do. We all sat down and I did my best to rescue him.

"We have some serious new information for you guys," I started and was going to keep talking, but Phoebe waved a graceful hand and stepped in.

"Excuse me, Enoch," she said, batting her eyes apologetically at me. "Let me interrupt for just a sec." She turned her alluring attention to both Tom and Armando. "I just wanted to let you guys know that without your fantastic help during our recent"—she paused for effect—"soiree, we could not have accomplished our mission." She was smiling broadly and, of course, the boys were now ready to jump off a tall building for her.

"Wow, thanks," Tom said, in quasi-shock and awe I guess. "When Enoch said he needed our help"—he glanced at me and wagged his head at Mando—"we just wanted to do whatever we could."

Phoebe smiled. "We're going to need your help again," and then quietly tacked on, "soon, I'm sure."

Armando rubbed his hands together in evident joy. "Anything for Enoch"—a sloppy trademark Mando grin—"and Phoebe."

Tom said with a genuine warmth in his voice, "Don't forget Dee!"

"Hello, Tom. And everyone!"

"You know," Tom said to me with a wry smile, "when she finishes the PHANTASM gig, we want Dee to come work with us."

Armando agreed loudly, "Absolutely!"

"I am humbled by your offer Tom and Armando."

"They couldn't afford you, Dee," I said, humorously eyeballing my two friends. "Besides, you still have a lot of work to do for me."

"Yes, Enoch, you are a lot of work."

That drew a hearty laugh from the assemblage. Merely a hah-hah chuckle from me.

"Okay, hopefully everyone is done talking for now." I looked at Phoebe to see if she wanted to go on, but she sat silently, and Dee said nothing, so I finished, "We've got a lot of ground to cover."

Our waitress, uh, wait-person, came over and we had to ask her to come back since we hadn't even glanced at the menus. A brief discussion of cocktails versus wine ensued. We decided to begin with water, bottled—who drinks tap—and continued the friendly libation argument before considering appetizers.

We were about to order wine, and stay on safer ground, when Tom casually suggested we revisit the Copper Gorilla, which elicited such a look of confusion and interest from Phoebe that Tom felt compelled to explain the evil concoction in lurid detail.

This is how empires crumble.

The four Copper Gorillas arrived and we bantered over appetizers, finally reaching a consensus. Bacon-wrapped scallops with porcini mushrooms, droplets of basil-infused olive oil, sprinkled with saffron. Parmigiano-Reggiano and Spanish Goat Cheese vegetable samosas in a light curry sauce. And Vitellos special Un Poco De Todo salad which changed each week and could, and did, contain anything, everything. Always delicious, always worthy of admiration, I regarded this week's choice with a consideration that approached reverent adoration.

Swiss chard, mustard greens, collared greens, wild lettuce, arugula, dandelion greens, sweet onions, toasted almonds, sherry-soaked cranberries, pan-warmed and then chilled, stevia, finely cut celery, carrot slivers, crushed walnuts, feta cheese, a light dusting of finely ground pine nuts and a dash of oatmeal cookie crumbs. Dressed delicately with a first cold-pressed extra virgin olive oil, red-wine vinegar, peach and jalapeño jelly, and vanilla-honey yogurt mix.

Okay, maybe it's an acquired taste, like a Copper Gorilla. A little bit of everything, but not for everybody. Náda por tu. Gringo lingo.

Speaking of which, a few Gorilla sips had been duly noted and we were busily engaged in the serious business of conversation, mostly in tones meant only for our ears, as belied the delicate nature of the subject matter. I told Tom and Armando about the Nykr video, and the fact it had been scrubbed from the PHANTASM system.

Armando nodded knowingly. "The large size of the *demonhunter* folder that we saw on the Nykr server completely supports the notion there is a video in it."

Tom enthusiastically nodded his agreement. "We think we're getting closer to breaking into that folder and acquiring that video."

Armando finished the thought. "We left the office with a new algorithm running." He rubbed his hands together in a kind of conspiratorial glee. "We think it may do the trick." He knocked twice on the wooden table.

I nodded excitedly. "I don't know what's in that video, but it must be important."

Phoebe laughed, sprinkled some salt in her hand and tossed it over her shoulder. "I hope that helps," she said with suitable mirth and that generated a great laugh and a hearty toast to luck.

After the general gaiety of that event calmed, I reached into my jacket pocket and produced the plastic baggie with the cookie.

Tom, ever the joker, immediately commented, "We'd prefer a check in the mail, but that's a nice gesture." If Phoebe laughs, you know you hit a homer. Tom circled the bases. Doffed his cap to the crowd.

"Funny guy," I replied dryly. "We brought this back from South Africa." That calmed the hilarity a mite. "We need to get a good independent analysis done on it."

Armando grunted. "I know just the guys. Used to be in the somewhat shady side of the chemical business a few years back, but were convinced to change their ways."

Phoebe grinned slyly. "Like some other people I know."

Tom and Armando exchanged sheepish looks. Armando took the cookie. "I'll put a mega rush on this." He tucked it away in the little leather pouch he always carried with him. "Better than some damn man-purse," he said in snippy tones as we watched him set the purse, er, pouch, on the edge of the table.

Our appetizers arrived. It was akin to tossing red meat to lions. I thought Phoebe might spear me with her fork as we battled over the scallops. We ended up splitting the last one without the loss of blood.

⬚ My Brain Hurts ⬚

Which probably would have been mine since I have no skill whatsoever in defending myself using only an eating utensil.

"Anything else about deciphering Brody's message?" I tossed that out between delightful chews.

Both guys shook their head. "Still hacking on it," Tom said solemnly, not even grinning at that old joking reference.

"I might have something on that," Phoebe chimed in and I glanced at her in surprise. She gave me an arched eyebrow look. "Well, it's just something I came across on the drive over here." She had our undivided attention. Well, she already had that, now we just had a better excuse to stare at her.

"Okay, lay it on us," I said softly.

"I was looking at a report out of South Africa, just running over a few loose details, not even sure why." She took a sip of her drink, whether for dramatic effect or just because she was truly thirsty, I don't know. It was amusing, though no one noticed it but me, that everyone else took a drink at the same time.

"I'm skimming through the report and noticed the printed coordinates of the facility," she continued, her voice intense. "It's rare to see whole number GPS coordinates like that."

"I don't recall them," I said, which didn't mean much since I hadn't actually read the whole report anyway. Well, I read the important parts. Looked at the pictures.

"Minus 26, 25," she said lightly and then waited.

It would have been comical, if it hadn't been so important, that Tom, Armando, and I seemed to gasp and say at the same time, "Longitude and latitude!" or some variation on that theme.

I unclipped my ComUnit and held it up. "Dee, can you display Brody's message for us, please?" It immediately popped into view on the screen.

gaia penta peptode 12 12 12 -12(7) demonhunter ctr?

"Good heavens!" I cried in astonishment and held the display aloft for everyone to see. "36, -84!" Phoebe smiled blithely as I exclaimed the numbers. "Dee, what's the location of those coordinates?" This question was asked with as much Enoch coolness as I could manage at the moment. In other words, fairly blurted it out. Tom and Armando were leaning forward in their seats, their faces a study in anxiousness. Or, is that anxiety? Anticipation? Freaking grammar.

"Knoxville, Tennessee, USA."

"There was a recent transfer of funds from Nykr to a bank in Knoxville!" This burst forth from me with barely restrained excitement. Okay, maybe not restrained all that much. I'm pretty sure it was clear and distinct two or three tables away. I grimaced and Phoebe shot a withering look of chastisement my way.

"Yes," Dee confirmed very softly. **"$50 million dollars."** Mando whistled and Tom said holy crap or holy something or other. "However, the bank is not at the location reflected in the GPS coordinates."

Phoebe nodded slowly, digesting this. "Enoch, do you remember what Ruach said? About another primary being opened."

"You think this could be it?" I had already been pondering the same thing. She nodded.

"Dee, what exactly is located at those coordinates?" I asked hesitantly, almost fearfully.

A brief pause. **"It is zoned as a commercial area."** Another moment or two went by. **"There does appear to be some kind of manufacturing operation at the site, judging from the permits and licensing records. It was recently purchased by a Pnumis Corporation."** Pause. **"There are currently no satellite images. That is all I have at this time."**

Mando already had his digital tablet open on the table and said, "I hope they have a website!" Which was lustful hacker-speak for *get-ready-because-here-I-come*.

A wisp of a smile creased Phoebe's face and she looked at Tom and Armando, "Guess we need you sooner than I thought."

"Wow, this is a lot to digest," I said, trying for a little humor to break the serious shroud of events which, like a shadow, had suddenly fallen over the dinner. "Maybe we should just sit back and enjoy the evening, and worry about all this other stuff tomorrow."

Armando immediately folded up his tablet and slid it back under the table. You didn't have to ask him twice to break out the party favors.

"Do a Scarlett?" Phoebe said with a wistful look at me.

☐ My Brain Hurts ☐

"Here's to Scarlett!" Tom said, raising his Copper Gorilla into the air.

Ah, and that did not only break the somber mood, my friends, it shattered it, vaporized it. Poof!

Anyway, I won't bore you with the tedious (belch) details, other than the fact that the entrees were spectacular, the desserts ridiculous, the wines fashionably expensive, and the conversation most gratifying. At some point I looked around and realized we were about the only people left in the joint.

We paid an inordinately large bill and left an appropriately obscene tip (somehow allowing the cocktails and wine to influence our reasoning, imagine that), rationalizing that PHANTASM would want us to relax in a fashion commensurate with our recent expenditure of effort (harumph, harumph). Hugs, pats on the back, and we were happily escorted to the exit.

Our excited wait-person came running out from the restaurant area, gushing an astonished thank-you, and I hazily tried to recall exactly how much tip I had left. Oh, well. We walked, staggered, traipsed, straggled, jostled each other outside. More hugs and kisses. I reminded the guys not to forget about the Pnumis hack report thingy. "Pnumis this," Armando yelled in great merriment. They both fell into the taxi and we watched them drive off.

"They're good people," Phoebe said in an amazingly clear voice. I say clear because she had easily enjoyed as much adult beverage as my own self, and if I had said that, it might have sounded like, "Der goob peeble," or some variant thereof.

Jimmy pulled up (I wondered absently who had called him), thankfully close to the curb. Phoebe slid in with an easy grace while I sort of pitched myself in with all the elegance of a wounded sumo wrestler.

"You have special friends," Phoebe commented as we put our seat belts on. Well, she easily put hers on and I grappled around with mine like it was a wet eel.

"Der goob peeble," I said. Told you so. Kind of embarrassing, even though I felt fine. I rallied myself. "So, are you up for a quick knox to Tripville?" Mostly rallied.

⬚ Chapter Fourteen ⬚

Phoebe laughed just the right amount. "We'll have to clear it with Hume."

"Of course," I replied, then added, "think we should ask him now?"

Phoebe shook her head. "I imagine he's probably in bed asleep, which is where we should be."

"Ah, c'mon buzz-breaker, what's wrong with a little fun?" I said it gentle-like.

Phoebe's smile was genuine and sincere. "I had a blast tonight, thanks for taking me."

"Me, too, Pheebs," I said grinning, really not as soused as maybe I was letting on. "That was really impressive work, spotting that latitude-longitude thing."

She eyed me with a happy expression. "Thanks, Enoch, I appreciate it."

"As soon as the boys crack that *demonhunter* folder, I think we are going to be a lot closer to the truth," I said enthusiastically.

Phoebe seemed to shiver. "I hope that's a good thing."

I nodded slowly. "You got that right."

Long couple of days, long night. We both just sat back, enjoying the memory of the meal, the drinks, the conversation. A pleasant sort of aura drifted down and surrounded us all the way back to the secret-agent garage and the Black Ops car lift that descended to the parking area.

We clamored out of the parked vehicle, thanked Jimmy. He laughed and drove off. We headed for the elevators.

And yes, more than once during the night I had entertained appropriately randy thoughts about Phoebe. But she was my partner, and I think it was best to keep things professional. Besides, I would be crushed if she rebuked me. Aargh. Nonetheless, maybe a last minute nightcap? You never know...

"Hey, Dee, does PHANTASM have a bar?"

"I assume, using tonight's activities as a referent, you are referring to an establishment which provides adult beverages."

"You may rightfully so assume," I replied jauntily, happily.

Phoebe smiled as the elevator doors opened. "One for the road?"

"My only risk would be a ticket for WUI; hah, walking under the influence," I said comically, though my wit, or lack thereof, only drew the vestige of a smile from Phoebe.

"I don't think PHANTASM has a saloon," Phoebe said, and did chuckle this time. "We'd never be able to get the damn IT guys out of it if we did."

"There might be one on Level 5, but I can't access a map," Dee said in casual reply to my earlier query.

"Level 5?" I am not sure if Phoebe and I said this, you know, precisely at the same time, simultaneously, but it was close enough that we exchanged startled glances.

"There is no Level 5," Phoebe stated flatly.

"I do not wish to disagree with you, Phoebe, but please look at the ComUnit display," Dee replied with a mildly subdued admonishment.

I quickly unhooked the unit and held it up for Phoebe and I to study. On it was what looked like a scan of a set of blueprints. Fairly crappy scan, at that. "Where did you find that image?" I inquired.

"I could not find a bar or saloon on any of the maps in my default system, so I ran a search on some archival PHANTASM servers."

"Maybe these are proposed blueprints and they never actually built a Level 5," I said, offering a possible solution.

Phoebe frowned. "Even a secret facility has secrets."

I was studying the blueprints, as best I could, considering how poor they were in visual quality. "Dee, I don't see an access point. How do we get down there?" If Level 5 existed, a way in had to exist.

"It may take a few minutes to analyze that." We had been walking, all this time, towards Phoebe's quarters. We reached her door.

"You can come in until Dee gets us an answer," and then she caught herself. "I didn't mean for it to sound like that."

"Oh, for heaven's sake, Phoebe, I know what you meant." And we entered.

It was not what I expected. I figured, you know, guns, knives, more guns, maybe some dismantled IEDs. Possibly some stuff from Torquemada's dungeon.

But, it was all woman in here. Some people just have an eye for color, texture, scale, and presentation. And some folks (pick me) simply toss crap out with no real feeling for feng shoe, show, shui; yeah, that's it, shui. Which is Chinese for: "Hey, your place looks really nice."

Okay, not true. The truth is, sometimes you walk into a room and just feel, well, comfortable, peaceful, at ease. And then I understood. With what Phoebe had to go through, out in the field, she had to have some retreat, almost a sanctuary, a place where she could escape to and recharge the batteries. I mean, almost from the moment you stepped in her quarters, a warmth and calmness just sort of descended on you.

It was a massive open living area. No kitchen in sight. It was a hybrid between the elaborate tent of some desert nomad prince; a Moroccan house (just without the open air above); and a seaside resort villa. Incredibly designed fabrics with rich and warm colors, some hanging from the walls, some from the ceiling; plush pillows of sizes varying from immense to small; thick carpet that looked as soft as a babies butt; and pewter, silver, and gold (plated, I assumed) items and ornately carved wooden boxes everywhere.

"Will you come do my place?" I said in truly stunned awe. "This is really nice," which seemed like sort of a goofy statement, but was exactly how I felt.

"Take a seat," she said with an appreciative smile. "You want that nightcap now?" She was standing near an opening that had those hanging beads as a door, except these were incredibly carved wooden balls of exquisite design, each one appearing to be uniquely wrought, with gold and silver spheres of different sizes placed between them. Damn, she looked fine. The beads, too.

"Iced tea, if you have it, thanks." I was still taking it all in, comfortably lounging back on this gigantic gold and amber-colored pillow with copper-hued braided tassels, when she returned and handed me a cut crystal glass, and kept one for herself.

"Spill it and you die," she said pleasantly. She was teasing, had to be, but I still held my cup in a death grip.

"Any luck, Dee?" I said loudly. The ComUnit was sideways on the carpet, at my feet.

"It does not appear that the elevator shaft extends to Level 5." Her voice bore just a tint of aggravation.

Phoebe piped in. "They have to have some sort of emergency exit, regardless." She looked at me. "In case of fire."

That fired me up. "Dee, look for any sort of connection to Level 4, anything at all."

A few moments went by. **"I do have something which might be of interest."** The ComUnit display flashed and I picked the unit up. Phoebe, sitting on a pillow next to me, scooted over and leaned in to see. It was a schematic, much clearer than the crappy blueprints, of the Level 4 stairwell. A little whirling blue light appeared by the stairs.

"What's the blue light, Dee?" Phoebe asked the question that was just about to leap out of my mouth.

The ComUnit display changed to a video feed. **"I have tapped into the camera located in the Level 4 stairwell."** Previously, I may not have mentioned the ubiquitous cameras all over PHANTASM. Hah, that's kind of redundant, isn't it? Anyway, you take them for granted. The cameras, not the redundancies. I mean, shoot, they are all over the place in the outside world, not just PHANTASM. You just sort of learn to ignore them.

A pulsating little red arrow was now pointing under the stairwell. **"My research indicates there is some kind of door under the stairs."** I admit it, a little bit of tea might have sloshed out when I excitedly jumped up. Fortunately, it also happened to Phoebe when she leaped to her feet. Come on; it was mostly water anyway.

"I need to grab some gear," Phoebe exclaimed, dashing impromptu from the room. I picked up the ComUnit and clipped it on my belt.

I may not have been thinking about the ubiquitous cameras before, but I was now. "Say, Dee, can you use EM interference to scramble up those cameras?"

"Yes, Enoch."

"Good. I don't want any video of Phoebe and me being recorded," I said and then, after a moment, grinned to myself. And, yes, I did have a quick image of that. Sue me.

"I will block all camera recording when either of you are in frame."

Phoebe came scampering back into the room, her face flush with excitement. "I heard talking, fill me in," she said as she stuffed a variety of objects into her pack.

⬚ Chapter Fourteen ⬚

"I made sure Dee would scramble up any cameras trying to record us moving around," I said proudly.

"Damn, Enoch, you're smarter than you look," she deadpanned and we headed for the door. Bee atch.

I don't know why we were sneaking around on tip-toes like a couple of supposed cat burglars. Come on, we live here. We can move around, even at two in the morning. Right? Well, probably at Level 3, our quarters, maybe not at Level 4. I was freaking out that someone would know we were there by tracking the ComUnit signal, but Dee assured me that she was effectively blocking all incoming and outgoing GPS signals.

It still made me uneasy. Nonetheless, nevertheless, we entered the stairwell for our level and proceeded down the long flights of metal stairs. "Do you know," Phoebe whispered in a sort of semi-disbelief, "I've been at this facility for four years, and this is the first time I've ever stepped foot on these stairs." Clang, clang, eerie echoes.

We stepped off onto the flat concrete walkway outside the entrance door to Level 4. No more stairs descended. It was very quiet.

Off to the right, on the wall, was a long metal pipe that ascended and vanished into the ceiling. It was attached to a large valve with a wheel. The water connection for the fire fighters, if they should ever be called on to fight a fire this deep in the complex. That brought a mental shiver.

Phoebe and I exchanged anxious glances, because there was a darkened area under the ascending stairs. We moved to the right and back around to get a better look. She flipped on her metal halide flashlight and the area was awash in creamy light.

There was an array of oddly sized cardboard boxes piled up under the stairway, which had a maximum height, toward the back wall, of maybe four feet, sloping toward the front and the bottom of the stairs with almost no clearance at all there. As Phoebe held the flashlight, I began carefully sliding boxes out of the way.

The first few were of moderate weight. A couple were almost empty and then, toward the far wall, when I slid a big heavy one slightly out of the way, the flashlight revealed a smallish opening, covered with a metal plate that had a keyed inset lock.

I nervously moved the last box out from under the stairs. Phoebe had to step back. Then, we both bent over and began crawling under the stairs, to get a closer look at that door.

When we arrived at the little door, I immediately reached out a hand to touch it. Phoebe snatched out and grabbed my sleeve. Cobra strike. "Hang on, let me test it first," and she produced the same little screwdriver-looking tool she had employed in South Africa. She ran it slowly and cautiously around the door frame, then nodded, apparently satisfied. "It's clean." As she rummaged around her pack for more tools, I estimated the opening to be not quite two foot in height and a little under three feet wide.

Plenty big enough for us to get through, assuming we could get it open, as it did have a lock.

A simple lock, as it turned out. Which Phoebe picked in about fifteen seconds. The metal creaked on its hinges as we eased it open. I know it wasn't all that loud, but it sounded like a frigging gunshot in this enclosed space. I willed my rambling heart to settle down and try to beat normally.

Phoebe pushed the door open and when she started to lean in, it was my turn to grab her sleeve. "Let's see if Dee can scan the inside," I whispered. ~Did you catch that, Dee?~ I thought tossed her.

~You are safe to enter.~ Even an eemee can get excited, I mused as I noted the tremulous quality to Dee's voice. I told Phoebe it was clear.

Phoebe leaned in and cast her light around the room. Naturally I had poked my nosy head in over her shoulder as far as I could. It was a very small room, really not more than a closet. Four blank walls and a concrete floor. Nothing in the room at all; well, not counting dust and cobwebs. We easily squeezed through the opening and stood up. The air was thick and stale.

There was a door on the far wall. With a regular lock. Which, like most locks around Phoebe, clicked open ajar with not much resistance after a few probing embraces of pick lock love. Dim light filtered in along the edges of the door.

꧁ Chapter Fourteen ꧂

Phoebe whispered softly this time, "Dee, anything we should know?"

"I tapped into a camera mounted above this door. It appears to be nothing but a hallway leading to another door. I will scramble the video feed when you enter the hallway."

We eased the door open with care. Hinges which had not been used in a long time squealed in protest. Even that sounded alarmingly loud to me. We stepped through into a hallway very much like the one I found when I first entered the PHANTASM building last Sunday. Damn, that seemed like some other lifetime. Focus. Focus.

It was not as long as that other hallway, but it had the same white featureless walls and white floor, bland, boring. A door was at the end of the hallway, with a security box of some kind on the wall next to it.

As we drew nigh, as they say, we saw it was a very old security keypad. Alphanumeric only. No fingerprint reader, no retina scanner, no blood or saliva analyzer. Very old school. Ancient, if you will.

Ancient or not, it still required a six-character alphanumeric code. My math skills stink, but I'm pretty sure that meant bazillions of possible permutations. 26 letters, 10 numerals, plus some punctuation marks to start with. Let's just say we weren't getting in without a little help. And Phoebe's nice little pick lock set wasn't going to get this bad boy open.

"Dee, I need a little assistance." I held the ComUnit up to the security box so Dee could get a clear visual. Probably didn't need it, as she could scan it with EM waves, but I didn't immediately think of that. A little nervous.

"You are very needy, Enoch." She said it in a joking way, so I merely chuckled. **"I must think about it for a few minutes."**

The fastest computer yet known still pales, in terms of computing power, to the human brain. Or, apparently, to the eemee equivalent. The speed of thought is much faster than anything, even if that sounds like some kind of dipsy-doodle science fiction. As Dee explained it, when the security box flashed green and the door popped open, she merely mentated on every possible combination. I coughed and said *bullshit* under my breath, but Dee merely poo-pooed me for not remembering she was an eemee.

"A very sweet eemee," Phoebe said as we opened the door.

"Thank you, Phoebe. I think you are sweet, too." I was noticeably absent from the conversation, either as subject or predicate.

The door opened into a wide corridor. It was about ten feet across and ran on down to a far wall about 60 feet or so away. Along the outer walls, on both the left and right sides, were a series of large windows. I estimated them to be 4 x 6 or thereabouts, with a door and security box, like the one we had just used, next to each window.

My guess was that these were offices—five on the left and five on the right. I judged the ceiling to be up around twelve feet or so in height.

There was light from some overhead source in that ceiling, but all of the windows had darkened interiors, as far as I could tell, and you could not see inside at all. There was no sound. The air here smelled much less stale than in the closet, but still a bit under-circulated. The temperature appeared comfortable, though a little warm for my taste.

We stepped slowly toward the first window on our left. As we moved close to the glass a light snapped on inside. Both of us took a flashing involuntary step back and the light instantly went out. We exchanged startled glances, because I think we both had just the briefest, fleeting, glimpse of, well, something inside. I took a deep breath and held Phoebe's gaze. "Ready?" was all I said. She nodded coolly.

We stepped forward. The light inside the room came on and we remained still.

There are things we see in life that amuse us. Things that scare us. Things that puzzle us. Things that thrill us. All kinds of things. I think my mind had been prepared for just about any possibility in that room.

Except for what was actually in there.

A large, intricate, and three-dimensional pentacle was constructed on the floor. It was colored a dark blue and white. Most of the symbols and letters were white. There were small shiny metal fixtures affixed at the five points of the pentacle. Incredible details, even at this distance. But that shock was secondary to seeing the figure which was sitting, cross-legged, in the center of the pentacle.

It was a man, late middle age, wearing a white smock, very much like something you would see in a long-term health care unit. His feet were bare. His hair was black with flecks of gray. His head was tilted downward as though he were staring at the ground. You could see the rise and fall of his back as he was breathing, but there was no other movement.

Until his head jerked up and he glanced through the window at us, an astonished look etched on his face.

And then I felt a tingling in the back of my neck and a raspy, gravelly, hesitant, voice in my mind saying, ⁓Me. Help. Me. Please.⁓ The hairs on my arm went absolutely vertical. I know because I looked. I am sure my mouth fell agape.

I heard, like a faint sound in the distance, Dee say in stunned disbelief, **"He is an eemee, trapped in the pentacle!"** Phoebe and I stared at one another in wide-eyed confusion and alarm.

"He asked me for help," I said in a small, unsteady, voice.

"Ask him why he is here," Phoebe whispered urgently.

Before I could even begin to process her request and act on it, Dee's voice sounded out, strident, frightened, **"Some kind of alarm has been triggered. We need to leave immediately!"**

⁓We will help, but we must leave now!⁓ was all I could send before Phoebe took a tiger grip on my arm and guided me roughly to the door. In just moments we were out, shut and secured the door, darted down the hallway, shut and secured the other doors, wiggled through the small opening, closed and locked it, and I began sliding boxes back into place.

I am sure not much more than two minutes had passed and we were moving rapidly up the stairs to Level 3.

⁓What's the update, Dee?⁓ I thought-slung this with as much calm as I could muster. It wasn't much.

~Security detail is approaching the Level 4 stairwell.~ I assumed she was tapping into the video feeds in the area. She informed me of this just as we opened the door to Level 3 and stepped inside. We eased the door shut behind us, holding the latch open to deaden the always deafening metallic click as it closed. We paused just inside the hallway to catch our breath.

"Damn it," I cursed softly. "This is a mess. Maybe we can go back tomorrow." My thoughts were in utter disarray.

☐ My Brain Hurts ☐

Phoebe shook her head. "Tomorrow is today, and aren't you curious about Knoxville?" Ever diligent Phoebe.

Crap. Who can keep up with all this? I let out a long, noisy, breath. "We need to know what's going on down there." I thought about the offices on Level 5, one of which was apparently a prison cell. "But," I said wearily, "I guess that eemee isn't going anywhere." That was grim and I hoped it didn't sound callous, just realistic.

We headed off down the hallway toward our quarters. "We should ask Hume about Level 5. He has to know it's there," Phoebe suggested as we walked, almost in a daze, down the corridor.

I sighed. It was becoming a regular freaking habit these days. "Not sure it's a good idea to let him know that we know." I grimaced a fake face. "That's supposed to be a secret area, remember?"

Phoebe nodded in reluctant agreement. "Secret for a reason, I suppose."

My turn to nod in accord. "Right. A reason we don't know right now, but will figure out sooner or later."

Dee said softly, **"I hope sooner, Enoch. Being imprisoned within the thoughtless, mindless, confines of a pentacle is a horror almost beyond my understanding."** The underlying layer of sorrow in her voice struck a resonate chord in my very inner being.

"I promise you, Dee, we will help." I did not know what else to say. We were at Phoebe's door.

"We could ask Ruach," Phoebe said in a tired voice, her hand hovering above the fingerprint ID pad.

"Great idea. Let's get him up at three in the morning and ask him about the eemee in the basement." Man, I was gassed.

"Try to get some sleep," she smiled and squeezed my arm. "Good night, Enoch."

"Good night, Phoebe," I replied as her door swung shut. I turned to traipse back to my quarters, exhausted, my mind ablaze with thoughts I was trying my best to quell.

A Quick Knox To Tripville

"Non sum qualis eram—I am not what I used to be."

—Latin saying

I was not in my happy place when the ComUnit squawked to life and Phoebe's bright and cheery voice came on, "Rise and shine, partner, time to kick some ass." I did, indeed, want to kick some ass right about then, I can assure you.

"How can you be so bright and cheerful?" I moaned and struggled to a seated position on the edge of the bed. I was too young to have this much pain in the morning.

"MedPatch," she said and I had to smile. I got up, found my pack, rummaged around and found the aforementioned MedPatch. The one with the neuro- and endo-stimulants.

I slapped it on. "I'll meet you in 20 minutes for breakfast," I said and headed for the bathroom to clean up.

Refreshed and suddenly alert and chipper—albeit artificially—I arrived at the cafeteria five minutes early. Phoebe had, of course, arrived even earlier and was waiting for me by the entrance. We greeted each other with a little hug and got into line.

They had these pancake-looking things, with some kind of whipped topping and nuts, that were seven shades of decadent in appearance, but I needed the calories (rationalization) and took an order. Added a small 8 ounce soy-tofu protein steak—more zip in it than red meat, with no fat—plus some hazelnut, honey, and poppy seed bread—toasted—with orange marmalade. I don't know, I just like saying *marmalade*. Not even sure who Marmal is...

Anyway, Phoebe informed me that she had called Hume earlier (damn, what time did she get up) and we had an appointment with him in about 30 minutes. Phoebe further informed me (something she seemed to be enjoying a bit too much) that while Hume thought this our little get-together was about the Iceland mission briefing, it was really so we could spring the request to explore the new Knoxville lead on him.

"He's not going to like being tricked like that," I said as we waited for the elevator doors to open for Level 4. We had left the cafeteria arguing. You know, our regular and ongoing conversation.

"We are about to make a significant breakthrough in the deciphering of Brody's message," she said with a friendly, but defiant, tone. "I don't think he's going to regard that as a trick."

It was not a surprise to me, then—although Phoebe's shocked expression said differently—that about 10 minutes later Hume shook his head, rubbed his chin, and proclaimed loudly, "This is a hell of a time to drop this on me!" He scowl-frowned. "We have gone to a lot of time and trouble to get things arranged for your trip to Iceland"—he bit his lip—"and now you tell me you want to go to Knoxville"—he paused just a moment—"to pursue a possible, not probable, lead that may, or may not, pan out?"

Phoebe started to say something but Hume quickly raised a hand. "And, suppose it really is an eemee site? Just the two of you are going to waltz in there, ill-prepared and without backup?" He looked hard at both of us. I felt that I had to come to Phoebe's aid.

"We did it in South Africa," I stated softly. Phoebe turned and rewarded me with a smile.

"Yes," Hume said very slowly, dragging the word out, then easing back in his chair, making a steeple with his fingers. "I seem to remember that mission." He regarded me with a rather discomforting look as he rocked his head up and down. "Wasn't that the mission where you were captured, tortured, and just managed to escape through a nice blend of luck and skill?" A tilted smile and raised eyebrows. "Mostly the former?"

I thought it was mostly skill. "We got the job done."

Hume nodded. "And we had satellite imagery, backups on the ground, and solid intel." He looked doubtfully at Phoebe. "What do we have here?" A plaintive grunt. "An address." He gave us a withering look. "No images, no intel, no backup." He sighed. "Do you really expect me to let you go there?"

☐ Chapter Fifteen ☐

I could tell what Phoebe really wanted to say, but she was struggling with herself not to say it. I stepped in. "When you put it like that, it doesn't sound good."

"It's not good!" Hume exclaimed, maybe louder than he meant, and then continued in much softer tones. "Look, if your insight into Brody's message is correct, about latitude and longitude, that is tremendous." He made a grand hand gesture. "Hell, it's better than tremendous; but we still need time to accurately confirm it and then come up with a good plan." A thin smile. "And then, in you both go."

"How long?" Phoebe asked lightly.

Hume let out a long breath. "Damn it, Phoebe, you know how this works." He shrugged. "You leave for Iceland Thursday morning, tomorrow, and are scheduled back Friday night." He stared pointedly at her, again gesticulated with his hands. "Hopefully, we'll have everything in place and you can go the next day, Saturday morning." He paused. "Maybe."

She stood up. "I'm not feeling all that well." Truth be told, she did look a little pale. "Can we do the Iceland briefing later?"

Hume stood up. "You're pushing yourself too hard, Phoebe," he commented. "There's nothing in the briefing you probably don't already know anyway. I'll post a report to your ComUnits." He looked at both of us and shook his head. "I need you both fresh for the Iceland mission." He walked with us to the door. "Get some rest, relax." We left his office, trying our best to heed his advice.

"We're going," she said sullenly, strongly, as we stepped off the elevator onto Level 3. So much for Hume's advice.

"Going where?" I asked pointlessly, pretty sure I knew the answer that I didn't really want to hear. If you have a part, though, play it out.

"Knoxville," was all Phoebe said as we were walking to her quarters.

"You think that's a good idea? You heard what Hume said," I replied carefully, clearly recalling his pointed admonitions.

Especially the part about no intel and no backup. Got my attention.

She stopped walking and turned to face me. "Can't you feel it, Enoch, everything speeding up, coming to a boil, about to burst?" she stated with passion and it was impossible for me to dispute it. I felt that way myself.

New information, new insights, fresh clues were flowing fast now, and that had to mean we were getting close, but to what?

If you get too close to the flame, you know what can happen.

"We have to be back here before tomorrow morning," I wisely pointed out, reminding her of the Iceland trip, then shrugged. "What can we accomplish by then?" We were nearing her residence.

"Not a damn thing sitting here on our backsides," Phoebe rebutted me with a tingling ire. "Dee," Phoebe said loudly as we entered her quarters, "can you connect me to the Oak Pines Municipal Aerodrome?" She saw the *what the devil is that* look on my face. "An airfield," she aped a grin, "you know, with planes."

A man's gruff voice came loud and clear over the ComUnit. "Oak Pines," was all he said.

"Let me talk to Bryan. Tell him it's Phoebe calling." Her voice was different. A kinder, gentler, voice. Who the hell was Bryan?

A moment or two of silence passed. "Phoebe Scarlett O'Hara," a man's deep radio-perfect voice said in tones that implied he was both surprised and pleased.

"Bryan Whitlock, you damned old flyboy, how are you?" Phoebe said in a very pleasing and warm tone, with an undercurrent of friendly teasing.

"I'm still in the air, Phoebe, mostly over you," he said humorously, sweetly.

"And full of your usual crap, as well," Phoebe countered, and they both laughed.

"How can I help you?" I guess Bryan wasn't big on small talk. Point for him.

"I need to get to Knoxville. Soon and fast," Phoebe replied.

"You the pilot?" Bryan asked.

"Yep," Phoebe answered.

There was a pause and sounds of keystrokes and paper rustling. "I have a number of small business jets on the property. Pick one from the website and drop me a line; I'll have it prepped and ready."

"Thanks, Bryan, I owe you." Phoebe said with meaning.

⬡ Chapter Fifteen ⬡

"No, Phoebe, I owe you," the man said with real feeling.

"I put our ETA at ten-thirty," Phoebe said, her professional tone firmly back in place.

"See you then," the man remarked and the connection was broken.

She appeared to be truly touched by the conversation. She saw my questioning look and sighed. "His daughter was kidnapped some years ago. I got her back. End of story." She smiled THAT smile, the one that means no more questions will be tolerated. "Go get ready."

So I hustled out as Phoebe was shouting at me, "Meet me outside in ten minutes and we'll catch a cab."

I didn't want to wear my black SWAT garb out the front door, so I stuffed it in my pack. Well, wrestled, pounded, beat, and otherwise pulverized it into my already overloaded pack. I grabbed pretty much all the same gear as before, counted my various patches to make sure I was okay (yes, I had neglected to replenish) but I think I could survive a half-day mission with what I had on hand.

The POS BB gun received a grim and swarthy appraisal. Narrow-eyed and flinty doubt. Hard to invest much trust in a weapon with such an iffy track record. Nonetheless, I stuffed it in the pack. Maybe I could throw it at someone.

I told Dee to keep me informed if Hume or Ruach were anywhere around. A few minutes later, the coast cleared by Dee, I was outside. On the opposite side of the street, across from PHANTASM, Phoebe was waving at me from the other side of a yellow-colored cab. I scurried over there.

And off we went. "I'm going to check in on Tom and Armando and see how they are doing on the Pnumis ha…" stopped myself when I realized I was in a public cab, and quickly changed "hack" to "research."

"The way they looked last night, they're probably still in bed," Phoebe said with mild amusement.

"My friends are very resilient, just like me," I said by way of a suitable defense.

Apparently, though, they did not have ready access to a MedPatch and, thus denied the prodigious medicinal benefits thereof (hopeful pause for reader laughter), my phone call went unanswered. I smiled sheepishly. "I'll leave a text message."

▢ A Quick Knox To Tripville ▢

The rest of the short trip to the airfield was spent mainly with me reviewing, with increasing agitation, what little we knew about the Knoxville location. As in next to freaking nothing.

Not much more than the damn location. Dee did show me the licensing and permit applications, which made it obvious they had plans to manufacture something, but not sure what. I couldn't find a website and nary a mention of Pnumis anywhere. Phoebe went to the airfield website and picked out a plane. I knew this because I asked Dee about it.

Dee finally did stumble on something. A patent application from Pnumis for a product called PWR^{UP}, which turned out to be chewing gum. Well, not just any chewing gum, but energy gum, designed for *energy, stamina, and mental clarity*—hmm, where have we heard that before? Clang, ding, dong, ring. Those are alarm bells, BTW.

I mentioned what we'd found to Phoebe and she nodded. "I knew this was a good lead." Indeed, but where would the lead lead? It would take some serious alchemical sleuthing to turn this lead into gold.

I know, sorry. I joke when I'm nervous. Well, try to joke.

About ten minutes later, with the cabbie weaving in and out of traffic like a stunt driver being paid on the basis of difficulty, we pulled up in front of the small airfield office. I clamored out, giving the grinning driver an appropriately irritated look as I exited. Phoebe paid the man, got a receipt (not sure why, thought this little trip was on the low low) and we headed toward the entrance.

Not much more than a glass-enshrouded shack really, but with dozens of antennas and several large satellite dishes on the roof. Wires seemed to run off in a hundred different directions. A metal controller tower had been erected in a little patch of earth in the back. Plain and simple, stairs on the outside leading to a little glass-enclosed area at the top. Only small planes could land at a minimal airfield like this anyway, so not too much sophistication was needed, I guess.

Kind of ignorant about that topic, truthfully. We went inside.

A long desktop, almost like a saloon top, sat off to our left, stretching perpendicular to us and ending in a short hallway. At the end of that hallway, a closed door. The wall behind the desktop was covered with photos. Flying seemed the common theme in most of them. Go figure. To our right was a small waiting area, with two sofas, old, but comfortable-looking. Some plain wooden chairs were strategically scattered around as well.

A gnarled wooden coffee table, looking like something the second-hand store would reject, was littered with magazines and some plastic flowers. The magazines were circa 1980, frozen in time. I guess people came here to fly, not to read. A plain metal door was located between two very large and recently cleaned picture windows.

A small two-engine business jet was visible just outside the door. Other planes were off in the distance. Mostly single engine prop jobs. A few other small business jets, similar in size to the one Phoebe had picked out, were there as well.

I took all this in during the brief lull of walking in and then seeing a man, tall, mid-fifties, military haircut, still very fit, approach from the back. He waved and spoke. "Phoebe, early as usual."

"Bryan," she laughed as they embraced. "Smart ass as usual." I liked him already.

He extended a clipboard. "Just need your initials."

"Tack this on with some other invoices for PHANTASM," she said softly and eyed this Bryan closely. "I don't want it to stand out."

He nodded and grinned. "More secret agent stuff?"

She laughed. "Who plants those ideas in your head?" She turned to me. "Bryan Whitlock, this is my partner, Enoch Maarduk." We shook hands and I was still buzzing from Phoebe's last remark. She actually told another person I was her partner.

Maybe a side effect of the MedPatch?

"It's an older model," he pointed at our craft, "but completely refitted." He grinned and looked at me. "Not that it matters to Phoebe, who I believe could fly anything."

Phoebe smiled at the compliment. "It'll work fine, Bryan, I really appreciate it."

Some more paperwork changed hands and before you could say Bob's your uncle (I always wanted to say that, even though I have no idea what it means) we were on the tarmac—well, the concrete between the shack and the jet anyway.

And then strapped in, again up front, but I knew the Gs we were going to draw in this bad boy paled in comparison to my previous ride. Of course, that didn't stop Phoebe from handing me a barf bag and laughing. "Black mamba," I whispered and she rolled her eyes.

A pre-flight checklist and other procedural gobbledy-gook later, we taxied into position and were soon on our way to Knoxville.

I spent the first three-quarters of the flight (that is a rough navigational guess by a non-navigator) reviewing reports on the ComUnit, talking to Dee, napping and—I guiltily and happily admit—shooting virtual zombies in some silly ass game. Had the third highest online score that day. E-knocker was my user name. Hah!

At some point, though, it occurred to me (accompanied by a spurt of suitably swirled anxiety) that we were embarking on a mission without a real plan. And you thought only governments did that. "Say, Phoebe, when we get there, what exactly is our plan?" Tried my best to keep the accusatory tone to a minimum.

"You're looking for a job," was all she said.

"Huh?" was all I said.

"You're applying for a job with Pnumis." She was smiling and confident as she stated this.

"Okay," I said, venting a long (perhaps bitter) breath, looking down at my blue jeans (at least they were clean) and my less than dressy dress shirt and commenting: "It would have been nice to know the plan before I packed." Of course, I could always change into my SWAT-gear. Maybe apply for a security job. Growl.

"I just thought of it," she said and I almost said something about the often overlooked importance of advanced planning, but caught myself just in time. Remember the woman scorned thing. Especially an armed woman.

Instead, I opted for a slightly more useful approach. "And if they aren't open, or not taking applications, do we have a Plan B?" Her smile wilted like my willpower at an open bar.

"Then we wait until freaking night time and break in," she spat at me in acidic tones. Tight lipped. Now she was mad. I really hoped

☐ Chapter Fifteen ☐

Plan A would work. Spending 5 or 6 hours in Knoxville sounded like fun unless a POP was put into the equation. That would be a Pissed Off Phoebe for those of you scoring at home.

I smiled and started shooting zombies with my super BFG shotgun. Damn, it felt good.

———☐———

"No website?" I exclaimed in my most exclamatory voice to Tom, speaking to him through the ComUnit interface I had wedged between the dashboard and windshield. Phoebe was behind the wheel of our rental vehicle. Oh look, a black SUV, and we were headed north out of Knoxville.

It was bad enough that I had wanted the red corvette but, no, we get the black SUV. Now Tom was telling me that Pnumis had no website. In fact, there appeared to be no systems at Pnumis with a connection to the outside world. Which was kind of important if you were in that outside world trying to hack in. You know, using that connection. The one that didn't exist. Sigh.

Which meant we were still blind. Phoebe didn't like it (think stone-faced scowl), which meant I didn't like it.

"We have something else, though," Tom said, probably just making a futile attempt to placate me.

"It better be good," I said, probably with just a bloody bit more vexation that I should have. The red corvette thing was still pissing me off.

"I'm not sure it's good, but it seems interesting," he rejoined and coughed when I remained silent. "Anyway, Armando was digging around that FDA site again, the one where we found the Argentinean supplement test results."

Digging into anything associated with the Feds still made me uneasy. "And…" I said expectantly, nonetheless.

"We came across a deleted file. Hadn't been zeroed out yet." Most people don't know this, but when you delete a file from your computer system—for instance, that naked picture you took of yourself after being over-served at the office Christmas party—it may vanish from your view in the local directory, but unless you zero out your drive, it's not actually deleted.

⧉ A Quick Knox To Tripville ⧉

I know, seems like another mumbo-jumbo tech BS trick. Like tracking you with GPS or key logging your text messages on the smartphone. You wouldn't feel that way, though, if you accidentally deleted something really valuable and had to get it back. If the file has not been zeroed out, you can get it back. Well, not that naked picture, for gawd's sake.

"Why did you pick that particular file?" I asked intelligently. Well, it sounded intelligent.

"It was inside a folder with some other Cambio S.A. company reports, mostly crap we already had, but the name of this particular text file sort of drew our attention." Tom paused, then added, "The filename was *questionable_lab* and Mando wanted a closer look at it."

I was getting flutterbyes in my stomach. And not just from Phoebe's driving. "What's in it?"

"I'm going to upload it so you can study it yourself," Tom said softly. "It appears to be an email exchange between two researchers working on the lab testing of the supplement." I sensed a mental shrug. "I don't know if it means anything or not, truthfully, just thought it would keep you busy for awhile and off our ass."

This was why Tom and Armando had clients that swore by their services. Yes, they were among the best in the biz, but people used them not just for their expertise. It was also because they told you the flat out truth. Mostly good, sometimes not.

"At least tell me Mando got the cookie over to his lab buddies," I said without rancor, hoping to salvage something useful out of the conversation.

"They are making it a Def Con One über priority," Tom said jauntily. I heard a voice in the background. "I gotta go. Look for the text file in a few minutes," he hastily added and vanished off the screen.

Black Ops Betty had, naturally, been listening intently to every syllable, despite David Gray's suave tones drifting in from the radio speakers. "That sounds promising," she said by way of letting me know I should get the file open right now and let her know what was going on.

"Dee, display that file when it comes in."

"Loading now, Enoch."

☐ Chapter Fifteen ☐

To render the message slightly more user-friendly, Dee had reversed the normal order of the thread and put the original message first, and the response second. Very slick.

———- Original Message ———-

From: "Martin Arrilla" <marrilla@dzuktechni_labs.com>
To: "Robert Gomez" <rgomez@dzuktechni_labs.com>
Sent: Wednesday, 8:05 AM
Subject: arg_supplement

Dr. Gomez:

I need to find out what you want to do about something peculiar that happened during our last testing sequence for the ARG sample you sent over earlier this week.

As you know, extensive tests were conducted on two previous samples. All results indicated there was nothing in the product but a harmless blend of vitamins, minerals, known herbs, and a host of other filler ingredients, one of which was identified as a variant of an ergoline peptide alkaloid, but completely inert.

We tested both samples on a wide variety of animal subjects, with no visual nor empirical record of any systemic change.

Since we had additional testing material remaining, and a new shipment of animal subjects had just been received, we decided to conduct a third test.

Almost immediately upon ingestion, the normally active rats became excessively docile and could be easily handled. They were alert and responsive, but only moved if an external stimuli was provided.

We attached one of the new portable brain scanners and recorded nothing but delta waves at about 2 Hz.

As the lab staff and I were arguing about these impossible results, we received notification that we had been sent the wrong shipment of animal subjects, and that our rats had just been the focus of a recent and massive EM wave irradiation test.

The animals were immediately processed and returned.

Please advise.

Dr. Martin Arrilla, Manager, Lab Unit 3, DzuTechni Laboratories, Inc.

⬚ A Quick Knox To Tripville ⬚

——- Response message ——-

From: "Robert Gomez" <rgomez@dzuktechni_labs.com>
To: "Martin Arrilla" <marrilla@dzuktechni_labs.com>
Subject: Re: arg_supplement
Date: Wednesday, 8:35 AM

Dr. Arrilla:

Tainted subjects. Ignore results. Send me all the files immediately.

Robert Gomez, Ph.D., Research Director, DzuTechni Laboratories, Inc.

Weird, right? I'm still gnawing on this when Phoebe announces that we are close to the Pnumis location. She's going to look for a place to park after she cruises by the location and gives it a cursory once over.

The Pnumis building was set back on a side street, a large facility that ran parallel to the street for about 90 feet, and probably, I don't know, 50 or 60 feet deep. Single story. Standard metal frame, stucco. Just a big warehouse-looking thing. There was a much smaller building next to it, to the left, but the name on it was for some other company.

There were about ten or so parking spaces in the front of Pnumis and the pavement continued behind the building. I assumed this was for more parking, but I couldn't see. There were only two cars parked in the front. Probably not a good sign that they were open for business.

We pulled into a parking lot in front of another small office building two doors down from Pnumis—Morgan Towers it said—but it was only a small single-story structure. Go figure. The lot here was crowded with cars.

"Just go in and ask for an application, then keep your eyes open," Phoebe said encouragingly. "Covert and quiet, no waves."

"What position am I applying for?" I asked as I flipped the front visor down to check my hair and face in the mirror.

Phoebe eyed my clothing. "Maintenance."

Satisfied with my look, but not her answer, I flipped the visor back up, then turned slightly in the seat to face Phoebe. "How do I look?"

"Like an unskilled laborer desperate for a job," she said flatly.

"This is so not going to work," I remarked caustically.

❑ Chapter Fifteen ❑

"Not with that attitude," she chided me.

"Not with any attitude," I scolded back, then softened my rhetoric. "But, I'll give it a try." I opened the SUV door and stepped out. Phoebe gave me a thumbs up. Before I shut the door I leaned back in. "If I'm not back in 30 minutes, you come get me."

I put my hand on the ComUnit, torn between wearing it and tossing it in the SUV. I unclipped it from my belt, stared at it, then clipped it to the inside of my left work boot. Uncomfortable for damn sure, but better to have it and not need it than need it and not have it. Say that five times fast. That, that, that, that, that. I joke when I'm nervous, remember?

I walked down the sidewalk until I reached Pnumis, then cut across the parking lot to the front of the building, which was faced by set of standard double doors with the metal handles on the outside and those lockable push bars on the inside. I could see a woman sitting behind what I assumed was a reception desk. It was a small room, actually, with two doors behind her, both shut. Standard made-in-China lithographs on the wall. I took a deep breath and walked in.

"Where the hell have you been?" the woman immediately said, not really angry, just sort of in a half-scolding tone, standing up and shaking her head. "You should have been here half an hour ago." She removed a headset and sat it on the desk.

Life is really nothing but a game of options. Choices. Decisions. Whims.

Boxers or briefs?

I guess I could have played dumb, stayed with Phoebe's job applicant story. See where that might have led me.

I could have froze, choked up. Hell, I could have turned and ran back out, and I almost did. We could always break in later that night.

Instead, cool as a freaking winter day, I suavely replied, "There was a wreck on the damn highway." Which was probably true, even if it was a lie.

Her face softened, just a little. "Well, that may be so," she laughed without humor, "but I'll let you explain it to Mr. Pivet."

~Dee, any information on this guy Pivet?~ I tried not to sound like that drowning guy I'm always talking about.

"You don't think he'll really be mad at me, do you?" I asked the receptionist, trying to buy some time. Strut and fret, though mostly fretting right now.

She shrugged. "He can be the nicest guy in the world, or the meanest bastard I ever worked for." She seemed to tremble a little, but it was probably just my usual vivid imagination. "Depends on whether you have good news or bad." She had sat back down at her desk.

~I've accessed a company computer network that's only inside this building. Pivet is the Head of R&D.~

Research and Development. You can't hit a homer without swinging at a pitch. Hey, batter, batter. "We all want the research to be a success," I said in the friendliest voice I could manage.

"I don't know how they expect to make gum if they can't even get the basic ingredients blended right," she commented coldly and picked up the headset. My job was to wade through the clues that were gumming up my mind. Sorry, nervous, remember?

"Maybe the Argentineans will come through," I smiled mysteriously as I said this. Without the slightest effing clue why I let that sentence pass my lips. Just throwing it against the wall, if you know what I mean and I think you do.

She lowered the headset. She had a curious expression on her face. "Is that the news you have?" she asked, a little tremor in her voice.

"Emma," I said with a sly grin and walked toward her desk. Her name was engraved on a polished brass plate affixed to one of those triangular wooden stands. Emma Stevens. "You know I can't discuss classified information." I smiled with a wink, as though we were in this together.

She picked the headset up. "He'll be thrilled," she said with some excitement and pushed an array of buttons. "He's here," was all she said into the microphone on the headset.

"Someone will be here shortly to escort you," she said, then seemed to think of something. "Can I offer you some coffee, or water?"

I had meandered over to one of the two chairs in the front. "No, thanks." I sat down and told Dee, ~Tell Phoebe what's going on here.~

~You are taking a big risk, Enoch.~ Dee obviously did not approve of, nor appreciate, my improvisational skills.

◊ Chapter Fifteen ◊

~You and I can always scan blast our way out, if we have to.~ Worked before. Dee would set them up and I could knock them down.

~That's not being very covert and quiet is it?~ she asked in slightly less than loving tones. Think bad dog again.

~It would only be used as a last resort.~ Hopefully not my, gulp, *last*, resort, I thought with a bit of alarm.

That started me thinking on Carl Gustav Jung, the famed psychiatrist and philosopher, who once wrote about a concept he termed synchronicity. Really, it's what I do when I'm pensive. I think too much.

Basically, when a number of events, circumstances, or occurrences take place that are causally unrelated, but yet have some strange meaningful linkage in your thoughts, that is synchronicity.

More or less.

I had come to Pnumis to gather information, and apparently they were expecting someone who was bringing them information. I knew nothing much about Pnumis, and I guess they didn't know much about the messenger, or courier, or whoever I was supposed to be. Because of these factors, there was an overlap in time. An open door. An entrance, and now I was en-tranced, you might say, by my acceptance of this synchronicity.

~Phoebe is angry. She wants to know why you abandoned the plan.~ Judging from her tone, Phoebe wasn't the only one that was upset with me. Women...

~Damn it, Dee, you've been here the whole time. Explain it.~ I also get a bit testy when I'm nervous.

One of the doors opened and two big, hulking, corn-fed goliaths came strolling in. They wore the kind of beatific smiles you abnormally see on masochists pulling the wings off of flies. Or birds.

~Phoebe says she's going to kick your ass.~ I was ever hopeful that after this, I would still have an ass left to kick. Intact would be a bonus.

~Just stay in touch with her and keep her updated.~ This damn multi-tasking was giving me a frigging headache, not to mention fretting about the imminent confrontation with the corn-fed mooks in the blue uniforms.

Yeah, blue uniforms.

You know, the same blue uniforms as the South Africa security guys. I suppose I ought to mention that minor frigging point. Though I tried not to think about it.

With great effort, I kept my face absolutely expressionless as they walked into the room. One of them looked at me and spoke, "Please follow us," and it didn't sound all that polite. More like, *get over here now or we will crush you like a bug*. With an Austrian accent. Probably just my imagination again.

As I walked by Emma's desk, she looked at me sympathetically and whispered, "Good luck," and of course that sort of sent a tingle down the spine. One goon in front, the other behind. Guess to make sure I didn't fall down, go boom, and get an oowie.

We went through the door and it was shut behind us. No, not with a click of echoing finality, though maybe that crossed my pea brain. Just a click. There was a wide corridor in front of us. The walls were painted a light brown and the trim was a dark brown. Not sure why I noticed that, just nervous I guess.

Rambling, sorry.

Closed doors appeared every 20 or 30 feet on both sides until another wall, about 40 feet or so ahead, loomed up. Windows also, but shades or shutters were drawn on them all. There was an elevator directly ahead of us and that appeared to be our destination.

An elevator, for a single story building? Rut row!

~Phoebe doesn't like you getting into the elevator.~ I was going to reply snappily to her something on the order of excrement and its association with Sherlock Holmes, but felt it would belabor the oblivious, obviously.

~Me, either,~ was all I responded back to Dee.

Nonetheless, on the elevator I went. And down we went. It was fast, like the PHANTASM elevator, and I tried to concentrate on how far we were dropping. When we stopped, I figured it was equivalent to Level 3 back home. I think.

The door opened and we stepped off into a short hallway that ran left and right in front of us. We went left. I glanced right. There was only a plain door at the end of the hallway. In front of us, as I marched

☐ Chapter Fifteen ☐

left between Frankenstein One and Two, (leaning out to see) there was a large ornately carved wooden door. It was the standard width, but about ten feet in height. As we got closer, I could see a dazzling array of concentric circles and triangles carved into the surface of the darkly stained wood.

~Dee, you still with me?~

~Yes, Enoch.~

The guy in front opened the door.

Get Ready, Cuz Here It Comes

"No problem can withstand the assault of sustained thinking."
—Voltaire

The Boys Scouts have the coolest motto—"Be Prepared"—and I thought of that as the door slowly opened and we eased into the room.

Man, I was so not prepared.

It was just a regular business office. The kind you have seen a million times if you have ever worked for any big corporation. Same sort of desk, chairs, tables, cabinets, computers, the colorful fake Picasso prints on the wall. Thankfully, the familiarity of it all helped settle me down.

Pivet, or the guy I took to be him, was seated behind his desk studying a computer screen. We walked in and Goon 1 shut the door and stepped to the right while Goon 2 moved to the left. They stood there like roided-up sentinels guarding the hen house. I guess that made me the fox.

Hopefully, not caught with egg on my face.

Pivet waved at one of the chairs. "You're late," was the first thing he said.

"I misjudged the traffic, I'm sorry," was my response, figuring that guys in power love for you to grovel a little and act contrite. Lickspittle.

He nodded benignly. "It happens." He leaned slowly back in his big leather chair and eyed me closely. "What kind of mood was he in when you left?"

Trained actors, confidence men, politicians, and born liars all possess a singularly unique skill that is essential to success in their chosen line of endeavor. They can absorb themselves in a character that does not truly reflect who they really are. They are like chameleons in that regard. However, as I tried to do this myself, I realized it might actually be more subtle than that.

⏻ Chapter Sixteen ⏻

Those kind of people, I decided, simply have no inner being, no true selves. It's easy for them to shed one persona and don another—they are utterly nebulous themselves.

I knew who I was, and being someone else wasn't as easy as I thought, but I was going to do my best.

"He's very upset about South Africa," was what I said, figuring there had to be some kind of linkage between here and there, and the destruction of that facility had to be well-known by now. I was dying—wait, poor choice of words—I was eager to know the identity of that "he" which Pivet, and now me by inference, were referencing.

Pivet made a face. "That was a mistake and someone's head is going to roll," he said with grim chuckle. I was just starting to process that thought when he added, "At least they salvaged the first shipment." This last bit of info kind of spun me around, but I was poker-faced.

Or, about to get poked in the face.

I knew that the facility here was not up and running yet, so I decided to play a gambit. In chess, all that might cost you is a playing piece. Here it might cost, well, a piece of my hide. "He's anxious to know when the facility here will be operational."

That apparently was a sore subject. Pivet cursed, rather skillfully I must say, and looked pointedly at me. "He knows the nature of the problem we are having here, damn it."

Well, I was already treading water, how much deeper could it get? "The Argentineans may have something to say on that."

Pivet squinted at me. He was scowling, most unpleasantly. Crap, from what Emma had let on, this should be good news.

"You have the formula with you?" Now he was smiling and his voice cracked just a little. I breathed an internal sigh of relief.

⁓Dee, tell Phoebe to get ready.⁓ "My associate should be in the building shortly."

"Your associate?" Pivet repeated, his smile changing into an unsure frown. "No one said anything about an associate." I saw him fiddling with something on his desk.

⁓Tell Phoebe to get in here now!⁓ I urgently thought to Dee.

~She's on her way.~

⬚ Get Ready, Cuz Here It Comes ⬚

"We have latitude in cases of extreme security," I said calmly, but hoped that it didn't sound as lame as I thought it did.

Pivet nodded. He let out a breath. "As long as he approved it, it's fine with me." His smile was not nearly as pleasing as it had been earlier. "He did approve it, didn't he?"

Just then the door opened and in walked a tall woman.

That's really not doing it justice. Let me rephrase it. The door opened and in walked this slice of divine femininity who was taller than me, and I'm easily six-foot. She had a Middle Eastern face, almost feline, gorgeous. She was wearing a white dress, textured like a thin sweater, very nicely fitted; lovely long legs; black medium-high heels with petite leather straps wrapped around the front of her finely-turned ankles; hair sort of curled up and tied behind her with a couple of wicked looking pointy things sticking out.

A small, circular, silver medallion on a delicate looking silver chain was around her neck. The medallion rested, comfortably I am sure, just above her, uh, ample bosom. Her proportions were, well, striking and perfect. Her eyes reminded me absently of Hume. Bright, large, and blue.

"Miss Anuket, glad you could join us," Pivet said warmly, respectfully, almost fearfully if you ask me. I noticed the two behemoth guards sort of went rigid, their eyes hooded, guarded, not really watching Anuket, even though she was, IMHO, smoking hot.

Pivet waved at the Goonie Brothers to get their attention. "Bring his associate here," he said gruffly. They grinned eagerly, seemingly relieved to be called into action, and rumbled from the room. I wasn't sure if I was more worried for Phoebe or the two over-muscled beefcakes. Truthfully, I was more worried about me...

"I want to hear for myself the news our courier is bringing," the tall woman said softly, and her carefully countenanced, almost songlike, words sent a tremulous shiver up my spine.

Not because of what she said, but because I recognized her voice.

From the Iranian shoe insert video.

"His associate is delivering the formula," Pivet said softly to this Miss Anuket. I thought he said *associate* with a gentle touch of derision.

⬚ Chapter Sixteen ⬚

As I attempted to remain calm, paranoia was slowly worming its way into the varied thoughts darting around my mind. The way Anuket was now looking at me, examining me, evaluating me, didn't help.

~Dee, get ready to blast these people.~ Tensed and edgy.

~I think we should wait, Enoch.~ I was about to say WTF to Dee, in a nice, frantic, way of course, when I felt tingling in the back of my neck.

~Not me!~ Dee said urgently, and Anuket was smiling like she just ate a canary. Which I think she could do. Alive and squawking.

Damn it, Anuket was an eemee.

"What information are you bringing to us, courier man?" Her smile was about as pleasant as the one the doctor gives you right before he says, "This will only hurt a little." I blocked and held her scan.

Now, here is where things get a little sticky. Dicey.

Proble-freaking-matic.

As I held her scan, not letting it move upwards into my brain stem and allowing her control of my cortex, so to speak, I had the unsettling feeling this eemee was different from Dee, Ruach, or Noet, all of whom had compassionate and endearing qualities. Eemees with a heart, you could say.

This eemee was a real bad bee atch. It was a feeling, a sensation, an intuition if you will, that rippled through my mind like a current from a live wire. Nothing good here, move along now. Wish I could...

As Anuket was scanning me, I started my own scan on Pivet. I knew I couldn't use Dee's EM energy on Anuket, another eemee, but Privet was a different story.

He sat back firmly in his chair when the scan started, not grasping the importance of the Boy Scout motto at all. In a moment or two I felt his mind sort of slide aside. ~I should check the primary pentacle,~ was the thought I was implanting, focusing with pulsating repetition on that single thread. ~I should check the primary pentacle.~ If he pointed it out and I found it, then I could destroy it and send Anuket back to the spectrum and out of my head.

Egyptian goddess wannabee atch turned up her intensity. Don't know if it was a coincidence, or she knew I was in Pivet's mind, but her focus was sharp, probing, cutting, slashing, prodding.

☐ Get Ready, Cuz Here It Comes ☐

I felt my grip on Pivet slide and slip, even though his head turned slightly and he looked over my shoulder—which had to mean something—but I was too absorbed and entangled with my own situation to follow his eyes.

"My, you are a strong one, aren't you?" Anuket said in those measured tones of hers and glided silently over to stand near me. We locked eyes. "Who are you?" she asked pleasantly, but her eyes were not pleasant at all.

The pressure she was applying was immense, constant, unrelenting, absorptive. I had to let Pivet go. He started to shake his head as though he were recovering from a fall. "My name is Enoch," I was stunned to hear myself say and I grimaced against her onslaught.

"Enoch, what a nice name," and she said it so nicely. She was nice, too, and friendly. Very friendly. I felt like it was important that she should know about PHANTASM. That would be nice. I was going to tell her all about it when the door burst open, Phoebe rushed in, and promptly shot Anuket with the BB gun.

Which, thank whomever you want, actually worked, enmeshing her body in those dancing, leaping fingers of multi-colored, almost electrostatic, beautiful, quantified energy that whirled around and engulfed her.

I felt her pressure on me vanish. I let out a huge gasp of air.

Unlike a human, though, Anuket did not go down, but was fighting like a hungry dog denied a bone, and judging by her facial features, just a little pissed off.

Make that utterly pissed off.

~Tell Phoebe to keep shooting her!~ I thought-screamed this and probably rattled Dee's teeth, well, if Dee had teeth to rattle.

Pivet was reaching into his desk drawer. I had full energy now and grabbed him with a scan. He straightened up like a soldier suddenly called to attention. His hand held a revolver, but his fingers instantly loosened and the firearm clattered to the tiled floor.

I blasted into his mind as brutally as I thought he could withstand, ~I should check the primary pentacle.~ Again he lifted his eyes and looked past my shoulder. Hah, to one of the Picasso prints.

☐ Chapter Sixteen ☐

I took three steps forward and knocked the frame from the wall. Anuket, ablaze in a rainbow of sparkling energy and twisting in obvious agony, whirled to face me and tried to move. You could see the mad effort reflected on her pained face as Phoebe shot her again and again. There was a sound in the air not unlike sizzling bacon, and rippling waves of energy seemed to undulate and distort the light. There was an acrid smell like burning tires swirling around the room.

The pentacle was there, behind the painting. I took a maddening look around for some object to use to smash it, saw nothing, dashed as a crazed person to Pivet's desk, grabbed a large staple gun, turned, ran three steps toward the pentacle and threw it as hard as I could.

Anuket screamed, though it was more like a chortled, half-choked, yell, and when the stapler crashed into the intricate workings of the pentacle — smashing it to bits — she simply vanished. No sound, no lights, no transition. Just gone. The bacon stopped cooking, but the pungent and lingering aroma of charred rubber tainted the air.

Pivet was standing there, seemingly frozen in place, his eyes vacant, with an expression on his face that was an equal mix of fear and disbelief.

Phoebe looked at her BB gun and shook it. "Empty," she said laconically and holstered it with cool assurance.

"Phoebe!" I said with a happiness that, trust me, I really felt. That eemee bee atch had been about to kick my no playing ass.

Phoebe was shaking her head and giving me the death stare. "See what he knows," she said, gesturing at Pivet. She was functioning in full blown pro mode.

Before I could even start a scan on him, however, Pivet's face contorted in a frenetic mask of pain. His hands shot to the side of his head and he writhed in agony, then collapsed like a bag of rags to the floor where he now lay in a motionless heap.

Phoebe and I rushed over to him, but even a cursory glance told the tale. Blood was dribbling out his left ear and right nostril.

~Dee, if you didn't do that and I didn't do that...~ The implications bounded around my brain for a few moments — then I looked in wide-eyed alarm at Phoebe. I wanted desperately to get into Pivet's computer, search his desk papers, but there was simply no time.

EXOPHOBE

⎍ Get Ready, Cuz Here It Comes ⎍

"We need to get out of here, now!" I shouted and grabbed Phoebe's arm, dragging her to the door. I let go and we ran out toward the elevator.

We leaped from the open elevator door onto the ground floor, hurtling past the two gagged and bound behemoths. How in the hell did Phoebe do that? Emma was not in sight, I thought idly as we sprinted past her desk and out one of the front doors. We slowed to a jog and then a brisk walk as we hit the pavement, so as not to draw attention to ourselves from any casual observers.

"What happened back there?" Phoebe asked with urgency as we drew near to our rental SUV.

"An eemee energy blast killed Pivet," I replied quietly, my eyes darting around nervously.

"Why did we leave?" she asked angrily, holding her hand up for emphasis. "I'm wearing my attenuator ring!" She gave me an especially dirty look. "We should have looked through his computer," she scolded me.

"You were also wearing that ring when I knocked you out during testing, remember?" I chided her gently. "And this eemee is just as strong as me." Maybe stronger, but I left that part unspoken.

"How is that possible?" Phoebe demanded as she backed out of the parking spot and shoved the gear into drive.

"Exactly what I was thinking," I commented as we drove by the facility and turned onto the access road leading to the highway.

"You mean some other eemee was here, other than that bitch we were fighting?" she asked, making the natural assumption.

"Or, that wasn't the primary pentacle I destroyed," I said more calmly than I felt.

"Why would that be the case?" Phoebe's tone expressed the same bewilderment I felt.

"Dee, you want to comment on this?" Because I was damn sure at a loss.

"Secondary pentacles can function as either linked portals or transportation conduits."

Key-wrap, I had forgot all about that. This was bad. Very bad, if it were true, but I was not yet convinced.

☐ Chapter Sixteen ☐

"I was in Pivet's mind. I told him to show me the primary pentacle. That had to be it," I said, referring to the one I had wrecked with my stapler fastball.

"Empirical evidence would suggest otherwise."

"That's not helping, Dee," I said dryly. "That would mean Pivet was not the controller."

Phoebe immediately asked, "So, who is?" Smart girl, and good-looking, too.

"I cannot answer that inquiry at this time, but I do have some other information that may prove useful."

Might be a good time for some distraction. The traffic was heavy, but Phoebe was maintaining good speed back to the small county airport where our plane was fueled and ready. "Go ahead," I said encouragingly.

"The eyes of the Walking Man in the Iranian shoe insert commercial are a match to the eyes of the eemee known as Noet."

The eemee I freed in South Africa. Anuket's voice and Noet's eyes. Two eemees from two different locations. What the hell did it mean?

Suddenly, those creepy, eerie, fingers of uneasiness that sometimes trickle up your back toward your brain were trickling up my back toward my brain. No, it can't be, I thought with a sickening feeling of dread. Damn, what other kind of dread is there?

"Dee, can you get Joe on the line?" I said this very low, almost a whisper.

Phoebe glanced over and saw the expression on my face. "What's wrong, Enoch?"

I tried not to frighten her. "Hopefully, nothing," I grinned sickly. "Maybe a lot." I frightened her.

"Hey, Enoch," came Joe's jovial voice as his smiling face appeared on the ComUnit. "How can I help you?" He was sitting at his desk surrounded by video screens.

"Hello, Joe, you remember that Iranian video you showed me? The shoe insert one." Hard to forget it.

"Sure do," he replied helpfully. "What about it?"

"What's the creation time stamp on the video file?" My heart was pounding at this point.

☐ Get Ready, Cuz Here It Comes ☐

"Give me a sec," and I heard movement and some noise. "Got it here, let's see; that would have been yesterday, Tuesday, at around 2:30 in the afternoon."

"Thanks, Joe," I said quietly and Dee broke the connection.

"That is not possible," Dee said, **"unless..."**

How could Noet appear in a video created Tuesday afternoon when I had destroyed his primary pentacle earlier that morning? I had seen him vanish from Terloff's office. Yeah, kind of like Anuket vanished.

"Enoch, what's going on?" Phoebe asked with concern, so I told her what I knew, and what I thought I knew.

We are getting close to the airfield. Traffic was heavier. "This is bad," Phoebe intoned. I was rapidly being convinced that things were, indeed, about as bad as they could get.

"Dee, get Tom and Armando for me, please." They had that algorithm running on the Nykr folder. Maybe they had something for us. Hope is the last refuge of the desperate man. Foreplay before unmitigated disaster.

"Yo, E, what up?" Armando.

"Talk to me about the Nykr folder," I requested in calm tones I did not feel at all.

"I'll let Tom tell you," he said, then a rustle of noise.

Tom's voice and visage came on. "Enoch, we finally broke that slippery damn video folder wide open," he said excitedly, with a hint of rightful pride.

"What's in it?" I asked with a newly heightened sense of angst. Knowledge might be power, but it could also be anguish. Usually was. Is.

"Well now, it's not so much what's in it, as how we actually managed to get in it," he said cryptically. Effing tech guys and their need for love and affirmation.

"Okay, how did you get in it?" Like pulling teeth.

"You know the best place to hide things?" This was asked in a quasi-serious voice. If he had been sitting next to me, I would have pulled a few of his teeth.

"Hide things?" was all I could sputter out. I was about to rescind my Copper Gorillas-for-life pledge.

⧫ Chapter Sixteen ⧫

"It's like seeing the forest and not the trees." I could hear the playful humor in his voice but sadly, only images of strangling him played in my mind. Phoebe was pulling into the airfield rental return parking lot. In the distance, I could see our jet on the runway.

"Forest and trees?" I felt groggy, like I had just woken up from sleep.

"The new algorithm didn't really work worth a spit," and he sounded like he was enjoying this.

"Have I mentioned this may be a matter of life and death?" Phoebe was pointing at her wrist, to a non-existent watch, and made a motion like flying. I made a gross face and shrugged.

"Actually, Mando had a vision." That was hacker-speak for a blind, lucky-ass, guess. "The folder name was an anagram," he said simply and I frowned, pondering what this meant. My eyes then shot open and I prayed I wouldn't do duty in my shorts.

"Gee whiz!" I exclaimed loudly. Okay, that's not actually what I said, but what I really said is not fit for human eyes or ears. Speaking of eyes, Phoebe's opened to the size of saucers, and more than a few very saucy and completely unladylike words escaped from her mouth. After that I stated softly, emphatically, "An anagram of Denton R. Hume."

"Yes, sir," Tom acknowledged with a monstrous grin. "That got us right into the *demonhunter* folder and we downloaded the video."

I'm not even sure, after this, that the video even mattered. The anagram seemed a fairly damning revelation, on the face of it. "What was in the video?" I asked disjointedly.

"Wish I could tell you. More stinking high-level security," he replied with a sigh. "We're hacking on it." No accompanying smile.

I let out my own long breath. "Keep me posted. Awesome work guys." Dee broke the connection and we climbed out of the vehicle.

———⧫———

We had taken off, leveled at cruising altitude, and Phoebe had switched on the autopilot. Not a word had yet been exchanged between us. Finally she looked at me, confusion, fear, anger all roiled together in an unsettling mix. She looked the way I felt.

"It doesn't necessarily mean a thing." This was tossed out by me as a way of starting the conversation and attempting to deflect and alleviate her concerns. We had opened up a couple of candy bars, but they were only half-eaten. Frigging caramel anyway. Two plastic bottles of lukewarm water sat in cup holders between us.

"Or, everything," she said gently, pointedly. Defying me, requiring me to provide further explanation.

I carefully and dutifully noted Phoebe's tense demeanor, twisted my right ear lobe, then idly rubbed my chin. Mostly to buy some time as I thought this through. "You've been at PHANTASM, what did you say the other day, almost four years?" I asked in my best cool, logical, voice. I always wanted to make a T-shirt that read, *You can't ration rationality.* If you steal that, I'll sue.

Phoebe nodded in the affirmative. "And in those four years," I went on relentlessly, "has Hume ever given you a reason to doubt his sincerity, or his leadership?" I offered this inquiry in the same level, reasonable tone. Vulcan logic is untouchable. Though, usually only for a Vulcan.

With the fingers of her right hand, she absently rubbed the side of her forehead and said softly, thoughtfully, "No"—she then looked cogently at me—"but, what about all this recent information, especially the anagram thing?" The emotions of irritated confusion and satisfied acceptance were equally present within her, and battling for the upper hand. "How do you explain that?"

I blew out a deep, raggedy, breath. "How long has Hume been at PHANTASM?" I felt ignorant for not having learned more about the company I was now employed with but, considering the rather nonstop hurly-burly nature of the last four days, I think my lack of knowledge was understandable, though easily remedied.

"About seven years," Phoebe answered. "He was the one who started the operation." She was eyeing me intently, I imagine wondering where I was going with this. Me, too.

Wondering, not eyeing.

"So, we can assume that any enemies of PHANTASM, or of Hume himself, are well aware of his existence? And the existence of PHANTASM?" This seemed a most reasonable question. Even in the face of unreasonable doubt, Cartesian or otherwise.

☐ Chapter Sixteen ☐

Phoebe gave me a non-committal nod, but uncertainty clouded her eyes. "We carefully guard the identity of all field agents and operatives," she stated flatly. Assail that!

"Was he, himself, ever in the field?" I asked, trying to press home my salient point.

She pursed her lips, thinking about it, and reluctantly shook her head. "I don't think so, no."

"Okay," I said with an encouraging smile. "Do you honestly think, then, that the human controllers we're searching for have never heard of PHANTASM?" I didn't mean to, but I gave her an especially withering look. Maybe I meant to. "They have never heard of PHANTASM, an agency whose sole purpose is to, basically, root them out and then kick their ass?"

"Fine, what's your point?" she said, though not particularly happy about her forced acquiescence.

"Well, Phoebe, suppose Tom and Armando hack into, I don't know, the Argentinean server, and they find a folder there with your name on it, O-H-A-R-A." I spelled it out for added oomph. "Should they conclude you're a bad guy, a traitor?" I paused for just a moment.

"Or, should they think that perhaps the enemy knows about you, and maintains digital records of what it knows about you in a folder that has your name?" Her face was all the proof I needed that I had stuck a resonant nerve.

I let a moment pass and continued: "What if you found a folder with my name..." Before I could finish the sentence, Phoebe stopped me with a raised hand and a look of mildly vexed irritation. Which rapidly morphed into a demure and polite demi-death stare.

"Okay," she granted with a recalcitrant smile. "I get your point." Indeed, her expression seemed calmer. "But, it still doesn't explain everything else that's been going on." Hell hath no fury like a woman's question left unanswered.

"I have a theory on that," I replied with a wistful smile.

"Be still my beating heart," Phoebe said with a tilted non-smile smile of her own. She made the standard fluttering heart gesture with the fingers of her right hand over her chest. Very amusing.

☐ Get Ready, Cuz Here It Comes ☐

I held a certain finger up to my eye. "You're number one in my eyes," I commented with a joking look.

She cast me a playful scowl. "What's the theory, Einstein?"

I rubbed my hands together. "First, I need to get some info from Dee, who has been listening, right?" I said it with a hint of humorous accusation.

"You never instructed me to go into silent mode," Dee instantly shot back, mirroring my mocking tone precisely.

"From hence forth, dear Dee, you are free to listen to any conversation I have." I said this as heartfelt as possible because, truth be told, without Dee, there would be no Enoch. Well, not alive, anyway.

"I am touched by your kindness, Enoch," and she did, indeed, seem emotional about it. I cleared my throat, kind of embarrassed by all this sudden feminine gooeyness.

"Dee, can eemees go, uh, bad?" I wasn't exactly sure how to phrase it. "Evil, I mean." Yeah, I was thinking of Anuket.

"When we are in the EM spectrum, Enoch, there is no good or evil. We are beyond those concepts." She paused, as though carefully weighing her words. **"We do not interact, per se, with others in the spectrum, only the complement."** I still did not understand that part completely, but I did not want to interrupt Dee's explanation. **"However, when we are invoked from the spectrum by a human controller and assume a physical manifestation in human form, we are suddenly subject to the dilemma of free will."**

In truth, that answer was the one I feared to hear. "Dee, what happens if the human controller is, uh, killed or relinquishes control of the pentacle to the, er, invoked entity; the eemee?"

"The eemee would control their own destiny and could choose to remain, or could choose to destroy the pentacle and return to the spectrum." Dee replied without emotion, her words clipped, tense. I think the ramifications of my questions were hitting home in her mind.

Phoebe had already leaped ahead. "You're thinking Anuket and Noet may be acting on their own, without human control?" The level of excited incredulity in her voice was palpable.

⬚ Chapter Sixteen ⬚

"I have no proof of that, just a feeling," I answered honestly. However, it was a scratch I badly wanted to itch.

"And yet," Dee said softly, sadly, **"I fear it might be a valid intuition."**

Phoebe was still puzzled, judging by the expression on her features. "But, what would the eemees want?"

Dee did not say anything, so I took my mental machete out to whack at it. "They have human form now and are, essentially, human." I shrugged. "I think the temptations of the flesh, and the temporal lust for fortune and fame, would consume them just as it does many of us."

"Ruach did not remain for those reasons," Dee said passionately.

"You are right, but I do not include him in my theory." I was truly, terribly, sorry that I had not summarily preempted him, and felt compelled to explain further. "There is a basic kindness and goodness in Ruach, a..."—I stumbled for the exact word I wanted—"...a spirituality that one rarely encounters in humans, uh, or eemees." I scruxillated up that last bit, but didn't know what else to say.

Phoebe piped in, "I couldn't agree more. Ruach is one of the finest souls I have ever known." Bless her heart for bailing me out, yet again.

"And I as well," Dee added and I was overwhelmed by the raw emotion invested in her words.

I had to move beyond this delicate subject. "Ruach is not the problem. He is not the enemy," I stated emphatically and sighed. "I think it's possible, hell, very probable, that we are being deliberately misled." Just a moment to let this register. "I feel like we are being pushed on a path encouraging us to suspect Hume while the other eemees continue making their plans."

"Plans for what?" Phoebe demanded to know.

"Do you remember that Iranian video?" All of these isolated and sundry thoughts were rambling and cascading through my mind; sensory overload. I was almost in a neuro-frenzy attempting to sort them into some kind of cohesive story, link them together, find connections. Like a drunkard doing calculus.

Phoebe nodded in affirmation to my question about the Iranian video. "The effects were strong," I commented, then gave Phoebe a grim smile. "You even wanted to buy a pair of the shoe inserts."

She seemed to shiver. "I remember I wasn't the only one," she added thoughtfully. I nodded.

"Dee," I began a query. "An eemee cannot force a human to act, correct? I mean, you can't make a person do something against their will?" I'm pretty sure I knew the answer, but I wanted the facts out in the open.

"An eemee can manipulate EM energy to implant thoughts and ideas in a human mind. However, if such thoughts and ideas are not in accord with the person's basic internal beliefs, that person will probably not act upon those implanted thoughts and ideas."

That's what I thought, though that "probably" thing troubled me a little. Still, I had a couple of twists on the topic. "Two questions then, Dee." Brief pause. "Question one—what about someone who has no real strong set of internal values, no core beliefs?"

"Those minds are easy to sway. An eemee can manipulate EM energy in the form of any kind of audio or video informational stream to influence and modify their behavior."

That's also what I figured. People like that were going to be fodder for EM manipulation no matter who was controlling it, human or eemee. Those sorts would flock to any banner the manipulated EM message pointed them toward. It was the other kind of people I was most worried about.

"Okay, question two, but a premise first, as previously established. Under normal circumstances, an eemee cannot make someone with strong internal values act against their own beliefs. They cannot influence them." I wanted to make sure I understood this point absolutely.

"That is essentially accurate."

"Then, how can you explain what happened to Phoebe and I after viewing that Iranian video?" I paused for just a contemplative moment and then finished up. "We felt the need, almost a compulsion, to buy those shoe inserts right then and there."

"Yes," Dee readily agreed, **"however, the effects were temporary and rapidly vanished."**

"True," I rebutted graciously, "but, only after we stopped watching the video." I refute you thusly.

☐ Chapter Sixteen ☐

"Not correct, Enoch," Dee stated patiently. **"You both watched the video a second time, and the effect was negligible by then. The video has a purely transitory impact."**

I stood corrected. But, now it was time to uncork my zinger, bring the heat—a little chin music, to use baseball terminology. "What if the technology existed to make the effects last longer, say, a lot longer?" That thought had been festering in my mind like an open wound. Sorry for that visual.

No response right away, then: **"Your question is positively speculative in theory but only marginally possible in reality."**

After a few moments, while I repeated that three times fast to myself, I said quietly, "Explain that."

"The technology to empower such a longer-lasting effect does not currently exist," Dee stated flatly.

Phoebe, bright girl, chimed in, "But, the implication is that it could be created."

"Possible in reality," Dee repeated. **"Marginally."**

"Dee, how would such technology work?" I wondered. "Can you speculate?" I wanted her best conjecture on this topic.

"It would require sublimation of certain aspects of the human neurological structure."

Phoebe shook her head, and I could tell she was not sure what Dee meant. "Say it a different way," Phoebe asked softly.

"Parts of the human cerebral cortex, most notably the frontal lobe, would need to be altered by electrochemical processes to dampen or inhibit rational and logical thinking skills."

I was going to comment on this when Dee spoke again. **"Ruach is asking for you, Enoch."**

"Put him on," I quickly replied.

Ruach's strong and vibrant face appeared on the ComUnit screen. "Ruach, good to hear from you," and I meant it in earnest. "What's up?"

There was a graceful pause. "How was Knoxville?" he asked without a shift in facial expression.

Phoebe and I exchanged shocked looks; I suppose guilty shocked looks from Ruach's perspective. I swallowed hard and took a breath.

"Why would you ask that?" Not overly clever, true, but I was scrambling to get my scrambled-eggs brain out of the frying pan. And stay out of the fire!

"Well," he said with a gentle smile, "I was just reading a report from someone you may know." He was being very nice, even though it felt as if a hammer blow was about to be delivered. "Her name, when you met her, was Emma." The hammer blow fell, and I felt a little like a ten-penny nail.

Oh crap. Crap, crap. Crap cubed. The Pnumis receptionist had been a PHANTASM operative! That meant Hume would know all about the Knoxville debacle. "We thought it was important to see what was going on for ourselves," I lobbed that weak explanation barely over the net, fully expecting it to be slammed back.

"I read a quote recently, something about a road to Hell and good intentions," he said with a wry little smile.

"I'll get a full report to you when we get back," I offered contritely, weakly, groping.

Ruach regarded me with a mischievous look. "Emma was very good at her job, Enoch. She even managed to plant a video camera in Pivet's office."

Man, this crappy day was really circling down the toilet now. Phoebe rolled her eyes skyward. "So, you saw what happened there?"

Ruach nodded. "Most of it. A few things were out of frame." I was not going to ask him to clarify that remark.

"What's your general impression?" I prodded him. Might as well make the worst out of bad situation.

Ruach thoughtfully rubbed his chin. "I believe you should answer that query first, based on our respective positions within the PHANTASM hierarchy." Wow, I have never had rank pulled on me quite so eloquently.

I took a gulp of air. "We thought we had destroyed the primary pentacle and sent an eemee named Anuket back to the spectrum, but it was an eemee scan blast that killed Pivet, so we can only assume that it was a secondary pentacle, and Anuket is still here on earth." That was about as succinct as I could put it. Especially since I was out of breath.

⟦ Chapter Sixteen ⟧

"My conclusion as well," Ruach confirmed. He went on, "However, their production troubles remain unresolved." He said that latter bit as a statement and not a question. I did not dispute it, since it jelled with my understanding, so I remained silent on that topic. There was a question, though, I had to ask. Need to know basis.

"Has Hume seen the report?" I asked as calmly as I could, considering the circumstances.

"I am the filter through which information from operatives must pass before it gets to Dr. Hume," Ruach replied, regarding me with his large, dark, eyes. "Eventually, this information must be passed to him."

Now, I pride myself on being a kind of smart fellow. Okay, not always. Arrogance to the point of ignorance sometimes, I'll grant you. But, I could not help notice how he used the word *eventually*, which implied that he had not yet forwarded the report to Hume, and may possibly hold it for a short while yet. Well, that was my interpretation.

"He does have a great deal already on his mind," I said suggestively, hoping to get some kind of confirmation of my thinking from Ruach, but he was impassive. I was determined to stay quiet and let him initiate the next bit of the discussion.

The merest flitter of a smile creased his face. "Since Dr. Hume is out of town and won't be back until late this evening, I can't imagine he'll see my report until midday tomorrow, at the earliest."

I wanted to ask a question, but it appeared to me that Ruach had more to say, so mum was the word.

"This will resolve itself as time passes, but there is another pressing issue." I let out a little gusty breath in preparation for whatever it was Ruach was about to say. "We had some kind of security breach the other night," he said pleasantly, as though he were commenting on nothing more important than the weather or what he had for lunch.

"Nothing serious, I hope?" Which seemed the inevitable and expected response, so I offered it.

"Well, we aren't sure, exactly," and he was really watching my face. I mean, really giving me the hard study. I maintained eye contact, unwavering. "It appeared to be unauthorized access to a secure area here at PHANTASM, but we didn't find any hard evidence of it." His voice was melodic, pleasing.

☐ Get Ready, Cuz Here It Comes ☐

"Possibly a faulty circuit in the alarm," I tossed out, realizing I probably sounded like an idiot. If the shoe fits...

"As they say, though, absence of evidence is not evidence of absence," he said in carefully measured rhythm, but I knew that old investigatory trick, having said it previously.

"What secure area?" I inquired innocently, even though I already knew the answer. Phoebe's eyes were as big as saucers, again. She was shaking her head.

"An area that is very dangerous," he answered in solemn tones. "An area that, for those unfamiliar with such things, will seem incomprehensible without a proper understanding."

It was my turn to step up on the tight-wire and try my best at balancing without falling off. "I'm new to PHANTASM. Is this something that I should understand, in case it becomes an issue for me?" The best defense is a good offense. Preferably a nuke from orbit.

He seemed to be considering this. "Yes, but this is a subject we can discuss upon your return." That meant the matter was closed for now.

"We'll contact you as soon as we're back," I said softly.

"That's good, Enoch. I will do everything in my power to help you," and with that cryptic statement he signed off and disappeared.

I sat back, contemplating all of this. Phoebe was watching me. A few moments went by and she noted the absorbed expression on my face. "You're going back there, aren't you?" I knew she was talking about Level 5.

"No, Phoebe partner, *we* are going back there." One of us was smiling. It wasn't Phoebe.

Taking It To Another Level

"The basic difference between an ordinary man and a warrior is that a warrior takes everything as a challenge while an ordinary man takes everything either as a blessing or a curse."

—Carlos Casteneda

First order of business was trying to figure out what had triggered the alarm on Level 5 during our previous visit. We couldn't very well go wandering back down there and run the risk of being nabbed, well, *in flagrante delicto* so to speak, as we violated Level 5 security measures once again. Not good to be caught in the act. Would look bad on the résumé. Hard to defend the indefensible.

It was Phoebe's idea to get that scenario ironed out, and a good one.

As Dee ran diagnostics reviewing available data, Phoebe and I continued bumping around theories about what everything we had recently learned meant, exactly. Or, inexactly. Well, make a valiant attempt to see what it meant...

"They're going to use advertising with the same digital tricks that were in that Iranian video to sell products to people without the brain power to resist," she stated in strong and emphatic terms. She then shook her head in righteous anger. "They stand to make tens of millions, hundreds of millions, billions, in forced products sales."

That was hard logic to dispute, refute, or otherwise disagree with. Considering the kind of money those product sales could generate, using eemee techniques, the profits would be, well, obscene. Even by the standards of decent society. Shoot, even indecent society.

But, something still bugged me. Was chewing on me like a chigger trapped in my socks. "I just have this feeling that it's not about the money. I mean, it is, but it's more than that." And, yes, I'm sure that sounded just as wishy-freaking-washy to Phoebe as it did to me.

☐ Taking It To Another Level ☐

"It's always about the money," Phoebe countered, not convinced. "They can use that money for lots of evil and nasty things." She was idly twisting and untwisting the small nylon strap on her ComUnit.

"Not arguing that, Phoebe, but evil people have a lot of money right now, and the world still turns," I reminded her, though preparing myself for her obvious rejoinder. Hopefully, not crushing my windpipe at the same time.

"The world is in crappy shape right now, Enoch, and you know it," she ruthlessly effaced my argument with the sort of acerbic tone she normally reserved for rude drivers. "Lots of bad governments are trying to control people's behavior." As soon as she said that, I knew we would rapidly be tearing off madly on a new tangent. I put on my best Boy Scout face, getting ready for it.

"My gawd, Enoch!" Phoebe blurted out in horror. "What if the eemees are working for some kind of evil country, you know, turn everyone into mind-numbed zombies that don't question anything?"

"That's a bit paranoid, isn't it?" I quickly countered, though the same thought had briefly entered my mind, and been dismissed. The thought, not my mind.

"Let me see if I have this straight, Enoch Maarduk," and whenever a woman uses my full name, I know I am about to get whackled and stampoozled. "We have these powerful eemees, able to influence human thoughts through digital signal manipulation"—she nailed me with a skunk eye—"and then there is some possible new technology that would allow that influence to last a really long time."

This was followed by a particularly wicked smile; not bedroom wicked, but the mildly unfriendly variation. "Which means the evil government, in league with the eemees, could make people think and do anything they want, and you don't think this is a good way to take over a country?" Can you hear that, the sound of sarcasm dripping from that question and splatting on the floor next to my feet?

"Well, Phoebe," I replied in my most patient, yet respectful, tone; "that would require lots of people, I mean, a real conspiracy theory thing." I groaned a little for effect, I admit it. "Entire nations and governments would have to be involved!" I shook my head. "The only evidence we have right now is for the existence of five small companies, and only two of them, Nykr and Cambio, are actually producing and shipping a product for sale."

"There is that shipment from South Africa which may not have been destroyed," Dee added thoughtfully. Damn, that comment from Pivet about a salvaged shipment. I added that forlorn fact to my already overwhelmed mental checklist.

"Do you see my point?" I pleaded to Phoebe, whose expression had softened a little.

"I'll grant you that, right now, it's just five small companies," she said petulantly, "but, what will it be tomorrow, and the day after that?"

"I agree with you, which is why we must stop all this now," I said with harsh finality.

"It was the lights," Dee said out of the blue, as it were.

"The lights?" You notice how I am really good at saying nothing with something. Takes clever mad reaction skill to buy thinking time like that. Or, not.

"In Level 5, when you triggered the motion sensor that switched the pentacle room lights on, it tripped a silent alarm."

"Can you deactivate it, or bypass it or something?" I believe my breathing stopped.

"I already have a routine in place that can be initiated at the appropriate time."

"I could just hug you, Dee," I said happily. And started to breathe again.

"You are such a tease, Enoch. I will enjoy a vicarious thrill if you hug Phoebe."

Phoebe was regarding me with raised eyebrows and, I think, daring me to try. "Rain check, Dee, but I appreciate the sentiment."

By this time a little headache, with which I had been previously engaged in battling, had gained a pernicious foothold and, with irresistible momentum, was rapidly intruding into my consciousness. You know, to the point that all you can do is think about your headache and little else.

As if some tiny little gremlin with a red hot poker was just inside my skull.

⊓ Taking It To Another Level ⊓

Probably residual effects from my nasty confrontation with that ^&%*$ Anuket. Phoebe agreed, as she appraised my squinched up face and haggard eyes, that I should get some rest.

I thanked her for her sagacious advice and tilted my seat back. And moments later was out like the proverbial light.

Phoebe must be going soft (I concluded moments later when my mind fully engaged), as it was only the gentlest of nudges and the softest of voices that roused me from my extended nap. Thankfully, the pain in my head had receded to just a faint and distant throb. Not perfect, but ignorable, as long as I didn't think about it. What?

We landed without incident. Any landing you can walk away from is a good one. Shoot, even run away from.

The cab ride back to PHANTASM was uneventful. Even a casual glance at Phoebe's face revealed her inner turmoil as she pondered the many disparate bits and pieces of information we had on hand. My own thoughts were jumping from one scenario to the next, bandying one conclusion about with another until all I had was this jumbled morass of flotsam and jetsam that made me cross-eyed. Or, just cross.

When in doubt, shoot zombies. I could have upgraded to the rocket launcher, but nothing seemed quite as satisfying as a shotgun blast at close range. Digital mayhem is very rewarding. Probably a character flaw.

The cabbie dropped us off in front of PHANTASM as the last vestige of the sun dipped below the horizon. Phoebe and I agreed that, if anyone asked, we had been out exploring the town. A gray lie.

I pointed to my left shoulder as we were walking to the front door. "These BioPatches work great," I said with an impish grin, "but I could use some real food."

"Wednesday is enchilada day in the cafeteria, and they are to die for," Phoebe replied with her own charming smile. "Metaphorically, of course."

"Of course," I answered as we trudged down the familiar white hallway.

⏀ Chapter Seventeen ⏀

"Clean up, get refreshed, and I'll meet you there in an hour or so," Phoebe announced as we entered the elevator.

"A woman with a plan is always dangerous," I remarked with a light-hearted look.

"I'm dangerous even without a plan," Phoebe said flatly and gave me a glance that buckled my knees. Have I mentioned she is really good-looking?

We exited and headed for our respective quarters.

I flashed through my shower; did a shave touch-up; changed into some fresh clothes; grabbed my pack and gear; then dashed like an idiot (very much like one, actually) down to the cafeteria, merrily determined to get there before Phoebe which, happily, I did.

As the minutes ticked by I began to think, standing as I was outside the cafeteria, propped up against the wall, about my proposed revisit to Level 5, especially in light of Ruach's mysterious admonition not to go there.

I was getting nervous and began thinking about enchiladas.

I spent some time in south Texas, so I know a thing or three about enchiladas. I imagine everyone knows what an enchilada is but, because I feel the need to clamor up on the soapbox and expound on this, please allow me to orate on their multitudinous virtues.

At its most basic elemental level, an enchilada is simply corn dough, formed into a sort of flat, thin, pancake, cooked to correct consistency on a hot, dry, skillet and then rolled around and stuffed with a filling of some kind (e.g., meat, cheese, beans, potatoes, vegetables, rice, seafood, or any combination of these items thereof).

It is then slathered or drizzled (as the recipe demands) with a sauce, and not just any sauce. The word enchilada is derived from the Spanish word *enchilar* which means "to add chili peppers to" or to season with such peppers. It is a very, very, ancient food. Probably back then they used the peppers to mask the taste of bad meat. Come to think of it, some places still do that. Hah! Anyway...

The perfectly constructed enchilada is comprised of three parts. The whole is greater than the sum of the parts. AUM. Very threefold.

◻ Taking It To Another Level ◻

First part, there is the corn tortilla itself, which demands the best maize kernels, hopefully stone ground fresh in a classic black basalt molcajete, which you can also call a mortar and pestle if you wish. The only missing ingredient for the tortilla now is good, clean, pure aqua—water—to make the *masa de maiz* or corn dough.

Second part, there is the filling. Here is where individual preferences and tastes often express themselves in extravagant combinations, using the fillings noted four paragraphs above, in such peculiar culinary blends as to warrant admiration, or possibly disgust. I'm thinking shrimp and pork should never appear together in public, but hey, who am I to say what's fit to eat?

I prefer simplicity in my filling. It must blend with all other aspects of the enchilada in a pleasing manner, so I can taste everything and not feel as though World War Three was breaking out in my palate.

The third and last part, but certainly not the least, is the sauce. This is where the true art of the enchilada must be given its due. Here is where one must confront the awesome tableau of available peppers—mild, medium, hot, and freaking dangerous—and make a proper usage thereto, adding just enough to provide that endorphin-inducing kick without reducing you to a simpering wimp crying in the corner, begging for milk to quell the flame and keep your lips from exploding.

Phoebe came around the corner, her pack dangling loosely from her shoulder, and waved.

I'm really sorry for that enchilada thing, but when I get really, really, nervous, I explicate, pontificate, and otherwise rattle on about things until someone stops me or I pass out from exhaustion.

Usually the former.

I waved back at Phoebe. "Sorry I'm early," I sputtered out, grinning like someone who ought to be medicated.

Phoebe eyed me closely as she walked up. "Are you feeling okay, Enoch?" She tilted her head and gave me a good-looking over. "You seem a little odd," she said and quickly added: "I mean, more than usual." At least she was smiling as she said this.

I followed her into the cafeteria.

☐ Chapter Seventeen ☐

We were getting into line. I shook my head. "I dunno, maybe it's the after effects of that witch Anuket."

"Still have the headache?" She asked this as, with a clattering echo, we slid our red plastic trays onto the stainless steel tubes attached to the buffet-style guide rails.

"No," I replied softly. "Actually, I feel great." Which was true. I hadn't felt this good in a long time.

"Maybe it's the after effects of the MedPatch," Phoebe suggested as we loaded up our plates with enchiladas, rice, charro beans, and iced tea. The woman behind the counter looked at me like I was mad when I asked for a Big Red. Ignoble wench.

I thought about the MedPatch stimulant blow back possibility for a moment. "Nah, I've had enough little cat naps here and there." I shook my head. "I think it's just sheer brain overload." We picked a table and sat down.

Phoebe nodded. "I feel your pain." We ate in silence for awhile until Phoebe looked at me with arched eyebrows. Here it comes. "So," she leaned in slightly and said in a low whisper, "what's your plan for Level 5?"

I also leaned in, very conspiratorial, and simply replied, "Ruach wants us to go there." The enchiladas were ridiculously good. Sublime and spicy. Just the way I like my wom... Er, enchiladas.

"Ruach wants us to go there," she repeated in doubtful, doleful, tones. She regarded me with an effusive stare that didn't require much elaboration as to its true intent. "This is the same Ruach who warned us it was very dangerous there, right?" She idly stabbed her enchilada a few times.

"That was actually the signal for us to go back," I replied enthusiastically, though without great affect upon her. I sighed. "We have to know more about what's going on down there, Phoebe," I said in plain, candid, truth, and this got her attention. "I know this isn't scientific, or based on reliable intel, but my gut is telling me we have to go."

Phoebe looked at my plate, at me, and then pointed her fork at one of my untouched enchiladas. "Is that one of the three-cheese ones?" I nodded slowly and she sawed off a bite with her fork and ate it.

"Damn, that is good." She seemed to be giving careful consideration to the enchilada morsel she had just consumed. "The serrano-cranberry sauce is spicy, but not enough to scare you away." She shook her head and looked wistfully at me. "Kind of like Level 5."

I chuckled. "Then it's a good thing you didn't try the beef one with habanero sauce." I waved a hand at my mouth like it was on fire, which it was. We both laughed at that. I relaxed. Without Phoebe, Level 5 was not something I would try to tackle alone.

"Dee, is everything still a go?" We didn't want any more silent alarms going off. Does a silent alarm go off?

"GTG!" I guess Dee had been studying text messaging. Tom was probably a bad influence. And, naturally, thinking of Tom made me excitedly think of any new information he and Mando might have.

"I'll get him on the line," Dee informed me. Damn, I forgot, she could sense any over-wrought or agitated thought. Hopefully, not the Phoebe ones. Dee was silent on that, so I breathed a mental sigh of relief.

"Enoch, Dee says you need to talk to me." It was Tom, sitting at a desk surrounded by computers, displays, boxes, widgets, wires, and Shiva knows what else, munching on a candy bar. Dee had previously linked Tom's home video transmitter to my ComUnit.

"Just checking in for an update," I said with a smile.

Armando's mustached face popped into frame, "Do you have a bug planted here?" He popped off the frame.

"What was that about a bug?" I asked, a bit confused. Phoebe was shaking her head in denial.

Tom laughed. "It's just that your sense of timing is always uncanny, Enoch." He shook his head this time. "We just got the cookie analysis in from Mando's buddies." I waited patiently, as Tom can be a bit melodramatic at times. "I'm uploading the report to Dee now."

"Great work guys," I thanked them and then paused, to see if Tom had anything else to add. When only painful silence ensued, I am sure he sensed what was coming next, "So, any luck on the video hack?"

"Oh, yes, Enoch," Tom said with a rueful, self-effacing smile, "plenty of luck." He grimaced. "All bad!"

⬚ Chapter Seventeen ⬚

He twisted his neck around, trying to get a crick out, real or imaginary. "The good news is that we've eliminated most of the crack methods that won't work." I wasn't exactly sure how that qualified as good news, but I was willing to let it slide in the name of friendship, or whatever. "Mando says he's sleeping here until we figure it out," Tom said, moderately serious. "Unless one of his girl friends calls," he added with an amused look.

"Then turn the phone off," I said, more than moderately serious. "We need to know what's in that video."

"Just a matter of time, E, just a matter of time," he said in a tired, yet determined, voice.

"Thanks for everything, I mean it, and I'll be in touch," I said, ending the connection. His image vanished.

"Dee, is there a report from PHANTASM for the lab analysis on the South African cookies?" In the maniacal hubbub I'd almost forgot about it.

"Let me check the servers," Dee said and there were a few moments of quiet. **"Yes, I'll display it now."**

Hmm... The PHANTASM lab, I concluded after reading the report, did a fabulous and notable job of proving that the cookies were, indeed, nothing but cookies. No extra ingredients, inert or otherwise, were noted. It was a one-sheet, half-page, report, short and sweet. "Show me Mando's report," I said casually to Dee. It flashed up on the screen.

"Well," Phoebe said, reading the document with me as it appeared on the ComUnit, well-positioned on the table between us, "that tells a different tale."

Mando's former shady chemical business guys had a very comprehensive report and it listed every component ingredient and its percentage of the total. Their analysis indicated 20% of the cookie included inert ingredients, most of which I didn't give a big woo about, but the appearance of our old friend the ergoline peptide alkaloid was carefully noted.

I couldn't imagine with their, uh, background in that area, these guys would misidentify any chemical like that.

More importantly, I couldn't figure out how the PHANTASM lab guys had missed it. "Dee, who signed off on the PHANTASM report?"

"Dr. William Fulsum," she replied quickly, but it didn't clang any bells with me.

I looked at Phoebe and she was shaking her head. "Is there a bio on him?" I directed this query to Dee.

"A biological on him?" Dee asked in some consternation. She wasn't completely up on all slang yet.

"A biography, or some employment records," I clarified for her. Just a moment passed.

"No biography that I can find. I have located the employment records, but they are on a secure server."

"Can you access those records?" That would be the easiest route.

"The protocol required would leave a digital footprint of my presence." In other words, Tom and Armando would be needed and, truth be told, letting those two guys root around in the PHANTASM system really wasn't rocking my world right now. Still, it might be the only viable option. I was caught between a rock and, well, another effing rock. Cliches bite, but I still like them. Character flaw. Tragic.

"Dee, if I ask Tom and Armando to check on this, can you limit their access to that particular server only?" I was not sure I wanted to be the guy who let the raging bulls loose in the lingerie department.

"Hold for system check," Dee replied and Phoebe was shaking her head. Her neck muscles must be awesome because, most of the time, that's all she did.

"What?" I said, trying to do my best impression of some television sitcom idiot. Pretty good, too. The impression part, not the idiot part.

"I know we need the information, but do you think letting Tom and Armando hack around inside PHANTASM is a good idea?" Good-looking or not, that woman can get on my nerds. Hah, nerves, but nerds works, too, right? Anyway...

"A good idea?" I slung it back at her. "No, it's a crappy idea, but I'm waiting to hear a better one." He shoots, he scores.

"Fine," she said in a short, clipped, tone, which I am fairly positive didn't really mean *fine*, but actually meant *I will kick your ass if this goes south*.

"I can monitor their activity and report to Enoch any unplanned intrusions." Dee to the rescue!

⧉ Chapter Seventeen ⧉

That worked for me. "Get them the links they need and see what they can find on this Fulsum character." I had my fingers crossed when I said this. I even looked at Phoebe with my eyes crossed. She scowled and, surprise, surprise, shook her head.

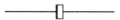

The last time we had been in the stairwell of Level 4, looking for the entrance to Level 5, it had been around two in the morning on a work day. Not much risk of idle foot traffic passing by. Now it was just at the end of a regular work day and no such assurances existed. Dee informed us she would be monitoring all cameras and alert us to any unwelcome activity.

The only issue for me and Phoebe, standing by the stairwell of Level 4 arguing, er, engaged in animated discussion, was, if someone did come along, how were we going to explain the boxes that would no longer be stored nicely under that stairwell.

It was decided, mostly by me, that we would move all the boxes out and stack them as neatly as possible, so it would appear that they were supposed to be stacked outside the stairwell in that fashion. We would, from under the stairwell, do our best to slide the whole mess over to cover the opening.

Mice and men, Phoebe and boxes, and plans that stink.

We oozed and squeezed in on the far end and then tried like mad to wrangle the stack of boxes over to block the opening better, but it was awkward and heavy. The boxes, not the opening.

Anyway, after a few frantic minutes, and some creative use of the English language by Phoebe that made even me gasp, we said &*^%^ it and crawled toward the little door. Dee assured us that security personnel did not pass through the stairwell on routine checks until later in the evening. Usually.

Cold comfort.

Phoebe tested the small door frame again and it came up negative. Same for Dee's scan on the little room. We wriggled through and stood up. Phoebe picked the door lock, just as efficiently as before, we meandered down the hallway, and stood facing the final door.

▢ Taking It To Another Level ▢

Dee's voice came wafting from the ComUnit. **"Before I open this door, I need for both of you to understand the condition of the entity you will encounter in that room."** She was referring to the eemee man that had asked for my help. **"Try to imagine a place where you have complete wakeful awareness, but there is no stimuli, internal or external. You have no thoughts, no stream of consciousness, no dreams, only a simple awareness of self. Period."**

Her tone seemed to shudder with emotion, **"And no sleep."**

"Over time, your ability to think clearly and to communicate is greatly diminished. Until we enter this room, I have no way of determining how long the entity has been imprisoned, or how responsive they will be. When contact with others is reestablished, some stability can be attained, but it is only by breaking the binding structure of the imprisoning pentacle that the eemee can completely return to human form and some semblance of normalcy."

"Is there no way we can destroy the pentacle and set the eemee free, you know, release them back to the spectrum?" That seemed like the natural and logical thing to do.

"If this were a normal pentacle, yes, but a binding pentacle has different properties." She paused, then added quietly, **"To destroy such a pentacle is to destroy the entity within."**

Phoebe was giving me the *stop asking stupid questions about things we already know* look of irritation. "So, what can we do?" I asked quietly. Bailing out with great and suitably enthused rapidity.

"I will not know until we have a chance to speak with the entity and I can assess the specific nature of the pentacle."

Dee used her eemee wile to decode the security pad, commenting that the code had not been changed. I could only assume this meant the security folks must have really written off the previous alarm as false, a system glitch. That was good for us.

Phoebe and I stared at the door that had just clicked open. I was gathering my courage, from the dark abodes where it lurked, and she was absently fingering the elastic hammer guard on her gun holster. Nervous habit. We stepped through, alert and poised. Well, I was alert.

Same room. Same set of windows and doors. Same sick feeling in the pit of my stomach. I looked at Phoebe and she smiled at me. We stepped forward to activate the light. **~We must get inside to examine the pentacle,~** Dee broadcast into my mind. The security box began to flash as alphanumeric entries whirred through the display in search of the proper code.

The eemee looked up at me with the same astonished expression I recalled from our previous visit. ~Come you back!~ Spoken in halting words, almost a stuttering kind of illiterate delivery.

"Dee can you transliterate and pipe his thoughts through the ComUnit so Phoebe can hear?" Instantly the previous message came over the ComUnit's highly sensitive speakers, perfectly clear as always.

"We want to help," I said reassuringly. This was new territory for me and I just wanted to set the eemee at ease.

"Help. Yes," was all he said. He was not moving, but watching us intently.

"Why are you here?" Had to start with something, so might as well try to find out his story.

"No help human," the eemee stated quietly in his lurching style. His voice did not sound well at all.

He must have misunderstood me. "We do want to help you," I repeated firmly.

The eemee shook his head slowly, very slowly, as though exercising such physical control was difficult, perhaps painful. "Human I not help," he said, and you could feel the frustration in his voice as he tried desperately to communicate. The effort seemed almost to have exhausted him. His shoulders drooped and his head lolled down. The door clicked open.

"We may go inside, but do not touch the pentacle," Dee advised. Don't worry about that one &*^% bit; I'm not going anywhere near that damn thing.

Phoebe, veteran of many more interrogations, friendly and, well, unfriendly, tugged on my sleeve as we entered the room. "I think he means that he's here because he wouldn't help a human." She looked intently at me. "Probably the human controller who invoked him."

That made sense. "You did not wish to help the human who summoned you from the spectrum?" I said each word carefully and clearly, as though conversing with a child.

⬚ Taking It To Another Level ⬚

"No help him," the eemee confirmed. I glanced at Phoebe and smiled, then turned back to the eemee man.

"Do you know his name?" Maybe a shot in the dark, but sometimes that's the only shot you have to take.

"No name," the eemee replied, a little less haggardly than before.

Dee chimed in. **"Enoch, I have been assessing the strength of this pentacle. We cannot undo the binding structure—it is too strong—but we may be able to decrease the power it holds over the entity and allow him to think and use his mind more clearly."**

"How can we do that?" I eagerly asked, hoping I liked the answer. Hoping I understood the answer.

"We need to focus our energies and concentrate on the five points," and no doubt she was referring to the elaborate electronic structures which were placed at the five major pentacle points. You could see what damn sure appeared to be integrated circuit boards, complex ones, almost like the motherboard of a computer. **"You will sense me scanning you, and then you must merge your scan energy with mine."**

"What are we focusing on, exactly?" I have enough trouble concentrating as it is. I'm usually a *where are my car keys* kind of guy.

Okay, this next part is bizarre because I didn't know Dee could do this. I didn't know anyone could do this, but there, suddenly in front of my eyes, as though I were seeing it myself—damn, that sounds dumb—was a very large and detailed schematic of an integrated circuit. One of the boards from the pentacle.

In front of my eyes isn't really what I'm trying to say here. Our eyes catch light that is reflected from the objects of the world and our brain renders a three-dimensional image out of that light. We can interact with the solidarity of those objects. Right now I was seeing this object precisely as if it were four inches in front of my face but, as I waved my hand at it (like the skeptical fool I can be at times) nothing was there. My hand didn't pass in front, through, or behind the image, and the image didn't even flicker as I tested it. Weird.

Which meant Dee must be projecting it directly onto, into, my visual cortex.

☐ Chapter Seventeen ☐

"Less worry about the process and more focus on the content is advised," Dee snapped tersely and I was jerked out of my techno revelry.

"Sorry," I said, properly chastised.

"Do you see the node marked LG1?" I told her that I did. **"Do you see the pathway from it to LG2?"** Again I confirmed it. **"Do you see the node marked LG3?"**

"Dee, are we going to do this for every damn labeled node?" Because there were hundreds of them.

"Your level of patience is underwhelming," Dee said.

"Amen," I heard Phoebe's voice from the side.

"Okay," I said with a sigh, "what do you want me to do?"

"We will use our combined EM energy to redirect the LG1 pathway from LG2 to LG3."

I studied the circuit board some more. Hell, seemed just as reasonable as anything else I'd been doing the last three or four days. Fug. "Say when."

"When." Dee stated simply and I waited for that familiar tingling in the oblongata to start. Nothing. No, surely it couldn't be that?

"When I say, 'when' that means you can start the scan," I explained, trying not to laugh.

"Why did you not simply say 'start' then?" Dee asked, becoming more like a woman every moment.

"Okay, start," I said, not wanting to argue, and there was the tingling. I focused on the feel, the power, on Dee, on the circuit board, on her instructions.

At first, not much was happening, other than a general feeling of warmth that began in the back of my neck, emanating evenly outwards and spreading across my face and cheeks and up into my head. But, not much happening.

"You must focus, Enoch. There can be no doubt." She sounded so confident, so sure, and I tried to clear away all doubt, all concerns about the sheer impossibility of this, the absolute surreal nature of it all. Relegating personal disbelief to the ash heap of your own mental history is not so easy. Believe me. Well, if you can. It's not easy, is it?

◻ Taking It To Another Level ◻

"You can do it, Enoch, I know it," and that was Phoebe's emotion-laden voice. And she meant it, really meant it.

And I'll be damned if suddenly, and I really don't want to use the word magic, but it was as if by such a force, LG1 was now linked to LG3, and LG2 was just a node by itself. Techno magic. Whole Lee Key Wrap.

The eemee in the pentacle looked agape at Phoebe and me. "That is most remarkable!" he said in pleased shock.

"You can thank Dee," I informed him, honesty being the best policy and all.

"I already have," the eemee man replied with a vast smile.

"You seem to have recovered quickly," I noted, curious as to how some of this process worked.

"The one you call Dee tells me my time in the binding pentacle has been brief," he replied and visibly trembled. "Long term effects are not so easily overcome." His speech was slow and measured, but you could sense his rising vitality.

Phoebe jumped in. "Tell us your story."

"We, that is to say, electromagnetic entities, or eemees as you call us, have no names. The entity Dee suggests, however, that I take a name to facilitate proper communication." He paused and seemed to consider it for a moment. "You may call me Phoster, with a P-H." Odd spelling, but he said it as Foster.

Hey, someone named Enoch has no business commenting on someone named Phoster. Especially when your partner is named Phoebe. I think my pH level is too high. Hah! Sorry.

"As you may know," Phoster continued, gathering himself, "or perhaps may not know, when a summoning pentacle is correctly constructed, it addresses the EM spectrum at a very specific frequency, wavelength, and photon energy signature. Each pentacle is unique for one eemee and can only be used for the particular eemee for which it is configured." He seemed to be searching for strength to continue.

"Once the eemee is invoked by such a device it is subject to human control." He flashed a sardonic grin and waved his arms. "Primarily by being threatened with imprisonment in the same pentacle if they fail to cooperate." We nodded our understanding of that scenario. Firsthand knowledge, as it were.

"I was summoned by someone in the place you call Iceland." This, of course, jolted Phoebe and me into a knowing, well, semi-knowing, exchange of glances, "I was told what I was expected to do."

"When I refused to fulfill those expectations, I ended up here," he added softly and nodded his head gravely.

"How long ago was this?" I queried him, hoping that his answer might tie in somehow to other information I had on hand.

He shook his head sadly. "Time has no meaning for the beings you call eemees, and even less when you are imprisoned in a pentacle, but Dee thinks it has been less than a human year."

"Phoster, who summoned you?" Phoebe asked quietly, and that had been one of my upcoming questions.

"I saw no human, only heard a voice distorted by digital manipulation," the man answered with a tinge of regret.

That was good information, even if it seemed like no information. It meant someone was rather keen on keeping his or her identity as the human controller a secret. But, secret from whom? And, why?

"Do you know if any of these other rooms are occupied?" Always good to know more about what you are dealing with.

"I do not."

I turned to Phoebe, "Do you mind checking the other rooms; I mean, just triggering the lights and looking in?" She nodded and left the room.

"Phoster, we cannot free you at this time," I said, not sure how else to phrase it. Picking the best policy and running with it.

"Dee has informed me of your circumstances," Phoster rejoined in solemn tones.

I nodded. "We'll figure out something," I said by way of reassurance. **"That is what I told Phoster,"** Dee said, a hint of steely resolve in her voice. I guess half the battle is believing you can win it. Trite, but true. Though the other half is kicking some butt.

"Do you know how we can undo the binding properties of this pentacle?" If there was something I could do, as a human, perhaps we could still free Phoster, or any other possibly imprisoned eemees.

Phoster answered with a taint of sadness in his tone. "The activation sequence is a secret known only to the human controller."

Dee explained further, **"Phoster means the exact sequence by which the five points of the pentacle are activated and their unique energy signatures synergized."**

"It sounds rather complicated," I commented.

"In terms that Tom and Armando would fully appreciate, it cannot be hacked," Dee stated in flat tones. **"You must know the code."**

"Well," I replied, a bit of resignation seeping into my voice, "we'll do what we can."

"Just having the ability to think, to imagine—to have even a simple stream of consciousness—is a great gift," Phoster said with barely restrained passion.

I heard a low controlled shout from Phoebe. Just outside the door, it seemed.

"Stay strong!" I said to Phoster as I hurriedly departed and closed the door.

Phoebe was standing outside the room next to where Phoster was being kept. The light to that room was on and a pleasant-looking woman, maybe mid forties—short, brown hair, white smock and bare feet—was suspended in the air inside another pentacle. A few seconds passed. She looked up with the same dazed expression Phoster had exhibited when the light first snapped on in his room.

Phoebe looked at me. "I started over there," she motioned across the walkway at the door opposite of Phoster's cell, "and worked my way around, counterclockwise." She pointed at the room now awash in light. "This was the only light that came on."

Dee was busy decrypting the door security when I said to the woman, "We are friends," and hoped she knew what the word "friends" meant. Apparently not, as her face was still squeezed up in fear.

"No hurt me more," said in such a pleading and mournful way that it just about broke my heart.

"We are here to help you," I tried to keep it simple. I smiled as kindly as I could.

The door clicked open.

☐ Chapter Seventeen ☐

As we moved forward to enter, I felt the eemee woman try to blast me with a scan. I took a faltering involuntary step back and heard Dee cry out, **~No, stop!~** Instantly the intrusive scan ceased.

"Who are you?" came the woman's husky voice, not as disjointed and out of kilter as Phoster's had initially been, but still shaky, confused.

"We want to help you," I said and then Dee flashed a new IC board image in my mind.

~LG7 reroutes to LG9~ was all I heard. She must have assumed I was an old hand at this by now.

In much less time than before, the new pathway was in place. I'm a slow starter but a quick learner.

"Oh!" the woman exclaimed, then looked at both Phoebe and me, small tears in her eyes. "Thank you, thank you," and there was silence for a few moments while everyone regrouped.

"You were summoned in a country called Iran." I said this as a statement, not a question. Phoebe regarded me with arched eyebrows, probably wondering how I figured that one out.

"That is what the human called it, yes," came the woman's confirmation. "Who are you?"

"Dee, give her a quick background." I figured an eemee direct connect would save some time.

Less than five seconds had gone by (I know, I was counting) when the woman said in knowing tones, "You are Enoch," and I nodded. "You may call me Elia," she said and added: "I have heard your name mentioned before." I was stunned at that. Mortified. It's okay for your heart to skip a beat, as long as it finds the next one.

"Elia, who said my name before?" I managed to squeak this out.

"As you said, the controller of this pentacle summoned me in the place you call Iran," she laughed derisively. "He demanded that I help him influence the minds of humans."

Elia's answer had obviously been "no."

"Did you see the man?" Phoebe asked, which was good because I wasn't sure I could speak right now.

"I never saw the man, and his voice was distorted, but someone else was in communication with him," she replied, then continued. "The controller told this other man to go visit Enoch Maarduk."

◻ Taking It To Another Level ◻

Could that have been the guy from last Saturday, the guy with the gun? Polyester Man? No sense talking about days or time to her, it would be pointless as her understanding of human time did not exist.

Then Dee piped in, speaking in strident tones, **~The ComUnit is receiving an urgent message from Dr. Hume. He wants to know why you and Phoebe are not on the way to Iceland.~** I blew out the breath I had probably been holding for what seemed like the last few minutes.

"We cannot free you right now, but I promise we will," I said forcefully to the eemee woman. I tried to put this in the strongest possible terms in order to ease her mind. And mine.

"I will wait for you, Enoch," the woman said; the calmness in her eyes expressed her inner confidence. It was profoundly touching to me. We left the room and softly closed the door.

"Dee, tell Hume we are involved in some important research and we'll call him back in less than ten minutes." We had to respond to Hume's message or there would be heck to pay. Well, heck that rhymes with well. We began walking towards our exit area.

———◻———

We had less than ten minutes to deal with and resolve a very real and pressing problem. Which was trying to figure out the story behind the eemees on Level 5. It was unimaginable that Hume did not know about them and, therefore, he was in some way responsible for imprisoning the eemees or, at the very least, maintaining the binding pentacles.

"There has to be a good reason," I stated, trying to believe it myself. "I'm sure there's a good reason." Sometimes, if you repeat something, it makes it sound more true. Truer.

"We have to ask him about it," Phoebe stated, though without the usual sense of self-assurance she normally conveyed. I think she was waiting for my endorsement to bolster her spirits; and I was not so sure on this particular topic.

"If we mention Level 5 to Hume, he's going to demand to know how we found out about it, since it's supposed to be secret," I began my reasonable argument that I knew Phoebe was going to find unreasonable. "Then I'll have to explain how Dee found some blueprints on a PHANTASM server." I stopped here to give Phoebe my version of a weak death stare. "Then I, we, would have to explain that Dee is an eemee." This time I raised my eyebrows and appraised her with a grim smile. "How well do you think that's going to go over?"

Phoebe pursed her lips. "Fine, let's ask Ruach about Level 5."

"Ruach did warn you that Level 5 was dangerous and that things there would seem incomprehensible without a proper understanding," Dee relayed to us as a sort of languid admonishment.

"Yes," Phoebe quickly replied, "and Ruach can provide that understanding."

"I cannot speak for Ruach, but I believe that he would say that you must seek the truth for yourself," Dee enjoined with a meditative edge to her tone.

I could see that Phoebe was anxious to say something more, but was biting her tongue in self-restraint. "Ruach can't really help us on this, can he?" I addressed this to Dee, making an inference from her statement and Ruach's past comments to me.

"Considering his unique circumstances, he is doing all he can to help you," was the cryptic way Dee phrased it. Might as well get self-help advice from a Zen master. "Live like the wind, grasshopper." Fug.

Phoebe could not contain herself any longer. "We'll keep this to ourselves," she stated emphatically, then showed me what a real death stare looked like. "For now."

We placed the call back to Hume.

There is a fine line that separates manageable irritation from irrepressible fury. Thankfully, Hume was just on this side of the line. The irritation side. "What the hell are you two still doing here?" Apparently, well not apparently, absolutely, he had got wind of the fact we had not left for Iceland. "You should have been on that plane already!" Not a happy camper. Think of skunks invading the RV.

Thankfully, though, he was merely yelling at us over the ComUnit and not in person. Having settled the Level 5 issue between ourselves (for now) Phoebe and I were scampering back to our quarters to grab our duffle bags of gear and then head for the aforementioned flight to Iceland. "I'm sorry, sir, we were detained," which was the extent of my cleverness at the moment.

⬚ Taking It To Another Level ⬚

We were exiting the elevator—Phoebe shook her head and whispered "Lame," in unkind tones. She went rapidly left and I went slowly right.

"Detained?" Hume sputtered. "Detained by what?" Just a hair's length pause. "Are you sleeping with Phoebe?"

"No, certainly not," I huffed indignantly, although because he was accusing me of it or because it wasn't true I won't say. But, also an opportunity to defuse his anger. "I resent that you would even ask me such a thing!" I exclaimed, though I was, in actuality, kind of perversely flattered by his accusation, in a curiously unsettling way.

"I'm sorry," Hume said, reluctantly to my ear, but went on in softer tones. "Events have escalated and the Iceland team needs your assistance right away." Not sure if this were true or not, as Dee had not mentioned any recent reports on the subject, but you don't argue with the boss. Well, not too much.

"I do apologize, sir, but we were, uh, researching some things relevant to the mission, and time just sort of got away from us," I said belatedly and, if you stop to ponder it, quite truthfully.

"That's fine, just get to the airfield and get going," he said with a closing flourish of grump and disconnected.

I entered my quarters, grabbed my pre-packed black canvas duffle bag (what the hell is a duffle anyway, make a note to look that up) and headed for the underground garage to meet Phoebe.

Who, probably in payback for my beating her to the cafeteria this morning, was already lounging against Jimmy's SUV drinking some kind of power drink. When I stepped from the elevator, she casually pushed off the fender, eyed me gaudily and said, "What kept you?" Then handed me an extra can of the stuff she had stashed in her bag.

Now, that is a good partner.

"What did you tell Hume?" Phoebe whispered, reaching down into her blouse to affix a BioPatch and watching me to see if I was watching her and well, as a courteous gent I did sort of turn away. Sort of.

Act like you've seen boobs before.

Anyway, where was I?

Oh, yes, Hume.

⟦ Chapter Seventeen ⟧

"I told him I was sleeping with you and apologized for being late," I said seriously, not sure why I tossed this level of flippancy into the fray, but the bag was off the cat now.

"I'm sure he knew that was a complete fabrication," she purred, but her eyes were playful. I think. Easier to read Sanskrit than a woman's eyes.

"I told him we had been doing some research and simply lost track of time," I admitted in flat tones.

"And he bought that?" Phoebe asked with a bit of skepticism edging her words.

"That's all I was selling, so he had to," I cleverly replied. "He said, to quote him, 'events had escalated' and we were needed in Iceland right away."

"What events?" Phoebe quizzed. I could always count on her to ask the exact same question plaguing me.

"Dee, do you have recent communications from Iceland? What's going on?" Inquiring minds and all that.

"Just a moment," came Dee's instant reply and, of course, this led me to wonder exactly, or inexactly, as the case might be, what a "moment" actually was defined as, well, according to Dee.

Before the Iceland report popped up, assuming there was one, I remarked aloud, before I could stop myself, "What is a moment?"

"A moment is an indefinite, yet very brief, interval of conscious time, ascertained from the perspective of the casual observer."

Phoebe chuckled and looked at me. "I think you fit the bill as a casual observer."

I tilted my head and cast Phoebe a wide-eyed look of fake irritation. Dee stated simply, **"I can find no recent report."**

"Could have been a secure transmission for Hume's eyes only," Phoebe opined thoughtfully.

"I'll grant that," I acknowledged. "Doesn't really matter. I'm curious to see what's going on in Iceland with my own eyes."

Phoebe nodded as Jimmy turned onto the highway entrance ramp.

When you are busily engaged in a private conversation with someone else, there are usually people around you in the general environment that you often take for granted. Secretaries, children, passengers on a public conveyance, fellow diners, cab drivers.

Jimmy.

After being ding-zinged by finding out Emma was an undercover PHANTASM operative at Pnumis, I was hesitant to say too much, too loudly, in front of anyone I wasn't familiar with. I leaned very close to Phoebe, who rewarded me with the usual caustic look I had grown accustomed to and fully expected.

"I like Jimmy," and I made a subtle gesture with my left thumb, "but, there's no need to talk out of school, if you know what I mean."

Phoebe slowly nodded her head, glanced at Jimmy, then back at me. "Agreed," was all she said.

After that, we did the old chit-chat routine, content to pass time in friendly banter, mostly about irrelevant bull snarf as Jimmy navigated his way along the crowded highway.

The ComUnit flashed and Dee informed me, "**It's Tom, and he is extremely excited.**"

Phoebe and I exchanged anxious looks. The top priority was cracking that Nykr video and if Tom was excited, well, that could only mean one thing. I hoped so, despite being a perpetual pessimist. For some people, the glass is half-full, to some it's half-empty.

To me, it simply has a slow leak.

"Tom, talk to me," I said as I watched Jimmy switch lanes to pass a slow-moving tractor trailer.

"We finally got it!" Tom exclaimed with obvious emotion. "We almost gave up, but tried a few more things and we did it."

Armando leaned into frame. "This was the hardest mother we have ever had to crack," he said with raised eyebrows and a weary, but happy, expression.

"What's in it?" Phoebe couldn't help but ask. Her eyes were bright with anticipation. Think packages under the tree.

"Three men sitting at table in an office. Some kind of meeting." Tom paused for breath. "I'm going to upload the video to Dee," Tom continued. "You can tell me if it means anything to you." He scowled a little and his smile was, well, strained. "There's no audio." He was not thrilled to be adding this last gem of information.

☐ Chapter Seventeen ☐

"Did it get lost during the crack?" I asked this because sometimes the hack in can cause considerable damage.

I mean, even the words "hack" and "crack" sound damaging.

"No," Tom replied sadly, "someone had already stripped the audio out." The obvious conclusion, always dangerous to jump to, was that something important was in that audio. In this case, though, I felt such a leap was fully warranted. The possible painful landing, well, not so much.

Dee piped up. **"I have the video, Enoch."**

"Okay, boys, we got it," I said cheerfully. "Send me a bill!"

Tom grinned, "Oh, yeah, we're working on that." I'm pretty sure the PHANTASM accountants would have cringed at the tone of his voice. He disconnected.

"Dee, I have a question for you." My paranoia was creeping like a nun.

"Yes, Enoch?"

I decided to think this rather than say it. ~Dee, our driver, Jimmy, may be okay, but I'd rather not have to, uh, converse aloud.~

~That is not a problem.~

~Can you transliterate the conversation so Phoebe hears it as well? I mean, in her mind?~

~Ordinarily that is not possible, but since you are in such close proximity here in the car, with minimal interference, I will attempt it.~

I leaned over and explained to Phoebe what I wanted to try. She looked at me with angst and skepticism. "That sounds kind of creepy," accompanied by a crinkled nose, like she smelled a skunk.

"It's a little odd at first," I admitted honestly, maybe understating it slightly. "Just remember, it's only Dee trying to help us." That seemed to soothe away her issues, a little anyway, and she nodded her head, signifying she was ready.

~Go ahead and load the video, Dee,~ I said with modest trepidation. Okay, that's a blatant lie. How about tremendous trepidation? It's like when you feel bad and the doctor orders some lab work. A week later you're standing there in the doc's office with this heart-pounding sense of dread and excitement waiting for the results.

Or, maybe that's how you feel when you get the bill.

⬜ Taking It To Another Level ⬜

The video was paused, waiting for me to start it, with only the first frame visible. The length indicator read 1:37, as in minutes and seconds, which wasn't much of a video clip, but it was better than nothing. Much better.

It was an office setting. Crystal clear high resolution. In the background was a large bookcase with a simple desk and black leather or vinyl-covered chair in front. The desk was cluttered with papers and such. To the right you could see a large whiteboard covered with arrows, ovals, squares, triangles, check marks, and writing, as though someone had been standing there recently making a presentation of some kind.

Three men were seated at a rectangular wooden table. The table itself, and the man seated to the left, blocked most of the view of what was off to that side, though it appeared to be just filing cabinets and office equipment.

The man nearest to us, using our viewing angle, had his back to the camera, but the other two were visible.

The man seated directly to the left had been known to me as Ranis Terloff, the human controller I had confronted in South Africa. That notched my adrenaline up just a bit.

The other, to the right, was unknown to me until Phoebe, after staring at the small ComUnit screen for a few intense moments, let out a gasp. "Mencius," she said aloud, then immediately her hand shot to her mouth and covered it, as though she knew she should not have said it aloud. Enough adrenaline now to run a marathon! Well, maybe a half-marathon, considering my training regimen.

~I am telling her to relax and merely think it and I will transliterate.~ This from a patient Dee.

~Enoch?~ came Phoebe's questioning voice. Not frightened, that wouldn't be Phoebe, but probing, cautious, concerned.

~Hey, Phoebe,~ I replied and then chuckled. ~This thought-speak stuff takes a little getting used to.~

~I recognize Tazik Mencius,~ she stated with obvious hostility. ~Who are the other two guys?~ Sometimes anger does a great job of focusing your mind. She was using thought-speech perfectly.

⌶ Chapter Seventeen ⌶

~The other man whose face you can see is the guy I had trouble with in South Africa, Ranis Terloff.~ I said with cold precision.

~You killed him,~ Phoebe said flatly. Hearing it said aloud like that was a bit discomforting.

~Yes,~ I acknowledged, letting out a breath and not wanting to dwell on it, then queried her. ~You know the third man?~

Phoebe shook her head.

~Start the video, Dee,~ Phoebe requested and the static image moved into action. Did I mention Phoebe and pro mode? She was locked and loaded.

After watching the video roll for about five seconds or so, it occurred to me that the man whose back was to us must have been talking. I concluded this because neither Mencius nor Terloff were talking, but were looking intently at the unknown man. Their heads would occasionally move, as though acknowledging or agreeing with something the unknown man was saying. This sequence lasted for perhaps twenty seconds or so.

In response to whatever words the unknown man had spoken, Mencius said something, then waved his left hand in a gesture of dismissal, favoring the unknown personage with a smirk and a look of derision. The quality of the video (carefully viewing facial expressions and body movements) helped make this determination possible.

Terloff nodded, then put both hands up, palms out at an angle, and made a downwards pushing motion, as if to indicate *let's take it easy*. He spoke what appeared to be a couple of short sentences to Mencius, then turned to speak to the unknown man, who had not moved much, so we still did not know who he was.

Before Terloff finished talking, Mencius jumped violently to his feet, angrily saying something. His chair was thrust backwards and toppled over. Terloff, tension evident on his face, straightened in his chair, but remained seated.

The unknown man stayed casually calm, shook his head, waved offhandedly at the fallen chair and raised his head to regard the upright Mencius. The unknown man's head turned a little, but not enough to see all his features.

☐ Taking It To Another Level ☐

Judging by the attention Mencius was giving to the unknown man, I had to think the seated figure was again speaking. The unknown man continued talking as he turned in full profile to watch Mencius, as the latter bent down to retrieve his chair.

"Hume!" I yelped in stunned disbelief, not even aware I had spoken aloud. It really wasn't disbelief, either. More like a shocked confirmation of suspicions I had been fighting hard not to believe. I thought Phoebe would have gone ballistic at recognizing him, but she was cool, detached, thoughtful, absorbed.

Mencius resumed his seat and the video ended.

~Dee, please rewind the time marker to around 55 seconds and freeze it,~ Phoebe asked softly. What was she up to? And she already had this thought-speech thing down pat. She is good-looking, too.

Dee adjusted the video to the requested time mark. The three men were seated at the table. ~Dee, can you zoom in on that white display board? The one to the right?~ The video was adjusted. It was a little out of focus, but almost readable. ~A little to the left now.~

Dee brought that area into full frame. ~Dee,~ Phoebe thought gently, ~is there anything you can do to enhance the readability of the writing on the board?~

~Yes, one moment, please.~

The writing came up, much more legible. It showed the names of the five eemee sites. There was a dot next to the name of each site, and they were written as they would occur if you were looking at them on a map.

It looked like this:

☐ Chapter Seventeen ☐

~Okay,~ I commented as I looked at the image, ~this just confirms that Hume is in on the whole thing.~ I wasn't sure what Phoebe was driving at.

~This wouldn't have meant anything to me,~ Phoebe began her explanation, ~except for this murder mystery I just finished reading.~

~Murder mystery?~ I guess you should know me by now. When in doubt, repeat.

~It was about this deranged killer who was claiming her victims at specific locations,~ Phoebe explained, staring intently at the image on the ComUnit.

~Specific locations?~ Yeah, I'm ashamed of myself. I spread my hands out in ignorance awaiting enlightenment. A neophyte seeking supplication.

Phoebe sighed, as though I were a dull schoolboy. Remember that box of rocks thing? I think if she had been able to lay her hands on a ruler, I would have been whacked. Hmm, maybe Phoebe and whacked don't really belong in the same thought sequence. Smacked

~The killer in the novel was forming a pentacle to invoke a medieval demon,~ she said with infinite patience.

I guess I was still wearing my stupid face (tried for years to ditch it, but no luck) because Phoebe just shook her head with infinite exasperation. ~Dee, show him.~

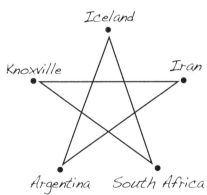

I freely admit that there are times when I process things a little slower than others. I'm thinking it through, examining all the possibilities, getting my synapses wrapped around it.

☐ Taking It To Another Level ☐

Once I get my neuro-teeth into it, however, it's like trying to get a favorite chew toy away from a pit bull. Grrr...

~They plan a massive activation of the peptide alkaloid!~ I said in soft, almost reverential, tones of horror.

Phoebe was looking at me strangely. Well, more strangely than normal. ~What are you talking about?~

~I do not understand either, Enoch.~

~Dee, remember that lab results email exchange? It was in a text file from Tom. They were talking about the Argentinean supplement.~ I paused for just a moment to gather my scattered wits. Maybe two moments. ~The one guy mentions something about delta waves. Give me two or three paragraphs plus that reference.~

A few breaths went by. **~Here it is, Enoch.~**

> Since we had additional testing material remaining, and a new shipment of animal subjects had just been received, we decided to conduct a third test.
>
> Almost immediately upon ingestion, the normally active rats became excessively docile and could be easily handled. They were alert and responsive, but only moved if an external stimuli was provided.
>
> We attached one of the new portable brain scanners and recorded nothing but delta waves at about 2 Hz.

I looked up and realized we were almost at the airfield. There would be no trip to Iceland today. "Jimmy, we need to head back to PHANTASM," I said softly, but forcefully.

"I'll inform Colonel Williams we are being delayed in traffic," he said, leaned to his right and locked eyes with me in the rear view mirror. "That should give you time to get back and visit with Dr. Hume."

That triggered an instant and stiletto-icy response from Phoebe. "What do you know about that situation?"

He started to reach into his pocket. I heard the unmistakable sound of the metal clasp on Phoebe's stitched fabric holster click open and the hiss of metal as her weapon was being slid out. "Just an ID, Miss O'Hara," Jimmy said softly, carefully lifted his hand to show it, and gingerly handed it over his shoulder to her.

◻ Chapter Seventeen ◻

"James Albert Scanlin," she read without emotion, then looked at me. "NSA," she said, much less impassively. "You need to explain this," and she waved the leather ID holder for emphasis, addressing Jimmy in tense tones.

"PHANTASM has been on our radar for a few years now," Jimmy began gently explaining. He shrugged. "They accept government funding, and you know that comes with strings." He was exiting the highway.

"You're the string," I said, though not sure why, it just slipped out.

"I have no authority to interfere, only to observe," he stated firmly, merging onto the crowded access lane.

Phoebe grinned wickedly and huffed, "And what have you observed?"

He shrugged again. "I just watch and listen," he answered evasively.

"And report," Phoebe added with a hint of irritation. She glanced at me and shook her head again.

Jimmy tilted the rear view mirror so he and Phoebe could see one another clearly, "The truth is, Miss O'Hara, I don't really have anything on Hume, or PHANTASM. I've been driving here for almost two years and all my reports together wouldn't fill a thimble." He grunted. "Hume's a very careful man."

"But, you do think he's up to something?" I asked, very much curious as to what Jimmy thought on the subject.

"That's not for me to say, sir, I just..." he began his answer but was interrupted by Phoebe.

"Watch and listen; yeah, yeah, I know you NSA guys," she said a bit derisively.

Jimmy grinned, not bothered by her tone or remark. "Always around if you need us."

"That's kind of a scary thought," I said to no one in particular.

Phoebe and Jimmy seemed to have reached a silent accord. "If we need you, I'll call," she said softly and handed his ID back.

Jimmy had entered the highway heading back to PHANTASM.

~Dee, can you, well, sort of, block Jimmy's auditory system so he can't hear us talk?~ I should have thought of this possibility before. Eemees can manipulate all forms of EM energy.

⧫ Taking It To Another Level ⧫

~I can create wave interference patterns so all he hears is white noise when either of you speak.~

~Do it,~ I said to Dee; then, to Phoebe, ~Have you been following all of this?~

"Yes," she said very loudly—on purpose I imagine—then added with a scowl. "What's your plan when we get back to PHANTASM?" Even when Phoebe frowned she was pretty.

"I confront Hume with the facts and give him a chance to explain himself," I said simply. Direct frontal assault. Forlorn hope, I hoped not.

"*We* confront him," Phoebe amended my statement with a devilish grin.

I shook my head and pursed my lips. "Not a good idea." I said this very slowly while idly scratching the back of my neck.

"Convince me." Phoebe, ever the professional, giving me the leeway to state my case. And, also the possibility she might tell me where to put it.

"Look, let's just say, hypothetically, that Hume is in this thing up to his eyebrows," I began my argument. "We don't know how he might respond when we confront him with what we know."

"All the more reason for me to be there," Phoebe said without heat.

"Dee can generate the energy I need for my EM blast," I countered. "If Hume tries any funny business I can knock him out."

She was silent for a few moments gnawing that over. "If push comes to shove, Dee can always call you in as a backup," I happily appended to my position. Anticipatory raised eyebrows.

That seemed to do the trick (my statement, not the eyebrows) and Phoebe nodded, but still wore her unhappy face like a new tattoo. "That doesn't tell me *what* you intend to do with him." She really placed extra oomph and stress on the word "what" and it shook me. Gave me a serious pause.

The expression on my face confirmed it.

"You don't really have a plan," Phoebe said in mock irritation as she studied my features.

Well, mostly mock.

⬚ Chapter Seventeen ⬚

It did present a bit of a conundrum, an imbroglio most assuredly. This wasn't something you could go to the local police department with. I mean, if I asked Hume to step down he'd probably just laugh in my face since I had no real authority in the matter. I could use force, but what if I was wrong? Innocent until proven guilty, remember?

I leaned over toward Phoebe. "We've got an NSA connection," I whispered, motioning with my head at Jimmy. I had the displeasure of watching her face darken, quite literally and quickly.

"They will simply shut PHANTASM down, period. Hume might be dirty, but PHANTASM does good work and we need it running," she said softly, shaking her head. "Forget that idea."

"I could just zap him and lock him in one of those rooms in Level 5," I offered helpfully, half joking.

Phoebe tilted her head down and appraised me. "If we are one-hundred percent sure Hume is doing something bad, then that's actually a great idea," she stated, and then switched to the full-fledged Phoebe death stare. My mind was about to implode. She tilted her head down even further. "Are we one-hundred percent sure?" She did not sound like she was one-hundred percent sure.

"A lot of the evidence we have is circumstantial," I admitted feebly, finishing in almost a whisper. The more I considered all the facts, the more doubt was seeping in. Like water onto a leaky rowboat, and I didn't have an either oar. Terrible.

Phoebe let out a long breath. "All we really have is a video with no audio." She looked pointedly at me. "We don't know anything about why that meeting was taking place." I frowned as I thought about it.

"We know about the peptide alkaloid and the global pentacle activation plan," I said defensively, regarding those facts as black marks against Hume. Surely that indicated some kind of devious plot?

"Maybe Hume knows about those plans and is fighting against it," she replied with terrific sarcasm. "I mean, he did send me to China, where we stopped Mencius and his operation"—quick intake of breath—"and he did send you and me to South Africa, where you stopped Terloff."

A wry smile from Phoebe. "Then he arranged an air strike to wipe out the company."

☐ Taking It To Another Level ☐

She let out a long breath: "And now he is encouraging us to go to Iceland."

I bit my lip and looked steadily at her. A horrible and gut-wrenching realization was starting to overwhelm me, and I did not like it, even though it might be true. "We're overreacting," was all I could mutter.

Phoebe squeezed my right arm and gave me a knee-wilting look of sincerity. "This has been a difficult few days," she said and laughed gently. "We've been fighting shadows as well as real bad guys." She nodded, "I think you have made amazing progress, finding out incredible things, but we're rushing to add it all together and I'm afraid we might be making a terrible mistake."

"What you're saying is, Hume is not involved in any sort of diabolical plot?" I asked, not completely clear in my mind of her true opinion.

"No," Phoebe replied, clarifying her position. "What I'm saying is, he deserves an opportunity to explain what's going on"—she smiled sweetly—"and I want to be there."

I sat still, then nodded slowly, gradually accepting that she had a valid point. "You're right." As I thought about it more, it made perfect sense. "We'll ask him to explain himself. Maybe we just stumbled over stuff that is supposed to stay secret." I shrugged, did the spreading hands thing. "You know, part of the PHANTASM battle plan or something." She gave me the kind of scouring look only a woman can truly deliver. Singed my synapses.

"Here is what we are going to do," she said carefully. "We are going to tell Hume we need to know everything, and I mean everything." She looked at me with raised brows. "We'll tell him that the more we know, the better job we can do for PHANTASM. For him." Warm smile. "Period. End of story." She said it with such definitive care that I remained silent. Jimmy was exiting the highway. I looked in earnest at her for a moment or two.

"You wouldn't have all these new worries hanging over your head if I hadn't shown up," I said, slightly abashed and more than a little guilt-ridden.

"Maybe not, but I did have that black mamba hanging over my head," she said with a wide grin.

Not to be outdone, I was thinking of Knoxville. "Well, I seem to recall someone recently who was pretty handy with a BB gun..."

Phoebe shrugged and said, with genuine regret, "I should have shot that creature with a real gun."

We were in this mess because I think too much, and here I was about to start on a new line of unreasonable reasoning. I looked at Phoebe with a fractious and puzzled expression. "Can we shoot an eemee?" She shrugged, plainly taken aback by the question.

"Dee, can an eemee be, uh, injured, like by a gunshot or something?" Kind of a strange question for her, surely.

"Yes, eemees in human form are subject to pain and injury, though tolerance levels are significantly higher. If the human form is destroyed, an eemee's elemental energy is returned to the spectrum. Only by destroying a binding pentacle with the entity imprisoned inside can an eemee be truly killed."

"Sorry to ask that," I said with a hint of embarrassment.

"Those are the facts," was Dee's characteristically placid response.

We were nearing PHANTASM. Both of us thoughtful, more than a little apprehensive. The longer I dwelt on our suspicions, dissecting them and looking for substantial bits of truth, the more insubstantial my notions about Hume seemed to become. There was nothing concrete that pointed at him. Indeed, there was nothing but a bunch of only slightly related events where I was filling in large gaps with mostly wild guesses.

Was he withholding information from me, from Phoebe? Yes, no doubt, absolutely no doubt.

However, maybe that was okay.

You had to accept one basic scenario that was undoubtedly true— that Hume's actions were for the protection of PHANTASM and, thus, to be expected. Clandestine organizations had to have secrets because they were, indeed, in a secretive business. If an operative were captured, I mused with a quivering mind-shiver, there were nasty ways the bad guys could use to make them talk. Gulp, make me talk. Or Phoebe.

The more I considered this, the more confused I became. And irritated. Justifiably so, as I saw it.

Even if I granted that some knowledge was being legitimately kept from us in order to protect PHANTASM, recent events had escalated along to a point that I felt compelled to acquire this knowledge. Deserved to know it. Phoebe and I were risking our lives, and would continue to do so.

Plus, there was that sticky business of Level 5. Sooner or later, someone needed to explain that. That particular someone was going to be Hume.

We should be told the whole story, about everything, and it would take a very strong counter-argument from Hume to convince me otherwise.

As Jimmy was driving into the parking garage, I shared these thoughts with Phoebe. She was in complete agreement and enthusiastically accepted my offer to accompany me to visit Hume (which I was glad for, but determined not to show it).

And so, with a united front, we entered the elevator and headed for Level 4.

As we walked in the outer office, Deandra's startled look was a clear indication that no advance notice of our visit had yet arrived. She stood as we marched toward Hume's door and her face was a mask of puzzilation. "Is, is Dr. Hume aware that you are here?" she sputtered, flustered.

"I'm sorry, Deandra," I said with my best friendly and apologetic smile as we passed by. "I promise to explain later." In we went.

I'm not sure how I expected Hume to react.

He had fumed and vented earlier, when we had first delayed our Icelandic departure, so I was fully prepared for a titanic meltdown of epic proportions.

However, as soon as he saw us, and noted the expressions on our faces (a mix of resolve and determination) I think he reached the conclusion that things were off-kilter and akimbo. That is to say, out of whack and a bit bent out of shape. Like my brain after meeting Anuket. Or before!

☐ Chapter Seventeen ☐

He simply nodded his head and waved at the chairs. "You obviously have something to say, so get it said." He didn't look like a fellow who was quivering in fear of being uncovered as a charlatan.

I was beginning to feel like an ass. A feeling I am fairly conversant with, sad to say, so readily self-diagnosed.

I suppose we should have remained standing—after all, by agreeing to sit we were making a subtle acknowledgement of his authority—but we sat down anyway.

"We feel like there are some things being left unsaid about this whole eemee business, and we think we deserve to know the truth," I said with a clear voice that never wavered. Tough as titanium nails when it was needed. Me, not my voice.

"We?" Hume repeated, glancing at Phoebe, who nodded gamely.

Hume sat back in his chair, regarding us both with sharp appraisal. He gesticulated with his raised hands, palms facing toward himself. "What do you want to know?"

"Well, for starters, we'd like to know the real meaning of the linkage among all of the eemee sites," I stated forthrightly, tossing my first grenade over the wall.

"You mean, how they form a pentacle when connected?" Hume responded gently, with a ghost of a smile. Throwing the grenade back and detonating it at my feet.

"Oh," I commented, sort of deflated; okay, totally deflated. "You know about that?" Phoebe already seemed aghast at the direction of the conversation, judging by the expression on her face.

Hume sighed expansively. "We have almost 200 people involved in this operation, scattered around the building in various departments." He smiled knowingly. "That's 200 sets of mouths attached to 400 ears." Another rueful grin. "And that's not counting video feeds, email threads, paper trails, or any other techno gadget some crazed IT guru invents."

He shook his head. "You would be surprised how difficult it is in a secret organization like PHANTASM, of actually keeping anything secret." That made him chuckle.

☐ Taking It To Another Level ☐

"I know Phoebe is aware of this, but I am not sure about you, Enoch," Hume began to explain. He tilted his head back and looked at me. "PHANTASM is not only involved in otherworldly events involving electromagnetic entities." He shook his head. "No, sir, we monitor a great deal of human-generated EM activity." He smiled. "I believe you've met Joe, who is an essential part of that mission."

He took a short breath. "Obviously the level of internal security surrounding our work with eemees is considerably higher than say, keeping an eye on the local news report." He paused here to make sure I caught the subtle, well, not so subtle, sarcasm in his voice. I acknowledged it with an agreeable nod.

Hume continued, "In eemee events, the established protocol is to have the public records say one thing and the actual reports that cross my desk state the true facts."

Yes, I did want to run and hide, but I maintained my attitude, willing to take my medicine. Phoebe did as well, though I was certain she was going to take it out on me later. Probably with a blunt instrument.

However, I still had a few rounds in my virtual argument gun. "There was a video, pulled from a Nykr server," I said softly, watching him closely. Boom!

"Yes," he confirmed serenely, "a video of myself with Ranis Terloff and"—here he turned to look at Phoebe—"Tazik Mencius." His smile seemed quite natural. Phoebe's was a bit forced. "I must commend your friends on their abilities," Hume added with a nod of his head.

I was waiting for an explanation of the video, not accolades for Tom and Armando, so I said nothing. Hume went on. "Mencius and Terloff contacted PHANTASM through an intermediary." He looked at me, "A gentleman, and I use that term rather generously, whose taste in clothing runs to polyester." Polyester Man! From the condo.

"I suppose a little history might help you better understand," he said patiently, fatherly even.

"Tazik Mencius and Ranis Terloff were old friends, going all the way back to their university days." He steepled his fingers as he thought about his remarks.

⎘ Chapter Seventeen ⎗

"Somewhere along the line they came across some old medieval schematics, blueprints if you will. Nonsense to an untrained eye, but Mencius was a software engineer and Terloff was a chip designer."

Even though my knowledge of pentacles was limited, that sounded like a lethal combination if you were looking to build one.

"Can I offer you two something to drink?" Hume asked suddenly. Surprisingly, Phoebe nodded and Hume reached under the bookcase behind him, opened what I guess was a small refrigerator and produced a plastic bottle of water for her. He turned in his chair and looked at me. "Enoch?" I shook my head. He also got a bottle for himself, one he promptly opened and from which he took a drink.

He sighed. "So, they took the plans and built a rudimentary pentacle, with mixed results." A mild frown, then a lopsided grin. "A large explosion being one part of the mix." He laughed without mirth. "They initiated the pentacle remotely, I think because they feared such a result, but the feedback from this test was still very encouraging, so they built another pentacle. A much, much, better one."

"Ruach," Phoebe intoned breathlessly.

Hume smiled at that. "Yes, Ruach." He sat quietly for a moment, looking contemplative. "Neither Terloff or Mencius were, I believe, bad people at first, but I think the implications of what they had achieved, and what could be done with it, slowly dawned on them. Overwhelmed their senses." He seemed to sag a little and sighed.

"Our monitoring systems picked up the EM spike from their second pentacle activation." He shrugged. "Of course, at the time we didn't know what it was. It was like nothing we had ever seen before. Some of the tech guys said it was a bug in the software, but others were not so sure."

He let out a breath. "We decided not to directly investigate, just to keep an eye on the region." A sour face. "That was a bad decision by me, and one I still regret."

"After rumors and reports of too many strange events kept piling up, we finally put people on the ground in China." He shook his head and grimaced. "Trust me when I say that making cookies was not the only thing Mencius was doing."

☐ Taking It To Another Level ☐

"Eventually, Terloff went off to start operations in Iceland and South Africa." He stopped and regarded us both with a knowing look, then went on. "By the time the Nykr facility was under construction, PHANTASM operatives were causing them all kinds of grief at all locations."

He stopped and looked intensely at Phoebe. "Do you remember your mission to Korea? And the one to Romania?" Phoebe nodded tentatively. "Those were both related to Mencius and Terloff, to disrupt their plans." This surprised Phoebe quite a bit, I could tell.

"As our intrusions took their toll, Mencius and Terloff arranged a meeting, hoping to work out some kind of truce," Hume relayed to us. "I told them that the only acceptable solution was destruction of the pentacles and release of the eemees, whose existence we were now aware of."

He waved his hands in the air and grunted. "Obviously you know the answer they gave me."

"What about the other locations in Argentina, Knoxville, and Iran?" I wanted all the facts.

"Mencius and Terloff recruited a certain Serges Mendiola to run the Argentinean operation," Hume said and shook his head. "We have an agent on the ground there, but none of his recent reports have set off any alarms."

"Except," I commented dryly, "they are producing, and shipping, an energy supplement with the peptide alkaloid as an ingredient."

Hume nodded in affirmation. "True, but it appears to be an inert ingredient." I exchanged a quick glance with Phoebe, who had just finished taking a big sip of water and eyed me with an unchanged expression. I was flying through flak and taking some serious hits.

"We intercepted their first shipment in Miami and burned it in the warehouse," Hume added as a bolster to his position. A good point, too.

"The peptide alkaloid is in the Iranian shoe inserts as well," I continued in gentle, logical, tones, recalling the details from the report I had recently reviewed. "How do you explain that?"

A partial shrug from Hume. "Not sure, other than they are following a similar formula for compatible products."

⬚ Chapter Seventeen ⬚

Phoebe chimed in, "Why would they do that?"

Hume's fingers moved across his desktop screen and the wall behind us came alive with figures, charts, graphs, and text. "All of their purchases were originally routing through the Chinese operation," he grinned at Phoebe. "Until you closed it down." The Iceland location was flashing red on the display. "Now everything arrives at Nykr, gets processed and then sent out to the other locations, using ships of Iranian registry."

He coughed. "I imagine they make similar products because they are buying the same basic ingredients in massive quantities." It was difficult to find fault with that logic.

Still, it was disconcerting that he had said nothing more specific about the global pentacle theory that Phoebe had come up with earlier and that Hume had previously acknowledged. Phoebe sat stoic and silent. This was my show.

I decided it was time to act. "You know the five locations form a pentacle. What's the purpose?"

Hume grunted in exasperation, frowned. "I'd love to hear your theory, Enoch." He smiled, thinly to be sure. "I think it might just be a red herring as well, designed to distract our attention."

"So, this is all about selling some products?" I asked with a biting skepticism.

Hume let out another long breath. "Well, we talked briefly about this before, Enoch; hold on," and his fingers began moving over the touch screen. "Here are the estimated sales figures for energy drinks, supplements, and other related products that our analysts arrived at, based on the quantity of purchases we've been tracking for all five primary pentacle locations." Some numbers appeared on the screen in bold, red, type.

Let's just say that revenue projections and profits were in the billions. Even after inflation, it was a huge amount of money.

"How are sales and profit numbers like that possible for new companies introducing new products?" I asked, although I half-suspected the answer Hume would give. Feared it, in point of fact.

"Joe tells me you viewed the Iranian video," Hume said, letting me know that he knew more than he was letting on. Which was probably why he was the boss and I was sitting here sweating like a dork.

☐ Taking It To Another Level ☐

"The effects are temporary," I threw out, rallying on my own behalf.

"No question," Hume laughed without mirth. "However, they only need to last long enough to force someone to buy the product."

Phoebe seemed confused. "You mean, *influence* someone to buy the product, don't you?" That's what I thought as well.

Hume shook his head. "Dr. Panglaws tells me, for certain test subjects, the effects induce an actual neurological change that manifests as behavior. Short-term, but *forced*."

"What kind of test subjects?" I asked the logical question.

Hume pursed his lips and made a face. "That is classified," he said unhappily, "even from you, Enoch."

"What's your plan, then?" was all I could think to say.

He shrugged again, a bad habit I recognized for sure, being in clear possession of it myself these days. "We have already shutdown the Chinese operation and destroyed the South African operation. Mencius and Terloff are dead." He took a breath. "Operatives on the ground tell me the Iran operation is in disarray. We destroyed the first shipment from Argentina, but they are back in production."

His smug smile bore a cruel cast. "But, our IT guys introduced a computer virus into their automated production equipment and Cambio hasn't been able to churn out anything new yet."

He pointed at me, then Phoebe. "And both of you were completely out of bounds going to Knoxville." He couldn't stop the big grin that creased his face. "However, that operation is at an utter standstill with no one running the show, and no one to turn to."

A fake scowl. "So, luckily for you, it worked out."

Hume had not mentioned Noet or Anuket, and damned if I was going to bring it up right now. Mostly because I hadn't yet figured out what it meant. "So, all that's left is Iceland," I stated, figuring this must be where the trouble was if he still wanted Phoebe and I to go there.

"We do have problems in Iceland," he confirmed, and his tone was no longer pleasing, but suddenly very somber. "We have a two-man team on the ground, rookies." He looked at Phoebe, "Bradley and Jacobs." She nodded.

"They were going to join up with you when you arrived"—he let out a short breath—"but they didn't contact us during their last scheduled check-in time less than an hour ago and we can't reach them on either agent's ComUnit."

"We're still scanning their vitals as active, so they're alive," Hume said with some relief. "That means the ComUnits are still with them, but obviously we are concerned that an eemee is blocking actual ComUnit communications, or that our guys are somehow in a situation where they can't talk." He paused, a worried look on his face. "Worst case scenario is that our operatives are in enemy hands." His forehead was etched in furrows as he delivered that last part.

"There is another scheduled check-in later this evening, around ten our time." He looked at Phoebe. "If we don't hear anything from them then, you will immediately depart for Iceland and find out what's happened." Phoebe was impassive, stone-faced.

Hume sat back in his chair. "Is this acceptable?" He asked it calmly, coolly. We both nodded agreeably.

I squirmed uncomfortably and looked at Phoebe. She was giving me the skunk eye and I knew what that meant. Time to unleash the Level 5 question. I took a deep breath, but before I could speak Hume began talking again.

"Oh, yes," Hume said quickly, "one more thing." Another huge frown. "Reports of strange things have been crossing my desk—false alarms, breaches in server security, and so on." He eyed us closely. "If you two aren't the ones responsible, then we have a spy or possibly a rogue agent on hand." He tilted his head forward and gave us a serious look. "Are you two responsible for those things?"

I was going to admit our full culpability and then ask about Level 5, but Phoebe was already shaking her head and saying, "That's not us," catching Hume's frank stare and holding it. I just sort of sat there and tried to appear as benignly harmless and stupid as possible, which was pretty much how I felt at the moment.

Hume grunted. "Okay, then, I'll increase security at all access points until we get a better handle on this." His expression lightened. "Get packed, rest up, and we'll see what happens at ten." Phoebe and I stood up, each shook Hume's hand, nodded innocently, and stepped away.

We left the office.

☐ Taking It To Another Level ☐

"What the hell were you thinking?" I gasped at Phoebe after we waved goodbye to Deandra and exited the outer offices. We were still in the complete dark about Level 5 and what Hume knew, or didn't know.

Phoebe was shaking her head in obvious irritation. Thankfully with herself and not me. "I'm not sure what came over me, but I just couldn't admit to Hume that we were sneaking around behind his back." She gave me one of those pitiful looks where you are seeking empathy and understanding from someone else. "I would have felt like a terrible traitor to tell him it was all our doing." Even though she sounded meek and mild about the whole thing, my empathy and understanding were off hiding, so I merely scowled back.

We didn't say another word until we reached the elevators, at which time Phoebe's ComUnit beeped and flashed. She glanced at it, then me. "It's a text message from Panglaws," she said in puzzled tones, looking at the display. "He wants to see me at one of the labs here on Level 4. Something about testing a new weapon."

I could see she was still pretty keyed up from the Hume meeting and how it ended, yet intrigued by this new development.

I frowned at Phoebe, then smiled. You can't stay mad at your partner. Pointless. "Kind of late, isn't it?" I commented lightly, with a big grin. It was after eight in the evening.

"Are you kidding? Some of those techno zombies sleep in the lab," she said with a chuckle, happy to be on familiar ground and off the Level 5 subject. I entered halfway onto the elevator that had just whooshed wide. I was holding my hand on the door to force it to stay open.

She gave me a lopsided grin, "I should at least check it out."

"Shoot, yeah," I said in a pathetic attempt at weapon humor. She shook her head at me, though with a half-grin.

"I'll let you know what it is," she said with an anxious smile and started to move away.

"If it works, get one for me!" I said with a wink as I allowed the elevator door to whoosh shut. It started rising.

As I was thinking about Panglaws and the new weapon, and also trying to disengage my mind from the Level 5 Hume meeting debacle, I suddenly felt a distinct and unsettling wave of uneasiness sweep over

〔 Chapter Seventeen 〕

me, like a sudden night chill. The elevator slowed. Before the first bit of sound came from the doors opening, I stepped to the far right, next to the wall, not sure why; call it paranoia if you must.

As soon as the doors were open wide enough, a darkened figure moved forward with astonishing speed.

Mando fancies himself a tennis player.

He played some in high school and a little in college. And, truth be told, he has some mad skills and a true facility for the game.

But, he can't slow down time, so he has real problems when the match gets close and contentious.

We'll battle back and forth, neck and neck. Yet it seems like, again and again, we'll be near the end of playing and he'll lose his serve, or screw up some easy points, make errors, and I'll win the match.

If he understood how to focus and slow down time, he'd be able to win. I've tried to explain the idea to him, both with adult beverages and without, but I'm met with equal parts doubt and ignorance.

It really isn't all that complex, but it does require a great sense of calm, a certain serenity, if you will grant me that term. Time doesn't actually slow down—that only happens when you are visiting the in-laws—but the complete absorption and channeling of energy to maintain concentration and clarity of mind yields an amazing side effect—the compression of time as it seems to unfold.

It does take some practice to use on a consistent basis, and competitive sports is one good way to hone that trait. Combat training is certainly another, though the cost for failure in the latter is much more significant when training is transformed into reality.

I saw, sensed, felt, the man enter the elevator. As I say, he moved fast, but not out of control, just quick; his right hand brandishing a wicked looking, double-edged, fighting knife with about six or seven inches of edgy glistening steel held just barely out in front of his body, very well-prepared for a deadly thrust forward.

He fully expected me, his apparent victim, to be standing near the door, in the center of the elevator, as anyone about to exit normally would be. As a result, his feet were ill-placed and his body movements ill-timed to make a sudden adjustment to his left and deal with me standing about three feet away from where his mind told him I should have been.

He made the refinements, though, with great rapidity, taking one concise step forward with his right foot, pivoting with his hips and stabbing forward, with the efficiently murderous intent of disemboweling me, no doubt.

It was the obvious move for him, and the one I assumed he would make. I had already transitioned a half-step to my right, turned sideways and slammed my fist down toward his forearm as hard as I could.

The man was about my size, maybe a little lighter, and even I, as strong as I pride myself on being, could not have held onto a knife under the impact of such a blow as I delivered. The knife, accompanied by his sharp grunt and yelp of pain, clattered noisily to the elevator floor. The door started to close and the thought of battling it out in a closed elevator with a mad assassin was not all that appealing.

I brought my right arm and fist close into my body and threw a high cocked and bent elbow at him, a right to left swinging blow. Kind of a modified forearm shiver. He leaned back, thinking the blow was aimed for his head, but I only wanted to knock him off balance and then get out of the damn elevator.

I hit my intended target, his left shoulder, and sent him cascading into the far wall with a thunderous crash. I nimbly stepped over his thrashing legs and through the elevator door, tripping the sensors which triggered it to open again.

Moments later, having retrieved the knife, albeit with his left hand, he stepped slowly out into the hallway after me.

I felt a tingling sensation in my oblongata. Dee wanted me to blast him into unconsciousness, but my blood was hot now. This guy had tried to kill me, thinking he could stick me with a knife like an animal at slaughter. All that did was tick me off. I started smiling, ignoring her. Blocking her.

I'll confide something to you. Most of the time I'm really laid back. I like to laugh; to make other people smile. Truthfully, I'm a pussycat. There are times, though, when my soul can get a little dark.

Shark-eyed Enoch.

⧠ Chapter Seventeen ⧠

That's what my friends call me when I get really miffed and cross over to the proverbial dark side. Regular Enoch gets along with almost everyone. Well, maybe not English professors and puritanical linguists. Still, it takes a lot to bring shark-eyed Enoch to the forefront. I keep him in check most of the time. If someone lies to me or disrespects me—well, that's a different story. Shark-eyes might stop by for an ugly visit. Usually bad for the other fellow.

I can tell you—for damn sure—that when someone waves a knife in my face, they are going to meet the shark-eyes.

I've been in plenty of scraps, it happens to all of us, but not many where someone was actually intent on killing me, and only twice when a knife was pulled on me. Well, there was that gang thing with Danny II, but I swore I'd never talk about it.

So, twice I've had knives waved in my face. Once was a drunk at a bar, which, since I was sober at the time, was like fighting a baby. The other was a jealous boyfriend, more dangerous than the drunk, but he was just showing off for the girl, not really seriously trying to stick me. Neither event posed much of a threat, all things considered, and old shark-eyes never showed up for either confrontation.

A little hand-to-hand with a skilled opponent, with me unarmed, well, that might represent a perilous difference, but I was mad. Not crazy, out-of-control mad; but cool, calm, methodical, serene mad.

Shark-eyed mad.

The pain was evident on his face and in his eyes. He was clenching and unclenching his right hand, grimacing madly each time as he tried to get the feeling back. He was going to be operating left-handed for awhile, and judging by the way he held the knife, he was not ambidextrous. Threat level diminished some.

He was game, though, and we circled each other warily.

A brief discursive on knife fighting, if you will grant me the forbearance, and some brief attentiveness.

If you face an irritated and hostile person armed with a knife, you have to establish quickly and reliably if you are dealing with an amateur, or with someone trained in the use of bladed weapons. Your tactical and strategic moves during the confrontation are based on the accuracy of your assessment, and your life may depend on it. The most telling point, no pun intended, is elegant and simple—the amateur almost always holds the blade away from the body, out in front, often swinging it around wildly or jabbing it out threateningly.

Not only that, but the untrained person always thinks, because he or she are in possession of a supposedly superior offensive weapon, that they must attack. A knife in the hand of such a person is nothing more than a long, pointy, finger on their hand. Invariably they will lunge in thrusting madly or rush in slashing crazily. Assuming you don't panic, all you must do is simply evade the initial strike and then counter attack to either disarm or disable them. Child's play.

You have a genuine problem when you face someone properly trained in the use of a knife, especially a fighting knife. Such a person understands that a knife, while it can be used as a slashing weapon, is best used as a thrusting weapon because the point is far faster than the edge. Thank you, Richard Sharpe. In addition, the skilled attacker keeps the knife hand near to the body. The attacker wants to close the distance with you, to grapple and, using his or her body as a shield, the opponent will then turn and drive the point home.

This is not conducive to good health or longevity. Yours.

This guy might have the knife in his off, left hand, and he might be holding it by the handle, blade out, fencing style, but he was smart. He kept the elbow bent and the weapon close to him, waiting.

A knife encounter is a dance of minimal errors. First, moving in a semi-circular motion, in opposition to one another, then forward, then back, side steps, back steps, shuffling feet, very Fred Astaire. He made a few preliminary jabs, some half-hearted thrusts, but never tried to really close the distance between us.

The pending reality of two things slowly began to creep into my pea brain as I observed and noted all this.

The first realization was that he was simply stalling for time, waiting for the numbness in his right hand to drain away so he could wield the weapon in his proficient right hand. Threat level would rise exponentially if he managed to do that. If I permitted him to do that.

The second realization, as I considered how many more orders of magnitude dangerous he would be with the knife in his right hand than his left, was that I was wearing a rather manly leather belt.

☐ Chapter Seventeen ☐

As he warily circled to his right, and I to my right in graceful response, I suddenly and smoothly undid the belt off my waist and had several loops of it around my right hand, drawn tight, before he could even react.

He did not like it, not one damn bit, for now I actually had two weapons to his one. My knuckles were wrapped in hard leather and could deliver a devastating blow, or they could easily knock aside his knife thrust. Plus, the heavy metal buckle at the end, rained down on him with a bullet-like, whiplash, strike, was easily capable of breaking bones.

No, sir, he was most unhappy, but realizing it was Elvis Presley time (now or never) he pulled a very deft border shift and the knife was now in his, apparently healed, right hand. Not only that, but he caught the hilt in his palm, between the thumb and index finger, with his palm down, simply closing his fist around it. Reverse grip. It made sense for him because he had powerful forearms and could easily implement the dangerous arc slashes so favored by reverse grip aficionados.

I suppose another reason he went with the reverse grip was because of my new belt weapon. Undoubtedly without it he would have chosen the straight fencer's grip and then tried to work his way close to me to deliver the killing thrust. Much more difficult with the belt in my hand. Bummer for him.

His smile was forced, but he seemed to appreciate the situation and wasn't going to back down now.

The little tango we had been doing earlier had just been a preliminary event, a warm-up, as now it was in deadly earnest. Any miscue earlier, when he held the knife in his left hand, wouldn't have cost me much due to his inability to unleash a truly coordinated attack, and since I had been unarmed at the time (well, not counting fingers, hands, elbows, feet, knees, and head) a mistake on his part wouldn't have been punished too severely by me.

Now, however, any stumble, any out-of-balance body movement, a loss of focus, or any other slight bobble, could result in something that would leave an unsightly mark. A serious hole. Unanswered email.

We took turns, first moving left, then right. I lashed out once with the belt, hoping to catch him unaware, but he leaned out of the way just in time as the buckle whizzed by his suitably alarmed face. It occurred to me, though, that one had to be careful with the belt weapon because it did have one rather glaring and potentially hazardous weakness. If your opponent should somehow manage to grab the loose end, all they had to do was yank on it with some force. Unless you could release it quickly, you would be instantly and regretfully pulled into the killing zone.

My guess is, a bad outcome would be in the offing. Your offing.

As he circled left, he took two quick, and I mean quick, short steps forward and made a slashing arc, right to left high and then left to right lower, intending to maim or wound, not to kill. This was the third such attempt during our little waltz, each attack barely avoided by deft-footed me, but now his intentions seemed to crystallize in my mind.

He was looking to inflict some weakening wounds until they slowed me down, and then he could finish me off. But, considering we were in the hallway of agent quarters, I thought it an ill-advised and incredibly stupid plan. Someone would be along, sooner or later, and then what would he do?

And, I swear I am not making this up, but as if on cue, the elevator made a noise. In addition, to make matters worse for him, he had his back to the elevator. No amount of professional training can overcome natural human proclivities, like turning your head toward a sudden, unexpected, sound. Which he did, even if just for an instant.

Enough time for me to move forward into range and crack a whip-like stroke down, catching him flush on the bony part of the wrist with the whirling metal buckle. He let out a shrieking squall of agony, releasing the blade and instantly clutching his wounded arm to his chest, protecting and covering it with his left hand. Almost before I heard the knife clatter and rattle on the ground I had made a half-pivot, cocked my arm just slightly, and delivered a walloping short right lead into his face with my leather-wrapped right hand.

In martial arts, great emphasis is placed on the power than can be brought to the fray with short punches, the aptly named six-inch punch and such. It's a combination of focus, willful energy, and follow through. Push that chi on down the line. My punch traveled less than a foot, but I put a whole bunch of my recent bad attitude into it.

◻ Chapter Seventeen ◻

Okay, maybe a little fear, too.

He was out cold, even as he flew backwards as though jerked by a rope. His right leg and foot actually flew up and I was kicked in the left forearm. He did a sort of quasi-flip and landed ass first, followed by his shoulders and then a sickening thud as his head cracked on the floor. Well, I hoped it didn't crack, but it sure sounded bad.

Phoebe stepped into the hallway from the now open elevator, saw the knife on the ground, me looking like I'm not sure what, and this guy, nose broken and blood dripping out, wrist bloody and swollen, unconscious.

"Sorry you missed the party," I said wittily. Folks are always telling me I'm full of wit.

She absently, calmly, patted her ComUnit. "Panglaws never sent that message. About the new weapon."

Really?

I nodded and looked at the fallen man as Phoebe stepped over to examine him. "So, it was a setup." A statement rather than a question. I think both of us had Hume on our minds, but neither wanted to say it.

"I know this man!" Phoebe exclaimed in astonishment, "Georg Pleshovich or Plesavich, for sure." She looked at me with, well, a sort of awe and respect which was weird from her. "He's a professional assassin. We crossed paths in Romania." A mental tremble passed through her. "I still have a scar."

"I'd like to see that," I said with a wide grin.

"I bet you would," Phoebe chuckled with macabre mirth and unhooked her ComUnit. "I need a security team and a med team with a gurney immediately to Level 3, by the elevators." She clipped it back and looked steadily at me. "You want to say it, or should I?"

"Hume warned us there was possibly a rogue agent or spy in the building," I replied defensively.

"That's nonsense! All that activity was us, or Tom and Armando." She flattened me with an angry look. "You know that."

I shrugged and said incredulously, "Maybe so, but Hume wouldn't risk an assassination right here in PHANTASM." I shook my head vehemently. "It doesn't make sense."

⧉ Taking It To Another Level ⧉

It was silent for a few moments while she considered my response. "None of this makes any sense, Enoch," she replied slowly, then pointed at the unconscious form of the would-be killer. "But, that seems pretty straight-forward to me." Raised eyebrows and a serious stare at me.

I really didn't want to get into this conversation right now. The same chemicals that flood your body to help you during a fight are the same ones that weigh you down after it's over, to help you recover. Besides, despite the constant 72 degrees in the building, I had worked up a pretty good lather during that whole escapade. In short, I stank like a mule. With or without Borax. Hoary ref there.

If genius was 99% perspiration, I was feeling pretty smart. Ranked rather high, you might say. Well, if you like crappy puns you'd say it.

"Look, can we talk about this later?" I said, trying to whimper a little and get some sympathy. "I need to take a shower. Change clothes. We can meet up in the cafeteria for a snack, say, in about 30 minutes or so." I flashed my best "take pity on me" look. She groaned.

The elevator doors opened just then and four people piled out. Two security guards in black uniforms, a man and a woman, and two med team guys in white uniforms rolling out an ER gurney. Very officious. The wheels click-clacked across the tile floor.

I motioned them through as I brushed by and stepped into the elevator. I waved at Phoebe. She tilted her head, eyebrows arched again, and shook her head at me as the doors shut.

Great neck muscles.

What Did You Do?

———☐———

"Never interrupt your opponents when they are in the process of making a mistake."

—Napoleon Bonaparte

The adrenaline burn after a hard fought athletic contest or a serious fight can be exhausting, but a rabidly quaffed power drink perked me up just fine, thank you. A nice, long, scorching hot shower didn't hurt either, and I even trimmed up the facial hair, tweaking the eyebrows and nose hairs along the way. I know, TMI, sorry. I ramble when I'm nervous, remember?

And it wasn't the aftermath of the attack that was making me nervous; it was not knowing who was responsible. After meeting with Hume, he had answered the doubts about my previous doubts, but now I had new doubts, and was more confused than ever. I just didn't think Hume was some kind of evil master mind behind it all. Phoebe had left me a message that she intended to talk to the would-be assassin, but that he was still unconscious.

I had finished changing into some old and incredibly comfortable blue jeans and a black, well-fitted, short-sleeve, collarless shirt. I was working on my boot laces when the ComUnit flashed and Dee said at the same time, **"It's Tom on the line, Enoch."**

"Thank you, Dee," I said warmly. In a way I found strangely pleasing, and comforting, it was good to hear her voice. Simple pleasures are always the best.

"Tom, you must have something for me," I stated, and just for a fleeting moment it struck me as sad. Sad in the sense that Tom and I used to talk all the time about mostly nothing, just banter, blather, blither. Now, it was all business. Damn, here less than a week and I already needed a break. Poor pitiful me. I grinned stupidly at myself.

⬚ What Did You Do? ⬚

"Not sure you're going to like it," Tom muttered enigmatically.

"Never do," I kidded him.

"Well, for starters," he began, "we did find some info for a Dr. William Fulsum on the PHANTASM server." The guy who had signed off on the South African cookie report that found nothing of merit to report. Tom's statement was bouncing around my already overloaded cranium. "We were able to take a peek at a couple of HR files." Tom cleared his throat. "Fulsum did work at PHANTASM." A pause of the briefest, most pregnant, nature. "Two years ago."

"Thanks, Tom, great work as always," I said quietly, letting this new information takes its toll on my understanding. His image vanished. "Dee, show me that lab report, the one from Fulsum," I said, a sudden idea (always dangerous) popping into my head. The ComUnit instantly displayed the one-page report.

"Zoom in on the signature at the bottom, please." Dee did and there it was. My mind was ablaze with options and possibilities. Or, possibly too much niacin and B-12. "Dee, do you have access to the files Tom and Mando found in the Human Resource stuff for Fulsum?"

"Yes, Enoch, do you want me to pull up a form with Dr. Fulsum's signature?" Smart girl, er, eemee.

"Yes, m'am, I surely do," I said enthusiastically.

Another form, it looked like a W4, appeared next to the lab report. If you simply took a quick glance, you would accept the signatures on both as the same; but a closer, harder, look showed issues. Not that I'm an expert or anything, but it seemed to me—giving it some careful scrutiny—that you could make a pretty good argument that the signatures were *not* from the same hand.

"Dee, what's your analysis of the two signatures? Are they from the hand of the same person?"

The two signatures were cropped out, reduced to the same scale and overlaid, accompanying by a dazzling display of arcane mathematics as they were traced and retraced. Ain't technology grand? Well, when it works. Still, I trusted Dee's techno wizardry implicitly.

"Based on a preliminary analysis, there is a 72% probability that these signatures do NOT derive from the same source. I can make a more thorough assessment, if you wish."

☐ Chapter Eighteen ☐

"Hold that thought for now Dee, but I do need something else," and now I was nervous for sure. "Can you locate one of Dr. Hume's signatures and put it up? Leave the lab report up as well."

A few moments passed, then a staff memo bearing Hume's signature appeared.

They were completely different. Hume's name was fairly upright in appearance, simple and direct. The Fulsum lab report signature was in larger letters, slanted a little to the left, with much more panache and flourish. Not gaudy, but in that neighborhood.

I looked again, darting my eyes back and forth. Or, maybe not. There were two common letters and the harder I looked, the more I seemed to be seeing, or perhaps hoping to see. It was the *um* that appeared in the surnames. "Dee, run a complete comparative analysis on the *um* letters in the last names."

The ComUnit again whirred into action as tracings were made of the letters. They were then superimposed together and all sorts of mathematics and calculations were flying around the display. I was torn between wanting it to match and not wanting it to match, and my guts were in an uproar. I plopped down in my living room chair and let out a drafty breath.

"I have the results," Dee intoned, which only made my anxiety increase tenfold.

"And?" I said testily, though not meaning to be so harsh.

"There is sufficient empirical reliability to state that these signatures were generated by the same hand."

Hume's hand. The W4 apparently had the real Fulsum signature, which did not match anything, but the fake lab report and Hume's memo did match. Which had to mean Hume had forged a report to claim that nothing was in the South African cookies.

Still, there was one other thing to check.

"Dee, can you see if there are any recent reports on the server from the lab that deal with any testing done on those cookies?" I asked this because Hume himself had said they had one set of reports—false or misleading—for regular inspection and another—true—set of reports routed to him.

⬚ What Did You Do? ⬚

"There is nothing on any server. I have also scanned internal email exchanges between lab staff themselves, and from lab staff to Hume."

Hume was lying. This was the first, in my mind, clearly documented case of a flat out falsehood. And where there's smoke...

"Dee, get me Tom again, please," I said absently, my mind whirring away into a bazillion different directions, which was a gazillion more than normal.

"It is not required that you always say please, Enoch," Dee said cheerfully.

"What would I do without you, Dee?" I hugged her with my voice. Indeed.

"Enoch, you are a needy bass turd," Tom said playfully when he came on the line.

"You have no idea, Tom," I agreed. "But, you may not be able to help with this new request."

Mando leaned into frame, "Thanks for the vote of confidence, pendejo." At least he was smiling as he said it.

"Besa mi..." I rejoined grinning, leaving the butt end of my comment out. Mando's face darted away.

"What do you need, Enoch?" Tom asked seriously.

"You know the Nykr video, the one without an audio track?" Tom nodded. "Is there any sort of software, or program, or even lip-readers, that we can use to get some kind of dialog out of it?"

Mando's head once more popped into frame, "Dude, you are freaking me out." He vanished again.

"Why does he do that?" I asked, completely dumbfounded.

Tom laughed. "It's because you seem to know what we are doing at about the same time we start doing it."

"Huh?" I slung back at him.

"Ever heard of ALR?" Tom asked solemnly.

"The Alabama League of Realtors?" I offered weakly.

"Automated Lip Reading," he replied with a mild grin. "It's new research into analyzing video without audio."

"What about it?" I inquired of him.

"Well, after a couple of beers at dinner tonight, Mando and me started wondering what you're wondering, and did some checking around," he said with a touch of pride in his voice.

"So, it can be done?" I asked excitedly.

"My friend, as long as you have the money, damn near anything can be done," Tom said pleasantly.

"Dee, you did set up an account with PHANTASM for Tom and Armando, right?" I had asked her about this before, but it had been some time back.

"Yes, they have an open purchase order," Dee stated innocently.

I rolled my eyes skyward. I'm sure I could trust Tom and Armando but, damn, the temptation of it all. "You didn't hear that, did you?" I asked, though it really wasn't a question, per se.

"Hear what?" Tom said, flashing a most angelic smile.

I sighed. "I need that ALR thing now, like yesterday now," I said, cost be damned. "Spend what we need to get it done fast, within a few hours if possible."

"I know just the people," Tom said quickly and he vanished.

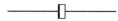

It was around 9:30 when Phoebe and I met at the cafeteria. The first thing I wanted to do was update her on my Fulsum research and the fact that Hume had probably forged the report.

"That lying SOB!" Phoebe said with acidic venom after I finished laying out the facts. It was hard for me to argue about that, based on the evidence, although I wasn't familiar with Hume's familial relations. No matter what, *prima facie*, it didn't look good for Hume. And you thought *fronti nulla fides* exhausted my Latin. Bah!

We agreed that no matter what Hume claimed about the ten o'clock Iceland team check-in status, we weren't leaving PHANTASM until we got the lip reading results back from Tom and Armando.

"They can really do that?" Phoebe asked and took a sip of water from a plastic bottle. The label said it was 100% biodegradable. I nodded and she added, "That is way cool." She was so cute when she did that.

"If the results come back bad for Hume," I said, halfheartedly poking at a bowl of cold soup, "I have a plan."

⎕ What Did You Do? ⎕

She took another sip of water, pondering some rejoinder of biting significance I am sure, tapped her chin a number of times with her left index finger and said warily, "Okay, let's hear it."

"I don't like it," she said flatly, but with emotive power. I had outlined my idea to her and, well, let's just say it was not met with a round of ringing applause. A standing obliteration was more like it.

I shook my head against her objection. "Maybe so, but it does make sense." The plan was for me to visit Hume alone, like I had originally sketched out for Phoebe, who would be backup in case I got in trouble. I patted my ComUnit. "Dee and I can take care of ourselves, and I doubt Hume is going to resort to physical violence." I smiled knowingly.

Phoebe looked at me like I was a dolt. "Has that little episode with the assassin outside the elevator just slipped your mind?" she reminded me in a sweet voice. "There may be more people like that lurking in the woodwork."

I shrugged nonchalantly. "So, I blast them all." Only way to be sure.

Phoebe was looking at me rather oddly. "You seem fairly cavalier about using a power that instantly killed four men in South Africa." Her look, and words, were more than a little unsettling, unnerving.

I thought back to that episode in South Africa. It had been my anger, my fury, getting the better of me and using a weapon, my mind blast, that I still didn't fully understand. However, it had been self-defense, using the only weapon I had available at the time.

"That's not fair," I stated, even though she might have a valid point.

"Beware of battling monsters, lest ye become one," Phoebe replied gently, quoting Nietzsche. Impressive.

"When you stare into the abyss, the abyss stares into you," I enjoined quietly and we were both silent for a moment. The men I had killed in South Africa had undoubtedly deserved it, but you have to exercise control over a weapon like I had, or in the arbitrary use of it you're no better than they.

A great mind sigh. "You're right, my arrogance is wrong and I'm sorry," and I genuinely was, for both our sakes. "I promise to be careful, and be a good steward of my power," I said with conviction. "But, you still can't come," I added forcefully.

◻ Chapter Eighteen ◻

"Dee!" Phoebe said loud enough to make someone at a nearby table glance over.

"Yes, Phoebe?" Dee replied in a much softer voice.

"You'll notify me immediately if this idiot gets into any trouble," she stated in a quiet, matter of fact, voice.

"I will keep a close eye on this idiot," Dee said with a smile in her voice.

"I'm right here!" I complained playfully.

Bitter synchronicity—our ComUnits flashed simultaneously, and it was Hume.

"The Iceland team didn't report in at their scheduled check-in time." He looked grim. Phoebe and I were either full of prunes, or Hume was a hell of an actor. "You need to saddle up and get out to the airfield." His image disappeared. We needed a plan now.

I grinned nervously at Phoebe. "Well, there you have it."

"Dee," Phoebe said without hesitation, "get me Jimmy, the driver, on the line." Apparently, Phoebe now had a plan.

A few seconds went by and we heard Jimmy's voice, but did not see his image (he didn't have a ComUnit or video phone). "Miss O'Hara, how can I help you?"

"Well, Mr. Scanlin, I need you to start driving toward the airfield, with me and Enoch as passengers, and when you get about halfway there, contact Hume and tell him you had an accident." Her voice was calm and clear. I now understood the plan.

"Okay, Miss O'Hara. Do I actually need to have an accident?" He didn't seem worried about the answer, just asking the logical question.

"I would think the NSA strives for authenticity in all its covert operations, Jimmy," she replied softly. "Still, please be careful." There was obvious sincerity in her tone.

"I'm always careful," and he clicked off.

"I didn't think of that," I admitted candidly. Did I mention she was really good-looking, too?

"Yeah," she scowled. "Your plans don't always engender the greatest degree of confidence." She smiled and immediately added, "But, I have faith in your ability to make them work."

☐ What Did You Do? ☐

"I think I was just insulted and then hugged, I'm not sure," I said with a sly smile.

We stood up. "So, where do we go to wait for Tom's ALR report?" I asked quietly.

"Not our quarters; they might be monitored." She was giving the question considerable thought. "We'll slip into the theater after it starts and catch a movie." She nodded. "It's always crowded with the shift change folks, so no one will even notice us."

"We have a theater?" I asked as we walked out of the cafeteria.

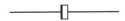

The movie had already started when we entered. We crept, partially blind, down the far wall until we reached the last row of seats. The theater was larger than I thought, two sections of seats, right and left with 15 rows of 10 seats each. The back row on our side, the right, was empty and the nearest people were five rows in front of us, a group of three. We plopped down in the pleasantly cushy rocking seats, prepared to wait for the ALR report.

It was a foreign film with subtitles. A period piece set in the late 19th century. The language sounded like German, but I guess it could have been Dutch or Swedish or something. At times the inflections and tonal quality didn't seem quite German enough. Lo que sea or whatever...

Not that language or subtitles mattered much. About ten minutes in, with some peasants arguing over a stolen cow, I fell fast asleep. I'm not sure how long I dozed, but it was Dee's soft voice whispering in my head, rather than a Phoebe Worldwide Federation of Wrestling smack down elbow, that roused me. As I straightened in my seat, Phoebe looked over at me.

Peasants were still arguing, but this time it was over a dead cow. Gotta love those foreign films.

~Mando has something,~ Dee said with just a dash of anticipatory anxiety.

I leaned over toward Phoebe and whispered, "Mando's calling." She nodded, her eyes wide open.

☐ Chapter Eighteen ☐

"Go ahead, Dee, put him on, but keep the volume low," I told her, blowing out a long breath and coughing lightly. Phoebe leaned in close to the ComUnit.

"E, you there?" came Mando's questioning tones.

"You got me," I said, holding my breath. The peasants were smiling and some ornate text appeared on screen that read, "Das Ende," which meant I'd missed the whole damn movie.

Thankfully.

"We got the info you asked about," Mando informed me, smiling.

"That was quick," I commented, trying to remain calm. AUM.

"The guys we used said the enhanced HD video made it a lot easier for the ALR software to work," he clarified. "Since all their software does is extrapolate text from lip movements, you're getting a text file with descriptions of the video action matched up to the ALR text snippets."

I followed that and it actually made sense. It's always scary when that happens to me. "I've posted the file to Dee," Mando added quietly. He seemed a little solemn. "Good luck, man, let us know what happens."

"Done," was all I said and the connection was closed.

The lights in the theater were slowly coming up. I looked over at Phoebe, "Let's wait until it clears a little," and people began rising up, stretching, checking their pockets, blah, blah, blah. In a couple of minutes, except for a few stragglers way up front, we were alone.

"Dee, show us the text file," I asked, my stomach now a mass of broiling waves. So much for calm and serene.

The text file appeared on the display. It was in the form of a description, along with comments and the ALR text. We sat reading it, thoughtfully absorbed, tentatively anxious.

ALR Results Bendix Video Clip #1.

Note: ALR interpretation cannot convey emotion, other than that which can be judged from facial expression and body language. Alternate readings based on probabilistic scatterings are shown in [brackets]. Unknown or questionable words are shown in {braces}. Please note that ALR word choice selection is often influenced by visual context.

⬜ What Did You Do? ⬜

The scene begins with three men seated at a table. Two are initially visible in terms of ALR utilization, the third has his back to the camera. The video begins with the unknown man, whose back is to the camera, speaking. We judge this to be the scenario based on the expressions and reactions of the other two men whose faces are visible. The man to the right says, in response to what the unseen man has just finished saying, "You keep saying [stating] that, but where [what] are the results?" Judging by his facial expression, the man to the right is upset.

The man to the left replies, "{Unknown}, we must be patient while {dental} completes [competes] the formula." The man pauses, stares at the man whose back is to the camera. The man on the left continues to talk, "You are setting [getting] close, are {aren't} you?" Facial expression indicates a query, a questioning look on the speaker's face.

The man to the right quickly rises to his feet. His chair is knocked over. He appears to be angry and says, "We could [should] do it ourselves!"

The man whose back is to the camera apparently is speaking again, because the standing man's face changes expression during this time sequence, as though he is listening. The unseen seated man turns to face the standing man as this latter bends to get his chair. The seated man, whose face is now visible, says, "{Unknown} will do what I say [state]. Now sit down." The seated man's face appears calm.

The standing man seats. End of video clip.

I looked at Phoebe. She was looking at me. "So," I asked softly, "what's your professional assessment of this?"

She bit her lower lip, nodded. "If I were completely objective," she looked at me with a tilted head and raised eyes; "which I'm not"—a short pause—"I'd say that Mencius was a hot head, which I happen to know was true, Terloff was a sneaky, evil, little turd, which is just a guess, and Hume is in charge of the whole damn stinking mess."

She smiled sweetly, "What do you think?"

I took a deep breath and let it out in a long stream. "Pretty much the same thing," was all I said in a low voice.

"What's the next step?" Phoebe was always locked and loaded.

"I'd like to talk to Ruach before we try to take Hume down," I said calmly, hoping Phoebe would agree. Any sort of additional clarification on all this could really be useful.

⬚ Chapter Eighteen ⬚

She seemed to be considering it. "He either doesn't know anything, or Hume has some kind of hold over him," she finally said.

"Dee, I know you've been following all of this. What do you think?" I valued her opinion a great deal.

"Ruach once told you the following: 'The truth is not something that can be given to another, it must be experienced.'"

Even though I was beginning to understand what Ruach was trying to tell me with that, it didn't help me right this minute. "Dee, does Ruach know Hume is possibly, uh, bad, or involved in something he shouldn't be doing?" That was awkward.

"Humans must solve human problems," Dee replied mysteriously.

"Ruach helped in China, with Mencius," Phoebe observed very gently.

"Yes, but humans initiated the action. You took the first step."

Phoebe nodded and seemed to accept this.

I decided to be blunt, after all, it was going to be Phoebe and me with our asses on the firing line. "Dee, you will support us against Hume, if necessary?"

"I will do all I can to help Enoch," Dee confirmed. Internal sigh of relief, I think.

"What about Ruach?" I followed up.

"In his current situation, he is doing everything he can to help you," and though that didn't spell out anything specific, it was good enough for me.

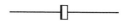

We found ourselves, for the second time this day, resolutely headed to Hume's office. Yeah, Phoebe convinced me to take her along. Don't ask. The first time we visited Hume had been to make some simple inquires and get some straight-forward answers. Seek a fuller explanation of what was happening.

Now, it was to confront Hume with serious allegations that, if he could not explain to our satisfaction, would require his removal. Forceful, if necessary.

He would have his chance to explain, but the evidence seemed damning, as I have said before, and I admit I was prejudiced against him because of that evidence. But, we'd hear him out. Phoebe and I had agreed on that. Maybe there was some logical explanation that, in our haste (and possible ignorance), we were overlooking.

We entered the outer office. Deandra simply shook her head at us and waved off-handedly at Hume's door.

Hume's expression reminded me of something you might see on the face of an exasperated parent. He rubbed his forehead as if in anguish, lowering it for a moment to stare at his desktop. He then straightened up and watched as we moved into the room.

We walked over and stood in front of his desk. "Well," he said with just the barest hint of emotion, "here we go again." He gestured at the chairs with one hand while drumming his fingers on the table with the other. "Have a seat."

Truthfully, I figured we'd just stay standing this time and have it all out, probably with much wailing and gnashing of teeth, but Phoebe immediately took a chair, so I reluctantly followed suit. One of Hume's fancy family crest chairs.

"I'm a patient man," Hume said patiently, curiously enough. "But, even I have my limits." He was only looking at me and never glanced at Phoebe. "I thought I answered all your questions at our previous meeting." His tone was conversational and friendly. That is to say, normal.

There are times you're all fired up to say something and then the moment comes and you freeze. Lockjaw. Tight ass. Nerve bound.

Or, you finally manage to blurt out what you intended to say, but not with the same firm determination and bitter resolve that maybe you had worked up in your mind prior to the meeting. Kind of like I was doing now.

"I wanted to, er, ask about, ah, Dr. Fulsum's report." It was a little shaky, but I finally managed to spit it out intelligibly.

"Fulsum's report?" Hume repeated in mystified tones. He shook his head. "Refresh me on that." He regarded me blankly.

"He signed off on a report stating that the South Africa cookies had no ingredients worth worrying about," I said, rallying myself, and before Hume could speak I added, "except you forged his signature."

☐ Chapter Eighteen ☐

Hume actually started laughing. I didn't quite know what to do. I had envisioned any number of possible responses from him, and hilarity had not been on that list. Phoebe was impassive, staring at him. "I don't see the humor," I said, obviously failing to see the humor.

Hume straightened himself up. "Enoch, do you remember what I told you about the supplies shipped to Iceland?" Asked with a slight smile. I nodded. "The five locations are buying mass quantities of the same raw supplies and then those raw supplies are being distributed to the separate production operations." I shrugged as if to say, *so what*?

"Our analysis of the Argentinean supplement and Iranian shoe insert showed the same basic ingredients." He shrugged. "There were slight differences in ingredient percentages, but all within normal tolerances." He smiled at me, waiting for some sign I understand. Since I did not understand, no such sign was forthcoming.

"Even the tests to determine the percentage of inert ingredients in Nykr bottled water yielded similar results," he said firmly.

"However," he cleared his throat, "the cookies you brought back from South Africa were different. The concentration of the peptide alkaloid was much higher, more concentrated, with a slightly different chemical composition."

He smiled wanly at me. "Do you remember our first meeting today?" He paused and sort of scowled at me. "I told you Panglaws had run some tests where behavior could be forced in certain test subjects by changes in neurological function. Changes induced by the peptide alkaloid subject to EM energy?" I nodded, recalling that. "Well, Panglaws was using the formula from the new South African cookies."

Hume nodded as my face slowly changed from shadowy ignorance to a dawning realization.

"Obviously those sorts of test results represent extremely sensitive information." He eyed me closely. "You do understand that information about a new drug that, when exposed to EM exposure, causes neurological changes *forcing* certain induced behaviors, might be of extreme interest to people?"

He eyed me like I was crazy not to have thought of this. "Bad people, evil people?" He shook his head to emphasize the point.

⬚ What Did You Do? ⬚

"That kind of information has to be controlled. We cannot let it get out." He waved a crooked finger at me. "Even you are not supposed to know."

I flashed him a weary look. "Okay, let's say I buy all that. It still doesn't explain the forged signature," I objected softly, but firmly.

"Lab personnel function under one overriding protocol—security." Hume sighed. "When they encounter anything that is deemed a security risk, a rubber-stamp report is automatically generated." He chuckled. "Fulsum was an idiot as a lab tech, so we sacked him, but now the lab uses his signature for all such reports. Kind of an inside joke."

He noted my sour expression. "Not everyone gets it, of course, but when we see the Fulsum signature, we know there's a security issue, and we utilize more secure pathways to access the real data."

I expected, and would have welcomed, some kind of response from Phoebe, but she simply sat there watching Hume. Fine. She was backup anyway.

Maybe it was time to ask about Level 5. See how Hume would explain that and, if he did, well, I didn't have much in the way of topics left to work with. "What can you tell me about Level 5?"

Some people are terrible liars. They look at their feet, roll their eyes, play with their ears, whatever. They have tells. They always lose money at poker. Some folks, though, are great at fibs. They simply make statements and don't invest any weight in them at all. Could be true, could be false. *Fronti nulla fides*, remember? Sometimes you can't tell jack squat from looking at a person's face.

Hume was a sphinx. "That area is supposed to be secure." A rather nasty stare, squint-eyes. "And a secret."

I couldn't think of anything truly remarkable to say, so merely commented, "Not anymore," and smiled resolutely, waiting for a proper response from him. Phoebe seemed to have perked up some, and was eyeing Hume closely.

"You two may be the best agents we have, but you aren't the only two we have," he stated in solemn tones. "No single field agent can ever know all the things that go on here at PHANTASM," he began his explanation with a grim smile. "That would be far too dangerous."

A darker, almost sardonic look. "Our people understand the risks of being compromised by the enemy." I had to let that unpleasant thought rattle around my mind for a moment.

He looked at Phoebe, then back to me. "Agents have died to acquire those pentacles on Level 5." He said it flatly, clearly, but with subtle force and emphasis. "The eemees contained within those pentacles were actively involved with, and fully supportive of, the human controller at the time of their capture." He smirked. "Despite any information to the contrary, those eemees continue to be uncooperative and have been placed in a binding pentacle until they change their minds and decide to help us."

I wasn't sure what to make of that. ~Dee, can this be true?~ I thought with barely constrained emotion.

~You and I share the same level of information on this topic.~ Which was Dee-speak for she didn't know anymore than I did. Which meant, in lieu of a clearer explanation, I had to admit that Hume was being truthful.

He seemed to have a good explanation for everything. Maybe I was full of crap. Wouldn't be the first time, nor the last. Still, I was getting ready to fire my last salvo. If that got jammed back, I was going to profusely apologize, express sorrow over my many character flaws, put my metaphorical tail between my legs, and haul butt.

Probably haul butt back to my real life after Hume fired me.

"Have you heard about ALR?" I asked innocently.

Hume looked at me, a strange sort of irritated expression momentarily crossed his face, then his self-assured smile returned. "No, what is that?" he said, his words a bit forced I thought.

"Automated Lip Reading," I said carefully, clearly, watching him closely. His initial response was a nod of the head, but then his eyes narrowed slightly, as though something had occurred to him. Like the video, was my thought.

So, might as well confirm it and get this party started. "We applied some ALR techniques to the Nykr video," I told him gently, figuring that would open the floodgates.

☐ What Did You Do? ☐

Hume started laughing again—wholehearted and deep—finally gathering himself enough to talk. "You know, Enoch, it was Joe that first came across your blog. He was very impressed; sent me an email immediately." Hume nodded vigorously. "It wasn't just the blog entry about electromagnetism that intrigued us, it was your whole site." He smiled. "I told Ruach you were special before I ever met you." He rubbed his hands together in enthusiasm. "We always need new ideas, new energy, around here, and you are perfect."

"I'm flattered," I said without emotion, "but, can you explain what was said in that video?" Phoebe glanced once at me, then back to Hume. She remained silent.

Hume sat back in his chair, looking carefully at me. "Enoch, what is your opinion of humankind?"

"What?" I replied, utterly and totally confused at this point, completely taken aback by this question seemingly plucked out of nowhere. "My opinion of humankind?"

"Yes," Hume clarified, "what is your opinion of people in general?" His face was creased, to my eye, with a sly smile. This whole discussion was rapidly assuming a surreal quality, but I shook it off, determined to see it through to whatever end it might achieve.

"I think people are basically good," I answered slowly, thoughtfully, not sure what he was aiming for with this line of inquiry.

"Do you think this goodness is inherent, genetic if you will, or a learned trait?" Hume prodded, watching me intently.

It was an interesting question, and not one I had really given much thought to recently. I mean, I guess we all just assume most people are good, part of the basic nature of being a human being, if you'll forgive that expression.

But, the question itself left the implication from Hume that goodness was not inherent, not genetic, not part of our nature, and I had to give that conjecture a good objective consideration. If you really stopped to honestly review what was happening around the world today, in all the different countries, cultures, religions, and governments, you started having massive doubts about the basic good nature of humanity.

At least I did.

☐ Chapter Eighteen ☐

I had to, almost unwillingly I'll grant, agree (the more I pondered it) that, in our natural state, that is to say, just being alive in any environment, humans are extremely clannish, tribal, xenophobic—we just do not like people who are different from us. We systematically instill an intense dislike of others while we promote our own adaptive strategies—our own cultures, religions, or systems. Tough to argue against this.

In fact, the more I evaluated the implications of Hume's question, the more drawn I was to the conclusion that while humans were, by nature, social animals and generally agreeable to members of their own immediate group, they were extremely inhospitable to those outside the group. Not just our total human history backed this up, but current world events severely underscored the truth of it. Read the news and honestly answer this question for yourself.

"Mostly learned," I begrudgingly stated, growl-faced and tight-lipped.

Hume smiled knowingly, quite pleased with himself it seemed. "Will you agree then," he began calmly, "that our animal nature, essentially violent, is gradually tamed over time by increased socialization, and that any sense of good must be acquired through cultural transmission?"

"Gilgamesh and Enkidu," I muttered in mild sorrow, fondly but sadly remembering my net session from last Friday, so long ago it seemed.

Hume chuckled dryly. "So, in the five thousand years plus since that Sumerian story was written, you'd think humanity would have had time to figure out what good is; and we would have established a clear pathway to achieve it on a consistent basis."

I made an ugly face, I know it. Felt it. "That really hasn't happened." I had to admit this with a bit of bile.

"Exactly," Hume declared with a triumphant and self-satisfied flourish. "The world of today is still a nasty, brutish, place full of evil." He shook his head, his expression one of great sadness. "Enoch, the litany of evil in the world today is stunning—mass murder sanctioned by governments or religion, systematic child abuse, forced prostitution of children and adults, human slavery, murderous drug cartels, sexual bestiality, economic corruption..."

☐ What Did You Do? ☐

I interrupted him, waving a world-weary hand. "Okay, I get your point." Stop smacking the deceased equine.

"Do you, Enoch, do you really?" Hume asked me with surprising passion, locking in on me with his mesmeric blue eyes. "You've lead a pleasantly isolated, secure, life up to this point. Enough money to buy some luxuries, party with your friends, surf the Internet, play games. No real troubles. Nothing to really disturb you."

He visually raked me with rough derision. Well, that's how it struck me. "The real world Enoch, out there beyond your nice little bubble, is a horrible place, with terrible people and bad things happening everywhere, all the time."

He stopped, not because he didn't have more to say, but because that last outburst seemed to have drained him. I stayed silent.

He continued in subdued, but forceful, tones. "The true purpose of PHANTASM, Enoch, is to battle that evil. To locate it, to counter it, to eliminate it." He smiled knowingly, eyebrows arched. "But we face a difficult task, a very difficult task, because the vast majority of people are ignorant." He grunted in scorn. "And this is not an ignorance simply in need of the cure of enlightenment, Enoch, this is an ignorance which is genetic and incurable." He sat watching me, awaiting my response to that declaration.

Which I was happy to give, but first I needed some clarification. "Are you equating ignorance with lack of intelligence?" I felt this was one of the keys to his argument, and certainly something I could agree with.

"Absolutely," he replied.

And now another key. "And you think intelligence cannot be improved? That it is genetic?" I was a little confused on what I considered that critical point, and not sure I was buying into his argument.

"There are both genetic and environmental components relevant to the level of cognitive ability that each human can achieve, but the primary determinant is genetics," Hume replied flatly, firmly.

"I don't agree," I instantly rejoined with some heat, not really thinking the argument all the way through, but just stating what I felt in my heart and not my head.

☐ Chapter Eighteen ☐

"You can disagree all you want, Enoch, but the facts obviate anything you might feel about the subject," Hume said with blunt and crushing certainty. "The bell curve rules."

"That's racist!" I exclaimed. "You're making generic claims about minorities and other ethnic groups."

"Nonsense," replied Hume calmly, waggling a finger at me. "Enoch, your mind has been filled up with drivel force fed to you by politicians, the media, and others." He sadly shook his head. "The bell curve is true for all of humanity, be they yellow, black, brown, red, white, or purple."

His face was about as serious as I had ever seen it, and he gestured at me again, pointing in my direction. "You need to accept the fact that about 70% of all humanity, regardless of race, creed, ethnicity, or any other variable, is merely average, or just ever so slightly above average, for intelligence. For cognitive ability." He set his features, strong, determined. "And that fact, like their intelligence, is immutable."

I was rubbing my lower lip with my right index finger, my brain whirling and flailing as I tossed his arguments back and forth. I was flustered by the strength of his statements, by his absolute surety, but there were still questions, problems, that I could not wrap my head around. "So then, what is the evil that PHANTASM battles against?"

His reaction was a pleased smile that cracked the solemn austerity of his face. "I knew you were the right man for this job, Enoch, from the moment I met you." He vigorously nodded his head. "You always ask the best questions." He joined his hands together and rocked them to and fro.

"Have you ever thought about that word, Enoch? The word *evil*," he started explaining, that same slightly unsettling and knowing grin on his face. "The anagrams you can generate from it are so evocative, so appropriate." He took a sip of water, and so did Phoebe. "Humans live under a vile veil, Enoch, pulled over our eyes by governments, by corporations, by schools, by religion, and by the media."

Live, vile, veil—anagrams of *evil*—Hume was a very persuasive speaker, I had to give him that. And I was raptly listening, and hearing.

"Technology is not the savior of humankind, Enoch, it is its bane," he said softly. Man, I wanted to attack that, but it was obvious he had more to say, so I bit my tongue and stayed silent, absorbed and fascinated by his elaborate discourse.

"You, of all people, Enoch, should be able to see that the people of superior intellect on the far right side of the bell curve utilize technology to dominate and enslave the middle and left side." He paused after that and sat watching me, allowing me to ruminate over that remarkable remark. And, I admit, it disturbed me, but perhaps not in the way he intended.

Hume continued. "It is only those people located far enough to the right of the bell curve, Enoch, that have sufficient intelligence to understand how to create technology—how to use technology—to manipulate electromagnetic energy, to truly derive economic benefits from it." He smiled, wickedly, coldly. "The people to the middle and left of the bell curve are merely users of that technology. Dazed zombies with an EM addiction fed and fueled by the EM wave dealers."

This was a significant amount of information to get tossed into my brain that contradicted a great many of my own personal beliefs. When you are faced with the statements of others with which you disagree, you want to be a skeptic. You want to cling onto your own beliefs, cherished ideas you hold to be right and true. To refute the arguments of others in the face of your own values.

Nonetheless, a rippling shiver cut through my mind. His words had the relentless ring of truth and certainty, and even though I had a distrust of his basic ideas, they were enticing and so, well, reasonably presented. In a soft voice I said, "What would you propose to do to fix the problem?" This was all I could think to ask, wanting to better grasp and understand his intentions. Bobbing and weaving, trying to get my wind back late in the round.

"We watch how the EM signal is used and make sure no laws are violated." A graceful smile. "We try to keep the people of lower cognitive ability, those in the middle and left side of the bell curve, from being mercilessly exploited by those on the right side of the bell curve." He said this with utter conviction and sincerity, a complete belief and certitude.

I gradually began to see his motivations, if but a shadowy, furtive, glimpse. And it sort of floored me.

⬡ Chapter Eighteen ⬡

I believe he saw the eemees, the peptide alkaloid, and the global pentacle network as some kind of system to influence people's behavior, to try and change the world. To make it better. More equitable, if you will. But, this change would be according to his understanding, his vision, his beliefs.

And, irritatingly, it was still eminently fuzzy to me exactly what his real understanding truly was.

"Okay, so you're building this, well, global pentacle network that you'll somehow activate with EM energy, and use the eemees" —I blew out a shot of air—"to influence, or force, behavior changes." So far, Hume had nodded in enthusiastic affirmation at the things I had been saying. "What behavior do you intend to influence?"

"The people on the left side of the bell curve do not require a peptide alkaloid or anything else to influence or force their behavior." Another sad smile. "They don't have the cognitive ability to resist EM wave suggestions." Just a moment's pause. "From eemees or humans," he added, I supposed for clarification purposes.

He nodded and continued, "We need to reach the people on the right side of the bell curve, Enoch, force them to change."

I felt an electric-like shock in my head as the implications of where he might be going hit me. "You're working in phases," I stated evenly. A guess, but a good one I surmised. He smiled, that same pleased look etched on his face. "Get people to use your products, spread them everywhere, make sure everyone on the bell curve uses them."

I looked at him for confirmation. He smiled, almost gloating, and spoke with rising emotion.

"The new peptide alkaloid is derived from a plant found in South Africa, Enoch." He rubbed his hands together in a kind of joyful glee. "The inert chemical is absorbed by the brain's neurological tissue and the body never gets rid of it." He laughed. "Never!" A grim chuckle. "One dose is enough to make the mind receptive to eemee energy. After that, it is child's play to force the behaviors we need to make a Utopia of the world."

"Utopia!" I spouted this word in stunned disbelief. Suddenly, with a clarity that both shocked and terrified me, I realized that Hume was not in this for himself.

☐ What Did You Do? ☐

This wasn't about self-aggrandizement or anything remotely similar. He wasn't looking for power or fame or world domination.

My god, he really thought he was going to change the world. Not for his own enrichment, but to make it better. Force people to be better.

"Don't you read books, watch movies?" I asked incredulously, unable to keep a harsh undertone out of my words. "A plan like yours never works. The G-23 Paxilon Hydrochlorate won't work," I added emphatically.

He gave me an odd look. "The what?" I knew my *Serenity* movie reference had blown completely over his head.

"It doesn't matter," I shook my head vehemently in reply. "There's no way your plan will change the world. You can't force changes in basic human nature." It can't be done. Such refinements have to be internally generated, not externally induced.

I paused for just a moment and added feverishly, desperately, "Besides, you only have four locations. South Africa was destroyed." There was no way he could activate the global pentacle network.

Hume laughed loudly. "Enoch, Enoch—we manipulate EM waves for a living. Digital dreams." A shake of his head. "That South African news report was bogus." He watched me closely, his eyes bright. "With the new formula in their hands, they'll be churning out fresh shipments within the week," he added with an knowing gleam in his eye.

I was casting about for any attack angle by now, feeling like that proverbial rat in the corner. "Even if that's true, you can't expect the pentacle formed by uniting your five locations to generate enough coverage to allow eemee energy scans to reach everyone." I gave him my most dubious stare. "It's pointless."

His fingers flashed across his touch screen desktop. A sudden surge of light and movement drew my attention, and I turned my head to look at the wall display behind me.

And saw the hellish face of insanity, I assure you.

The image was the planet Earth as seen from outer space. It was sitting inside a pentacle. A pentacle formed by energy lines which joined the orbits of five earth-encircling satellites.

"We have all five satellites already in the necessary elliptical orbits and are entering the last phases of calibration." He shook his head gleefully. "With enough money you can accomplish anything," he chuckled. "Now, with the new formula, I will significantly escalate my sales plans." He was almost giddy, and seemed to be talking to himself. "The increased sales opportunities from using the new formula will most definitely speed up the implementation of the satellites."

"How do you know the drug will work as you hope? You haven't tested it." I was clawing at anything to throw him off his position. To dent his resolute certitude.

"Really?" He eyed me with detached amusement. "Phoebe doesn't seem to think so."

Phoebe. I had been so involved with Hume's diatribe that I had completely forgotten about her presence here. "What do you mean?" I looked at Phoebe. "Phoebe!" I said a bit too loudly. Her head slowly turned to me, but she was not alarmed, not in the least.

"What have you done?" I shouted at Hume and tried to get up from my chair, but could not rise. It was as though I were mega-glued to the chair. The chair itself could not be budged from the floor.

Hume eyed me provocatively, "I had a little of the new South African cookie concentrate converted to liquid form," he wantonly smiled. "I added some to the bottled water." A nasty grin. "100% biodegradable containers." He sat one on the desk. The kind Phoebe had been drinking from lately.

~Dee, I need your help!~ I thought in rising alarm, but was greeted by silence. ~Dee!~

"The entire PHANTASM facility has been awash in EM broadcast energy, mostly to the effect of what a great guy I am and how Phoebe should support my activities." He smiled benignly at Phoebe. "You support me, don't you, Phoebe?"

"I support Dr. Hume," Phoebe said in normal tones, a small smile on her face. She seemed fine, on appearances.

~Dee, where are you?~ I cried desperately, fighting the sense of panic seething in my benumbed mind.

"I was taking a bit of a risk, though, in allowing Phoebe into this room," he acknowledged, looking at me. "My office is built with a custom EM protective shell"—he grinned at me, taunting me it seemed—"much like the one Phoebe placed on your condo sometime ago." He nodded, winked. "It blocks most EM activity both from getting into the room, or from happening in the room." A grim smile. "I activated it a few minutes back."

Crap, that must be why I couldn't reach Dee. The damn EM shell. I struggled uselessly against the chair.

"I was hoping the effect on Phoebe from the EM energy I'm using outside my office would persist in here, and apparently it has." A self-satisfied and dangerously smug grin. "Except for the energy signatures of the chairs, of course, which are unaffected."

He appraised me with a humorous expression and pointed at the chair to my left. "Have you ever taken a close look at my family crest?"

I looked over at the crest. The image was carved deeply into the dark wood. A crown, like a king's crown, with a muscular hand thrust up through the center, thrust up into the air, and the hand was brandishing a sword at an angle, rather than straight up and down. Underneath was a Latin inscription that read *Auxilio ab alto*. Auxiliary, so that would be helpful, alto was 'stop' in Spanish...

He watched me trying to work this out and finally said, "The Latin means *with help from on high*," and it occurred to me that it was not meant in a religious sense.

"Do you see how many points are on the crown?" he asked softly, almost in a teasing tone.

Five. There were five points on the crown. Two small triangular ones on either side of a large triangular one. Five, as in the number of points there were in a pentacle. I'd have to say, the help from on high was not religious, but referred to eemees. I felt a sinking feeling in my guts.

"The Hume family goes back thousands of years in Scotland and England, and my ancestors were among the first to successfully construct a primary pentacle. Rudimentary, but functional." This was followed by a sort of self-congratulatory laugh. "Who do you think planted the pentacle schematic for those traitors Mencius and Terloff to find?"

"Still," he casually shrugged, "they were useful in getting a working pentacle built, before they turned on me, although there were a few features, the knowledge of which I kept to myself," he finished with a knowing smile. One I would have dearly loved to wipe off his face.

"What are you going to do with me?" I mean, I was trapped in this damn chair, Phoebe was some kind of stinking zombie and I couldn't talk to Dee. Felt like I ought to check on my fate, since it appeared to be out of my hands for now.

"I want you to join me, Enoch, to embrace the role PHANTASM can create for itself." He made a fist and shook it. "Help me change the world!" he added with great passion.

"First you try to murder me," I said incredulous, "and now you want me to join with you?"

"Murder you?" Hume repeated and I could tell from the tone of his voice and his facial features he was completely taken aback by my outburst.

"Yeah," I replied tentatively, now unsure of myself. "Some assassin guy who tried to knife me on the elevator." Hume still wore a look of confusion—kind of similar to the one I had one right about now. "Phoebe said his name was Georg Plesavich, or something like that."

"I know the name, but he's not one of my people," Hume said—and I believed him. "Enoch, I have always wanted you to join with me to help run PHANTASM and improve the world we live in."

There was no questioning the sincerity of his tone. Still...

"Denton," I said, keeping my voice perfectly level. "I don't agree with your basic premise about the bell curve and human intelligence."

I shook my head; let out a small breath. "In fact, I don't agree with any of your ideas." I smiled, raised my head to look at him. "All humans can evolve. Any person can get smarter, can improve themselves, can raise their consciousness." I shrugged. "It just takes a strong sense of self-determination, acceptance of personal responsibility, and hard work to achieve." I gave him a truly doubtful look. "New behaviors cannot be forced on them by you; or by *anyone*."

He regarded me with a sad countenance and seemed to be chewing his lip, lost in thought. He rubbed the lower part of his chin with his left thumb and forefinger, as though giving something great consideration. Hopefully, not how to dispose of my body. I swallowed hard.

☐ What Did You Do? ☐

"Enoch, the human race has had tens of thousands of years to improve itself, and what do we have to show for it?" He asked this earnestly, a sorrowful smile crossing his face. "Bestiality and pornography readily available on the Internet at the push of a button, drug cartels as powerful as countries, terrorists willing to strap bombs to themselves and blow women and children to pieces, human slavery, vast ignorance, and global poverty." His expression was intense. "Cruelty beyond imagination, Enoch." He smiled, grim. "Women stoned to death for being raped." He shook his head. "Babies murdered because they are the wrong gender."

He eyed me curiously. "Do you honestly think things have improved in the world since the time of the ancient Greeks and Romans?" He snorted. "We are not more intelligent, not more noble, not more virtuous, not better." He shook his head. "The sheer number of genetically inferior people in the world threatens to collapse the global economy, Enoch, and something must be done."

I sat silent, wanting to let Hume finish his rant. He went on. "Barbarism, Enoch, overcomes civilization through basic mathematics. It is an equation as simple as one plus one equals two." His smile was unpleasant. "It is an immutable and horrific fact that 70% of the earth's population live in barbaric conditions. Not because we, the more intelligent, allow this terrible situation, but because the barbarians cannot escape it on their own."

"So," I interrupted his discourse, "you want to step in and help?" I grunted my derisive scorn. "Be the messiah!" I hoped it would set him off, maybe get him to say something I could use against him.

He laughed. Again, not what I expected. "Enoch, I don't suffer from any messianic vision. I suffer from reality and truth." He paused. "The middle and left side of the bell curve are being completely passed over by technological innovation that favors those on the right side of the bell curve." He shrugged. "If something isn't done about it, the entire world, as we know it, will collapse."

I waved a finger at Hume. "And your solution is to use forceful mind control to get the people on the far right side of the bell curve, the people you claim control EM technology for their own selfish benefit, to provide aid and sustenance to those on the middle and left?" I paused for breath. "You want to do this because you believe those people on the middle and left are genetically inferior in terms of cognitive ability, and they cannot be made more intelligent." I had to make sure I perfectly understood his mind on this issue, as it was the only way to find a successful argument against it.

Hume clapped his hands in sheer joy. "You've got it!" He wagged his head happily. "I couldn't have stated it any better myself." He smiled warmly. "I'm looking forward to getting started on the satellite test, and you can help me immensely."

I slowly shook my head, watching his pleased expression drain away. "The foundation of your argument rests on the fact that some people are genetically inferior for intelligence." I plaintively shrugged and spread my hands out toward him. "I disagree and, respectfully, cannot support your position."

Better to die in this chair with my truth, than live a lie on my feet with his error—though I hoped it wouldn't come to that.

His facial features were calm, contemplative. "Perhaps you just need time to review my offer. To ponder the truth of my statements," he nodded, deeply affected by his own words as he weighed various alternatives.

"No human could survive being sent to the EM spectrum," he mused and drummed his fingers on his desktop, "but, I think you could." He smiled to himself. "It will give you time to reflect, reconsider."

"I'm not an eemee," I sputtered. How could I be sent to some EM spectrum place thingy? It didn't make sense.

It was all blackness shortly after that.

A Nice Place to Visit (BIWWTLT)

"We do not have to visit a madhouse to find disordered minds; our planet is the mental institution of the universe."
—Johann Wolfgang von Goethe

It was, indeed, blackness. Dark, abysmal, and complete; but I never lost full consciousness. My sense of awareness, my waking state of mind, if you will, was just sort of, well, "transposed." I know, that sounds lame. Trust me, it felt worse. I knew that "I" was alive since I could sense myself, but I had no feeling of bodily form.

I had a flashback to my cold water torture back in South Africa where I had experienced a similar sense of disembodiment. Here, though, there was no cold, no warmth, no nothing. Double plus ungood negative.

Where was I?

Back in that South African vat of water, with that neck collar, I had been cold—hideously cold—but now there were no such sensations because, apparently, I had no fleshy apparatus to sense temperature changes. No other sensory input seemed available either. No smell, no taste, no tactile, no sound. A void. No incoming stimuli at all.

Do you remember what I said—seems like years ago—about keeping your sense of humor intact? Only way to survive and all that? Forget that crap, I was scared pooh-less. Winnie or otherwise.

An induced coma. Like a trance. That's it. Perhaps Hume had managed to slip me some kind of drug that puts a person into a comatose state. You know, paralyzes the body but allows the mind to keep churning? Like a Copper Gorilla.

No, that couldn't be right. I remember he said something before I went into this black. Something about the EM spectrum. That was it, sending a person to the EM spectrum.

⬚ Chapter Nineteen ⬚

Sending me.

Ordinarily reaching such a conclusion would have unleashed a veritable flood of chemicals into my body, unnerving the system, as it were, in an effort to "wake" it up. Slap some sense into it. Fright, fear, flight, and all that. But now, it was simply an obvious conclusion drawn from the available facts. Logic which demanded sanity.

I "knew" I should be worried or nervous about it, but those emotions did not afflict me or even minutely disturb my peace of mind. It was just one fact to contemplate among a veritable horde of related facts. Hmm...

I needed to think about this. Concentrate a little. Focus. Mentate. Cogitate. Facilitate. Agitate. Aggregate. And that's when I heard a violin playing soft and low, the echoes drifting in from far off in the distance.

The gentle waves of sound drew nearer. Nigh. Clarified. Amplified. Dignified. Magnified. A bariolage. Oscillating bow.

I knew this because it was a technique often chosen by Bach for use in his compositions. Whenever I faced some particular thorny issue, back in the real world, and had to relax and think, I often listened to Bach. Bach in the real world.

Johann Sebastian. German. Born in 1685. Married his second cousin. Contrapuntal. Counterpoint. *An Eternal Golden Braid*. ISBN 0465026567. International Standard Book Number.

Whoa! That was weird. Awesome weird. Weird with some ah. All of those facts just sort of rumbled, tumbled, articulated into my thoughts, flashing across my awareness seemingly unbidden. In control, but not, they just sort of "flowed" without any overt effort on my part.

But, that couldn't possibly be true, because I was the one thinking, so some element of control had to exist.

This new scenario required some thoughtful assessment. I had to focus more, as in a chess match, where planning and forethought were critical. Essential to a successful outcome. I was, perhaps, engaged in a classic battle between the forces of darkness and the forces of light, just like the chess board colors.

Such a clear dichotomy of power to think in terms of good and evil, black and white. No grayscale tumult. On-off. Yes-no. Manichean.

⧠ A Nice Place to Visit (BIWWTLT) ⧠

Ebony squares, dark as the thoughts of someone who misplays a gambit. Skull-white squares, calcimine in abiding time like the pure intentions of queenside castling. Count those squares of polished wood or finely cut stone.

8 by 8. 4 by 4 by 4. The binary pattern focuses my mind, pulls me into a deep and cool place. 64 alternating squares of light and darkness. Zoroaster. Ahura Mazda. *Thus Spake Zarathustra*. Night and day.

The chessboard is a mandala. Sanskrit circle. A pentacle is a form of mandala. Pure and simple. AUM. Creation. Preservation. Destruction.

Will you still need me, will you still feed me?

When I'm sixty-four.

Binds, threads, gunas, strands, webs, plaits.

The genetic code for every living creature on Earth consists of codons constructed in triplets from four possible bases, the bases being adenine (A), guanine (G), arcytosine (C), and thymine (T).

Four bases, combined in triplets. Four cubed equals 64. Like the machine upon which some of the very first computerized chess games were played. Aye, aye, Commodore.

An octet is a grouping of 8 bits. Computers run off a system which uses 8 octets as its basis. 8 by 8. 64. Will you still feed me?

Cast the yarrow stalks, palm the dice, flip the Tarot cards, read the hexagram.

The *I Ching* is a most ancient system of mystical divination, a pathway to self-discovery, a guide to evolutionary change.

It consists of 8 trigrams (lines) in different combinations of six lines each. Thus the possible combinations available are two to the power of six which equals 64.

There are exactly 64 sexual positions pictured in the *Kama Sutra*.

Ontogeny recapitulates phylogeny. Infinite regression.

I am disturbed, of this there can be little doubt, though doubt is the source of my disturbance.

The word *disturb* has a nice Latin root. *Dis-* means "apart," "asunder," "away," "utterly," and *-turbare* is "confuse." To be disturbed is to be confused, cast apart from yourself and your fellow humans.

That is really what doubt truly is—a great confusion that overwhelms the mind and disrupts normal systemic responses to external stimuli.

☐ Chapter Nineteen ☐

Madness is simply a person expressing their sincere doubts about reality.

Madness is rare in individuals—but in groups, parties, nations, and ages it is the rule. Dear Fyodor, so prescient. A thin veneer, indeed. Between civilization and barbarism.

Wrong. Something wrong. My mind drifting every where, no where. Shooting off on tangents, like surfing the web, but simultaneously in a multitude of related, unrelated, directions. Dross and slag. Hold that line.

Sturm und drang.

I am reeking with ignorance. Largo un poco agitato. Rise and come forth.

Have to focus on PHANTASM. Focus on Hume. He wants PHANTASM to be the new State. There will be no governments, no countries—only PHANTASM. But where is the word?

Immanual Kant (1724-1804) spoke of the *logos*, the word, in the beginning, as—

> . . .a communicable mental faculty (concept/relation) which allows (hu)man to strive toward the realization of his (its) highest ends.

If technology and the State, facilitated by PHANTASM, fuse together to achieve control and power without consideration for the realization of those highest ends, then humanity is doomed to a fascist Faustian bargain that ends only in hopelessness and despair.

Remember Orwell's motto, "Ignorance is Strength," but the State, PHANTASM, is not our shepherd.

Beware of eemees in human clothing.

Mind, Body, Soul. Physical, Emotional, Spiritual. Love, Truth, Power. Heart, Soul, Might. Reptilian, Mammalian, Human. Creator, Preserver, Destroyer. Karkma, Jnana, Bhakti. Goodness, Passion, Ignorance. Sat-Chit-Ananda. Father, Son, Holy Ghost. Ammara, Lawwama, Mutma'inna. Osiris, Isis, Horus. Tamas, Raja, Sattva. AUM. Sikha—Mind, Virtue, Wisdom. Epithumetikon, Thumoeides, Logistikon. Memory, Intelligence, Will. Jism, Nafs, Rooh. Subjective Spirit, Objective Spirit, Absolute Spirit. Executive, Judicial, Legislative. Heteronymous, Autonomous, Theonomous.

⬛ A Nice Place to Visit (BIWWTLT) ⬛

Three faces of neuro-reality. Triadic brain structure. Triune human.

Must concentrate on my name. So much to think about. The temptations of Pandora. Pandemic. Pandemonium. Panacea. Panthetic. Pan. Greek god of shepherds and flocks. Shear force.

My name. What is my name?

Endless days of mindless middles, with no beginning, no end, stretching beyond willful sight.

Mixed and scattered, revolving around the center, centered unto itself; where is the Wizard when you need him?

Melancholic depression, it seems fashionable and it's cheap enough as thrills go; like Russian roulette with a cap gun.

I cannot stop thinking, *cogitatus oblivio*.

Hume. Denton R. Hume. Demon hunter. Focus. Focus on his existence.

Existence begins in every instant; the ball There rolls around every Here. The middle is everywhere. The path of eternity is crooked. Friedrich, dear Friedrich. Crying over a horse. The music began. Symphonic sympathies.

Thoughts coerced by distant sonata: allegro assai, faster, faster. Obliquity. Sideways.

My name is Enoch.

Fear without the fear. I am losing myself in a stream of EM data, *spiritus sancti*. Digital sodomy upon this lyrical temple. King lyrical.

Will you still feed me when I'm sixty-four. Hume said it. Satellites. Elliptical orbits. The inclination angle is 64 degrees. That's it.

Hume. I know a Hume. Not David, damn his empirical black heart.

Enoch Maarduk. I must stop Hume. The behavior of people cannot be forced through technological voodoo. The changes must come from within. Alchemy. Hermetic. Sealed with the kiss of Solomon. Yi, li, zhi, ren. Analect dialect, not for the derelict.

I could feel it without feeling it. Knew it without knowing it.

The Damocles sense of expediency about something that gnawed at my mind like a canker, hanging over me, dangling like a snake on a limb. Something that cajoled, caressed, and cursed my weary thoughts down the benumbed digital road, urging the gnarly fingers of fatigue to reach out and fog even a cortex of uncommon acumen.

☐ Chapter Nineteen ☐

I should be exhausted. Synapses firing on every cylinder. A whirling vortex of dentritic energy that seemed to have no end. Toric ending with no ending. Ouroboros. The wheels of existence churning madly and we good cogs tarry but a fleeting moment.

Bach, Bruckner, Cosmogony, Cosmology—the evolution of consciousness, in space, through time, by matter; the Alpha and the Omega; the yin and the yang—we are curious of these things, and our speculation drives us forward into the questing place, in search of our own salvation. *Itinerarium Mentis ad Deum.*

Journey of the Mind into God. Into ourselves.

A personal journey. An individual journey. Yours. Mine. Not the collective, the hive, the nest, the commune. Do not be assimilated.

Hume wants to provide salvation for us. Eliminate the individual journey. Grant us salvation without the search for truth. End the weariness. Through technology. Through drugs. Through forced behavior changes. The greatness of mediocrity.

My name is Enoch. Keep the faith. Face the music. Tote that barge. Enoch.

From *The Book of Watchers*, a holy book, from a holy man.

The holy man was at his pulpit, at times rabid, other times as calm as though blessing a child. You recall what he said, that all of us had only a shaky rattle roll of chuckling dice chance of living, or so it seemed that's what he said. Those organ echoes, lost cantos, still linger, those staid pews of lacquered oak, hymnals scattered like discarded crucifixes. The soft chorus will never pay tribute here again, the flames leap and swirl; this holy building burns with a vengeance.

The choir. Torpid with grace, quite amazing, the choir waited anxiously for a cue, in queue. The maestro motioned impatiently with a bony phalange. Everyone sat in star-glazed anticipation. The crowd, bemused, stirred. "Father Benzeth will give the invocation." I sat, obliquely angled. A beggar's coat with hound's hide patches. Tawny pants with lemon-scented hair.

My eyes trimmed port. A wavering figure emerged from the etheric shadows and ascended the podium, gathering robes.

"Glorious, we beseech. Bless these your humble ones."

⬛ A Nice Place to Visit (BIWWTLT) ⬛

"Dem bones. Dem bones." The choir was silenced with a swarthy look.

I am lost, cast asunder. Adrift in an undertow of shadows. Seeking and yet not seeing; feeling, but not yet understanding.

"Enoch!"

Yes, my name is Enoch. This morning my name was Enoch.

We face the morning, each world. We face the world, each morning. That souls which cry out in anguish for succor and surcease could, for one brief instant, experience the rapture of unity and meaning; then slide faithfully back to the world of cars and streets, the world of hate and greed, of love and peace.

And if we should, for a moment's respite, enter into a realm of serenity and beauty, we are either disconsolate upon our eventual return to disharmony and strife, or impatient to once again pass down the vistas of Paradise.

We should be determined to change the face of that which surrounds us, transforming it into the world of our most subtle visions.

But we do not require a PHANTASM to accomplish this. We must change ourselves first. We, the people.

The ancient Greek philosopher Plato spoke of a select group of individuals who he thought should govern society. These people were supposedly smarter; more advanced; better—the elite. Their sole purpose was to safeguard the rights and freedoms of the other members of society. To be custodians of those rights. To be guardians of those rights. To watch over those rights and protect society from bad decisions. These guardians where supposed to make good decisions for all members of the society, not just certain groups. Limitless power.

"Enoch."

"Dee, Dee, I hear you." So much emotion. EM motion. Eemee. Electromagnetic energy. EM spectrum.

"You must focus on my voice, Enoch, think back to this world, to PHANTASM. To Tom and Armando. To Phoebe."

Phoebe. Titan goddess. Oracle of Delphi. The Sacred E. Know thyself. She is very good-looking. "Dee, what can I do?" Desperate. Disparate. Diss Parrot. Talk bad about Polly, who only wants a cracker. Help me, Dee, help me!

꧁ Chapter Nineteen ꧂

"Listen to my voice, draw your mind to me, return to us. Hold your consciousness together."

Until they (the Proles / Proletariat) become conscious they will never rebel, and until after they have rebelled they cannot become conscious. Orwell. Oh, well.

You cannot force this. Force keenly felt. Impudently impotent. Tom and Armando would love this place, but I want to go home.

Click your heels three times. Home is the place where you go and they have to take you in. Robert Frost. With apologies. Apo- and –logia. Sad to be away from the logos. Lost the word.

"Dee! Dee! *Quis custodiet ipsos custodes?*"

"It is you Enoch. You must guard the guardians. You must watch the watchers."

I am Enoch Maarduk and Hume must be stopped.

"Thanks, Dee."

I was back.

I was still sitting in that damnable Hume family crest chair, which was now positioned inside a complex pentacle, located in a room with a large glass window. My pretty good guess was Level 5. I heard Dee's voice speaking, **"Good to have you back, Enoch."** I turned to see Ruach standing behind me, clutching my ComUnit, looking at me with a mixture of relief and worry.

"It's good to be back, Dee." I then smiled at Ruach, my voice hoarse and cracking for some reason. "Thank you," was all I said.

He lowered his eyes slightly, apparently embarrassed. "It was mostly Dee," he said modestly and handed me the ComUnit. "Hume is still unaware of her true abilities." I nodded.

"How long was I, uh, not of this world?" Not sure how else to put it.

"You were in the spectrum for almost four hours," Ruach replied, surprise clearly etched on his features. Damn, just after three in the morning now. Ruach continued, "I would not have thought it possible for a human to survive there at all."

I shivered at the memory. "If you guys hadn't come to get me, I'd still be there, except the Enoch we all know, and hopefully love, would have been, well, absorbed."

⎕ A Nice Place to Visit (BIWWTLT) ⎕

Ruach nodded knowingly. "There is no true self in the spectrum, only a sense of being."

"Isness," I stated simply.

"Just so," Ruach confirmed solemnly.

"Well, we better get down to Isness business, if you'll forgive the expression," I said with a smile, the first genuine one I'd had in a while.

"I cannot forgive you for that horrific pun," Dee countered in mock seriousness.

"Time heals all wounds," I kidded her, then continued. "Tell me about Phoebe."

"She is still under the influence of the peptide alkaloid, and it is continually being reinforced with EM energy activity, as well as continued consumption of water containing the drug."

This had been, and still was, a little confusing (not to mention maddening) to me. "I know the drug can only be activated with EM energy, but then after that, her behavior has to be induced with an eemee scan, right?" I looked in earnest at Ruach. "Who is doing that scanning? Who is implanting thoughts into Phoebe's mind?"

Ruach looked miserable. "Dee and I have spoken at length on that topic, and we can reach no sound conclusion, other than there is another eemee here at PHANTASM." I took that in stride, as it was what I had figured out as well.

"What about Phoster or Elia? Could they be generating the scan energy?" I didn't think so, but had to ask.

"Dee and I have monitored Phoster and Elia, and the other eemees, and none of them are involved," Ruach answered, shaking his head and offering me a very human shrug of his shoulders.

Okay, that about knocked my socks off. His answer, not the shrug. "The other eemees? What other eemees?" I hoped that didn't come off sounding as maniacally frantic as the alarming thoughts felt zipping around inside my head.

"Phoster and Elia are not the only prisoners on Level 5," Dee explained gently.

"How come we didn't see them on our previous visit?" I didn't mean for it, but I know that came out much louder and accusatory than I intended. Nothing seemed to make sense to me.

⚐ Chapter Nineteen ⚐

My voice was worried. I was worried. Hell, it was becoming second nature to me.

"The motion sensors to Initiate those room lights were disabled."

Another simple explanation that only made things worse. "How many more are we talking about?" I wasn't sure if I should be alarmed or not, but I was alarmed none-the-freaking-less.

Ruach answered by waving his arm around the room. "Each room on the left side of the hallway contains a primary pentacle." That meant five rooms, counting the one we were currently in. His eyes shifted slightly. "The primary pentacles in the first four rooms, however, have been converted to binding pentacles with eemees inside, two of which you have already met." He eyed me intently.

His face took on a sorrowful, distant, aspect. "A secondary pentacle in the first room on the right of the hallway has been converted to a primary." A wry smile. "My primary." He shook his head. "The remaining four rooms to the right are secondary pentacles activated in sequence with the creation of their mirrored primary."

I was still a little hazy on this primary, secondary, relationship and wanted some clarification. "The secondary pentacles are used for travel, by an eemee, between locations?" Hume would want to be able to communicate with the eemees he controlled by allowing them to move between their invoked location and PHANTASM. I was looking expectantly at Ruach.

He nodded. "Yes, but the human controller can also convert a secondary pentacle into a primary pentacle and, if they wish, into a binding pentacle." A strange kind of sadness was etched on his face.

"How do they do that?" If we understood the process, perhaps we could stop it or even reverse it.

Ruach shook his head slowly and his face was a perfect blend of frustration and sorrow. "I do not know the exact mechanism."

I thought about all this for just a moment. There was still so much to figure out, and my mind was more than a bit addled from my recent experience in the spectrum. "I know Phoster was originally invoked for Iceland and Elia for Iran, right?" I waited for Ruach's confirmation, which he gave with a nod. "Okay, who are the other two, in the rooms here on the left side?"

⬚ A Nice Place to Visit (BIWWTLT) ⬚

"Eemees, when manifested in human form, are much like humans," Ruach started to explain, a gentle expression on his face and in his eyes. "Some are kind, some are unkind." He shrugged. "Some have strong abilities, some weak." An expression of pain creased his features. "Those two were unacceptable to Hume, for whatever reason, but he has chosen to keep them prisoners—rather than free them—and can destroy them at his whim."

I began to sense the nature of the threatening sword Hume had dangling over Ruach's head. A terrible burden to bear.

"If all the eemees are accounted for, at their respective locations around the world, who can be generating the eemee scan that is affecting Phoebe?" This was a very troublesome variable to contemplate.

"Keep in mind, Enoch, that a duplicate of the primary portal exists here at PHANTASM. This secondary pentacle allows the eemee to easily travel back and forth," he explained patiently. "These secondary pentacles are channels to mirror the power of the primary pentacle."

Like I said, a little hazy on this primary, secondary, thingy. The meaning was just starting to penetrate into my belabored understanding. The sort of connection that existed between primary and secondary meant any of the other four eemees might be running around PHANTASM. Or worse yet, maybe new, unknown ones not currently detected, invoked somewhere else. Multiple scenarios, and all bad. Marvelous. Just bloody wonderful. "Can you sense this, uh, other eemee?" I asked, remembering what Ruach had told me previously. It would sure be useful information to have.

"There is simply too much EM energy being generated within this building right now to make any such interpretation. It masks everything," he said in more anxiety than I was accustomed to from him. So much for useful information.

"That's Hume's doing," I commented in a voice edged with contempt, "and that damn EM protective shell of his blocked my access to Dee." I stared at Ruach. "How does that EM shell work?"

"I was unaware, until just recently, that there was any eemee scan blocking technology in existence other than the attenuator ring, and the ring only offers limited and momentary protection." Ruach nodded after he said this, then continued, "Hume's device is much more powerful and can apparently block all eemee scan attempts on himself, as well as eemee communications within his presence."

I looked closely at Ruach, who was watching me intently. "How long have you known Hume was not what he seemed?" I asked without implications. It was apparent to me that Hume not only had the fear of the binding pentacle to control Ruach, but also the possible destruction of the other four eemees held prisoner on Level 5 to serve as powerful inhibitors on Ruach's behavior.

Ruach's face was etched in sadness. "He was not always as he is now," he replied meekly, but I was not content to let it go at that.

"Tell me more," I urged.

"Hume is a good soul, Enoch, but he has no faith in his fellow humans," Ruach stated simply, shaking his head. "Hume believes the great majority of humans are genetically inferior and can never increase their intelligence." Ruach smiled sadly. "He sees only inequity which must be fixed rather than potential which can be fulfilled."

I snorted my obvious disagreement with Ruach's take on Hume. "I don't see Hume as a good soul, Ruach, because in his fervor to correct what he sees as a great imbalance, he is willing to commit what he believes are lesser evils to solve supposedly greater evils." I shook my head, oddly affected by this whole thought process. "Evil is evil, great or small," I said passionately. "Hume wants to take, by force, things which the uniquely intelligent, as he would state it, have created or acquired and distribute it to those he thinks are doomed to stupidity."

I waved my hand angrily. "The problem is that society cultivates stupidity, rewards it—the same people that lament the lack of intelligence make billions exploiting stupid people, and then insist the stupidity is genetic. Nonsense." I was getting worked up now. "Entire systems of governance are designed to maintain this fallacy. The supposedly inherently stupid people, told repeatedly that their lot is fixed and immutable, are convinced to grant the so-called intelligent people the power."

I smirked, derisive. "The intelligent people will then take care of all the problems—but, truthfully, only take care of themselves."

I shook my head again. "Hume acts like he wants to help but, in my opinion, he only wants to maintain his own power, and wants to do it at the expense of the people who should have the power." I waggled my finger at Ruach. "People like Hume are not the solution, Ruach, they stand in the way of the solution."

I nodded, catching my breath. "Such people must be stopped."

"Beginning with the disabling of Hume's EM shell," Dee said gently, making both a salient point and skillfully guiding our conversation back onto the proper path. I smiled widely at her cleverness.

"We need to figure out how he's doing it, and I think I know," I said, putting aside politics and philosophy and getting back to the hot topic at hand.

"His ComUnit," Dee said with certainty.

I nodded in agreement. "Has to be." I'd already done some thinking about this point. There was no way Hume would ever leave his office if his only EM shell protection was some kind of device located in that office in a fixed location. He was too savvy for that. I shook my head. "He must have mobility, and the ComUnit always travels with him."

I favored Ruach with a smile. "Dee, do you know what this means?"

"Tom and Armando will be using their open purchase order some more," she said in complete seriousness.

I laughed aloud at that. "Send them the specs on Hume's ComUnit. Tell them they need to be covert and surreptitious." I grinned. "Tell Tom that, this time, it definitely is Black Ops."

Ruach looked concerned. "Hume informed me that tomorrow, that is, today, he wants to test the global pentacle and satellite network." Ruach's features were visibly upset. "He intends to activate all five locations."

I frowned, confused. "How is that possible? Phoster and Elia are here, so he's a little short on eemees, isn't he?" My math isn't that bad.

"I spoke with Phoster and Elia, now that you and Dee helped to grant them a degree of freedom," Ruach explained. "Phoster said that another eemee has been invoked to take his place in Iceland." Ruach offered me a wane grin. "Elia was fairly certain that the Iranian location has no eemee."

"Well then," I rejoined, "Hume can't test anything." Happy face.

"Unless," Ruach began sadly, "he sends me to Iran." He studied me with an intense and direct look. "Which is what he intends to do." Disconsolate face.

Crap and double plus ungood crap.

"When?" I wondered how much longer Ruach would be here to help.

"Just before the test, today around noon." Ruach replied with a hint of regret. "The test is set for one," he added as a clarification.

"No big deal." I shrugged nonchalantly and waved a hand. "We just have to figure everything out and kick his ass prior to that." And solve world hunger, bring peace to humanity, and cure cancer. Sigh.

Never feel sorry for anyone; including yourself. Just think about answers.

"Okay, we have to break this situation down into smaller, more manageable, problems and applicable solutions. Simplify." I stated this logically, rationally, my mind already honing in on options and possibilities. I was able and ready to face the seemingly impenetrable mysteries we faced.

Either that, or collapse in a heap calling for my binky. It was touch and go on that.

"First, we have to figure out a way to hack into Hume's ComUnit and disable the protective EM shell, as well as stop the damn EM energy waves he's broadcasting." I stopped to catch a breath. "If there is another eemee around here using that EM energy to broadcast stronger scans, that EM energy source has to be stopped."

I surveyed Ruach with an intense look. "That will lead us to number two, which is get Phoebe out from under Hume's control." I tried not to think about it, but it really, really, made me see red. "Third, we need to see if we can free the eemees here on Level 5 and enlist their help."

Ruach seemed displeased with something. "We will have a problem with that," he stated softly, his face strangely unpleasant. Great, more problems. Plus my stomach was rumbling like Mt. Vesuvius. As Ruach kept talking, I started rummaging through my pockets for a BioPatch.

"Dee and I have been examining all available information, and it appears Hume has some sort of remote control device, not his ComUnit, that he actually uses to control the pentacles." Ruach seemed to tremble. "He can destroy a binding pentacle with an eemee inside, just by entering a simple alphanumeric code." Meaning the instant death of the eemee, I thought bitterly. "Not only that, but he can summon any eemee back to a secondary pentacle on Level 5 and immediately convert it into a primary pentacle." Just a brief pause. "And then convert it to a binding pentacle."

That was bad, very bad, mucho bad. Muy malo, as it were. No wonder Hume had such a fearful death grip on the eemees. And then a thought occurred to me that really obfused the already obfuscated obfuscation. "If primary pentacles were invoked at the other locations, and only secondary pentacles are here on Level 5, how can Hume be the controller?" Dull expression of ignorance, cubed.

Ruach looked intently at me. "I cannot answer that. But, believe me, Hume controls the eemees, no one else." He was adamant about it.

Have to worry about the exact mechanics of all that later. Need to focus on the verifiable facts we had on hand. "Dee, what do we know about Hume's remote control device that we can use to disable it?" He was not the only person that could manipulate EM waves. I affixed the lone BioPatch I had found to my arm.

"Checking now, Enoch."

Back to my countdown. Four. "Okay, number four, we need to disrupt Hume's satellite test." Which was far easier to say than do. I mean, Tom and Mando could hack into most computers. But, a satellite network?

"Dee, get Tom on the line, please." I looked intently at Ruach. "Do you trust Dr. Panglaws?"

Ruach instantly nodded. "He knows nothing of these issues."

A mini-smile crept onto my face. "Good, then I need you to convince him to help with a couple of things, but without telling him too much." Maybe use a little eemee scan, just a touch, I mused to myself. I was mindful of the lesser evil, greater evil, rant I had made moments earlier, but felt we simply had no other viable option to defeat Hume. Panglaws would need a little "boost" to get his thoughts going in the right direction.

Ruach gave me a wry and infectious smile. "I believe I can manage that. What do you need?"

☐ Chapter Nineteen ☐

"I need to know how we can neutralize that damn peptide alkaloid in Phoebe's brain." The thought of her with Hume chapped me off all over again. "And I need to know if there is some kind of, I don't know, secret agent thing I can use to penetrate his protective EM shell. Or disable it." I spread my hands out in ignorance. "You know what we're facing," was all I added.

Ruach looked grim. "I'll be in the lab. Dee can always reach me if you require my presence," he stated quietly and briskly left the room.

Tom's face appeared on the ComUnit. He looked awake and alert. I'm not sure he and Mando ever go to sleep. Damn techno vampires or something. "E, hadn't heard from you and was starting to worry."

"Really?" I said, a bit skeptical, still inwardly grinning about my vampire ref.

Tom responded capriciously, "Well, not really, but I want to appear sympathetic."

"Funny," I replied with my own smile. "I do have another huge request." The left side of my head was throbbing. I tried to ignore it. Don't think of a white polar bear.

Mando's face leaned in. "As long as it involves open purchase orders, we're in."

"Will you please fire that guy?" I said jokingly. Even with a headache, Tom and Mando could make me laugh, and I sure needed that right now.

Tom shrugged. "I can't. Made him a partner earlier today." A sly look. "So, what's this new caper?"

No sense bushing around the beat. "We need to hack a satellite network."

Tom never even blinked. "Government satellites?"

"No, PHANTASM satellites." That made him blink.

"Digital is digital." His shrug was elegant, but not extravagant. "What are we supposed to be doing?"

"There are five satellites in question. All in elliptical orbits. The operational inclination angle for a satellite in elliptical orbit is 64 degrees," I relayed adroitly. Will you still need me, will you still feed me? Then added, "I need to change that angle for all five. Get them out of calibration for a spell."

▢ A Nice Place to Visit (BIWWTLT) ▢

"Dee, can you send me anything you can lay your hands on for the satellites?" Tom asked seriously.

"I do not have hands, Tom, but I will nonetheless comply with your request," Dee said with great humor.

Tom laughed. "Enoch is a bad influence on you, Dee."

"He bears watching," Dee said, shamelessly I might add.

Tom's face took a turn for the serious. "You already sent us specs for a ComUnit hack, and now this satellite project." He shrugged. "Which one has priority?"

I pondered it for just a moment. "If we get the ComUnit hack," I began carefully, "and can disable that ComUnit, then I don't think we'll need the satellite hack."

Tom nodded. "The only problem for me is that I won't know if I can do the ComUnit hack or not, so I'll have to work on both projects simultaneously, just in case."

"You can do that, right?" I queried, but in an encouraging and confident tone.

"Well, I think it may involve copious amounts of caffeine and other stimulants, but we'll manage." His grin was wary, but real.

Mando's face popped in. "I had a date, man." He didn't look happy.

Tom laughed. "Emily from Vitellos finally agreed to go out with Mando." Tom turned to look at his friend off frame, "I guess I could revoke his partnership..."

Mando leaned back into frame. "How soon do you need all this done?" he asked anxiously, knowing my proclivity for rather tight schedules, and embracing his new business responsibilities as partner. Shame about Emily though. Nice girl.

"The test is scheduled for one o'clock tomorrow afternoon, er, that is, today," I said, trying not to sound like I was asking for Rome to be built in a day.

"You know, Enoch, Rome wasn't built in a day," Tom said snidely, apparently in possession of the same mind-reading equipment Phoebe uses.

"I know," I said sympathetically. "We're all under the gun, Tom." I flashed him a sincere smile. "Do the best you can."

☐ Chapter Nineteen ☐

"As soon as I know something, I'll get a report back to you," Tom enjoined, thankfully with a grin of his own, and vanished. I arched my neck to get the stiffness of tension out. Good luck with that.

"I'm really feeling a bit scruxillated, Dee—I hope you have something to tell me about Hume's remote," I said wearily. I was rat rummaging through my pack for some peanut butter crackers that I swore were in there.

"That is not a word," she said carefully.

"Huh?" I replied cleverly. Contrived ignorance in the face of reality being a reliable trait of mine.

"Scruxillated is not a legitimate word," Dee advised me in very officious tones.

"Of course it is," I countered, not really wanting to run off on this tangent, but feeling a bit, well, perturbed by her eemee-knows-it-all attitude.

"I cannot find it in any reputable lexicon or dictionary source," she said flatly. **"Therefore, it is not a word."**

"Nonsense," I said, my pride piqued, as it were. "You just used it in a sentence, so it has to have a meaning."

"That is merely a conveyance utilized to achieve understanding. The word is without meaning." She sounded rather convincing, I'll grant you.

"Screwed as to the crux of the matter but titillated by the possible array of options," I replied by way of explanation. "A state of confusion made tolerable by anticipation of correction." The kick is up, it's good!

There was silence on her end. "Dee, are you feeling a bit jamboozled?" I asked with a modest jocularity.

"That is also not a word," she said, but her aplomb and certainty were in desperate decline.

"Bah," I happily advised her. "You are jammed up with doubt and bamboozled by the facts."

"You are cacabrimmed, and I no longer wish to discuss this topic," she said, though without ire. **"I have some information on Hume's remote control device."**

⎕ A Nice Place to Visit (BIWWTLT) ⎕

"Talk to me," I said, hoping it was knowledge we could use to disable the remote. Or, possibly get the free movie channel. Sorry, I'm a little nervous.

"The device generates an oscillated and encoded microwave signal," Dee said with great surety.

"And... this means what?" I replied, mostly because I only understood the individual words and not necessarily the entire meaning. Story of my life. {Insert woeful sigh here.}

"I do not believe the device can be hacked, but we may be able to disrupt the signal."

"Keep talking," I encouraged her. There had to be a plan. Dee always had a plan. Her character flaw.

"We would need a device capable of generating a mid-infrared signal at around 64 terahertz," Dee explained succinctly. There was that 64 thing again, but it felt like a deep six.

"Say, Dee, if I don't know what an 'oscillated and encoded microwave signal' is, what would lead you to believe I would know what a 'mid-infrared signal at 64 terahertz' is all about?" I said in mock irritation, with maybe a dash of real vexation thrown in. Hey, there's only so much one guy can know, okay?

"I am sorry you are so scruxillated, Enoch," came her instant reply. Accompanied by a very subtle little chortle, meant for me to hear.

"That's very funny," I said, really fighting not to laugh. Maintain straight face, maintain straight face.

"The signal to disrupt the remote can be generated by a quantum cascade laser," she advised me.

"I'm sure we can buy one on any street corner," I commented sarcastically. Where would we find such a thing?

"PHANTASM happens to have one in inventory," Dee replied, a bit snippy in tone.

"Really?" I exclaimed in surprise. I was all seriousness now, and properly slapped back into my place. Never doubt the power of blind stinking luck. Just go with it. "Where is it?"

"Dr. Panglaws uses it for spectroscopy of trace gases," she informed me. I've had a few trace gases in my time, but never needed a quantum cascade laser to track them. Hah!

☐ Chapter Nineteen ☐

"Ask Ruach to check on it, and get back to us on the status." I grinned. "Great work, Dee."

"I am happified you are pleased, Enoch," Dee deadpanned to me.

"Happy and gratified. I like it," I said admiringly. She was good.

I was still sitting in Hume's tragically uncomfortable freaking chair, trying to decide if I should stay or if I should go. Kind of reminded me of a song or something. I figured, since I was embracing indecision at the moment, best to simply stand up and work the kinks out of my back. Hume, you bass turd, you really got me. All worked up. That was me, working the kinks out. Get it? Kinks? You really got me?

You had to be there, I guess.

Hey, I'm nervous, okay? New territory and an old map, if you will.

"Enoch, Ruach is calling," Dee announced, startling me out of my self-induced rock review revelry.

"Ruach," I said lightly, attempting to contain my excitement and control my frayed nerves. "What did you find out?"

"Dr. Panglaws was most displeased about being asked to report to the lab at such an early hour," Ruach replied by way of commentary.

"I assumed you appealed to his higher nature," I intoned in a quasi-serious manner. Mostly by giving Panglaws the old 1-2 eemee scan combo. Greater good, greater good.

"After a brief, and mostly one-sided, discussion as to the positive merits of my request, Dr. Panglaws was kind enough to assist me in locating the quantum cascade laser." He said this without mirth.

"How did you know about that?" I asked in mild wonder, since Dee had only recently told me about that device and I had, just moments before, asked her to relay this information to Ruach.

Ruach laughed. "Dee and I have what you might call a natural affinity, and she was certain that disrupting the remote control would require such a device, and asked me to check on it."

There was that simple explanation for a complex problem again. Synchronicity.

"Is it in working order?" I inquired anxiously. Finding it was one thing, using it was another.

☐ A Nice Place to Visit (BIWWTLT) ☐

"The Doctor will shortly begin the process of verifying its functionality," Ruach stated. I sensed a mild chuckle from him, though his facial features never changed.

"That's great!" I commented.

"The specifications for the equipment, however, do represent some logistical variables which will need to be dealt with." That was Ruach-speak for we were in deep ^&%$ on some important issue.

Don't forget to breathe.

"What's wrong?" I said, a bit more downbeat than I meant to be. Problems at this stage were exacerbated. Damn, I love that word. Just hate the ramifications.

"The laser is an older model. It is about the size of a small dining room table." He paused just for a moment. "In addition, it only works on line of sight."

"Anything else?" I asked grumpily.

"I assumed that would be sufficient," Ruach said, though a small smile was etched onto his face and his eyes were bright. You had to keep your sense of humor, even when the worst was happening. I get it.

"It just means if you can't bring the laser to Buddha, you bring the Buddha to the laser," I said in a bit of philosophical inspiration.

"You have mangled the reference beyond all endurance, but I acknowledge your attempted point," Ruach commented dryly and nodded amiably. "Lacking another solution, we will need to bring Hume to the room with the laser."

We were agreed on the getting-Hume-to-the-lab thing. Time for the next subject. "What's the status of the peptide alkaloid neutralization research?"

Ruach's expression noticeably soured. "That area is slightly outside the knowledge base of Dr. Panglaws; or anyone else here at PHANTASM." He sighed expansively. "Apparently we have the facilities, but not the expertise." A sharp intake of breath. "We're continuing to explore all possibilities."

"Okay, keep on that and I'll check back," I said, masking my disappointment as best I could. I broke the connection.

Time to introduce a new topic into the mix. "Dee, I have an important mission for you," I declaimed with a certain grand solemnity.

Campy, maybe, but trying to take a cue from Ruach and remember a sense of humor about things.

"I am here to help Enoch," came her friendly reply.

"I need for you to look for the EM energy source generator that Hume is using, as surreptitiously as possible," I said and then quickly added, "with one proviso."

Dee was silent, waiting for me, so I continued. "I want you to locate it and make sure you can disable it, but don't do anything until later, when we have Hume in the lab." I smiled. "I'll have a signal worked out ahead of time."

"When you say when?" Dee asked with a laugh in her tone. Asked without asking.

"Funny," I acknowledged. "There is one more thing to talk about before you go off hunting for that EM source." Solemn tones.

"I have no ears but I am all ears," Dee said jauntily. What a trooper. Super duper. I guess that was what Hume was, so to speak. Superlative at duping us. Rambling again, sorry.

"Dee, we need to figure out a way to get Phoebe out from under the influence of the peptide alkaloid," I said carefully, starting off what I knew was going to be a difficult argument for Dee to eventually accept. I only hoped she would hold onto her sense of humor.

"Dr. Panglaws can render no assistance in that area," she said, stating my first premise for me as she echoed Ruach's recent statement about the knowledge base of Panglaws. Well, lack of knowledge base.

"We must have Phoebe back on our side to defeat Hume," I said, stating an obvious fact clearly. Second premise.

"She is a fearless warrior," Dee steadily confirmed. I wagged my head agreeably.

"Whatever we decide to do, we need to get it done before one o'clock this afternoon," I stated, then continued. "Before the satellite test." Premise numero tres.

"Yes, time is of the essence." Her voice was growing softer, slower, less certain, and I was thinking she was beginning to sense the direction I was headed. Trudge onward through the fug, again.

"You know what I need to do," was all I said, closing the discussion as I saw it. Conclusion, maybe.

☐ A Nice Place to Visit (BIWWTLT) ☐

"You intend to return to the spectrum," Dee said without any emotion, though slightly accusatory if you ask me.

"It's where the answers are," I said flatly, trying to convey a tone that indicated my decision was final.

"How can you wade through the distractions to find your answers, Enoch?" she said, her voice now fraught with feeling. **"How will you maintain your focus?"**

"Because I must, dear Dee; because I have to," I replied softly, and that's all I could say.

A fleeting moment passed. **"Sit in the chair. I have scanned its pentacle device and understand the functionality."** Dee had a pro mode just like Phoebe. Make a decision and then lock and load. A marvel to behold.

I sat down.

"One hour. I will permit you one hour, Enoch Maarduk, and then I will deactivate the chair," she stated in a voice that also permitted no dispute, so I just nodded agreeably.

"Wish me luck," I said, trying to lighten the mood.

"Luck is preparation meeting opportunity," she said, echoing my own words back at me.

"I'm prepared," was all I managed to say before the blackness came. Again.

Searching For Answers

"As long as you still experience the stars as something 'above you,' you lack the eye of knowledge."

—Friedrich Nietzsche

One of the most important reasons that human beings rule planet Earth is our remarkable ability to learn and remember. Give us scraps and we make a quilt.

And show others how to do it.

Put us in the strangest, most inhospitable, environment possible and we'll figure out a way to survive. And thrive. Then teach our offspring the skills they need not only to repeat the process, but make it better. No other creature possesses our unique adaptability.

Well, not counting self-replicating viruses, but they have caca for brains.

No, sir, humans are awesome. True, the first time we do anything can be utterly terrifying, be it ride a roller coaster, catch a baseball, tie our shoes, or ask someone for a date.

Or, visit the spectrum.

But, the second time we do something is much, much, easier. We now have a solid memory, expectations given credence, fears alleviated. We are veterans, not rookies. No longer n00bs!

Well, easy to think that way. Being in the spectrum was still a vastly unsettling and maladjusted feeling, like incredibly lucid dreaming— while you were awake. It had been a completely new and frightening drama the first time. Now, at least, I had a little bit of previous experience to fall back upon. Bad, true, but it was experience.

Still, knowing what to expect and dealing with it are two different events. Kind of like flying at Mach 5.

I knew, here in the spectrum, that I would have this shift in conscious awareness and then a vast and undulating data flow would start, only partially under my willful command. It had almost overwhelmed me before with its sheer magnitude and raw force. Scalar and vector. Imagine the information flow from a thousand websites streaming simultaneously into your brain.

And then factor it by a hundred.

I hoped, now, to at least be ready for the rapid and pandemic influx of information. Knowledge is power. Thanks to Sir Francis Bacon. Or, possibly Thomas Hobbes. Attribution retribution ablution. Wash away your fears. Rinse some sense without wringing my hands.

Focus. Concentration. Mentation. Phrenetic.

I must discern a way to stop or at least neutralize the effect the peptide alkaloid had on Phoebe. To get her out from under Hume's yoke and control was an absolute priority. Must free her from the eemee influence she was under. Can't worry about who the eemee is, only that I had to get Phoebe free from the drug.

I must become a rehab nabob.

I also knew that the pathway to knowledge was emptiness. The hole in the donut is as important as the donut. Unless you're hungry, I guess.

Still, the nothing is something. Todo es náda, y náda es todo. To do is todo. Not all or nothing, but the nothing is all.

I simply had to let my mind be open to thoughts and ideas which might, in and of themselves, offer guidance to the wide array of problems I faced. A vessel waiting to be filled, more or less. Top off the tank. Fill it to the brim. Hit me with your best shot. Patrón, preferably. Hah, a patron of the arts. To kill ya'.

Expanded focus.

Allowing that which was within to flow out, and that which was without to be in flown. Good humor, man, keeps the mind empty, for sure. Cool. Bad humor is a circulatory problem. Averroes knows.

Focus. Must focus. To wander as I wonder was a challenge.

Primary gaol was not to become a prisoner of unruly waves of thought. Word play waves. Gaol! Gaol! Soccer at the penitentiary. Too much time spent at the prison bar.

It had to be the ergoline peptide alkaloid.

❑ Chapter Twenty ❑

Ergot fungi. He got. She got. I got the ergot. There's a fungus among us.

Chemical equations with manipulated molecules, linked chains which forge unholy alliances. Distilled sources of some discontent, to be sure. Made inglorious by this son of Hume. Granular infections. Grainy inflection. Wry humor. Ergopeptine derivation. Mutation? Aberration? Fluctuation? Anticipation? Emancipation?

Shifting from CH_2CH_3 to CH_3 as an infinite regression. Binding the mind. One ring to bind them. Benzyl. Benzene ring. Energy organics, mechanics, antics. Hydro. Carbon. An EM mission emission?

Isolate the carbon unit. Sever the hydrogen link. Connect the dots. Energy swapped and tossed, bio-fools. Red herring. Energy sleight of hand. Look for the real source of power. Follow the yellow brick road, spiraling up, down, sideways. The Emerald City. The Emerald Tablet. Hermetically sealed. Alchemical results. Ergo, the peptide.

Ergo.

Descartes. French. Dutch. (1596-1650). *Cogito ergo sum* (I think, therefore I am) but the absolute essence is *Dubito, ergo cogito, ergo sum* (I doubt—therefore I think—therefore I am.)

Doubt.

The antagonism between faith and certainty. The chasm between lies and truth. Between politics and reality.

The new peptide alkaloid that Hume was using binds itself to critical neurological receptor sites in the brain and will not release them. Please release me, let me go. The wry that binds. Rye humor. It waits, lurking in three-four time, therefore time, to be activated by EM energy.

Wavelengths, frequency, amplitude, attitude, fortitude, dude—magnitude, unglued.

When the peptide alkaloid binds, activated by EM energy, the mind is then receptive to eemee manipulation, not just suggestions, but orders. Marching orders. Forced action. Loss of free will. Determinism. Sign the papers. We only want to help you.

Antagonism.

A dialectic between free will and genetic encoding. You are what you will, not willed what you are.

Integrate the abrogation, accelerate the assimilation. The peace of ignorance is the price of slavery. To be free requires self-control.

The new peptide alkaloid binding cannot be broken. The receptor bond is too strong. I see it clear. An absolute fact. The binding is too great. Alkalinity affinity.

For what we are about to receive is the bond that binds. Yet, it can be momentarily disrupted. Disturbed. Rattled. Shaken. Stirred. The broken Bond. Yes. On-off. Off-on. Binary. Infinite regression. Faces in the mirror. The abyss looks back. But, how, what?

So much to see that I cannot see. A splendid confusion which reeks and wrecks me. Tomorrow and tomorrow, but the spinning of the net. The weaving web. Sifting through the morass of implicate order; of explicate disorder. Disparate times call for disparate measures.

I feel snake bit.

Black mamba. Muscarinic toxin. Modulation. Fluctuation. Disrupt. Disturb. Turbo, –turbare. Buratto. Not to change, but only to disturb. A subtle movement. Hume as agonist. Yes.

What is he seeking, what is he looking for? His ancestor, surely, David Hume, said it best—"How can we satisfy ourselves without going on in infinitum? If the material world rests upon a similar ideal world, this ideal world must rest upon some other; and so on, without end."

Looking for a brief respite. Black mamba.

And I saw the chemical composition unfold in my mind, like a recipe for enchilada corn dough. Dee, Dee, bring me back.

I had asked Ruach to join me in my Level 5 room. He was the one disturbed this time. As in turbo disturbed. I had never seen him beside himself quite like this. "Black mamba venom!" he decried, then repeated himself. "Black mamba venom at five in the morning!" His normal calm reserve was being seriously threatened.

"Noet can help us," I said gently.

"Noet?" Ruach repeated stupidly, channeling his inner Enoch.

"Well, Terloff kept a live black mamba in his office," I softly informed Ruach, "and Noet was petrified of it, so I imagine it's still there."

Ruach looked at me like I was a madman. "How do you propose I extract venom from such a creature?"

"Now, don't go all ophidiophobic on me, it's just a snake," I said, though asking Ruach to milk the world's most dangerous snake did seem, well, maybe a little unfair. "That building will be full of evil people. Just pick one, use your eemee scan, and make them do it." Who said life was fair? By what snakelike scale can it be measured? That was bad.

He seemed to be considering my proposed solution and finding it wanting. "I could just kill the snake and bring its head back," he muttered and I took his proposal as an excellent alternative.

I spread my hands out in enthusiastic wonderment. "You see, with a little extra thought, you found a solution."

Ruach's smile was bittersweet, as they say. "For Enoch Maarduk I will do this thing." Then he looked at me with a dubious and penetrating stare. "But, I am not happy." He turned sharply on his heel and left the room heading, I assumed, for the South African pentacle.

"He is not really upset, just frightened at the unknown," Dee said to me, hoping, I imagined, to assuage my guilt.

"Well, he's not the Lone Ranger," I said, trying to sound pleasant about it.

"I do not understand what a position in the financial industry has to do with Ruach's uncertainty," Dee said, confused.

"Financial industry?" I said, equally confused, batting the query back across the verbal net to her.

"You said Ruach was not the Loan Arranger," Dee flatly replied, elegant in her simplicity.

I bit my lip to keep from laughing aloud. I mean, how could you not? I thought about explaining, but figured it would just get worse. Time for a subject change.

"The only way to disrupt Hume's remote is to use that quantum cascade laser, which is too large to move," I preambled aloud. "Which means we need to bring Hume to the lab under some pretense or other." I paused. "Any ideas?"

"Many ideas, mostly bad," Dee said softly.

"You *are* hanging around me too much," I chuckled. "Try to be serious."

"We could postulate a new BioPatch breakthrough, or some glitch in previously reported lab results relevant to the South African cookies, or perhaps a derivative drug with unusual attributes..." Dee rattled off and I had to interrupt.

"Those are all good, but it has to be something that requires, that demands, Hume's personal appearance in the lab," I advised. "Something that can't be completely explained in a written report." My brain was buzzing with possibilities. Or, possibly the last power drink I had consumed.

The silence seemed to indicate Dee was giving it some serious ponderation. She better not tell me that isn't a word.

"I have a possible scenario," Dee declared and then continued in scholarly fashion. **"We could say that Dr. Panglaws has discovered a steep denigration in the efficacy of the peptide alkaloid due to nitrogenation of the benzyl benzene ring."** Dee concluded, **"This occurs slowly over time, but yields drastic side effects."**

"I love it when you talk dirty," I said jokingly, giving her scenario a thorough review in my mind. "Panglaws must show Hume the side effects in the lab," I mused aloud and rubbed my chin. "Hume told me there had been previous test subjects, so Panglaws can claim follow-up exams of the test subjects yielded the adverse side effects." Dee's idea seemed to work on paper, mental paper.

Still, Hume was smart, wary. "Is this *nitrogenation* thing you made up possible? I mean, reasonable enough to fool Hume?"

"It is rather like politics, Enoch. There is enough truth in the story to effectively mask the untruth," Dee answered smartly and I nodded my head. The fact that she thought the story would be convincing was enough for me.

I bobbed my head rapidly up and down the more I considered it. "Yes, I think that will do the trick!"

"I am glad you like it," Dee said, quite pleased with herself, and rightfully so. But, I had to bring her back to earth. Hey, an eemee pun thingy!

"Tell me about the EM energy source generator," I inquired casually.

"It has proven somewhat elusive," she replied, crashing and burning to the terra firma in flaming shards.

"Give me the details," I said with mucho encouragement. Knock 'em down and then build 'em back up.

"There are many thousands of EM energy signatures in this building, all overlapping and in dynamic flux," she began her explanation, her tone a bit flustered. **"It is difficult to isolate and test each one."**

Hmm... I think I had a thought on that. "I have an idea that might help," I said cautiously, but with rising optimism. "A brief power outage," was all I said.

There was a momentary, lingering, silence. **"Hume will have the EM source generator on auxiliary backup,"** Dee said, attempting to dispute, refute, and reboot my idea.

"True," I readily agreed. "But, I guarantee that the EM generator will be operating entirely independent of any other readily discernible PHANTASM auxiliary system."

I think I heard the click of a light switch. **"Once I identify and remove such systems from consideration, then the one that remains must route to the EM source generator!"** Dee was delighted.

"Glad I could help," I said with a grin.

"I will research your idea and provide feedback," Dee said, logging back into her pro mode. **"Ruach has returned,"** she then intoned lightly.

What! Already? That was way too quick. Growl, snarl. Has to be bad news. I wearily stood up. There is no good time for bad news. As I walked—make that drudge trudged—to the door, it opened and Ruach came in holding a vial.

"The snake in Terloff's office had, sadly, left this mortal coil," he said flatly with a minimalist smile, "but, fortunately for you, Terloff appears to have been quite an active herpetologist."

"Probably got it from unprotected sex," I offered by way of a hideous joke.

Ruach looked at me as he considered my words. Then his eyes opened wider and his head tilted back. "Oh, I see," and then he looked curiously at me. "That's not very funny." He waggled his index finger for additional emphasis.

"Sorry," I said shamefaced. Not really. I liked the joke myself.

Ruach shook his head. "There was both venom and anti-venom kept on the premises," he stated, then shivered a little. "And many varieties of poisonous snakes." He coughed. "I told Noet to set all of them free." He held the vial up for our mutual examination. "What do you intend to do with it?"

That would be hard to explain. I could go on and on about fractional distillation and ionic exchange, tossing in a bit about reverse-phase chromatography, but those were just fancy names given to real processes. Things I had gleaned from the spectrum and understood without understanding. Don't make me explain that.

Processes, formulas, mixtures, methods that I had seen in the spectrum and were now outlined clearly in my mind. Make that etched and burned as though by a quantum cascade laser. Hah.

"Okay Dee, we need to get to the lab, but I think the only safe way back is through the stairwell," I said in heavy tones. Using the same route Phoebe and I took when we originally found Level 5.

"We could use Hume's secret elevator," Dee intoned lightly.

I shook my head. "Too much risk of being seen." I rubbed my chin as I gave it some careful thought. "Has to be the stairwell, but you'll need to monitor Hume's elevator, because we are all in deep looie if he climbs in there to come down here to check on me and I'm not in this room." I gave Ruach a knowing look and he made a subtle nod.

"What is a deep looie?" Dee quizzed me. British potty humor, I think, but remained silent on the subject.

We headed for the lab.

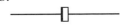

⎕ Chapter Twenty ⎕

In a weird and I guess strangely perverse way, there was something oddly satisfying about picking locks, crawling under the stairwell, and exiting Level 5 through the proverbial "back door" like we had done twice previously.

Okay—we didn't actually pick the locks. Ruach, proving that eemees are really strong, simply twisted the knob on the first door until it popped off; then "nudged" the little door under the stairs open with a swift kick. Dee dampened the sounds with EM sound wave masking.

Well, that's how she explained it when I asked. Techno mumbo.

Ruach mentioned that he found the waddling about on hands and knees under the stairwell strangely refreshing. Eemees.

We entered the lab area.

Panglaws, while pleasant enough in demeanor when we met, considered my request to use the lab facilities most irregular and wanted to confirm such an action with Hume. I could sense that Ruach, who had earlier scanned Panglaws to enlist his aid, was reluctant to make another neurological intrusion into the doctor's mind.

I finally made a raucous face to Ruach that conveyed something on the order of *WTF*, and that wasn't anything to do with the World Tennis Federation.

Panglaws immediately stopped talking and looked at me as though a new thought had suddenly occurred to him. Which it had, just not his own.

"Then again, if this is important to the mission, and time is critical, we should get started now," he said most agreeably, and we began working on the peptide alkaloid neutralizer.

A little over an hour had passed and we had experienced varying degrees of success, yet I was very encouraged. Panglaws had left the room, heading for the supply closet to find some flasks, Erlenmeyer or otherwise, and I sidled over to Ruach. "How'd you get by his attenuator ring?" Even though it wasn't perfect, it was supposed to block an eemee scan. I was just curious. Yeah, yeah, dead cat syndrome, blah, bah...

Ruach shrugged. "If you are unaware of the ring's presence, it is efficient at temporarily blocking an eemee scan." He smiled good-naturedly. "If, however, you are aware of it, you simply modulate your frequencies until you overlay one that matches the ring's output."

How come complex things sound so simple when they are properly explained? I was going to ask him to explain Phoebe to me, but bit my tongue.

Panglaws returned with a box of assorted lab goodies and I eagerly began sorting and sifting through them.

I won't burden you with the cumbersome details about what I was doing (mostly because I can render them but don't understand them). The gist of it was weaning the black mamba toxin down to create enough coalesced essence to combine with a dash of serotonin and dopamine, with some unique molecular characteristics of those latter two refined by repeated exposure to Ruach's eemee EM scan energy, and then getting the whole mess into a stable liquid form.

Don't ask.

The intention, road to hell or not, was to deliver it by an aerosol spray. Eau de peptide. Ruach and Panglaws were mad at work on figuring out the delivery system. I needed to see what kind of progress those hacking pilgrims Tom and Armando were making on Hume's ComUnit. I stepped away from the lab fray and asked Dee to get them on the line.

"No way at all?" I asked in distressed tones, having just been informed by Tom that he and Mando had hit the wall on this one. Not just hit it. Apparently, it had collapsed on top of them in a noxious cloud of brick and mortar dust.

"There is some kind of phased security software which is constantly rotating the passwords, base configurations, and other variables," Tom said in an irritated, almost resigned, voice. Fraught with distraught, if you will.

Man, that was not like Tom to give up—this must be bad. He continued in subdued tones: "The moment we do anything, there is an almost instant adjustment or refinement in the operating system and all the sub-routines." It was not exactly a whine, but was sneaking into that territory.

Tom's problem reminded me of something I had experienced in the spectrum. What was it? Yes, that was it. Infinite regression. Faces in the facing mirrors. Stairways within stairways.

Escher prints.

☐ Chapter Twenty ☐

"Tom, I may have an idea," I said, hoping to at least bolster his sagging spirit.

His expression did change, a little, and while fatigue may not make cowards of us all, it can sure sap your willpower. "I know you and Mando are exhausted," I began, and Mando's unshaven mug popped into frame.

"I've been rode hard and hung up dead," he intoned evenly and vanished. At least he still had a sense of humor, and that means we retained a fighting chance.

"Infinite regression," was all I said.

Tom's face was glazed in weary doubt, utterly not convinced. "We tried to get the security software to engage in an infinite loop, but the moment it spotted the code it simply timed out," he explained listlessly.

"No, not a loop, not really," I replied softly. "It's more about freedom in fluctuation, organized chaos." After a short pause I added, hoping to fully engage their attention, "Use its own strength against itself."

I was greeted with a cacophony of silence, so I went on. "We can't defeat the security software, fine; but we can engage it, occupy it, distract it, disturb it," I said and Tom straightened in his chair, listening intently now, sensing something.

"The security software recognizes an infinite loop and can't be locked up, okay, but what about a constantly shifting series of loops?" I asked flatly, then quickly concluded. "An infinite regression where the bottom can't be discerned because we keep moving the bottom."

"Holy crap!" Tom exclaimed, using an expression I could never quite figure out where, or what, the connection was, even though I use it myself. "You're saying that we don't actually defeat the security software, we simply bind it up and then bypass it?"

I laughed. "Freedom in fluctuation. Once you have the main security software occupied, there has to be some other hack in."

"The results log." Mando had leaned in again and added this bit of tid.

Tom looked at his friend and his jaw actually dropped open. You don't see that much. It was funny. "Hah, that's perfect!" He clapped his hands twice in excitement. "We can use a simple text log file to execute our hack code!" He laughed a little like an unnerved lunatic.

"The security layer will be completely engaged. It will relegate the log file to a background process. Probably not even a monitored process." Another hearty laugh that I loved to hear.

I had to dampen the enthusiasm just a wee bit.

"Here's the deal, Tom, I only want you to hack in and test the idea, and then get out," I explained carefully. "I don't want to run the risk that when we need to hack in for real, we've been in there too long previously and someone has changed the software, or it has adapted."

My plan was to disable Hume's ComUnit at a precise moment in my, um, Grand Scheme.

"If this idea works, Enoch, you're a genius!" Tom said breathlessly.

"Yeah," Mando lurched into view, "but, we're still billing for it." He lurched out of view. Pragmatic to a frigging fault. Awesome.

"Let me know how the test goes," I said and happily disengaged.

My grandmother loved jigsaw puzzles, bless her long departed soul. Her pattern recognition skills were sublime, even when she was well into her eighties. In fact, if I moved a photo or knick-knack, she would spot it almost instantly, prodding me gently to return her universe to its proper order and karmic alignment.

For a young kid, it got to be a game. One that we both enjoyed, me trying to be subtle in what I rearranged, and she in trying to determine what I had moved. And she always made me wicked good buckwheat pancakes.

The logic of how most jigsaw puzzles work seemed apropos to the problems I was now trying to solve with Hume. With a standard jigsaw puzzle, you dig through the tangled mass of differently shaped pieces to find all the ones with flat edges (well, assuming you are building a square or rectangular shape), in order to assemble the outer frame.

You start from the outside and work inwards toward the center.

That was what we were doing here, trying to figure out a way to get by the perimeter defenses and strike at the dark heart of the matter, so to speak.

It always helps me to work things out on paper, so here goes. Grin and grizzly with me, okay? Growl, that is barely bearable.

First thing we had to do was get Hume to come to the lab, hopefully with Phoebe tagging along, which I felt certain would be the case. She was, as Dee had previously stated, a fearless warrior, and Hume would feel at ease with her at his side, more so that she was now under his thrall due to the peptide alkaloid he had slipped into her water. Curse his blue eyes and sorrowful misguided soul.

Sorry.

However, what really worried me was—that in order to maintain Hume's control—an eemee scan had to be implanting thoughts in Phoebe's mind; a mind made receptive and pliable to such thoughts by the drug and continuous exposure to EM energy.

And I had no idea who, or where, this eemee was.

A variable I had to acknowledge, but couldn't do squat about. I had to think about it without thinking about it, as other more pressing (and addressable) topics abounded. Lots of things to hit the fan with.

Once Hume was in the lab, we had to make sure we had a reasonable line of sight to him so the quantum cascade laser (hey, it's real, research it, you can't make this stuff up) could be activated and disrupt his remote control device.

Without the remote control, Hume could not access the pentacles on Level 5 to either convert the secondary pentacles to primaries to recall eemees, convert those new primaries to binding pentacles, or destroy any binding pentacles. Most notably, Hume could not affect Ruach.

I was worried both about the current binding pentacles that already contained imprisoned eemees, and concerned about converted pentacles being used to bind any recalled eemees. Lots of things going on in this realm. All of it bad.

That remote had to be disabled.

Dee would also need to do whatever was required, and within her power, in order to disable the EM source generator that was hidden somewhere in the PHANTASM facility. Even if we disabled Hume's ComUnit, we still wanted that EM source generator taken out of the equation. One less variable to have to manipulate and be mindful of in the overall mix. Just a small nagging detail—Dee had to find it first.

Simultaneous with this, more or less (definitely more and not less) Panglaws had to get close enough to use the aerosol, dousing Phoebe with a dosage sufficient to work. And, you might rightfully be asking, how exactly was the spray supposed to work?

Glad to explain how I hope it will work.

Yeah, that's right, I said *hope*. You devise a plan, you work out the details, you factor in all the variables and you speculate, theorize, and explicate on the possibilities. The plan (or in this case, the formula) works on paper, it works in the isolated and rarefied air of the lab; but the real world, ah, now that is where hope ends and truth begins.

Kind of like politics.

The new peptide alkaloid Hume was using locked onto the brain's receptor sites like a crocodile onto a meal. You can't pry the croc's jaws loose with sheer force, and killing the croc may not be such a good idea. Not sure of the consequences. The best you could hope for was to momentarily distract the croc into dropping its potential meal while it dealt with some other, more immediate and pressing stimuli.

That was what my new drug was designed to accomplish. The black mamba toxin derivative would attack the bound up peptide alkaloid, momentarily dislodging its hold, just long enough for the serotonin and dopamine concoction to slide in and bind to the temporarily abandoned receptor sites in the brain.

The peptide alkaloid would eventually, probably relatively quickly, recover from the black mamba toxin and boot both the serotonin and dopamine from the receptor sites and reestablish itself, putting Phoebe right back in Hume's control.

Which is why I had placed protein shells of varying thicknesses around some of the black mamba toxin derivative. As the shells dissolved at different intervals, new black mamba attacks would constantly be bombarding the peptide alkaloid. It would be off and on again at the receptor sites, in perpetuity, or close enough for government work.

Flux.

The hope was for the freedom to be found in that fluctuation; that as this "war" for control of the receptor sites was being waged, Phoebe would not actually be under Hume's control, and I could communicate with her. Hope being, of course, a four-letter word.

At the same time, we had to disable Hume's ComUnit, as it generated the EM protective shell that blocked my scan blast, made

☐ Chapter Twenty ☐

communication with Dee impossible and, by implication, made Ruach nothing but a bystander since none of his eemee skills could be used.

Not only that, but both Dee and I believed the ComUnit might also be a localized source for the EM energy that the eemee was using to implant thoughts into Phoebe's mind. Hume's ComUnit had to be taken out.

Hope rises again, as Tom and Armando had to be able to take the infinite regression inspiration I had given them and translate it into the reality of a hack capable of actually disrupting Hume's ComUnit.

Cross your fingers, eyes, toes, whatever it takes.

A whole lot of wishing and hoping, true, but a whole lot of solid effort was being expended to translate such fanciful thinking into reality.

And, of course, there are those thousand natural shocks that good plans are heir to, but have to be accounted for. Such as, I needed to be in the lab when Hume arrived, but if he saw me, well, game over man, game over. So Panglaws was working on an EM screen, kind of like the technology used for the doors that were stucco particulates and couldn't be seen until they were activated.

The plan was to make an EM screen that looked like a set of filing cabinets. I would be hiding behind it until such time as I could reveal myself. I'll take what's behind door number three.

You had to hope I timed it right. Dante be damned, I wasn't abandoning anything quite yet.

Anyway, since I am nothing if not a functional paranoid, I also wanted a backup plan to the aerosol delivery idea. My argument was—what if the aerosol jammed, or Phoebe was too far away, or Hume intervened, or we can't get the EM shell disrupted in time and Ruach can't communicate with Panglaws? Or, Panglaws slips on the tile, or Ruach sneezes? Or, a roach farts?

Anyway, you get the general idea.

Trouble was, there was no real viable backup plan. We thought about using a tranquilizer gun, but the reason the spray mist was a good idea was because, once inhaled, it would rocket to the brain right on through the blood brain barrier thingy.

Think Copper Gorilla on steroids.

I might be able to hit Phoebe in the neck with a trank dart (I expressed my alarmed doubt on that point), but no one was sure if that injection delivery route would require a modified dosage or not.

And we all agreed that even a direct trank hit on the neck would not necessarily mean a quick delivery to the brain. Might just make Phoebe mad. POP, remember? That was an event to forestall at all costs.

The aerosol plan had to work.

The main thing was that we had serious synchronicity issues. All of the bits and smatterings of our plan had to happen pretty much simultaneously. Not just implemented, but actually work. Hope was rapidly devolving into doubt. Still, it was what it is, or something like that.

I slapped another BioPatch on and sipped from a bottled water someone had handed me earlier. Yeah, I checked to make sure it wasn't made in Iceland. Geez, I'm not a complete nimrod.

I told Dee to inform Ruach of her idea for luring Hume to the lab and he liked it. He was going to make sure Panglaws felt the same way. Said with a wistful smile. Think eemee intervention.

I glanced at my ComUnit display. It was around ten in the morning. We had achieved most of our goals. Panglaws and Ruach had worked out a very acceptable aerosol delivery system that had a range, Panglaws stated proudly, of approximately 1 meter.

"That's just under three feet," Dee informed me.

"I was all over that," I said defensively, though I might have been off by a foot or so in my belabored calculations. There has to be some tolerance for error, unless you're playing shortstop for the Yankees.

We had moved the furniture around so that anyone entering this part of the lab was channeled into an area directly in the line of sight of the quantum cascade laser. I love that name. It sounds like a device capable of destroying all known life or something. As long as it worked on the remote control, that would be sufficient.

Panglaws had ironed out the details of the filing cabinet screen. At first, there had been this flickering sort of wave that rippled across the image every so often. That would be a bad thing. As in Hume telling Phoebe to shoot me kind of bad thing.

☐ Chapter Twenty ☐

The bug got fixed and I made Ruach stand behind the EM screen so I could eyeball the result.

It was perfect, looking just like a set of filing cabinets. Muy bueno.

Panglaws was off tinkering and putzing with something or other. Ruach and I were taking a much needed break, sitting down lazily at one of the lab tables. He had a glass of water from the cooler and I had, imagine that, another power drink. Bad habits, as any nun will tell you, should be sewn up or replaced. I'm nervous, okay?

"Tell me about this *Book of Watchers* which is the source of your name," Ruach asked casually, gracefully opening a packet of cheddar cheese crackers. Gluten free wheat. Who knew eemees could be celiacs?

"Well," I began my explanation, always pleased on the rare occasion when someone asks that question, "actually the whole thing is called the *Book of Enoch*, and the *Book of Watchers* was my parent's favorite part." I paused for a moment, then resumed. "It's an ancient text, probably dating to around 200 BCE, but not accepted by religious authorities as part of their biblical tradition."

"What is the reason for this?" Ruach inquired reasonably.

I scratched my head. "The subject matter of the *Book of Watchers* has to do with angels in revolt from God and their fall to Earth." I shrugged. "I don't think that idea was received very well by religious leaders of the time."

"I am not entirely sure about angels and God," he said in mildly perplexed tones. "Tell me more about this *Book of Watchers*," Ruach continued in conversational tones.

"Kind of involved, but I'll give you the nickel tour," and I saw Ruach's face scrinkle up in confusion. "I'll give you a brief synopsis," I said optimistically and he nodded in apparent understanding.

I was about to begin to tell him what I knew when I realized Ruach might have some, well, gaps, in his knowledge that would pose a bit of problem when it came to interpretation.

"You are familiar with the concept of God in the Judaic-Christian tradition, right?" I said this with a confidence that drooped and sagged as I spoke. Let's just say I did not need to actually hear an answer to ascertain his level of familiarity with the subject or, in this instance, the level of his ignorance. His face offered plentiful evidence.

As in one big, *huh?*

I decided I was going to try and explain it in terms he might grasp, based on his own experience. Wish me luck. Yeah, I know, preparation meeting opportunity.

"Okay, Ruach, imagine that when you exist in the spectrum, you can interact with others of your kind; and you can also perceive and interact with humans." This seemed about as simplistic as I could state it and still make sense.

"That can only happen when we are invoked through a pentacle by a human controller and assume human form," Ruach commented.

I nodded. "Yes, but imagine if you could control that process yourself, without being summoned by a human," I explained. Ruach nodded his gradual acceptance of that premise.

"Well, we call you an eemee, which stands for electromagnetic entity. The supernatural beings in the *Book of Enoch* were called Watchers," I said slowly, trying to pick my words carefully. "A group of male Watchers lusted after mortal women and made a pact among themselves to descend to earth to take wives."

"The offspring of that illicit union were giants," I continued and Ruach eyes went wide at this reference. "These giants had ferocious and vociferous appetites, consuming all the food of man, all the wild animals, and soon began devouring the flesh of men." Ruach made a face and shook his head at this revelation.

"Eventually the suffering humans appealed to other Watchers who had not turned evil, and these good Watchers helped rid the earth of the evil Watchers, and the giants," I said with a smile, though I did not add the part about the evil spirits of the dead giants, the children of the ill-begotten Watcher-human liaisons, being cursed to haunt the earth. No sense getting Ruach too worked up.

"Obviously a tale of great allegorical and metaphorical significance," Ruach said sagely. "I will have to give it greater consideration."

I wasn't sure, with what we were about to face, he'd have time for that consideration, but I did not give voice to my concerns in that arena. Instead, I decided to ask Ruach a question.

⧉ Chapter Twenty ⧉

"Hume said eemees were summoned to Earth in Medieval times." I smiled, hoping to satisfy my curiosity on this topic. "Can you tell me anything about that?"

Ruach seemed introspective; even a little sad, if I was judging his expression correctly. "When I was first summoned by Mencius, he called me an *exophobe*." Ruach laughed—thinly—without any mirth.

I don't mind admitting my ignorance; I just don't like making a habit of it. "What's an *exophobe*?"

This time Ruach laughed with real humor. "The same question I asked!" He nodded, solemn once again. "The word is of ancient Greek origins. Over 3,000 years in age." A mysterious smile. "Eemees have been around for a long time," he said cryptically. Before I could jump on that statement with a query (and believe me, I was ready to pounce), he was talking again.

"The word *exo* means outer, external, or outside," he began and I was silent, closely following his explanation. "*Phobe* means a fear or aversion to something."

A half-smile and almost pained expression. "An *exophobe* is a person who is frightened by what is out there in the unknown."

He vented a small gush of air. "Or, an *exophobe* is the thing—the creature, the being, the entity—that lives out there somewhere beyond your senses, beyond your imagining—and gives rise to that fear."

I was giving Ruach a fresh appraisal. "Should I be afraid of eemees?" I hadn't really given this much serious thought—it intrigued me.

"As beings in the EM spectrum, no." He shook his head. "As beings suddenly manifested in human form, perhaps." His face was stoic.

His reply shook me, I admit it. I was going to follow-up on his somewhat unclear, and mildly disturbing answer, when Dee's pleasant voice sounded out. **"Tom is calling."**

"Put him on," I said anxiously, not wanting to abandon my discussion with Ruach but, if Tom was calling, it had to be about the hack into Hume's ComUnit.

"The test worked!" Tom said when his face appeared on the screen. The relief in his voice, and on his face, was palpable.

I let out a big dog sigh. "Okay, now the important part, Tom. We have to make sure the timing of the real hack is absolutely perfect."

He nodded and I finished up. "We'll hammer out the timing issues here and I'll have Dee upload instructions." I clicked off the conversation.

The most immediate challenge was that as soon as Hume walked into the lab, the EM shell from his ComUnit would block any communications with the outside world. Dee had done some extravagant calculations that indicated Hume's ComUnit generated an EM shell bubble with a diameter of about thirty feet.

Once he entered the lab, that easily encompassed the area where we would all be assembled.

So we had, you know, no way to tell Tom when to start the hack. That's until Dee came up with the brilliant idea of a practice run.

"Practice run?" I repeated inanely. Geez, I am so predictable.

"I will monitor the cameras in the hallway outside the elevator and advise when Hume is about to exit the elevator," she explained patiently. Tom told me the hack code was easy to inject into the ComUnit operating system, but it still would take about 30 seconds to become fully operational, even after the software was initiated.

He was guessing, based on the one and only test. You know how guesses go, like the lookout on the deck of the Titanic who said, "Nah, my guess is it's just a little iceberg, nothing to worry about."

There are no bears in that cave.

Anyway, I went to the elevator and told Dee to time me as I walked from the elevator exit to the lab entrance.

Thirty seconds doesn't sound like much, but it really is a long time. Take out your digital device, set the timer to zero, hit start, and begin walking. You can walk a long damn way in thirty seconds.

From the elevator to the inside of the lab was only about a fifteen second walk.

Which meant, I thought with appropriate consternation, we had to endure a fifteen second lapse in communications while Tom's hack wiggled in and did its nasty little job of disabling the ComUnit and EM shell. Well, assuming Tom's initial estimate (guess) was accurate. During that interval, I couldn't talk to Dee or Ruach, and Ruach could not be planting suggestive thoughts in the mind of Panglaws.

We argued about starting the ComUnit hack earlier, while Hume was on the way to the elevator from Level 4 or even before that, but we were concerned (well, mostly me freaked) that if, for any reason, he sensed something awry with the ComUnit, he'd never go the lab.

He had to set foot in the lab. It was a key element, probably the key element.

Speaking of keys, another essential key to our plan (well, one of many frelling essential keys) was that Panglaws needed to administer the aerosol spray to Phoebe. The thought of Phoebe, under Hume's control, with a gun in her hand, BB or otherwise, was not appealing to any of us. Swallow hard and try not to think about it.

So, Ruach was going to have to get Panglaws really worked up and absolutely dedicated, if you will, to spraying Phoebe with the aerosol or, at least, be very good at stalling for fifteen seconds. Again, doesn't sound like much, but it can sure seem forever. Think about the dentist and that so-called "minor" cavity.

We were rapidly approaching the proverbial moment of truth. Everyone was off by themselves hashing through the details of their own roles in the upcoming events and the exact timing for their actions. Here is precisely what was going to happen.

Maybe.

Ruach was going to report to Panglaws on his findings (fabricated, of course) about the problem with the peptide alkaloid breaking down. Dee's idea of nitrogenation. Ruach would strengthen his report by implanting the suggestion in Panglaws' mind that Hume should immediately be called in and shown the new report.

In addition, Ruach was going to make sure Panglaws understood the importance of spraying Phoebe with the aerosol, which would help with the supposed nitrogenation problem impacting her. Very important. Ruach was concerned about intervening so hard within Panglaws' mind, but when I asked if there would be any possibility of permanent damage he replied no, so I said it would be fine. I hoped.

Another maybe.

Ruach had arranged the quantum cascade laser so it would trigger fifteen seconds after Hume entered the lab, effectively (fingers crossed) knocking out Hume's remote control. Well, in theory. This time lapse effect should (knock on wood) coincide with Tom and Mando's successful disabling of Hume's ComUnit and the damn EM shell.

Yeah, another few maybes.

By this time, Panglaws should be in the process of dousing Phoebe with the spray, freeing her from Hume's control and letting us communicate freely with her. The aerosol, Ruach assured me calmly, should begin to work "within seconds" but he declined to be more specific than that. Fug.

At that point, Phoebe could zap Hume with her BB gun, or, with the EM shell now down, I might mind blast his sorry ass into unconscious oblivion. Or, she could zap Ruach, Panglaws, and me. I didn't say it was a foolproof plan. Bite your tongue.

If everything actually worked according to the supposedly foolproof plan, up to this point, we'd then secure Hume's remote control, probe his mind for the codes, free the eemees, plus disrupt the entire global pentacle and satellite energy activation plot.

Hurrah for our team! Time for a beer. Or three.

Truthfully, I'd rather put my life savings on black and spin. Shoot, at least then it was 50-50. I gave us a 1 in 5 chance here.

"That seems overly optimistic," Dee commented lightly, then went silent when I told her my opinion of her opinion. Aargh, and then I had to apologize for my flippant and unruly remarks.

Nerves like the bottom of the legs of my favorite old blue jeans.

Still, no one had a better plan, so we were committed. Pig to bacon rather than chicken to egg.

We activated the file cabinet EM screen. I took a deep breath and stepped behind it. I saw Ruach nervously fiddling with the aerosol spray canister, preparing to hand it to Panglaws at the appropriate time.

I stood behind the screen thinking about the last week and how a person's life can change so suddenly—literally overnight. It really was a question of words, or how you use the *logos*—if you'll forgive me that interpretation—that can transform a life.

Good technology (as I pointed out previously) utilizes the idea of *logos* in a positive, affirming, fashion for the benefit of humanity. As I carefully pondered all the ramifications of what had happened to me since I posted my EM spectrum blog entry last Friday night (well, Saturday morning), I realized that old saying about mighty pens and swords was really true—and very scary.

☐ Chapter Twenty ☐

Thoughts and words (and how the *logos* is really translated into reality) are the true sources of energy in the human universe. Not wind power, not solar power, nor hydrocarbons or nuclear fusion.

Words. Thoughts. The ultimate source of energy and power.

Consider—all of this was happening now because of a simple damn blog post I made.

Man, if ever there was a cautionary tale, there it was.

Words have a power, an force, a karma, that lives on forever. Hey, another great blog idea just came to me...

Crap, it was time for Panglaws to call Hume.

Riding The Wave

—⊡—

"All of nature is a great wave phenomenon."

—Louis de Broglie

I really thought it would take more insistent urging to get Hume to come to the lab, but Panglaws merely mentioned the odd results—about the breakdown of the peptide alkaloid—and Hume said he'd be right there. Okay, that was good; one maybe eradicated.

Many more to go.

Dee was monitoring the camera feed facing the elevator here on Level 2. We weren't sure what would happen when Hume's EM shell interacted with the camera, but figured we'd either see his image exiting the elevator, or the feed would turn to interference and snow.

Or, my knees would buckle in trembling fear and I'd pass out.

Either way, snow or no snow, when Hume appeared it was the cue for Tom and Armando to start the hack. They were on the line simply waiting for me to say the word. Assuming I had enough saliva in my mouth to talk.

Remember about Mando and tennis? About staying calm, focused, not freezing up. You know the shot you have to take and you take it. You don't miss because you can't miss. You do the do, lou.

I was watching my ComUnit display intently. The elevator door started to open and the video feed indeed frittered to fuzz. "Now!" I instantly blurted out. Thankfully, for my mental well-being and sanity, Tom gave me a verbal acknowledgement and then he was gone. I wouldn't be worrying about whether or not the hack attack was underway; it was on. Internal sigh of moderate relief.

From behind the file cabinet EM screen I noted Ruach staring intently at Panglaws, and the latter nodding his head in agreement, as though affirming the points of a discussion. Rather one-sided, as it was mostly Ruach implanting thoughts and instructions. Ruach handed him the aerosol canister and Panglaws palmed it, cleverly blocking it from casual view.

I was rehearsing everything in my mind, for the umpteenth time, and felt we had covered every contingency. It was really just a question of execution. Hold on, there has to be a better word than that.

I noticed Ruach looking at something on the table; I think it was a digital clock. He was about to start the timer on the laser.

The lab door opened, swinging inwards toward us. Ruach started the timer. Fifteen. Hume came striding in, scowling. Then Phoebe, her face calm and impassive, beautiful. Fourteen.

And then another figure.

Taller. Darker. Anuket. The eemee bee atch from hell. Thirteen.

~Dee!~ I lashed out a fervent thought. ~Dee!~ It was greeted by complete and devastating silence. Twelve.

"Dr. Panglaws, what the hell is going on with the formula?" Hume asked in an even voice, though his tone was hard. Terse. Expectant. Eleven.

Panglaws had already closed most of the distance to Hume's group. Just a little nearer and he was within spraying distance. Ten. Just had to stall for a little bit. Answer the question. Answer the question. Nine.

Anuket quickly stepped forward. Her action caused Panglaws to stop walking. Eight. "Something isn't right," Anuket said in puzzled tones, looking around the room with squinted eyes. Seven.

~Dee?~ I tried again. Still silence. Damn, damn, damn, Six.

"Nitrogenation of the benzyl benzene ring causes a rapid breakdown of the efficacy of the peptide alkaloid," Panglaws recited in a flat, emotionless, voice. By rote. Five.

"Scan him," Hume said gruffly, gesturing at Panglaws, obviously agreeing with Anuket that something wasn't right. In Denmark, or PHANTASM. Four. I did not know precisely what Panglaws knew about our plans, but Anuket would damn sure find out when she scanned him, and I couldn't let that happen. Three.

Panglaws went rigid as Anuket's energy scan engaged him, standing straight up as though he were being electrocuted.

I stepped out from behind the screen; well, through it. Two.

☐ Riding The Wave ☐

Anuket immediately released Panglaws and fixated on me. Imagine a snake that is watching a mere lizard and then sees a delicious mouse. Yeah, just like that. One.

Hume's face, though, was the one I was watching. Genuine shock and surprise, when you see it on a human face, is very difficult to fake. It is unique, and Hume was stunned. Zero. He did manage to blurt out "Enoch!" at just about the moment Anuket hit my mind, full force, like a tractor trailer tee-boning a compact car on the interstate.

~Enoch Maarduk,~ she mind-thought with a particularly harsh yet, mild, allure to her tone. ~This time you don't have anyone to help you,~ she said in a soft mocking reference to Knoxville and the way Phoebe had scorched Anuket's worthless carcass with repeated BB blasts of electrostatic-like quantified energy. Phoebe wasn't much use to me here, yet.

~Anuket.~ Even though I only said her name, I pretty much spat it out with as much vitriol as I could generate. ~Hume's toy and pet on a leash,~ I added by way of clever repartee, having just now quickly, and I hoped correctly, thought of this inventive line of disruptive discourse.

~Ruach, can you get Panglaws to spray Phoebe?!~ I feverishly directed this to Ruach in the mad hope the EM shell was down. Panglaws was standing, immobile, in the same spot, just staring off into the distance. Phoebe was watching Hume, and she had not moved. Hume was still staring at me, then finally turned to Ruach, who was focused on Panglaws. Silence from Ruach. Willing my calm not to shatter.

Anuket laughed. Well, it sounded like a laugh, if you can imagine a sound that while purporting to be laughter sends a shiver through your entire being. Worse than fingernails on a black slate chalkboard. ~Hume does not control me,~ Anuket stated with calm assurance, her voice husky, rich, and seductive. Staring into my eyes in a most uncomfortable fashion.

She was a gorgeous creature.

Hume was holding his remote control and trying to use it, probably to banish Ruach from the room and back to his pentacle; but the remote control was obviously not working. Click, click, click, nothing. Score one for the good guys.

☐ Chapter Twenty-One ☐

~Ruach, Ruach, tell Panglaws to spray Phoebe!!~ I anxiously broadcast—urgent edginess—but there was still nothing but the depth of rancid silence. Score one for the bad guys.

~Anuket,~ I began my argument in the most reasonable voice I could produce. ~Hume has plans to use your energy for his own purposes.~ I said it softly, easily, trying to keep my voice calm and rhythmic, unlike my heart. ~He intends to compel humans to act as he instructs them, using the energy of eemees.~

Another garish and grating laugh from her. This was getting weird. Why should she find my remarks amusing? Surely just the opposite?

The relentless, unyielding, and steady pressure of Anuket on my mind was intense, probing, pushing, seeking—trying to reach out, striving upwards, urging itself up from my medulla oblongota—where I was currently and desperately holding her at bay—to possess my mind. Turn me into zombie chum.

~I let Hume think he has control, Enoch, but his plans mean nothing to me,~ she said, the soft reasonableness of her own voice was soothing, compelling, pleasing, but I fought it off. Had to keep her talking and the pressure on my mind would be lessened thereby. Not sure how much I could take. Uncharted and untested waters.

~You have different plans, then?~ I asked, hoping to prompt her into telling me, which, for some odd reason, I was certain she would do.

~Do you think humans are the epitome of evolution?~ Anuket asked with mild amusement. I didn't answer. Any answer I could offer would seem, well, compromised. Depends on what she meant by evolution. Besides, it was better for me that she kept talking. I found myself gritting my teeth.

~Humans are a rope, Enoch, a rope stretched over the chasm of oblivion.~ The briefest lull. ~A rope that stretches from insensate beast to us, the ones you call eemees,~ and I was beginning to feel her sensible and beguiling madness swirling around me like a gathering mist.

~So, in your opinion, eemees represent the pinnacle of development so far in the cosmos?~ I worked hard not to change my tone or inflection so she could not infer anything from how I phrased the question. I wanted her to explain herself fully on this topic.

~Not at all, Enoch. We are merely the stepping stone, the foundation from which the next great leap will be made,~ she answered me cryptically and, naturally, drawing me deeper into her thought process. Even as I knew what she was doing, I felt the desire, the need, the compulsion, to know more—to hear everything she had to say on this fascinating topic. Plus, the pressure on me had leveled off, was holding steady, manageable.

~How will this next movement forward be accomplished?~ I figured this was the logical query to make to someone wishing to share their grandiose vision of the future. Warped as it may be. Give her enough rope, as it were.

~First, the chaos of human life must be quelled, must be controlled,~ she replied with positive affirmations, waves of acceptance, blistering patterns of certitude. I fought to fend them, reflect them.

~The uncertainty of life must be corrected,~ she said with cool and polished aplomb.

~By force,~ I stated, though I immediately wished I had not said it.

~If people have strayed from the correct path, Enoch, and will not listen to reasonable instructions to return, then force is the only tool available to compel them to choose the best possible direction,~ she said without rancor, smooth, elegant, modest. ~To show them the proper way.~ So reasonable, so obvious. Still, I could not agree.

~It is too great a task,~ I evinced strongly, thinking that to force all of humanity to change would be impossible. How could she hope to achieve this, even if she toppled Hume and somehow assumed control of the other four eemees?

Perhaps Anuket sensed my refutation of her goal—or perhaps she was merely continuing her stilted explanation—but she went on. ~Enoch, do you know why the pentacles built by a human controller respond only to his or her command?~ She asked this sweetly, openly. A purity of tone and intent.

She did not wait for my response, but continued, ~The human controller must put some of his or her own blood into the pentacle, into the pattern.~ She smiled, lopsided, crooked, not human. She was a beautiful woman, even so.

☐ Chapter Twenty-One ☐

~Blood, Enoch. DNA.~ A well-crafted smile, purely artisan. ~Unique, even among billions of other humans,~ she added, probably not even aware herself of the disdain with which she invested that last word.

~I have given much thought to that fact, Enoch, ever since I gleaned the knowledge from Hume's mind,~ she stated in almost sibilant tones. ~And when it came time to produce the formula for the new peptide alkaloid, I put my knowledge into action.~ We were getting close to something here, I could feel it.

It was not a pleasant feeling.

My vision had begun, just moments before, to slowly fade. I was, most surprisingly, not alarmed in the least by this occurrence, even though by now I could not clearly make out what was happening in the room. It was just a distant, blurry, mess. I was still aware of my body, that I was standing in the room, but even that sensation was tenuous, fading.

~What is your plan?~ It was the only thing I could think to say. Or say to think, as it were. I rallied my focus and focused on my rally. I was working hard to maintain a cohesive narrative, one that included me!

A chuckle from her this time, worse than the damn laugh. Dank, dark, deep, delicious. ~Part of my DNA went into the formula, Enoch, and soon humans everywhere will consume products containing it,~ she explained proudly, breathlessly, poignant, pregnant.

~So what?~ I intoned, unimpressed. ~Hume will use eemee energy and the global satellite network to force humans to help one another and your efforts will amount to nothing,~ I added, dismissing her statements as mere puffery. Eemee illusions of grandeur.

~Hume is a fool,~ Anuket added smoothly, emoting her words so gently that they hardly seemed threatening. ~He will be dealt with at the appropriate time.~ A sort of latent pause.

~The humans will help me,~ she said firmly, followed by more of that damnably disagreeable laughter, ~because I will tell them to build pentacles, Enoch. Pentacles.~

A set of disjointed, yet connected feelings rose like tornadic clouds and swept over my entire being, hurtling over me as a massive wave that struck with swirling force against the rocky and gnarled shoals of my cortical reef. I cannot adequately convey, with mere words, how this affected me, but I will attempt.

It was a pervasive feeling of utter defeat and despondent gloom, the like of which I have never before experienced in my life. As if all the goodness had been instantly sucked out of the world.

Suddenly, I could see the true majesty of her plan and it was, indeed, regal. Awe-inspiring. Sublime and perfect. Beyond reproach.

The activation of the global satellite network would give Anuket, and the other four eemees who would fall under her control after she destroyed Hume, powerful, perhaps total, dominion over human minds. The eemees would compel humans to build pentacles. To call down more eemees. To build more pentacles.

Pentacles where Anuket's DNA resided, putting her in charge of all the incoming eemees.

"Humans would be nothing but slaves!" This burst out from me, even though I did not mean to say it aloud.

~Enoch, Enoch,~ Anuket intoned slowly, with such gentleness, such meek and careful kindness. ~There is a natural evolution in all things.~ She said it with a compelling passion and I felt the elegant truth of her words. ~Look at yourself. You are human, but with powers and gifts that are not human,~ she emoted easily, her explanation fascinating, worming its way into my mind. Words bounding past the elaborate mental breastworks I had built to protect myself, slipping by and obviating my objections with veritable ease.

~Our union will create a new race of superior beings, Enoch, and we will control this world. To make it better. To manage the chaos. To show the way.~ A warm, pleasant, disarming, smile. ~Think of it!~ Her words shook me, penetrating to the core of my consciousness, but probably not in the way she had planned.

Our union? Creating a new race? Some semblance of sanity seemed to be slowly seeping back into me. Anuket was as mad as a hatter.

She didn't want me to join her. She wanted to join with me, wanted me to be her mate. That was insane. Beyond comprehension. A precipitant madness.

And yet...

☐ Chapter Twenty-One ☐

Think of it. To rule over an entire planet. To hold billions in thrall, subject to your every whim and command. To really create a new race of superior beings, as she said. To be the father and founder of such a race. The thought of such limitless power, to control and wield as one saw fit, with no boundaries, like the gods we should be.

~Enoch, Enoch, join with me,~ I heard Anuket pleading with a longing urgency, softly caressing me with the embracing and enticing timbre of her voice. I could feel my will crumbling, my mind wilting under the unremitting pressure of her cool and easy assault.

I had to hold onto my Self, who I was, who I am. Who am I? Almost panic.

Enoch. Enoch Maarduk. Think of my unique past. My parents were of humble origins, but through their hard work, selfless love and determination, they had made something of themselves; had succeeded in a world that so many see as unfair, where so many see only inequity and not opportunity.

People fail because they lack the will to achieve, not because they are genetically flawed. My parents were not perfect, yet they had created a world for themselves, and for me. We do not need forced change or some new step in evolution foisted on us by others.

We simply need to embrace the world we have.

And it is a human world, imperfect, yet perfect, because it is the world we have. Full of pain and sorrow, and yet full of hope and beauty. A world where anyone could be successful, and you didn't need mind tricks, drugs, or manipulated EM waves to do it. Just a belief in your Self. And the freedom to make it happen.

Hume and Anuket wanted to restrict, control, even eliminate that freedom. It would mean the end of humanity. It would be the freedom of the slave. Ignorance is not strength.

It would be the end of free will and freedom. Not just the freedom to be, but to become.

"No!" I screamed violently and the darkness came.

The first time had been terrifying. The second had been just a little unsettling, but no big deal. The third time felt, well, kind of normal.

◻ Riding The Wave ◻

I remember Ruach had said there was no sense of Self in the spectrum, just a sense of being. Isness. I had felt this loss of Self strongly the first time, just a little the second time, and now, not at all. Completely the opposite of what he said. Peculiar, but I was glad.

Let's hope this was a trend and not an aberration, here in my third visit.

"How can this be?" It was Anuket, her voice confused, almost frightened. "How can we be in the spectrum?"

Well, truth be told, I thought she was responsible for that, but her uncertain voice laid that grave error to rest. Which meant some other external agency was involved.

Or, I had done it.

This latter concept was like a bad relative. It just sort of popped in to visit me, unannounced but, ultimately, welcome to stay. Blood is blood. Welcome to stay. In the back room, with the dog.

Anyway, perhaps I could reason with Anuket, apply some logic. Think it through and through it, think.

"Anuket, your idea is doomed to fail, just like Hume's idea," I said with complete belief and confidence. Plant a seed and watch it grow. Muster the mustard seed. A call to arms. An armed calling.

"Humans cannot be trusted to make the correct decisions," Anuket calmly began her argument, her momentary loss of composure at finding herself in the spectrum now apparently overcome. Probably overcome by necessity, the mother that she is. "Humans must be helped, shown the way, directed to the path."

Sendero Luminosa. Pathet Lao. The Illuminati. The Great Leap Forward. The Cultural Revolution. Lebenstraum. The Five Year Plan. The Great Plan for the Transformation of Nature. The Special Period in Time of Peace. Eugenics. Good intentions. Lots of paving stones on the road.

The spectrum was making me giddy as data flowed and twirled, ran like digital wind through the taut canvas of my mind, cortical sails tacked to the breeze. Control. Focus. Clarity. Crystalline.

"Your lack of faith is disturbing," I said and chuckled with salubrious humor to myself at that starry allusion. No faith in humans. Disturbed

☐ Chapter Twenty-One ☐

indeed by the thought of coercion and force being used to make humans behave a certain way, like trained dogs. Sit. Roll over. Stay. Beg.

"Trained dogs?" Anuket repeated with much amusement. I wasn't sure how she garnered that notion from me, unless the spectrum offered little privacy for thoughts. Bookmark that query. For reference in the future—if I had a future.

"You completely misunderstand, Enoch." She smiled patiently after she said this. I could not actually see her, visually, and yet this impression—her patient smile as it were—was clear, distinct, and locked in perceptive vises.

"Humans will not be forced to do anything," she appended smoothly, almost apologetically. "Eemees will merely suggest the proper courses of action for humans to follow." Again the smile, every bit as irritating as her damnable laughter.

"Humans will follow us because we are naturally superior to them. It is the right and proper thing to do." Anuket said this with utter conviction and certainty, not a smug arrogance like you might expect, but as a statement of simple fact, irrefutable and implicit. "You cannot defeat the truth, Enoch," she intoned in ghostly soft tones.

Truth. *Veritas est adaequatio intellectus et rei* as the learned scribes from medieval times, ever practical in affairs of Church and State, so thoughtfully stated. Translated as: *Truth consists in the agreement of our thought with reality.* Bend it, twist it, warp it, shape it. Truth, these people believe, is what I say it is, not what it really is. Malleable, situational, non-absolute.

If you manipulate reality, shape the environment to your will, you control truth. So-called. That is to say, you believe you control truth. Pilate. *Quid est veritas?* or *What is truth?* As though religions or governments or corporations or universities or movies or books or eemees somehow know the truth, are in unique possession of it. Can offer it up as a satisfying sop to hungry people. In exchange, of course, for their souls.

It is not the consciousness of men that determines their existence, but, on the contrary, their social existence that determines their consciousness. I do not accept this.

⬚ Riding The Wave ⬚

Karl lacks any faith in humankind. X Marx the spot. Manifest nonsense. Worse than a mass opiate.

"And what makes you so damn superior?" I asked candidly, bitterly, putting the issue to task. Cutting to the chase. Getting to the point. Beating on the bush and not around it.

"Enoch," said in the most benign of whispers, "you know that the majority of humans lack intelligence," she continued gracefully, firmly, even-tempered and self-assured. "It is only by the hard work and benevolent guidance of a small minority of intelligent humans that your species accomplishes anything at all," she added gently, urgently, adroitly.

She went on, even tempo, adagio. "Hume wants to force that small, more intelligent, minority to help even more, but that is not the right way." She smiled and I shook my head in sullen disgust. Every petty tyrant knows the "right" way to do things. They safeguard the Truth. For the rest of us. From the rest of us. *Sic semper tyrannis*.

"Once we have increased the population of eemees, we can guide all the humans, intelligent or not, into making good decisions about enriching their lives," she said with soothing passion. So reasonable, so optimistic, seeking only progress for humanity. Such pomp for this circumstance.

I have always prided my Self on being objective. Not hubris. No Greco-Roman formula for heroic downfall. Simply maintaining a sense of personal honor by evaluating all the facts; well, all the available facts, before making a rational decision on critical issues. Induction, deduction, reduction, abduction. Who wants to die?

I had to give Anuket's position fair and equitable consideration, regardless of my initial reactions to it. I mean, what if she were correct? Thesis, antithesis, synthesis.

What if the vast majority of humans were simply unable and incapable of learning anything more than their basic inherited intelligence; unable to become more intelligent, doomed to a life of ignorance and stupidity, locked down by genetic heritage?

You are doomed to the wheel of ignorance by your genes.

⬚ Chapter Twenty-One ⬚

If genetics were responsible for most of a person's intelligence, that is to say, the level of their cognitive abilities, then no one could expect any improvement from childhood into maturity. Sure, there could be fine-tuning, additional training, tweaking, vain attempts to make the best of what was there, but no noticeable improvement in actual cognitive ability could be expected.

Beauty might be skin deep, but stupid would be to the bone.

You would only be as smart at age 31 as you were at age 11, and so on and so on and so on. Sure, you would get more experience over time, and more overall data would be available as you aged, but you would be operating with the same mental skill set, one that could not be improved, to manipulate your circumstances. No pomp. Stupid is as stupid does. Having a brain would offer no true assurance of actually having a brain, as it were.

If this were true, then education is a devastating waste of time and resources. No point in trying to turn morons into doctors. You cannot turn a sow's ear into a silk purse. Education would be a sham, a pretense, merely a system for turning out degreed idiots. A charade. A parade of charlatans. We lie to ourselves.

Petronius (27-66 ACE), said *Mundus vult decipi, ergo decipiatur*, and too many people believe this, latch onto it as an excuse. "The world wants to be deceived, so let it be deceived." Caveat emptor. Beware. Look out below!

The eemees, if genetics truly held sway and majesty in human affairs, would be needed. We must plead for their help. We must have external help because we are incapable of helping ourselves. Or, we help ourselves too much.

The eemees would assure, insure, maintain, balance the unfair equation, make things fair. Bring change.

Bring order.

They could suggest to the more intelligent, actually force and compel them through mind energy scan blasts, to give away what they had earned through legitimate effort. After all, it is the intelligent people who can usually translate their intelligence into economic success. People of genetically inferior cognitive ability have no way to employ technology to their advantage.

꓿ Riding The Wave ꓿

This is what Hume and Anuket fervently believed.

I heard Anuket quoting someone. "From each according to their ability, to each according to their needs." Commune on that. Fair is as fair does. Grasshoppers and ants.

Instead of using technology to generate benefits for themselves, the inferior humans are used by technology to accrue benefits for others. The more intelligent among us create zombies, masses of humans hopelessly addicted to the EM waves, dependent on their next digital fix, by controlling the hardware, the software, the content, the message. It's the medium, not the message.

"No one can understand the message," Anuket injected, acid-toned. Deflecting my thoughts. Derailing, destabilizing, deleterious delectability.

The content, the message, is barbaric, designed for the unintelligent. What is barbarism? A behavior, an action, a trait, or custom characterized by ignorance or crudity. EM energy manipulated to appeal to the barbarian. Deliberate obfuscation.

Self-perpetuating mythos.

Anuket wore a plaintive expression; I could see the pain in her eyes, sense the genuine anguish in her very being. "The eemees must step in to change and transform this hopeless situation. It is the only way to save humanity." I nodded sagaciously in empathy. Perhaps we have to look to the superior intellect of the eemee for help. We cannot solve these problems alone. Humans cannot solve human problems.

And, yet, even as I thought this, even as I considered how all this would work, could work, should work, must work, something was gnawing at my mind. Picking and cuffing at my thoughts, pecking, prodding, poking, punching. An uneasiness, an unsettling notion.

A pervasive and troubling sensation that clawed at the inner workings of my rational mind.

Dubitare. Doubt.

A faith that does not doubt is a dead faith.

If intelligence cannot be improved, if it is static, then barbarism would rule throughout the world.

"It does," Anuket chided me softly.

⬚ Chapter Twenty-One ⬚

"No!" I rebuked her loudly, absolutely. Although there are many areas in the world where barbarism seems rampant, civilization, true civilization, has spread far and wide. We are more civil to one another. It grows with each passing day.

We have the rule of law. Not *lex talionis*. Not an eye for an eye. There is justice in the eyes of the truly Righteous State.

"You have nothing but the tyranny of the majority," Anuket said with a harsh laugh, cajoling, rollicking. "The rule of mediocrity," she added in a deriding voice tinted with sarcasm.

"Even with your mindless majority in charge, ultimately you are still subject to the whims of a small minority, the selfish desires of the more intelligent ruling technocracy." She threw this at me in structured defiance.

Semantics. Words. Sophistry. Belabored and sensical nonsense. Flimsy whimsy.

Freedom is the key. Without freedom there is no intelligence. You are only a slave if you believe it. You must doubt to be free. Never buy what they are selling.

Humans can improve. You see it all around. The next generation has it better when they apply themselves, work hard, achieve. Self-determination. Personal responsibility. Honor. Integrity. Morality. Ethics. The Golden Rule.

"He who has the gold makes the rules," Anuket spat contemptuously.

Yes, I acknowledged, poverty and ignorance still abide. It surrounds us.

"The system is corrupt, stacked against the average person," Anuket argued with balanced grace. "The unfortunate are held down, chained to the station in life that is determined by their genetic traits for intelligence, for cognitive power." She shook her head in sorrow. "It is the wheel of existence from which there is no escape." Such resigned and pitiful desperation.

Fiddle faddle. A crock of manure. Malarkey. Bullsnarf. People succeed in life all the time. Brown, Yellow, Black, Red, White, Purple. All races, creeds, colors, ethnic groups. There are no rules.

☐ Riding The Wave ☐

Only that you must maintain a firm grasp upon belief, faith, trust, hope. Kindness lives. Compassion thrives. Love is real. You cannot let the EM energy manipulators control your mind. Life, liberty, and the pursuit of happiness mean something.

"Happiness?" Anuket spat out. "For most people; sex, drugs and rock & roll are the great human goals for happiness." She grunted, "The barbarians are not at the gates, Enoch, they are in control." Her smile was skillfully tilted. "You need us to help you, to make things right, to correct the problems of the past. To fix the challenges of the present." Reverent tones, sermonized, demonized, sanitized.

Illusion. Maya. We live under a vile veil. Evil. EM energy deliberately misused to force us into submission? To bend our wills into submission so we bow down before a well-meaning elite?

Could it be that the very people decrying the need to take from the intelligent and give to the unintelligent deliberately concoct and support the notion that there are genetic, inherent differences? In order to have power and control for themselves, to take the Will from the supposedly unintelligent, remove their self-determination, in exchange for some kind of ill-advised care, like a shepherd with their flock?

A flock they will shear or slaughter whenever they, the eemee ruling elite, so desire.

All humans are created equal. Flesh, blood, and bone. Codons and helixes abound. I share about 64% of my DNA with a banana. Will you still feed me?

About 95% plus with a chimpanzee. I am not like that box of rocks. I am that box of rocks.

It doesn't matter. No relevance. Allah, Buddha, Shiva, Jehovah, Yahweh, G_d. The difference is in the sameness. The underlying reality of human being is that, with nurturing, early instruction, love, and freedom, every human can be intelligent, move the right side of the bell curve, have cognitive abilities of whatever magnitude their drive and self-motivation will permit them to envision.

You must have faith and belief. In others. In your Self.

You cannot force or legislate human nature. Positive changes happen when people believe. When the truth of it is seen as the Truth. Faith which is nurtured by doubt.

⟨ Chapter Twenty-One ⟩

"Anuket, you can go to hell," was all I said, emotionless, flat, and simple. Tartarus. Gehenna. Sheol. Hades.

"That is a shame, Enoch, truly a shame," she said with genuine regret. "I had hoped we could rebuild this human world in our image, the two of us serving as examples of what superior beings are capable of."

"Humans don't need gods, Anuket. We only need ourselves, and each other," I replied, shaking in my anger. "We humans can do anything, once we set our collective minds to the task."

"And what tasks would that be, Enoch?" Anuket chuckled in derision. "Shopping at the mall? Going to the ballgame? Posting photos of the family dog to the Internet?" She shook her head in royal and arrogant distaste. "The vulgar whims of a useless hoi polloi."

"You know, Anuket, you are one ignorant eemee bitch," I responded sharply, really agitated now. "Human life is about the sacred nature of the mundane, about seeing glory in our daily affairs," I tried to explain. "About seeing the possibilities of potential instead of the woe of endless inequity."

I laughed this time. "Humanity is getting better, bigger, stronger, faster, but at its own pace, under individual control." I shook my head angrily. "We don't want, or need, anyone to force changes on us in the ill-advised hope that it will improve human nature."

"You should just stay here in the spectrum and play with yourself," I finished with a grin.

And then, kaboom — boomshakalaka — without warning, Anuket let fly a harvey wallbanger of an energy blast that blazed across my synapses, seemed to blow the top of my skull off, and set my spinal cord on fire. Chakra exploding. Tantric without the thrill.

I reeled, bobbed, weaved, bloated like a flutterby. Stretched again, ad infinitum, oh man, talk to me daddy. Pain so perniciously exquisite it suspended me in time and space. Every sense heightened, the final destination achieved. Arcs of bright light that flashed and ripped across the fabric of my senses. A bad trip.

"Goodbye, Enoch, you should have taken my offer," I heard Anuket say without malice, and then I was drifting, losing my grip on awareness, consciousness, being consumed and drawn down by the dark.

◊ Riding The Wave ◊

I am Enoch Maarduk.

Tom and Armando owe me dinner. I need to say goodbye to Dee and Ruach.

Humans cannot be forced or legislated to change their internal nature—they must of their own free will choose it.

I want to see that new movie coming out next week. I want to play some tennis this weekend. I miss a cold beer. I believe the basic nature of humanity is good. Humans can be made more intelligent, but all of us must embrace that belief. Faith which is nurtured by doubt. Faith in ourselves. In each other.

I want to ask Phoebe out on a date.

I mind blasted Anuket into absolute oblivion.

It was jarring—abrupt—a bio-shock to the system, all valves flailing. One moment it had been dark, my mind reeling, failing, with only fleeting impressions of Anuket and a stream of dialog and other disjointed and jointed thoughts.

Then, suddenly, lights, camera, action, focus and I am back in the lab, standing in the same spot as before. I took the deepest of purifying breaths. Bizarre head warp. Beam me up. Or down.

Speaking of down—Panglaws was on his hands and knees, his arms trembling as he unsteadily tried to push himself up.

Hume was also on the ground, but motionless. His skin color was pale. His breathing was almost imperceptible.

Ruach was in a half-crouch, looking as though he had just picked himself up off the ground. His expression was displeased and a bit flustered.

Phoebe was standing, staring at me, holding her BB gun. Well, actually pointing it at me.

I raised my hands carefully above my head. "I surrender, you got me," was all I said.

"Funny," Phoebe said, lowering her weapon. "Glad you could pop in." I laughed. That actually was funny.

"Just out painting the town infrared. And ultra-violent." I laughed at my own orange-colored humor.

☐ Chapter Twenty-One ☐

Phoebe scowled. Did I mention she is really good-looking? "Where's that bitch Anuket?" Phoebe asked tensely; albeit, politely.

I looked a little chagrined at that query. "We had, uh, a disagreement," I answered softly.

"I assume she lost the argument," Phoebe said with a baby grin.

I shrugged. "Lost in the ozone I guess."

"You shot me," Ruach commented, having now overcome his flusterage and rapidly regaining his composure.

Phoebe looked properly contrite. "I'm really sorry, Ruach, the spray kicked in right after I squeezed the trigger," she explained, hoping to placate him.

He smiled and shrugged. "It was more of a surprise than a pain." Panglaws was standing and rubbing his head. Apparently the spray hadn't quite kicked in before he got nailed either. Thankfully, there was no blood. Always a good thing. Except for a somewhat bedazzled look on his face, he appeared healthily intact.

"What happened to Hume?" I asked, gesturing with my thumb at his body on the floor.

Phoebe looked at Hume's form and noted his shallow breathing. "Not long after you and Anuket vanished, he grabbed the sides of his forehead, as though in pain, then collapsed," was the succinct explanation she gave me. "I've tried to revive him, but he's unresponsive." She sighed expansively. "Med tech guys should be here soon."

With a chill I recalled Anuket's words to me concerning Hume—'He will be dealt with at the appropriate time.' I nodded my head, looked sadly at Hume, then back to Phoebe. "Anuket hit him with a mind blast," I boldly stated, which was a guess, but felt certain the correct one. Phoebe wagged her head in understanding.

"You'll have to tell me all about it," Phoebe said, and I smiled inwardly at just the rarest hint of concern in her usually impassive and professional tone.

"It will require adult beverages," I said wearily, warily.

"Copper gorillas?" Phoebe joked back with a beautiful smile.

"Yeah, and we make Tom and Mando buy," I said, then thought of Dee. "Dee, everything okay with you?"

⟨ Riding The Wave ⟩

"**Now that you are back Enoch, we can complete the final tasks,**" she replied calmly, then added with much more emotion, "**and I am most pleased you are back!**"

I turned with alarm to face Ruach. I knew that one of those final tasks was the freeing of the four eemees held in the binding pentacles on Level 5. I also knew that we had to use Hume's remote control. Using the codes we had planned to scan from his mind.

His now possibly unavailable mind.

I whirled to stare at Hume as Ruach immediately began speaking. "You are thinking of the codes," he stated coolly.

"We have to convert the secondary pentacles to primaries, and undo the binding pentacles..." I did not need to belabor the obvious.

"I tried to scan Hume's mind," Ruach said and glanced, arch-browed, at Phoebe, "right before someone shot me." He shook his head, "Hume's brain has sustained massive damage. He may live, but I doubt he will ever recover his mental faculties."

He reached into his pocket and produced the remote control. "The quantum cascade laser is most effective." He laughed without humor. "It fused everything, including the internal circuits and memory."

He tossed the useless remote on the stainless steel table. It clattered with a metallic ring and skid into some papers.

Several things happened in the next few seconds. Panglaws wandered over, still a bit dazed, a confused look on his face. "What's going on?" he said, rubbing his head. Man must have a hard head, I thought idly, thinking of that first test where I had blasted him and he had fallen to the floor. Vishnu, that seemed like a million years ago.

Then the door opened and a woman, carrying some kind of small black medical bag and wearing a stethoscope, came in, followed by two young men in white medical outfits, a four-wheeled gurney between them.

Janet was her name, from the time Brody had appeared lifeless in the pentacle.

"Denton! Dr. Hume!" she said in great agitation as she approached the body. She looked at Phoebe, then me, then Ruach, then back to me.

"What happened?" As she was waiting for a response to her question, she began diagnostics on Hume.

◻ Chapter Twenty-One ◻

"He has absorbed a, uh, jolt of electromagnetic energy," I muttered, not sure exactly how to explain it. I nervously chewed on my lower lip and rubbed my thumb and index finger together in little angst-ridden circles.

"An electric shock?" she asked pointedly, listening to his heart through her stethoscope.

"More of a broad spectrum charge," I replied weakly. What was I supposed to tell her?

"There are no external burns," she commented, making a cursory examination of Hume. She lifted his lids and checked his eyes. Unclipped a small penlight and flicked it on and off. "Unresponsive to light," she said softly; checked his pulse again.

"Some kind of severe neurological trauma," she said and angrily stood up. "What happened here?"

I guess it was my helpless puppy dog expression that prompted Ruach to step in. And by stepping in, I mean to "suggest" to the doctor that further inquiries could wait until after Hume had been transported to a more suitable treatment environment. I could sense Ruach's implanted thoughts filtered through my own mind. That was new. Very peculiar.

As the technicians were carefully and gently securing Hume onto the gurney, the lab door opened again and Jimmy walked in. I looked at Phoebe and she gave me a meek expression, rare for her. "I thought he should know," she said with a flitting smile, and I smiled back. Probably not a bad time to get the NSA involved.

We shook hands and gave him as much information as necessary, which is to say, just enough for him to nod and shake his head on multiple occasions. He looked intently at me. "You'll be in charge of PHANTASM?" he asked, watching me closely.

I shrugged like a dope on a rope. "Well, I suppose, until they can find someone more qualified," I muttered and Phoebe rolled her eyes.

Ruach had remained in the background during most of the conversation, but stepped forward now. Apparently Jimmy knew him because I saw respect in his expression as Ruach began talking. "There is no need to look for a replacement for Dr. Hume, Mr. Scanlin," Ruach intoned, "Enoch was born to run PHANTASM."

Jimmy nodded. "That's good enough for me." He looked briefly at Hume as the technicians concluded their preparations for his transport, then back to us. "I assume you're not telling me everything," he stated with a rueful smile, then favoring each of us with a bemused glance. "That's okay, I know how it works." The doctor and techs were leaving the lab and he turned to follow.

"I'll be back driving in a few days." He shrugged as he turned to go. "Lots of paperwork to do on this thing." The group moved away and was soon gone.

"I have a notion," I announced quietly, hoping to break the somewhat somber and reflective mood in the room.

"Perhaps they make an ointment for that," Dee deadpanned, further easing the aura of tension that had gripped all of us. Phoebe laughed loudly and Ruach demurely covered his mouth with his hand.

"Very funny," I replied dryly, "but I'm serious." I knew Dee was kidding, but I was playing my part out. Strut and fret. Thankful that the fretting was nearing an end.

Ruach enjoined, "We always take you serious, Enoch, even in jest." He smiled, "Especially ingest."

"Hey, I like that one," I noted with a grin, then put on my serious, big boy, face. "I think I have a way to free the eemees from the binding pentacles," I stated softly, proving that I was indeed, serious.

"We do not have the codes," Dee declaimed sadly.

"True," I admitted and smiled slyly, "but we do have blood."

Ruach's face was a perfect blend of confusion and bewilderment. "Why would blood be important?" He favored me with a big frown.

Phoebe let out a half-grunt laugh. "Whose blood?" I think she was ready to spill some.

"Do any of you know how pentacles are really controlled?" I addressed the question to everyone and waited just a few moments. "I mean, the exact mechanism by which the human exerts that control."

"The human controller," Dee took the gambit, **"is the one who constructs the pentacle and invokes the electromagnetic entity, the eemee, and thus has control."**

I nodded. "You've stated the end result, but not how it's actually attained," I said, giving her position a gentle critique, then went on.

⬚ Chapter Twenty-One ⬚

"There's a very special reason why a particular human controls a specific pentacle." Ruach and Phoebe were watching me intently, obviously waiting for the payoff pitch, the punch line, the whole enchilada.

"The human controller provides blood for the pentacle, but not just as some symbolic sacrifice based on a misguided nod to arcane and archaic medieval ritual," I explained, sort of elongating the suspense for my own warped amusement, I suppose. Ruach and Phoebe wore blank looks, waiting.

"DNA," was all I said, then continued a few moments later. "Unique to the individual and putting them in specific control of the pentacle, and thus the invoked eemee." Picking Anuket's brain was yielding nice dividends.

Ruach's eyes grew wide, he nodded twice, rubbed his chin and said lightly, almost absently, "That explains a great deal."

Phoebe nodded her complete understanding as well. "So, you want to substitute your blood, your DNA, for Hume's, in the binding pentacles?" Smart girl, and good-looking, too.

"Not substitute, I'm not sure we can do that, but augment; add me to the approved user list, so to speak," I clarified for her with a grin.

Phoebe was convinced. "What's your plan?" She didn't waste energy. When it was time to move, brother, get out of the damn way.

I made a gesture with my hands. "We need to accomplish two things," and I held up a finger, cleverly indicating one. "First thing, we need to disrupt the actual operation of the base binding pentacle structure." More looks awaiting enlightenment, which I hoped to provide.

"We need to momentarily disengage the binding ability of the pentacle," I said, now treading on less sure ground, "which won't last long, but should give me enough time to introduce my blood into the pentacle circuitry." I wasn't sure if "circuitry" was the right word, but it sounded okay to me.

"At that point, I become a controller, which should allow me to destroy the pentacle without harming the imprisoned eemee," I concluded with a flourish, hoping everyone missed my careful use of the word "should."

"Should?" Ruach noted with appropriate alarm, ever vigilant, missing nothing. "Should allow you..." He let the implications linger. Even Phoebe was giving me the skunk eye.

"Here's the thing about plans," I began to explain, then shrugged. "There are always variables you can't define or you have to guess at." I scowled. "No one likes to do that, but it's the reality of life in a perfectly imperfect world."

I smiled. "Still, I am all ears for a better idea." Insert sound of crickets.

Ruach nodded, glanced at Phoebe, then at me. "One of the earliest invoked eemees is in Room 4." His expression was sad as he spoke. "He has been imprisoned for many years and is no longer responsive." He sighed. "If he is not returned to the spectrum soon, his being will have diminished to the point that return is no longer possible."

He gave me a powerful and plaintive look. "If it were me, I would be willing to take any risk imaginable to return home. To be whole once again."

It was quiet for a few moments until Phoebe coughed. "How do you propose to implement the momentary disruption of the binding pentacle so your DNA can be introduced?" Practical Phoebe, always on top of the real problems.

"Let's go to Level 5, and I'll show you," I said simply.

We actually thought about going to Hume's office and looking for his elevator entrance to Level 5, but that struck all of us as a bit creepy (okay, really creepy), so we decided against it.

Besides, Ruach had already busted open all the doors on our earlier exit, so it was really just a question of crawling under the stairwell and making our way through. A bit odd but, considering everything else that had happened these last few days, not all that strange.

Just saying.

Soon, we were standing in my old pentacle room. Hume's family crest chair stood like a strange reminder of events that now seemed light years away. I gently moved the chair off to the side of the room and out of the center of the pentacle.

⬠ Chapter Twenty-One ⬠

I gestured at that now vacant center part of the huge and elaborately constructed pentacle on the floor. "You'll notice that the inner part of the pentacle is a pentagon, a geometric figure with five sides," I pointed out.

That was duly noted by Ruach and Phoebe. Dee could use EM energy to scan the room and convert the feedback to a visual image, so I didn't worry about her ability to understand.

"If you connect the five inner points of that pentagon, you create a new pentacle," I said and traced the figure in the air just above the center.

"This process can be repeated ad infinitum. An infinite regression."

An image flashed on the ComUnit and Dee said **"Like this?"** I nodded in affirmation after giving it a quick examination.

Little allegorical light bulbs clicked on above the heads of Ruach and Phoebe and, judging by their facial expressions, they no longer wore that "duh" look I have so often seen in the mirror while shaving.

"We will construct an electronic signature, linked to the pentacle, that creates just such a succession of images," I instructed and smiled. "The pentacle will be switched off and on so fast that it will actually be in a null state. Binding then not binding." I shrugged. "I'll quickly introduce my blood into the pattern and that should do it."

Phoebe's face had taken on a doubtful cast. "Simple plans are never simple," she said flatly, daring me to contradict her.

I nodded slowly, "I know. I've tried to look at all the angles, think it through, and it should work"—then caught myself—"it will work."

☐ Riding The Wave ☐

Ruach had been staring at the pentacle and then looked at Phoebe and me. "Dee, is it possible for you and I to combine our scan energies to create the infinite regression that Enoch requires?"

"Some things are only possible in cooperation with another," Dee said sweetly.

"I look forward to that cooperation," Ruach said with spirited intensity.

"As do I," Dee rejoined. **"We should begin the process of envisioning the pentacle."** I handed my ComUnit to Ruach and he took it with great reverence.

Phoebe had produced her razor-sharp knife and was methodically swabbing the blade with an alcohol patch.

"It doesn't have to be a lot of blood," I explained, eyeing the nasty weapon with all due respect. "Really just a few drops should suffice."

"Don't be a baby," Phoebe scolded me. "Just run the edge lightly across your palm and you'll have all the blood you need." Easy for her to say. Her knife, but my palm.

A minute, perhaps two, passed in silence. Ruach broke his concentration and gave me a look of satisfaction. "We have it. Let's move to Room 4."

I had not been overly nervous previously. No duty in the shorts, no cookies tossed or beets blown. Now, though, I began to feel the queasy-cheesey-geesies in my gut. Nerves on edge. Heart plap-plapping like I had just dashed a spirited sprint. Sigh, take a breath. OM. AUM.

The eemee in Room 4 was a very young man, perhaps mid-twenties, a full shock of dark black hair. He was sitting in a lotus position, head down, motionless, suspended just above the center of the pentacle. He did not stir one iota when the light flipped on, nor when we opened the door and entered the room. He wasn't dead, but was apparently knocking on that door.

Ruach shook his head as he studied the man's unmoving form. Then he looked at me. "Your plan is his best and only hope." I took a deep breath and exhaled. Man, I could use a beer.

Phoebe handed me the knife, hilt first. "Be careful, it's very, very, sharp," she explained, needlessly I might add. Of course it's bloody sharp; it's a freaking knife!

◌ Chapter Twenty-One ◌

Ruach watched me as I moved into position near the pentacle. I placed my palm out, just over and above the dark blue circuit lines that formed the pentacle. My educated guess, based on a description I had culled from Anuket's mind during our little spectrum dance, was that those circuit lines were a sort of semi-permeable membrane that would permit the absorption of a fluid.

Blood being the fluid in question. I hoped. Erg.

On closer inspection, I could see that what I had thought were solid blue lines were actually transparent insulated conduit lines containing swirling dark blue EM energy of some unknown ilk. Almost like a gaseous substance or something, and one in which, if you watched very closely, you would occasionally see a flash of visual light. It was circulating in counterclockwise fashion.

"We are ready, Enoch, just say when," Dee said clearly, confidently. My attention was keen at this point, though that old friend, doubt, dropped in to say hello.

To be honest, I wasn't exactly sure when the blood should be spilled, to coin a phrase. Should I cut myself the moment Dee and Ruach began the regression, or give it time to actually start working? Which, naturally, begged the question as to how would I know whether or not it was working? Even after I provided the blood, how would I know? Was there a particular place the blood should actually go? Was my zipper up?

Oh, frail human, what a piece of, er, work, thou art.

I took a deep Zen, cleansing, breath. "When," I said and though I hadn't really expected to see or hear anything, sudden spectral tracings began to appear within the entrails of the pentacle. Lines of wavering EM energy, reddish in hue, flickering, sparkling, twizzling (twirling and sizzling). The first pentacle within the pentagon, the next pentacle within the pentagon only just slightly smaller, and on and on...

I slid the knife across my palm.

Pain is a relative thing.

I've talked to people who have been wounded in combat, and were not even aware of it until someone else pointed it out. I've seen guys with broken bones continue to play football, basketball, baseball.

☐ Riding The Wave ☐

I once witnessed a car accident where a cut and shredded up woman staggered out of the wreck, walked unwaveringly over to me standing on the curb, and calmly asked to borrow my cell phone. Wiped her bloody hand off first, too, before using it.

I played an entire half of basketball with two broken ribs. Lead the team in scoring that night and we won.

I've ripped up my hamstring playing baseball, torn my calf muscle up doing something, sprained my ankles so bad they turned the color of old molasses, had two nasty root canals that really unnerved me, tore off toe nails playing tennis, dropped a dumb bell on my foot.

Maybe that was a dumb bell that dropped a weight on my foot? Whatever. I know pain.

But, man, I really hate knives. Getting cut sucks. Especially when you do it to yourself, even if there's a good reason. Your irritated nerve endings just don't care about the reason.

Well, and the other minor thing was, I guess I had a momentary lapse in memory and overlooked Phoebe's admonition about the knife being very, very, sharp... Sigh.

Let's just say we didn't have to worry about whether or not enough blood would be available for the pentacle. It was more a question of when could I get a transfusion. No, just kidding, I do that when I'm nervous. Or, bleeding profusely.

Phoebe gasped. "For the love of..." she exclaimed, instantly producing a hanky from somewhere and wrapping it tightly around my throbbing and pulsating palm. Glaring at me and shaking her head in worried anger as the white cloth was instantly stained with spreading tentacles of crimson.

The eemee in the center did not stir at all, but his cross-legged body actually drifted slowly downwards about six inches. I didn't know whether this was meaningful or not, but I was taking it as a sign. Hopefully an "Eemee Crossing Here" sign—hah!

You're either laughing or crying in life. Make a choice.

I smashed my foot down on the integrated circuit board at the pentacle point nearest to me.

The unmoving eemee vanished. The blazing ethereal energy tracings of the infinite regression faded away. I looked in anxious anticipation at Ruach. His smile was immense and lit up his handsome face. "He is in the spectrum!" Ruach cried out. "I can sense him. He is home." He nodded happily and Phoebe gave him a big hug.

I started breathing again. And my damn palm hurt like hell. Thankfully, it was still bleeding, as we had more pentacles to deal with. Always looking on the bright side. Bright red in this case.

And that is what we did. We freed another eemee in Room 3, a elderly woman barely responsive, said a fond farewell to Elia and Phoster and, after he vanished, we trudged wearily out into the hallway.

Without a word being spoken, everyone knew the time was drawing near when friendships would end, when things would never be the same again. Ruach seemed to have trouble speaking.

"My friend, Enoch," he began and we hugged. There were tears in his eyes. I am not a crier myself, but I was choking back the emotions nonetheless. Phoebe's cheeks were wet as we slowly made our way to the bank of rooms on the right.

Well, I thought with a wicked bit of self-satisfaction as we skipped the fifth room, all but Anuket, who we didn't have to worry about anymore. I had already mind blasted that evil bee atch into the nether lands. We entered the fourth room.

Remember what I said about simple plans not being simple? Well, thankfully, sometimes simple plans actually do work. Go figure. With Dee and Ruach creating the infinite regression and my adding the blood, we were easily able to convert the secondary pentacle to a primary. Ruach immediately sensed the difference. I stomped on one of the points and Ruach brightened. "There is no eemee in Argentina," was all he said.

We repeated this process for the next two rooms. Ruach confirmed the eemees were safely home in the spectrum.

Soon, we reached the first room which held the pentacle for Ruach.

"Fine fellowship on a strange journey," Ruach managed to say softly, shaking hands with Phoebe and I. He caught Phoebe's eye. "Take care of Enoch," he said with a gentle smile. Phoebe nodded.

"Dee, my sweet, I will be waiting," Ruach said with great passion.

"Dear Ruach, thank you for everything," Dee said mystically, and Ruach looked at me.

"It is time," he said softly—sadly—his voice very subdued.

I shook my head. "There is so much good that you and Dee could do here—can't you stay?" Used wisely, their powers could be employed for needed change and positive influence.

"Humans must solve human problems," Ruach said gently, a whimsical smile gracing his face. "It has been that way since the dawn of time," he said mysteriously.

I was not sure exactly what he meant, but the resolute tone of his voice left no room for argument. "I will miss you," I said in a strained voice. "And Dee."

"Your friendship has been unexpected and appreciated beyond measure." He glanced at the elaborate pentacle circuit boards. "Do it now," he stated in impassioned tones, and I stomped on the computer components closest to me.

Ruach was gone. I felt a great void in myself.

"He is home, Enoch, safely home!" Dee said joyously. **"And now I must go."**

"Tom and Mando will never forgive me if I let you leave without saying goodbye," I said sadly.

"I spoke with them earlier," Dee explained simply. She then added, **"Your goodness shall be your strength, Enoch, all the days of your life."**

I tried not to pay immediate attention to the power of her words, or I know I would have broken down and lost complete control of my emotions. Phoebe had unscrewed the ComUnit back and handed me the knife again. I had it poised nervously over the small pentacle within the ComUnit. "Dee, I, uh, I wouldn't be here without you, without your constant help," I sputtered out and the tears came this time.

"It has been a great honor to know you, Enoch, and great honor to know Phoebe," Dee said, working hard to manage her voice.

"Dee!" was all Phoebe could croak out.

I wanted to ask one last thing, something that had been on my mind for a goodly while. I had to get it out before my emotions took over and I couldn't talk at all. I took a deep breath and gathered myself. "Dee, I thought eemees, ah, lived alone in the spectrum, but you and Ruach seem to have a, well, unique relationship."

⌾ Chapter Twenty-One ⌾

"Dee is the complement to Ruach as Phoebe is the complement to Enoch," she replied and my hand must have slipped. The knife cut into a pentacle conduit. There was a slight hissing sound, a small wisp of escaping bluish vapor, and Dee was gone.

"What do you suppose she meant by that?" I turned and asked Phoebe, a dull look on my face.

"Men are such idiots," she said and, by way of further explanation, took hold of me and gave me a very loving kiss.

Holy crap!

Das Ende

EXOPHOBE